The
Titan
was

A Triple Threat Novel

KRISTEN CASEY

The Triple Threat Series

The Titan Was Tall

The Doctor Was Dark

The Hero Was Handsome

The Triple Threat Box Set

About This Book

Being in charge is a pain in the...

Posterior. Rear end. Junk in the trunk. Those were some of the words that came to mind when the captivating woman walked into Red's office that day. But now wasn't the time to contemplate her ass...ets. Red need to focus on the fact that his huge conglomerate had just bought out her dinky publisher—and this sexy little author was the key to a smooth transition.

For all intents and purposes, Piper was his new star employee—so Red should not have cleared his schedule to take her dinner. He shouldn't have flirted like it was his freaking birthday, and he sure as hell shouldn't have gone and fallen for her. One more thing he shouldn't have done? Omit the fact that his company owed her a lot of money.

When his dirty little secret gets out, more than Red's new acquisition is on the line—his hard heart is hanging in the balance, too. Unfortunately, his golden way with a merger might not be enough to save him now.

Can Red convince Piper that her tentative trust in him wasn't misplaced? Or will their new relationship go the way of her missing royalties?

There's only one way to find out.

Step into his office and let Padraig "Red" MacLellan show you why he's the boss.

One

I T WAS A bad time to develop a case of the nerves. Not that there was ever a good time, but developing the jitters when you were about to meet the person who could make or break your career did seem to be especially inconvenient.

Perhaps Piper was being dramatic. Her new overlord had merely contacted her lawyer a week ago, suggesting a perfectly civil "meet and greet" between Piper and the fearless leader. Perry had informed her that it wasn't the kind of suggestion one generally rebuffed, so here she was. She was sure there was nothing to worry about in the least.

PKM Industries—the conglomerate that had acquired her publisher several months earlier—had flown her up to New York for a three-day stay. They'd arranged for a driver to ferry her from the airport, installed her in a swanky hotel, and had even provided a generous meal stipend. They'd emailed an itinerary of who she was meeting with on each of the days, and assured Piper that it was not necessary to have her lawyer present. A good thing, too, since Perry was sharp and astute—but also somewhat…elderly.

Regardless, all the fuss didn't seem like the kind of thing they'd do if they were about to cut her loose. And why should they? Her books had sold well, almost from the moment she'd begun publishing. She would be a valuable asset to them.

However, Piper was not used to dealing with an enormous company with deep pockets. She'd been an author in Trident's stable for the entirety of her career, from the moment she'd graduated and submitted her first manuscript to an agent. And little Trident was no juggernaut—just the labor of love of a kindly old couple who simply adored books and authors.

The Dentons weren't flashy, but they had been committed to the stories they sold. She'd been lucky to land with them. They had graciously helped her learn the industry and ensured that Piper did pretty well for herself. She owed them everything.

PKM was an entirely different kind of entity, though. As far as Piper knew, they rolled out the perks for every person they were about to sack. While it did seem as if the CEO could find someone a bit lower on the totem pole to do his firing for him, maybe he was just sadistic that way. Maybe he enjoyed it.

Piper fiddled with the buckle of her attaché case as the elevator chugged upward, and she tried not to let her worries get the best of her. She wasn't some green author who didn't know the ropes. She'd been doing this for eleven years and had the benefit of both a top-notch intellectual property lawyer and a reputable, experienced agent in her corner.

If this Padraig MacLellan guy was going to look at the work she'd done for Trident and decide to get rid of her, Piper would still land on her feet. Someone else would take her on because her fans would settle for nothing less. *She* would settle for nothing less.

She hoped it didn't come to that, though. It might be fun to see what she could accomplish with the resources of a larger company in the mix. She could expand her distribution, maybe, or get a few more translations of her backlist done. Maybe she could even work out a signing or two overseas. Who knew what PKM could do?

In the CEO's suite, she checked in with an extremely efficient young man named Wayne, dapper as a menswear ad in his gray plaid suit and pink dress shirt. He had clearly been waiting for her.

Wayne virtually leaped from his ergonomic chair to escort her straight to his boss, the estimable Padraig K. MacLellan. Or, as the tabloids claimed he was known, "Red." Piper straightened her spine as she stepped over his threshold, ready to do battle.

She was startled to discover that the head of the entire billion-dollar company was not an older, graying man, as she'd anticipated. Okay, fine—she'd searched for him online, but this man wasn't the one whose picture she'd seen. This was a lion in his prime, preening in his lair.

The man who stood and rounded his large mahogany desk to greet her looked to be about her own age, tall and broad-shouldered, with thick, auburn hair and intense brown eyes. Piper's step hitched as she got closer. He was, in fact, larger than life—maybe 6'5 or more. He *loomed* over her. MacLellan was disconcertingly attractive, too, his grip firm but not bruising when they shook hands.

Wayne slipped discreetly out of the office, shutting the door behind him. Piper tried to ignore the way the touch of MacLellan's hand sent sparks up her arm, her nerve endings firing off a series of electric aftershocks that made her grateful for the large leather armchair he directed her to. She took an extra minute to arrange herself, locking down her composure while she was at it.

MacLellan eased into his own chair and smiled.

"Ms. Corelli," he began, "I'd like to thank you for coming up to see us. I hope your flight went okay?"

Had that been a royal *us*? "Yes, absolutely." Piper almost added, *thank you for having me*, but given how gorgeous MacLellan was, the phrase suddenly seemed laden with innuendo. She couldn't make herself utter it with a straight face.

"All the other accommodations to your liking? Hotel, and so forth?"

"Yes, of course. All of the arrangements have been lovely, thank you."

"That's a relief. My assistant can occasionally get creative with things like that."

"I see." Piper set her bag on the floor and folded her hands in her lap. She kept her knees together and crossed her ankles off to the side, infinitely decorous. She was a professional, but sometimes people got the wrong idea about her when they discovered she wrote erotic romances. Piper liked to do her level best to refute their assumptions.

Well, most of them at least. She wasn't going to go out of her way to hide her black lace tattoo, curving around her ankle. And she certainly wasn't going to attend a meeting of this magnitude without wearing her lucky shoes—which happened to be four-inch, leopard-printed calf-hair peep-toes. She *was* a romance writer. Come on.

"It says here you live in Maryland?"

"That's right."

"I've never been. What's it like?"

"Well…I'd say it has a bit of everything. Within a two-hour radius, you can find city and farmland, skiing, sailing—you name it."

"Sounds fascinating. How could I have missed that?"

"Ah, well. Something for your bucket list," she tossed off casually. Oh, yeah. She was cool as cool could be. MacLellan would never guess what she was going through.

He laid his hands on his desk, and Piper immediately noticed his long, elegant fingers. He stared absently at her, a slight furrow forming between his eyebrows, and she agonized over what he might be thinking.

She cleared her throat. "Let's get started."

"Forgive me," he muttered. "It's been one hell of a week." He shuffled some papers around and refocused on her. "Let's, uh—let's start over."

"I'd be delighted. But I must admit, I'm not entirely clear why I'm here right now."

A small smile quirked up one corner of his mouth, turning him even more roguishly handsome. "Maybe I can enlighten you." He reached for a file laying to the side of his desk, centered it in front of him, and flipped it open.

"Ms. Corelli, when we acquired Trident Publishing—"

Piper held up a hand to stop him. "I'm sorry to interrupt. I just wanted to make sure you realized that 'Antoinette Corelli' is my pen name. My real name is Piper Fulham."

MacLellan shuffled a couple of pages around, read one with a frown, and peered back up at her. "Piper Mae Fulham. So it is. I overlooked that. I apologize, Piper Mae." His mouth twisted slightly.

Piper waved him off. "Happens all the time. And please, just Piper is fine."

"Excellent." He waited to make sure she had nothing further to add, then proceeded, "When we acquired Trident and started really combing through the nuts-and-bolts of how to stabilize it, we came across some surprising details. Maybe you already know."

The former owners of Trident might have loved books, but they weren't exactly business-savvy sharks. Piper was not at all surprised to hear the company wasn't up to this man's standards, so she simply nodded politely.

"I'd already reviewed the industry, and I knew that eBooks were major drivers. But," the CEO continued, "I was fascinated to discover that the highest grossing segment of this company was its romance division." He glanced up at her from the papers spread in front of him, allowing that tidbit to settle.

Piper sat patiently and refused to pity him. He ought to have known that, but no matter. *She* knew what she did for a living, and why it mattered so very much to people. Love truly did make the world go around.

"And who, amidst that whole division," he asked, "would you guess was earning us more money than any other author?" He consulted his notes, then elaborated, "More than the next four authors combined, to be precise."

Piper smiled thinly. Oh, she knew all right. The Dentons had made no secret of the fact. "Why don't you tell me?"

MacLellan ignored her little flash of smugness. "I will. It's you. Your books alone appear to have kept afloat an entire, wildly-mismanaged publishing house that was hemorrhaging money from nearly every other line of business."

"I've been very fortunate," Piper agreed.

"It seems so. But…I will admit to having felt some chagrin at never having *heard* of you before. Not one media profile, not one article, not one book review. Not even a whisper of your name crossed into my purview."

Well, he didn't have to be quite so emphatic about it. "You aren't exactly my target audience," Piper pointed out wryly. Though he'd make an excellent character study.

MacLellan sat back and regarded her carefully. "I'm not so sure about that."

"You're not?" The dissonance between their actual conversation, versus the one transpiring in her head, was throwing her completely off-kilter. She had to pull herself together before she missed something important.

"No. Because once it became clear that I had never heard of my highest-selling author before, I also realized that I'd never cracked open a single romance novel of any kind before. That kind of ignorance does not sit well with me, so naturally, I set about educating myself."

"You didn't." This interview was taking a decidedly unexpected turn, and Piper didn't have a clue where it was headed next. Was this guy some kind of holy roller, about to tell her all the ways her books were paving the way for the devil's work? Or was he about to get skeevy on her?

"I most certainly did," MacLellan assured her. "First, I read the current releases of several chart-topping authors at other publishing houses. Next, I sampled what some of the bigger indie writers had to offer. Laying some groundwork, if you will."

Piper watched him, trying to get a read on his expression, but it was impossible. "And?" she prompted.

"*And*," he said, "then I read yours."

"I see," Piper replied, though she didn't.

He asked, "Do you? Because once I read one, it seemed like maybe I should read another. From there, it definitely snowballed—pretty quickly, too. Took me a month and a half, but I read them."

"Which, uh…which ones?" Piper's mind was spinning with scenes from some of her more risqué stuff, mixing in some very unhelpful images of the man before her *reacting* to them. As one of her characters might say, *Oh, God.*

MacLellan made a show of checking his report once more. "All of them," he reported.

"In a month and a half?" Piper blurted. That was no small feat.

Her new employer's mouth twitched up at the corners again. "I found them very compelling."

"Clearly," Piper laughed, but it was thin and nervous-sounding.

He waited for a full beat, then two. Watching her. Waiting. She gazed back and tried to school her breathing. There was no hope for her heart rate, though.

"Forgive me," he said. "I've flustered you."

Crud. Not only was MacLellan smoking hot, but he was perceptive, too. Worse, he appeared to be one of those uncomfortable conversationalists who felt the need to drag awkwardness out into the open and shine a light on it.

For an introvert like her, that made him virtually a monster. If she'd learned anything, though, it was how to be a good faker. Her whole image depended on it.

When she replied, "What makes you say that?" it was blasé. So convincing.

He didn't respond directly. Instead, MacLellan inquired, "Was it me veering into odd superfan territory that did it, or was it just my unnaturally large size?"

Piper couldn't help it. Her eyes flicked down toward his lap, hidden behind that colossal, weighty desk, for only an instant before she wrenched them back up to his face in a panic. She blinked rapidly, plum out of snappy comebacks.

MacLellan's mouth stayed serious, but now his eyes twinkled with laughter. "It's okay. I like to get out in front of the elephant in the room, so to speak, so we can get past it. I realize that I'm a tad too enormous to be considered normal. I make people uncomfortable. Especially ones of your stature," he mused.

Piper could feel her face flaming. No way could he read her mind, but did he have any conception of how dirty he sounded? She had to get her mind out of the gutter. Piper decided to feign indignation at the height jab, if only as a deflection.

"Now wait just one minute," she muttered, then winced at her tone. Her voice was too freaking breathy to sound anything but flirtatious.

"I'd like to say that I'm a gentle giant to make up for it, but then I'd be lying to you within five minutes of meeting you, and that hardly seems sporting." Then the bastard winked. *Winked.*

Piper nearly swallowed her tongue. What the hell was happening here? Was he flirting *back?*

"I'm sure you're a perfectly fine person, towering or not," she managed. If MacLellan was a perfectly *proportioned* person, issues with endowment would not be a problem for him. But she was Not. Going to. Dwell on that. For crying out loud.

"Anyway." The head of PKM cleared his throat and shifted his gaze to the side, looking thoughtful. "It goes without saying that hanging on to you—particularly through this transition phase—is imperative for Trident. I wanted to meet with you face-to-face to get your thoughts on that, as well as to deliver this new contract to you." His eyes, when they returned to her, were a deep brown, like chocolate.

Piper took the packet and flipped absently through the first few pages. Numbers jumped out at her, and she felt her eyebrows notch upward.

"I…have no current plans to leave Trident," she said. Not now, anyway.

He chuckled—a low, delectable sound. "I'm relieved to hear that."

Quickly, she added, "But naturally, I'll need to review this with my attorney before I sign it."

MacLellan smiled wider. "Of course. That copy is yours. We'll forward another to your lawyer and let them know when we need it back." He shuffled through his file. "Perry Shanahan, correct?"

Piper nodded, and he began gathering the papers on his desk, arranging them neatly back into their file. All the facts and figures breaking down her career, her passion, and who knew what else for him—all encased in their slim, brown cardstock folder. If only her real life could be arranged so easily.

Their meeting was clearly at an end. Piper wondered briefly if MacLellan would be sitting in on any of the others she had scheduled, but decided that would be more of a nuisance than anything else.

She slipped her new contract into her bag. "Thank you for this, and for taking the time to meet with me personally. I appreciate the effort," she began. Though not as much as she planned to appreciate some of those zeroes she'd spotted in the new contract. PKM wasn't messing around.

"Of course," he said. Then, like he really could read her mind, he added, "I have no doubt the other meetings Wayne set up for you will go equally smoothly."

In the next couple of days, Piper would be talking to employees who would have a far more direct influence on her career—PKM's new editors, cover designers, and audiobook performers. Getting used to an unfamiliar crew would be an adjustment, but they could hardly be more difficult than the disorganized set-up she'd had to deal with before.

"I'm sure they will." She would probably never lay eyes on this man again. It would be insane for him to get involved in Trident's business at such a microscopic level. She frankly couldn't believe he'd even gone through with this meeting.

"You're heading back to Maryland afterward, I assume?"

"Yes." Piper set her bag in her lap and prepared to stand. Now that her uneasiness had mostly subsided, she was realizing that she'd never eaten lunch. She was hungry and more eager than ever to get out of there so she could go find something to eat.

MacLellan drummed his fingers on her file. "Any other plans while you're here?"

Again, Piper tried not to notice what great-looking hands the man had, but it was hard. Noticing superior male traits like that, then writing about them to perfection, was kind of her jam.

His wrists were oddly tantalizing, too—tan and lean where they peeked out from the starched white cuffs of his dress shirt.

"No," she blurted abruptly, then added sheepishly, "Not really." By way of explanation, she tacked on, "I wasn't sure what I'd have time for." Right. Not lame at all.

MacLellan contemplated that information, then seemed to make a decision. "Listen." He hesitated, then plowed on with a determined look, "You're my last appointment of the day. Why don't we grab some dinner?"

"I…that's not necessary," Piper stuttered out. "I'm sure my hotel has a restaurant downstairs." She tried to picture it but came up blank. "Or something." There was a bar, she knew that for sure. "The front desk can direct me somewhere, either way. Or, I can just get room service." And why was she rambling, exactly?

MacLellan stood behind his desk and reached to shut down his laptop. He looked amused, and warmer than he'd been. "I'm fairly confident that I can do better than room service if you're amenable. What do you say? Do you trust me?"

The giant of the business world was gone, replaced by a smiling, friendly man who was too toweringly handsome for anyone's peace of mind.

Piper would be no kind of romance author at all if she turned down the chance to study him a little longer. Opportunities like this one, needless to say, were a bit thin on the ground where she lived. She suspected by the end of a meal with this man, she'd have good ideas for a new character, a new story—heck, a whole steamy new series.

"Yeah," she replied, trying to focus. "Sure."

MacLellan came around the desk and led her out of his office, locking his door behind him. His hand was a barely-there hint of warmth at her lower back. When they passed his assistant's desk, Wayne popped out of his chair like an agitated preschooler.

"Where—" he began.

"Clear my schedule," MacLellan instructed blandly. "I'm leaving for the day. Could you ring down for the car?"

His startled assistant sank back into his seat. "Okay," he said. Wayne glanced at his monitor with a wild, desperate sort of look. "What should I—"

"Handle it," MacLellan ordered.

Piper got a glimpse of his assistant diving for his phone when MacLellan ushered her out, and then the office door swung shut, blocking her view.

As they reached the bank of elevators, Piper turned to her companion. "Last appointment of the day, huh?"

"Yup," he grinned.

She had to laugh. "Mr. MacLellan—"

"Call me Red."

"Okay, Red. Why are you doing this?"

He chuckled, handing her into the elevator and then pressing the button for the lobby. "Curiosity?"

"If that's true, prepare to be underwhelmed," she told him. She'd discovered the hard way that the reality of a romance novelist simply couldn't live up to the hype.

The doors closed, surrounding them in gleaming brass and mirrors on all sides. Piper swallowed against her sudden hyperawareness of Red, his height and intoxicating male scent.

And, *damn* it, she had to stop thinking like she was writing. This man was not one of her heroes. He was her *boss*.

Red's eyes flickered down, apparently snared by what should have been the imperceptible motion of her throat. It was just long enough for Piper to glimpse his lashes, and quite long enough for her heart to lurch alarmingly in her chest.

And then it was over, and he was smiling at her again. Awareness went both ways, it seemed.

"Hungry?" Red inquired. His voice was dark. Seductive. It was as if they'd traveled to an alternate, far-sexier plane of existence when they'd entered this shining little box.

You have no idea, Piper thought.

"Always," she said aloud, and the blasted man went and laughed.

"Do you have any preferences? Likes, dislikes, that sort of thing?" Red studied her in that unnerving way of his, as if he could discern her answer just by looking hard enough.

"I can find something to eat almost anywhere," Piper hedged. "I'm not terribly particular, I'm afraid."

She took in his raised eyebrow and slightly annoyed look and sighed. So, indecision wasn't going to work.

"Okay, fine," she said. "I especially like Japanese, Italian, and Mexican food. Does that help?"

"Much better."

He smelled ridiculously good. It wasn't fair. She asked, "Do you know a good place?"

"I know the best place," he said smugly.

"Then I am very much in favor, kind sir."

His scent infused the enclosed space, drifting around her, and clearly making her crazy. Piper knew this for a fact, because her next words were, "Do you mind if I ask what cologne you're wearing?"

Oh, God.

She stumbled on, "I'm sorry. I only ask because I'm very sensitive to smells, and I don't often enjoy perfume. I noticed yours and it's…"

Piper could almost hear the sound of the shovel as she dug a deeper and deeper hole for herself. Nerves. This was only nerves. Once they were out of this infernally small space, she'd be better.

Red looked uncomfortable and checked the floor numbers flickering over the elevator door. "Forgive me. Is it bothering you?"

"No! No," Piper assured him. "Actually, I'm surprised by how much I like it."

At another arch look from him, she appended lamely, "Usually I don't."

Red's concern morphed immediately into an amused smirk. "Are you telling me I smell good, Miss Fulham?"

"Great. The word you want is *great*."

He chuckled, and her heart pounded harder. Mercifully, the elevator door slid open on the ground floor, saving her from making an even bigger ass out of herself.

The doorman wished them a good afternoon, Red whisked her across the sidewalk, and then he opened the back door of a sleek black sedan idling at the curb. When Piper moved past him to enter, she felt the warm whisper of his breath near her ear. She turned in confusion to find him very close indeed.

He grinned, unapologetic. "Turns out you smell great, too."

Two

THE THING WAS, Red reflected that morning, he'd probably always known he loved women. He loved their bodies and their mannerisms, he loved the infinite number of ways they could express themselves, and the feel of their hair against his skin.

What he'd taken longer to figure out, however, was why not every woman he found attractive had the ability to light his fire. As it turned out, many of them simply left Red admiring but cold, and it had taken him years to put the clues together in any meaningful way.

Red eventually discovered that he needed a little something *more* than most guys to really get into the horizontal gymnastics with a woman. Once he'd recognized what that extra magic ingredient was, he'd thought it would be smooth sailing from there on out. He'd found his niche. His kink. Game over.

There was a big problem, though. His supposed niche? It wasn't working out for him. Red had come to the sullen conclusion that it was a very bad time to try being a dom in this city.

Thanks to the runaway success of one infamous book, an absolute glut of popular erotic titles had hit the shelves in recent years. And while those books were helpful in the legitimizing arena, they had made Red's tentative forays into the lifestyle a bit problematic.

It was complicated, to say the least. Here he was, a guy in his prime in a city of millions, and he just kept coming up empty-handed. The odds had to be at least a little in his favor, right? Especially once he'd scrapped the idea of real relationships—the strings were a headache he didn't need right now. The whole dom/sub thing *should* have been a practical solution.

Of course, in the beginning he'd had no idea how to go about it. Those aforementioned books had given him some pointers, but Red wasn't so damaged that he wanted to actually hurt some poor woman in exchange for paying a few of her bills. He just wanted some kind of mutually-satisfying arrangement between two consenting adults, without all the detritus that usually accompanied that.

Enter the internet. Even when you thought you knew everything, you never could guess what was out there until you put on some waders and went trawling through the muck.

He'd found some forums, and then some clubs. Red's first forays into the life had not gone well, though. The shopping for props had turned out to be more interesting than the actual using of them. And the women he connected with had been nothing like he'd expected.

He'd had no shortage of willing partners for some of his edgier tastes. Most of the women were merely dilettantes, though, curious about trying things their girlfriends were whispering about but not committed to the lifestyle in any real way.

Occasionally, Red stumbled across a woman he could consider an actual submissive, but as yet, he hadn't found one who really pushed his buttons. Or rather, one who pushed the *right* buttons. They'd been awfully disappointing so far, like milquetoast doormats. While that should've worked for him—probably worked for other men—Red had merely felt...frustrated.

The first he met had played her role to the hilt, but Red had never doubted for a minute it was a role—there hadn't been a real reaction anywhere to be seen. He'd suspected she was a budding actress, perhaps, but aside from her looks, she'd done nothing for him. Flush with the false confidence of a novice, he'd been certain he could do better.

Door number two was a different story. Red had gotten the hang of the process a bit more. She'd had a sweet face and a nice figure, and she'd *seemed* to be on board—until it became eminently clear that the whole concept of dominance and submission went against every bone in that woman's body. So much for contracts—no matter how one refined them, they'd never cover everything. When she and Red had parted ways, it had been a relief for both of them.

The less that was said about the third and fourth women, the better. As he'd reflected, it was tough times in the dirty neighborhood these days. Rough out there for a dom. Or whatever the hell it was the little shitheads on the street liked to say.

He wasn't clueless. He recognized that he might be a stubborn, domineering bastard. He'd certainly been told that by a girlfriend or two. He could be jealous, possessive, and territorial—protective, when it was warranted. However, all that should not have presented a problem.

The bigger issue seemed to be that the unknown thing he was searching for hadn't yet been found. Some empty corner inside him was still seeking fulfillment, seeking relentlessly and without satisfaction. Whatever mysterious attribute Red hoped to discover in a woman—which would allow him to relax into some semblance of romantic contentment—he couldn't quantify, and he couldn't find.

That pissed him off.

Red could tell the potential for it was still there, though. The friends he'd made in the life had assured him that finding a good fit was only a matter of time. Once that happened, all the pieces would fall into place. He had to learn patience.

ALL THAT ASIDE, he had learned that it was an excellent time to be a publisher of books about being dominant. Books about getting naughty, books about finding true love amidst all the sordid crap in the world—books that hit you in the groin and the heart. Red was going to be making a pretty little penny on those books, whether or not he ever figured out how to make their fantasies a reality for himself.

When he'd begun making forays into the arts last year, using some of PKM's income to prop up little companies that needed the kind of boost only Red could provide, he'd never expected to find himself here. His decision to bail out the struggling house of Trident Publishing—to bring it under the mighty wing of PKM Industries and turn it into a healthy, profitable business like all his others—was looking better every day. At least, it was if his recent reading binge was any indication of what was to come.

He couldn't wait to prove the naysayers on the board of directors wrong. Red had an instinct that was as strong as his father's when it came to these things, and the sooner they realized that, the better. He hoped his new author was going to make great strides in helping them on their way.

Red flipped through his reports one last time and glanced at his watch. The primary reason for his good fortune, the absolute belle of the ball when it came to making big bucks writing dirty books, was due in his office in five more minutes.

He wasn't entirely sure why he'd insisted on handling this meeting himself. Curiosity, he supposed.

Trident had a decent portfolio, and that was what had grabbed his interest at the start. Once they'd cracked the books, though, it had become clear that the publisher was mostly being kept afloat by the virtue of only one author's spectacular sales. One author, with a pretty raunchy backlist. Red did love a puzzle.

And the numbers, suffice it to say, had been intriguing. Since Red wasn't a man to leave the important research to others, he'd dug deeper. He'd blown through Ms. Corelli's entire library of smut in a matter of weeks, and it had been *quite* the eye-opening education.

She was a talented writer, he'd give her that. He'd never imagined that the florid covers he saw in airport markets were hiding the kind of nuanced storylines he'd just taken a deep dive into. Red had always been an avid reader, but he'd never thought one way or the other about the romance genre.

It was a failing. If anything, he ought to have been impressed by the sheer quantity of books sold, which translated rather nicely into some staggering dollar signs. He hadn't been. Red had been oblivious to the sales figures, to the fact that most of the women of his acquaintance probably read the books, and worse—he hadn't considered for a moment that women might want that stuff in real life.

He'd hoped, certainly. He wouldn't have tried the whole dominant lifestyle thing if he hadn't. But lately, Red had been forced to confront the fact that the *idea* of bondage was infinitely more attractive than the *actuality* of it. He'd had to pause for the cause—his wannabe submissives weren't aroused, and neither was he. Dreary and discouraging all around.

He checked his watch once more, growing impatient. He'd been jumpy when he'd gotten in this morning, not liking how little information he had on his cash cow. A quick internet search had provided only a small thumbnail photo of Ms. Corelli, but it hadn't been enough to get any sense of her as a person. He was having trouble wrapping his mind around who he was about to enter into negotiations with, and that did not sit well with him.

The income her books brought in was crucial to revamping the faltering finances of Trident. If Red was going to whip the newest part of his sprawling empire into shape, he needed this meeting to proceed perfectly. He paused, smirking at his choice of words. *Ha. This was one leopard with some predictable spots.*

Perhaps Corelli would strut into his office in tight leather and too many buckles, wielding a whip and black lipstick. That could be either interesting or terrible. What if such a look sat uneasily on her? *Not sexy.*

There was also the possibility that Ms. Antoinette Corelli was a wallflower—a forgotten mouse of a woman, tucked into a dowdy sweater, and slacks with an elastic waistband. A spinster getting her thrills from being naughty in secret. *Possibly sexy.* It depended.

God. He laughed uneasily. Red had lost his mind and this meeting couldn't be over fast enough. Whoever Corelli turned out to be, he only had to hand over the new contract they'd drafted, assure her that she was the jewel in the crown, and move on with his life.

Anyway, it never took Red longer than a few minutes to figure people out, and this would be no different. Business, plain and simple.

Corelli would naturally be wary, having a new commander looking over her shoulder. But making nervous people get comfortable, making them offer up their reservations and worries to him like gifts to a god—that was kind of what he did best. Red's superpower, as it were.

He wasn't going to spend the next hour thinking about all the intriguing things this woman had imagined in the pages of her books. He wasn't.

The expected knock from his assistant Wayne rapped a staccato rhythm on the wood of his door. It was time.

"Enter," Red called. He wasn't nervous. And he wasn't half hard already. That would just be flat-out insane.

Red stood as Wayne ushered her in, his whole body snapping to attention when Ms. Corelli cleared the doorway. Desire for her began to smolder right then, as she strode across his office and he realized that the recent mental image he had concocted of her—dowdy, middle-aged suburban housewife—was woefully inaccurate.

It wasn't until the first touch of her skin, when Corelli extended her hand confidently to shake his, that Red's want of her turned into a full-bodied blaze. His scurrilous brain supplied him with an image—one he supposed he ought to feel guilty for. Instantly, he imagined that instead of releasing her hand, he yanked on it, pulling her forward across his desk.

In his mind's eye, Red rounded the hulking piece of furniture in seconds and stood behind her, his palms smoothing up her long legs and pushing Ms. Corelli's slim gray skirt up over her hips. He laid a hand lightly on her back, and he gazed down at the pale, bared skin of her thighs. His other hand reached to stroke her between her legs, and…

And Red's little fantasy ground to a halt. He sat heavily down in his big leather desk chair and gestured for the woman to take a seat opposite him. He was annoyed to realize that he could not at all envision what sort of underwear this woman might wear. Even more weirdly, he didn't know what kind he *wanted* her to be wearing. Right—because *that* mattered right now.

He gave himself a mental shake and tried to refocus on the conversation. His star author presented herself very professionally, poised and confident. She was seductive, too, he noticed—which was not something he'd usually say about a woman built like her. Corelli was on the petite side, but slim and graceful nonetheless—long-legged and willowy, without the supermodel height.

Not an inch too much skin showed anywhere, nothing clung too tightly, and her posture was ladylike without crossing too far into demure. Red was excruciatingly conscious of her figure, her beauty, her allure. She was perfect for what he wanted. He had to be *nuts* to think it.

He desperately wanted to wrap a hand in her shining, shoulder-length hair—which was the light brown of…he struggled to come up with an adequate analogy that didn't involve rotting autumn vegetation or alternative meat products. The best Red could come up with, though, was wood—the soft color of a cask, the sort that a fine bourbon might be aged in.

He doubted she'd appreciate that. He hadn't been able to compare her hair to the booze itself, after all, merely its weathered receptacle.

Her eyes, on the other hand, those were something else entirely—those would burn nicely going down. Her eyes could lay his six-foot-five ass out on the ground, all on their own.

Corelli was saying something to him with just the faintest touch of amusement in her brandy eyes and on her lips. Red ought to be more careful. He supposed a woman like her might very well know the direction of his thoughts. She was obviously sharp as a whip.

The phrase struck him with an arrow of desire straight into his gut. The rest of his insidious fantasy dropped into place suddenly: she wouldn't be wearing any panties at all, and his large palm would smack her on the ass. Hard.

Red jerked, suddenly uncomfortable with his wayward thoughts. Uncomfortable, period. This sort of intimate awareness of a woman had never happened in the office before. Not here, not like this—and truly, only rarely anywhere else in his life. Never when it was supposed to, that was for damn sure.

He could tell by the look on Corelli's face—no, wait, she was called Piper—that she thought he was acting strangely. He needed to pull himself together and regain control of the conversation.

"Forgive me," he murmured, by way of explanation. "It's been one hell of a week." When Red realized that he truly had no idea of what had been said so far, he took a deep, fortifying breath.

He launched into the backstory of his research and explained some things she likely already knew about her own industry. It made him feel grounded to recite the facts, though. More in control. And as he told her about how he'd read all her books, he recalled how unexpected they'd been.

Red had thought they might be the idle (though skillfully-rendered) daydreams of a lonely old lady, or possibly some past-her-prime cougar. Now that Piper sat before him, however…he wondered. Maybe she knew exactly what she was writing about. Perhaps there was more reality in her novels than he'd supposed.

Red drummed his fingers and considered her. Did he want there to be? Despite her whole unflappable veneer and her professional clothes and manner, her shoes were not entirely respectable, were they? In fact, they were so sexy they bordered on slutty—and did unholy things to her slim, lovely ankles, and the curve of her calves.

He wanted—no, needed—to know more about her.

Red told himself it was because she was an outlier. An anomaly who didn't fit easily into any of the customary categories he usually sorted people into.

Piper was pretty without seeming to be aware of it, sexy without apparent effort, and had a complicated, naughty mind that he'd love to get lost in.

Red wanted to know where she came from. What did she like? What made her tick? He wanted to unwrap her layers like it was his birthday, and none of that had the least bit to do with PKM, Trident, or his bottom line.

For fuck's sake. He'd unwittingly waltzed right into the world's oldest, most worn-out trope, the one so many of his idiot brethren seemed so fond of: *the lady in the streets and freak in the sheets*. And Red had gone and done it at work.

Again, he wondered what the hell had gone wrong here. What mysterious sorcery did this woman possess, that she'd tossed him into such unfamiliar territory? Red hated not having all the information he needed. He didn't enjoy not being one hundred percent certain of his next move.

Which likely explained why, before he quite knew what was happening, he'd wrapped up their train wreck of a meeting and cleared his schedule. Without thinking about it—without much conscious thought at all, really—Red was walking Miss Piper to the elevators like he could do it in his sleep.

He was done for, that was clear as fucking day.

Three

W HEN THE TOWN car dropped them at the curb twenty minutes later, Piper couldn't help but notice the way Red MacLellan snagged the gazes of so many people out on the street. After the meeting she'd just endured with him—not to mention the car ride—she could hardly blame them.

Red was hard to miss. He was literally larger than life, with uncommon coloring and a commanding presence. It was no wonder he stopped traffic, and probably hearts. Piper could barely manage to take her eyes off him herself.

But she did not need the headache of another alpha man. *Been there, done that.* Her former fiancé Kyle had a similar effect on people, and she knew now where that led. It might have taken her too long to figure it out back then, but she wasn't likely to forget the lesson soon. It had been hard enough to stomach it the first time.

It was funny how an innocuous get-together could transform into a social minefield so quickly. There'd she'd been, cheerfully mingling at Kyle's college reunion, telling everyone about the wonderful things they'd planned for the wedding.

When the whole time, those people had known a different story—a more pertinent one. A tale in which Kyle, her supposedly devoted man, was infamous for blazing a trail through the beds of cocktail waitresses all over town. A tale in which Kyle's junk never rested and he never told the truth.

A story in which Piper, somehow, still filled the role of antihero.

Ever since, she'd wondered how difficult it had been for Kyle's crowd to force those indulgent smiles onto their faces. Had they speculated about Piper afterward with their spouses or taken bets on how long she and Kyle would last? Had they debated whether she knew what kind of person she was marrying, or whether she cared? Whether *Kyle* cared?

Piper had only discovered the true thoughts of one woman, after all—the one who hadn't quite managed to keep her judgments to herself. Piper could no longer remember if it had been a former classmate or an ex-girlfriend, and it hardly mattered anymore.

The only relevant part was the way the smirking woman had demanded to know how Piper had become a porn star in the first place.

Piper could remember the way her next words had felt in her mouth, even now. "I'm…not. I'm a writer."

"Oh really?" had been the arch response. "And what do you write?"

Piper had been confused, naturally. "Just…romance." She still chafed at her unfortunate choice of words. Not *just*. Never *just*. For her, romance was everything.

The woman's expression had said it all, though. Piper was speechless in the face of it, desperate to defend herself but so caught off-guard she couldn't summon the argument.

But…why bother trying when it would make no difference? That woman's mind—all their minds—were already made up. They'd been fed a litany of lies by a man they admired, and they'd swallowed them whole. Kyle had led his acquaintances to believe Piper acted in pornos and then relished the inevitable result.

Everything crystallized into one sickening revelation for Piper, then. The truth was, the man she intended to spend her life with fancied himself an author, too. And, while Kyle never seemed to finish his own magnum opus, he was always more than happy to weigh in on Piper's writing.

He'd called her *inauthentic*, but she realized he might've been jealous of her and had found a way to put her in her place. Maybe he'd simply been bitter that Piper wasn't the sexpot he'd expected her to be. Maybe he got off on being the guy with the slutty fiancée.

Whatever his motivations were, his words had been misleading enough that people jumped to conclusions. He hadn't corrected them. Instead, Kyle fed their misconceptions—nurtured them, even.

If he couldn't stand to see her succeed where he himself fell short, why try to marry her, then? Piper assumed it was his way of keeping her down permanently. *The bastard.*

After those light bulbs had gone off, Piper's life had devolved into a painful blur, and one long, ugly mess.

By the time she tried to tackle the final book in the series she'd been working on, her confidence was at an all-time low. Piper struggled from start to finish, and for the first time ever, Trident had brought in story coaches and developmental editors. She had wondered despondently whether the man she'd given her heart to had ruined her for good.

PIPER SHOOK OFF the memory and pushed herself to catch up with the long stride of the man charging up the sidewalk in front of her. All of that was in the past. Piper only needed to be concerned about her future now—and her dinner date held that in the palm of his very large hand. She'd do well to pay attention.

The fancy Japanese restaurant Red led her to was dimly lit, with dark wood walls, small fountains burbling softly, and a giant golden statue of some god or another looming on the back wall.

"This is so pretty," Piper breathed, looking around. "I love it. How did you know?"

"You said Japanese first. Whether you realized it or not, that was your preference. You were trying to be accommodating, but deep down, you knew what you wanted," Red informed her.

"It looks like you did, too."

His smile was cryptic, but his words were easy enough to understand, "You'll see—the food here never disappoints."

A beautiful, kimono-clad hostess glided up and bowed. "Mr. MacLellan, what a pleasure to see you."

"Hey, Miko. I don't suppose you have anything available this evening."

"For you? Always," the hostess assured him. "Table for…two?"

If Piper hadn't already been watching the other woman closely, curious about the fact that Red had called her by name, she might've missed the way Miko's eyebrows twitched just a tiny fraction when she inquired about the number in their party. Miko was too much of a professional to comment outright, but why did she seem surprised?

"Yes. Something private, if you have it."

"Naturally. Right this way."

Red winked at Piper and murmured, "Pays to be a regular."

The hostess ushered them to a row of curtained-off alcoves lining the side of the restaurant. She indicated the one on the end, then drew open the curtain and waited.

Red gestured Piper up the two wide steps but stopped her at the top with a hand on her arm.

"We should take off our shoes first," he told her.

Before Piper could figure out how in the hell she was supposed to accomplish that gracefully, the man dropped into a crouch in front of the entire restaurant to help her. Red's hands dwarfed her ankles when he slipped first one heel off her foot, then the other. His thumbs brushed almost imperceptibly over her anklebones, and then he set her shoes aside.

Red rose to toe off his wingtips and lined them up neatly beside her pumps. He handed Piper down into the dropped seats and sat across from her. She tried not to think of their exposed feet, mere inches apart under the table, because that would be *weird.*

Instead, Piper congratulated herself on remembering to paint her toenails a sexy dark red last night, and for choosing to leave off the stockings this morning.

Her lucky leopard heels had obviously increased in potency since the last time she had employed them. Piper probably ought to remember that the next time she decided to pull them out.

Miko had procured a small clay teapot from a sideboard nearby. The hostess leaned in quietly to fill their cups, set the teapot beside their menus, then departed.

Red watched Piper intently as she shrugged out of her sweater, then assessed the lacy charcoal-gray shell she wore underneath with his measuring brown eyes. He turned away. A waitress had appeared suddenly at his side.

Piper glanced at the menu, and her eyes snagged immediately on the list of fruity cocktails. *Ah.* Liquid courage.

"Can I get you something to drink?" the woman inquired.

"I'll have a Singapore Sling," Piper told her cheerfully. Even the name was fun to say.

"And will you be having your usual, sir?"

Red nodded. "Yes. Thank you."

Once the waitress closed the curtain again, Piper commented drily, "I'd never guess you came here often."

"I know. But, more importantly, what the hell is a 'Singapore Sling'?"

"No idea," she shrugged.

He frowned. "Then why would you order it?"

"It sounded interesting. Besides, how bad could it be?"

Piper was saved from elaborating by the rail-thin man delivering their drinks. He liberated Red's *usual* from a nest of straw in a small wooden box, then poured it with great ceremony from a beautiful stone bottle. Sake, Piper decided, and a special one at that. Had to be.

The waiter hovered expectantly. Red took a sip and smiled, then turned to ask Piper, "Any particular favorites on the menu?"

"I love tuna tataki. Also, hand rolls with eel."

"Are you open to trying new things?"

"Absolutely." And, now her mind was back in the gutter.

"Okay if I order?"

"Knock yourself out," Piper told him. She got busy taking her first slug of the Sling, and it was…*whoa*. Strong. It was *strong*. Strong like Red's hands. Strong like his personality.

The second sip went down easier than the first. She would have to be careful if she didn't want to morph into a horny, giggling teenager by meal's end.

Piper clued back into Red's discussion with the waiter right in time to hear him remind the guy, "You remember about the peanuts?"

"Of course, Mr. MacLellan. We'll be very careful, as always."

Piper held up a hand, looking between them. "What about peanuts?"

Now Red was the one shrugging. "Deathly allergic," he intoned, like it was no big deal.

Piper turned immediately to the waiter. "Please make sure my food is safe for him, too," she asked. "In case we want to share."

"Certainly." The guy bowed slightly, stepped off the stairs, and pulled the curtain mostly shut. Through the opening, Piper watched him stride quickly toward the kitchen.

Red studied her and asked, "Why did you do that?"

"What do you mean? Don't you like sharing?"

"I have nothing against sharing. I'm just surprised you bothered about the nuts."

"I can't imagine why—it's common courtesy. I should know. My little brother is allergic to cashews."

"Ah." He sat back abruptly, but Red's eyes didn't leave her face.

"Besides, it's been a long day," Piper sighed. "I'd rather not top it off with my new boss's death on my hands."

"Now you're being dramatic."

"Do you think so? You were the one who said, *deathly allergic.* All I'm doing is taking you at your word."

At her tart tone, Red conceded, "I stand corrected. But can you please stop referring to me as 'your boss'? I'm not even in your direct hierarchy. There's got to be ten different layers between my position at PKM, and yours."

"How kind of you to point that out."

Red smirked at her. "Maybe we ought to change the subject."

"If you say so," Piper agreed. "Tell me how it is that you come here often enough for everyone to know your name, your allergy, and your drink order, yet they're surprised by you showing up with company."

Red finished off the rest of his drink in one large swallow, then reached over to twitch the curtain further closed.

"I suppose because…it's been a while since I brought a woman here." He poured himself another measure of sake. "Usually, I'm by myself, or clearly conducting business."

Weren't *they* conducting business? How very interesting. "I can't imagine you are hurting for dates."

"Well," he muttered. "You'd be surprised."

Piper's Singapore Sling spoke for her next. "Oh, come on. You're telling me the inimitable Padraig MacLellan doesn't have a devoted person clinging to the hull of his ship like a lovestruck barnacle?" she scoffed. "Whatever."

"You know, you really do have a way with words," Red commented.

Piper rolled her eyes. *Duh.*

He took a deep breath, for the moment more amused than offended. "I can confirm that I have no barnacles—romantic, complicated, or otherwise," he chuckled. "What about you, Ms. Fulham?"

Piper smiled back, then let her eyes shift from his face to the delicate porcelain cup beside her plate. She stared into its depths, watching the tiny leaves in the bottom swirl lazily through the faintly green liquid. So, they were laying out romantic statuses, were they? Her heart notched into a higher speed.

Three years ago, her heart had eventually healed. She'd exorcized Kyle's demons when she'd written her next book. Piper saddled a bad guy for the ages with Kyle's name, then killed him off with a particularly grisly duel at dawn. She'd made the fateful bullet miss its mark. The faux Kyle had lingered—and suffered—for days.

Naturally, the heroine of that tome had found a man who kept her quite happy between the sheets, and that had been an even bigger arrow flung at Kyle. He might have been a prolific lover, but Piper could say with certainty that his competency had suffered for it.

As far as she was concerned, Kyle could go suck it. Now that she was back to trusting herself, Piper was done with trusting men.

"I, too, am free of entanglements," she stated firmly, then immediately wished she'd put it less baldly. Barnacles were significantly wittier than entanglements. At least Piper hadn't pointed out exactly how long she'd been free of either thing. There was nothing funny about that.

Red simply said, "I'm delighted to hear it."

They sat in silence for a couple of minutes, drinking their beverages. Piper hoped that Red's *sake* wasn't as boozy as her Sling. At least then there might be one person still standing at the end of this.

He cleared his throat and jerked his movie-star chin in her direction. "I noticed that tattoo on your ankle. Do you have any more?"

From singlehood to tattoos. *Well, well, well.*

"There might be one or two more," Piper smiled. Right. Mystery—mystery was good.

"You aren't sure?"

"No, I am. But it's all interconnected, and one part is about ten years older than the rest. So, I guess an argument could be made that there are two more tattoos, rather than one."

"I see." Red did seem to be trying, as his eyes traveled over every exposed inch of her. He refrained from asking where the tattoos in question were, though.

"What about you?" she wondered. "Does the power suit have any ink under his businessy threads?" Piper found that unlikely and it must have crept into her tone—because Red's eyes jerked back up to hers, amused once more.

"As a matter of fact, I do." He defended himself lightly, calling her bluff, though he also chose not to enlighten her further. Piper had to acknowledge that the *mystery* thing definitely worked both ways.

She forced her voice into the same casual tone as his. "Assuming none of them are of the Tasmanian Devil, or a zombie trying to claw its way out of your skin, I believe my opinion of you just improved," she teased.

"We're safe on that count," Red chuckled. "Though I probably don't want to know what your original opinion of me was, do I?"

Piper stared pointedly at the curtain. "Did you see that? I think I saw a ninja out there."

"Nice try," Red laughed again. She grinned back at him, unaccountably giddy. No more Sling for Piper. She obviously couldn't handle its mischievous charms.

Under the table, Red's pant leg brushed her calf, despite her dutiful efforts to stay on her side. Piper shivered. It probably wasn't his fault—his legs were about a mile long. She wouldn't let it distract her. Much.

In a lower voice, Red asked, "Did I just spot two dimples over there?" The corner of his mouth lifted in a crooked smile. "Woe to the man you unleash the full force of those on."

At that, Piper giggled outright. Red gripped his chest, feigning injury.

"You act like I'm Medusa," she said.

Now the other side of his wide, tantalizing mouth ticked up, too. "The one who turns men to stone? How incredibly accurate." He held her gaze as his meaning gradually became clear.

Piper felt a hot flush wash over her neck and face. Red was flirting with her. Red was flirting *hard* with her. What good deeds had she done, that led to her deserving such a thing? She'd obviously forgotten them.

"And she blushes, too," he murmured drolly. "Pulling out all the punches, aren't you, madam? I bow before your mastery of torture."

And he did. Red kept his hand on his chest and bent low over his plate like he was dining with a queen.

Piper frowned. He had her so off-balance that she blurted out a shaky question she very well knew the answer to. "Why on earth should me turning beet-red torture *you*? I'm the one in agony over here."

Red paused while the curtain was drawn back, and the waiter delivered an exquisitely-arranged wooden boat of delicacies. The man topped off their teacups then plunged them into privacy once more.

"Really?" Red asked her then. "You can't guess why a man would be fascinated by a woman's blushes? Come on, Piper—you're the romance author, here."

She shook her head. She was acting like a numbskull, but between the sheer magnetic force of Red MacLellan, and the insidious Singapore Sling, her brain seemed to have taken an untimely vacation.

What a surprise. It was always easier for Piper to act sophisticated on paper, living vicariously through her characters, than it was in actuality.

Unfortunately, Red took her silence as leave to explain the obvious. "When a woman's aroused," he murmured, "Her skin flushes in some very interesting places—and I have an excellent imagination, Piper. *That's* what's torturous."

"Oh." Oddly, she noted that Red had managed to go *there*, without seeming the least bit skeevy. No, he'd gone there and sounded damn hot doing it. Maybe if she kept still, he'd go into a bit more detail.

"But," he intoned, "I suspect you already knew that."

Piper did. Oh, she really, really did. And she wanted to blush for Red in all the right places.

At last, he relented. "Try this. It's one of my favorites."

Piper accepted the piece of deep yellow fish absently, then tried to ignore how he watched her mouth when she bit into it. Under the table, his shoeless foot slid alongside hers.

"Do you like it?"

"Very much."

"I've never seen it anywhere but here and in Japan. I took a business trip there a couple of years ago." He served her a few more things from the boat between them.

Piper gazed down at her plate in rapture. "It's almost too pretty to eat."

"Almost." Red didn't even glance at his food.

She wondered how their supposed business dinner had gotten so far off track. This gorgeous, successful man was hitting on her, there was no doubt about that. He wasn't being cocky about it, though, and that intrigued her.

It was like Red was flirting with her despite himself. Like he was trying not to but couldn't help it.

Piper couldn't imagine what had gotten into him, and she had to figure out a way to regain some semblance of control. After all, she was *her*, not one of her characters. Although maybe that was the explanation—maybe Red was confusing Piper with one of her heroines.

It wouldn't last long. Eventually, men always figured it out, and she went back to being plain, disappointing Piper. She watched Red finish off a mouthful of yellowtail, then take a long swallow of tea.

That little pottery cup was dwarfed in his hand. He had large, graceful hands and slim, elegant fingers. They looked strong and capable. She'd bet they were talented, too.

Piper bit her lip. Red had been teasing her, but there was something else under the surface—like he truly cared about her answers. She forced herself to really look at him, but nothing she expected to see was there—no arrogance or self-absorption, no sense of entitlement, no pretension. None of it.

Red was confident and self-possessed, that was true. He was sexy as hell and nice, to boot. His obvious interest should be a good thing, but right now it made Piper about as nervous as a turkey in November.

Four

H EY," RED SAID, watching Piper gnaw on that lush lower lip of hers. "Tell me something about yourself. Besides the usual work stuff."

"Me?"

Like the concept was so hard to fathom. Red shot her a look.

Piper inhaled and stared slightly over his left shoulder for a beat or two, then met his eyes once more. "You mean, like, hobbies? Or…"

"Sure. What do you like to do?"

"Well," she hesitated. "I like to knit, but I haven't had much time for it lately. And I read a lot. Romance, obviously. And…" she faltered and peeked at his face again. It seemed to be a more difficult question than he'd intended. Red raised his eyebrows, urging her on.

"And I like taking long walks. In the…woods." Piper trailed off and winced, managing to look self-deprecating, pained, and adorable all at once. She clearly understood that she sounded like an escort service ad.

He couldn't resist poking at her. "Let me guess—in the gentle rain?"

"Yeah, no," Piper grimaced. "That would get really wet."

Red fought back a grin. "Muddy too, I imagine."

"Okay, wise guy," she balked, mounting a less-than-valiant defense. "What about you?"

He shrugged.

"Rock climbing? Space exploration? *What?*" she demanded testily.

Red thought about it. "I like rowing," he offered mildly.

"On the river?"

"Mostly. And…" *Huh.* As it turned out, answering the hobbies question was, in fact, a bit challenging when you were a grown-up who worked all the time.

"I like playing cards." At least, he'd enjoyed it in college, back when he'd still lived with Tate and Luca.

"Cards? What, like poker, you mean?"

Evidently, Red was not supplying Piper's inquisitive brain with enough detail. "No," he laughed. "Just, you know, gin rummy. That kind of thing. Oh, and I like backgammon. That's good, too."

Aside from the rowing—which, strictly speaking, should be classified as exercise rather than a hobby—the things he was listing all required other people. He did not hang out with other people much.

Red gazed into space, then added, "I did a puzzle once when I was visiting my grandmother. That was pretty cool, too."

"Once," Piper huffed. "You did a puzzle one time, and that makes it a hobby?"

He laughed again—he had to. His sudden social ineptitude was turning this conversation into a fucking train wreck. "No, I know," he acknowledged. "But if the opportunity ever presented itself, I would totally do one again."

Piper snorted. Actually snorted. *God.*

Red wanted to kiss that incredulous expression right off her pretty face. Maybe she wouldn't think he was such a tool if he banged her on his antique backgammon board. Hell, Piper could even wear her sexy leopard heels to round things out. Just the sight of those things, sitting innocently next to his own shoes on the restaurant's bamboo floor, was enough to drive him mad.

Saying any of that out loud would not be strictly polite, however. Red roused himself from his reverie and cast around for a topic, eventually coming up with, "Tell me something else. What about your family?"

Piper gave him a questioning look. "What do you mean?"

"Seems like everyone has a family story. I'm curious about yours."

"Not much to tell, I'm afraid. Irish on my dad's side, Italian on my mom's."

"How long have they been in the U.S.?"

Her nose scrunched up as she thought about it. "Maybe...early 1800's for the Fulhams. But my maternal grandparents didn't come over until the Forties."

Red considered that. "You've got the Irish coloring, but the Italian bone structure, don't you? Your eyes are very Italian, too. The effect is very..." *Seductive.* "Fetching."

"Is it?" Piper was nonplussed by that. She did something Red was coming to realize was a nervous tic—she deflected with a question of her own.

"What about you? At least part Scottish, I imagine, what with that name of yours."

"All, actually. The whole crew came from the mountains right outside Inverness."

Piper couldn't hide her amazement. "The *Highlands*? You've got to be kidding me."

He nodded, not understanding at first.

"Just to be clear: you're a very successful man, who looks like..." She gestured wildly in his direction with her chopsticks, "...*that.* And you're a Highlander, to boot? That's quite the trifecta." Piper added, "The leering kilt jokes alone must be horrendous. However do you endure it?"

Comprehension dawned. In Red's research, he'd read a handful of books about Scottish Highlanders, each raunchier than the last. He had absolutely preened at finding himself part of such illustrious company. And now his star romance author had been kind enough to acknowledge it, too.

He grinned and dropped the register of his voice. "Quite nicely, thank you very much."

Piper turned pink again, but at least she smiled. "No need to be smug about it."

"Those dimples," he couldn't help mentioning again. He shook his head and gazed heavenward. Much more of those and he'd be in need of some divine intervention.

"Hooligans, all of you," she retorted. "You don't have to be charming on top of it—give the other guys a chance, why don't you."

As if. "You've never done a Scottish book, have you? No pirates, no cowboys, either…why not?"

Piper sighed. "I get seasick, so pirates are out. And the whole cowboy thing—I dunno. Seems kinda dusty, I guess."

Red laughed. She was a trip. "And the Highlanders?"

Another sly grin from across the table. "I may have to tackle the Highlanders."

Maybe just one in particular.

TOWARD THE END of the meal, Red finally found an opening to ask Piper something he'd been wondering about for weeks.

The PKM board had nearly rejected the Trident proposition out of hand when they'd learned how prominently romances figured in the publisher's portfolio. He and Wayne had worked more than a few late nights, putting together the numbers that finally convinced them.

There'd been significant snark from his friends, too, when Red mentioned what he'd come to think of as "The Trident Surprise." Interestingly, the most derision hadn't come from Luca—a native Italian and probably the most traditionally macho man Red knew.

Instead, it had come from Tate, and that probably figured. The third member of their little fraternity was mostly-evolved but had been wallowing in the testosterone-heavy confines of the Army since graduation. Red knew it was hardly a "woke" atmosphere.

Now that Red had gotten a feel for Piper's personality, though, he was dying to know how she'd respond to critics who alleged that romances, with their steamy interludes, were basically porn for women. He ought to have known she would have a lot to say.

"I'd argue that romances are, in fact, the antithesis of porn," Piper mused.

"Why is that?"

She took a deep breath. "Think about it this way. Pornography is sex, absent emotional intimacy, right? It's fornication that is completely divorced from the concept of love, existing solely for the purpose of titillation. Which is fine."

"Okay." Red was thoroughly enamored with the matter-of-fact way she explained herself. Unlike before, there wasn't a single blush or stammer, while Piper expounded on a topic that others might find uncomfortable.

Red wondered what else he might get her talking about. What else she'd be sanguine over.

"Whereas romance novels use sex as a means to illustrate the growing emotional intimacy between a couple. Romances use sex as an expression of love. In my opinion, it's the complete opposite end of the spectrum from pornography."

"God," Red sighed, staring at her. "You have no idea how much I wish I'd had you there when I was trying to win over my board last year. It just took you two sentences to explain something that Wayne and I couldn't manage in an entire PowerPoint presentation."

She smiled, "Suffice it to say, I've had plenty of chances to hone my message. Practice makes perfect."

"Apparently so. Remind me to rope you in, the next time I need to convince someone."

"At your service," Piper said, twinkling cutely.

Red watched her flirt and could barely remember to breathe.

WHEN THEY EMERGED from the restaurant after dinner, the car was waiting for them. Red handed Piper inside and slid in beside her, then spent the next twenty minutes trying not to get caught staring at his star author's long, toned legs.

As his driver wound through the remains of rush hour, the city lights cast flickering shadows across Piper's face. Red wondered if the air felt as thick to her as it did to him. He wondered how hard it would be to cross the inches separating them and take her face in his hands.

In too few minutes, though, they pulled up outside Piper's hotel. Red followed her onto the sidewalk and jammed his hands into his pockets so he wouldn't do something stupid—but he forgot to put a lock on his mouth.

Next thing he knew, he wasn't saying goodbye, so much as insisting on escorting Piper up to her suite. She looked somewhat confused but didn't put up much of a fight. Which probably meant she was packing mace in her handbag and wasn't afraid to use it.

On the one hand, the city was a dangerous place. Red had noticed the way other men's eyes followed Piper on the street, as obviously taken with her fresh prettiness as he was. He'd really rather she didn't get assaulted in the hotel his company had arranged for her. *Safety first*, and all that.

On the other hand, Red was forced to admit to himself that he desperately wanted to spend this last ten minutes with her. And given his edgy proclivities, perhaps the threat didn't come from others, but from him.

In the tight confines of the elevator, Red had to wonder what he'd been thinking. Trying not to kiss Piper in here was even more of a challenge than the car ride had been. Red stared at the flashing floor numbers and gripped hard on the rail. He prayed fervently for deliverance.

When they got to her suite, Piper smiled sweetly up at him.

"I had a really nice time tonight. Thank you."

"I'm glad you could join me," he said. "I had a great time, too."

She kept looking up at him with those whiskey-brown eyes of hers. Calm. Waiting.

He blurted out, "I should probably go."

"Okay," she whispered.

What emerged next from Red's mouth was a bit startling to him—and possibly to her. "I probably shouldn't kiss you goodnight. Even though I'm dying to."

She didn't recoil or frown, though. Piper just smirked and murmured, "Is that so?"

Red's eyes narrowed as he studied her. "On second thought, maybe I should."

She laughed. Damn her.

He ignored all common sense, plus the roaring in his head, and did what he'd been aching to do for the last three hours—he bent and pressed his lips to hers. Piper's mouth was exactly as soft and sultry as he'd imagined it would be.

Red could tell she was holding herself in reserve…until suddenly she wasn't anymore. Suddenly, her mouth was opening and welcoming him in, and Piper was kissing Red back like her life depended on it.

He yanked his hands from his pockets, gripped the back of her head and one tantalizing hip, then held her in place so he could explore her with his tongue.

Red was finally, actually, kissing her. It was dazzling.

But then she jumped like a startled cat when a room service cart rattled across the other end of the hall. He pulled reluctantly away, to find Piper flushed with what might be desire—or possibly mortification.

In contrast, Red felt ferocious. Ravenous, even. Before he could grab her again, she laughed nervously.

Piper's head tilted toward her suite's door. "Maybe we need to move this inside."

He hadn't expected that. Hadn't expected any of this. Off-kilter from the intensity of that kiss, he gasped, "No." Perhaps a bit too firmly.

Piper went pale. "I'm sorry. I didn't mean like…like *that*—" she stammered.

Red cupped her jaw in his hands, anxious to keep contact between them. "It's okay, I know what you meant. It's just that I don't trust myself to go in there with you right now." Even so, he couldn't resist dropping another quick peck on her lips.

"Well, there's a little sitting room," she tried. "And a door that separates it from the bedroom."

He had to smile. He got it—he didn't want to stop either. At. All.

"Regardless," Red explained. "I'm a dude. I'll know a bed is in there."

"Geez, I must be out of practice," Piper laughed unsteadily. "I mean—"

He cut her off again. None of that nonsense. "No," Red said. "You aren't."

She felt like a bonfire of wickedness, burning away all sorts of civilized things like restraint and propriety. Red would be lost in seconds if he went in that room with her.

Piper merely frowned in confusion and murmured, "Oh."

"I'd still like to see you again," Red offered. "If you're interested. I have a couple of meetings down in D.C. this week." Or he would, once he had Wayne set them up. "If that's close to you, maybe we could set something up for when I'm done."

"Seriously? That's lucky."

Red believed in making his own luck, but whatever. He said, "I agree. Should I text you the details?"

In answer, Piper fumbled quickly for her purse, digging through it for her cell. Moments later, he'd given her his personal number, she'd texted him a gif of a bespectacled secretary typing on an old-fashioned Corona, and Red was tucked into the hotel elevator sailing down to the lobby.

What in the world had just happened? He'd been jumpy as hell, waiting to meet her, and then Piper had been nothing like he'd expected. Red had commandeered her evening in some half-cocked effort to figure her out and then ended up with his tongue down her throat.

The *one* person in the world he could not fuck up a relationship with—the one and only person who could make or break the Trident deal besides himself—just had to be a stunning, intriguing woman he couldn't walk away from.

Red groaned. Karma was an evil, evil bitch.

Five

P IPER SANK AGAINST the back of her hotel room door and
pressed two shaking fingers against her lips. As business
meetings went, she was positive she'd never had one go quite that
way—not outside the pages of her books, at least.

She pulled her phone from her pocket and peeked at the
screen, just to confirm that she hadn't imagined that steamy scene
in the hallway. *Yup.* Red's text was still there, glowing brightly in
the dark. Piper clutched it to her chest and took a deep breath.

She tried stepping further into her suite, but her legs weren't
as steady as she would've liked. She staggered over to the small
loveseat and dropped into it. Her purse slid from her shoulder,
and her attaché sagged against her leg. She'd—she'd just made
out like a hormonal teenager with a man she'd only met hours
before. *And* he was her new boss.

Red had been pretty insistent that he wasn't exactly her direct
superior, and Piper could sort of understand where he was
coming from. Sort of. If he was a god on Olympus, she might as
well be a lowly shepherdess. Not a ton of opportunity for
interaction, there.

But who was kidding who? If the head honcho at PKM
Industries took a sudden dislike to her and her little story lambs,
Piper would bet her grandma's house that he'd find a way to toss
her fat new contract right in the trash. And, given the way her

royalties had been declining in the last few years, she could really use that influx of cash.

Piper had so many awesome ideas for her new series, but she was counting on PKM to add the extra push she needed to get her income back up to where it had been.

After all, her grandparents' house was going to need some serious work soon. When her parents retired last year and Piper moved into the place, she hadn't realized quite how much deferred maintenance she would be on the hook for—she'd only been determined to keep the farmhouse in the family.

Perhaps her mom and dad hadn't warned her because they believed Piper could afford the needed repairs better than they could. It probably served her right. If her dad hadn't been so dismissive of her career, Piper might not have had to act so proud whenever it came up in conversation. Maybe instead of rubbing his nose in her success, she could've been more honest about the ebb and flow of royalties in the publishing industry.

She sighed. There was nothing to be done about it now. Piper would fix up the home that her grandpa had built so painstakingly, and PKM would help her.

She reached down into her attaché and pulled out the new contract, then switched on the lamp beside her. After she'd combed through the first several pages, she couldn't resist calling Perry.

Her attorney picked up, as he always did, on precisely the second ring. "Shanahan," he barked.

"Perry, it's Piper. I know it's late, but I just wanted you to keep an eye out for…"

"Already got it."

"Are they for real?"

"I'm still going over it, but it certainly seems so. Nicely done, Cupcake."

"Thank you." Piper paused. "Do I need to remind you again that you cannot ever call anyone else *Cupcake*? You'll get in trouble, you know that, right?"

Perry laughed, a low, gravelly sound. "What do you take me for? I know that. But you and I—we go way back."

They certainly did. Perry had served in the Army with her father before beginning his legal career and had known Piper and her brother since they'd been in diapers.

"That's true," she admitted.

"So, you're my Cupcake, even if you are also a fancy pants author these days."

"All right, fine. But listen—do I sign this tonight and hand it over before I leave? Or what?"

"No, let them sweat for a bit. This contract makes it patently obvious they don't want you to walk. No need to rush anything. I'll check in with their legal team tomorrow, and then we can send it back to them in a week or two. I might be able to swing a couple more perks for you."

"What else is there?"

"You'd be surprised."

Piper smiled. Hiring Perry had truly been one of the best decisions of her career.

"You're the boss," she said.

"Speaking of…how was MacLellan, anyway? Did he seem like a good egg or is he some groovy Romeo who thinks he's God's gift to publishing?"

"He's…" Piper touched the pads of her fingers to her lips again and paused. "He's quite the force of nature."

"I'd heard that, but you know how the papers can be. They get it wrong sometimes."

"Not this time," she said.

Truer words had never been spoken. After she hung up with Perry, Piper laid awake for a long time, trying to unravel the murky motivations of Red MacLellan.

From a business standpoint, he had a definite reason to keep her happy—to keep her willing to work for his company and to make sure she kept producing the kind of product that would give him a good return on his investment.

From a personal standpoint, Red had no reason whatsoever to flirt with her, to kiss her like it was his job, and to ask if he could see her again. It nagged at her.

Maybe Piper had been tipsier than she'd realized and confused calculated charm with flirtation. It was quite possible she'd been projecting—transmuting her own scorching attraction to the man into a mistaken sense that he had a thing for her.

But…then Red had *kissed* her. He'd kissed her hard, like the world was ending and the house was on fire, and they'd both die right there on the utilitarian hotel carpet if he didn't do it correctly. And, oh God, had he done it correctly. Red had kissed her more correctly than any man ever had before, and probably ever would again.

Then he refused to come into her room.

Then he asked for a second date.

Piper huffed in frustration. None of it made a lick of sense. She flopped over for the umpteenth time and willed herself to fall asleep. Would she see him again, she wondered, during one of her meetings the next day?

By SIX THE next morning, Piper had parsed every statement Red had made in her presence in the prior twenty-four hours and convinced herself that it must all be one big chess game to him.

Red had a reputation as a ruthless negotiator, after all. He wouldn't be afraid to use any and every weapon in his arsenal to get what he wanted. If he thought Piper was going to make his Trident deal a success, he would want her happy.

What else would make a lonely romance author happier than a little nookie of her own? Red's efforts had been eerily accurate. She'd fallen for his seduction routine like she'd never met a grown man before.

Piper wanted to groan at her naivete—she was useful to Red, nothing more. Hadn't he said he wished she'd been on hand to convince PKM's board to go ahead with the Trident acquisition?

Red hadn't been gazing lustily into her eyes and playing footsie because he *liked* her. He'd done it because he needed her, and Piper could absolutely handle that. She needed him, too.

They would simply have to need each other's talents without any of the kissing, because that could get out of hand real quick. *Could.* Ha. *Would* was more like it.

She showered and dressed, drank a perfect latte from room service, and then marched downstairs to eat a very reasonable and business-like bowl of oatmeal in the hotel's café. The front desk staff called her a cab, and Piper set out for Trident's offices feeling very much in control.

She could do this. Of course, she could. Hell, Piper probably wouldn't even see Red MacLellan again on this trip, and he certainly wasn't going to follow up on visiting her back in Maryland. Why would he bother? Piper would show him that he could get what he wanted from her without all the sexy nonsense.

She barely noticed the city streets that rolled past her window. By the time the cab pulled up to Trident's building near Rockefeller Center, Piper was a woman on a mission. She strode into the lobby like she owned the place, and only missed one—okay, maybe two—steps when Red's assistant appeared out of nowhere to stop her.

"Good morning, Miss Piper," Wayne grinned. "Ready to make some new friends?"

Piper took in the man's gray suit, pale blue shirt, and bright green tie with an approving nod, and reached out to shake his hand. Firm grip, but not crushing. She liked him. Reluctantly, Piper scanned over his shoulder for a certain tall, auburn-haired drink of water, but Wayne appeared to be quite alone.

"Only if I can start with you," she teased.

"Honey, I'm gonna be your best friend, by the time we're through. Nice shoes, by the way." He led her to the bank of elevators and hit the button.

"Thank you. Nice tie."

"It is, isn't it?" Wayne smoothed a hand down the strip of silk and smiled warmly. Then he continued, "I figured I'd bring you by Legal first, so you can meet Anika. If you have any questions about the new contract, she's the one you should ask, but I doubt she's expecting anything final from you today."

"I hope not. My lawyer and I will be looking it over for a while yet."

"Good. After Anika, I thought I'd bring you to meet some of the new people we have in the design department."

"Sounds good."

"By then, I'm hoping you'll be hungry, and we can go find somewhere fun to eat."

"Wayne, I should probably tell you now. I am almost always in favor of food."

"See?" He elbowed her. "I knew I liked you. I mean, not as much as that British earl with amnesia you wrote about—but really close."

Piper goggled at him. "Don't tell me you read my books, too?"

"Only a few of them. Mr. MacLellan insisted." He held open the elevator door while she entered, then followed her inside before continuing, "I'm in law school at night, so most of my reading is of the dry, torts variety. But what I read, I approve of, Madam. I definitely approve."

ANIKA, AS IT transpired, was a beautiful, yet harried, drill sergeant. Tall and slim, with waves of sleek, glossy black hair, the head of PKM's legal department looked more like an exotic supermodel than someone who spent her days knee-deep in corporate litigation.

When Piper and Wayne entered Trident's third-floor legal offices, Anika was beelining across the room, barking orders right and left, and sending her soldiers scurrying in every direction to bring her what she wanted. She was younger than Piper expected, and not a little daunting.

Anika zeroed in on them immediately and headed over.

"You must be Piper," she said. "Red told me you'd be coming."

Wayne said, "Piper, this is Anika Faroughi, the head of PKM's legal team. She's here at Trident this week, trying to help with the transition."

"Trying, being the operative word," Anika commented drily.

"Nice to meet you," Piper smiled.

"Likewise. I'm sorry I don't have more time to chat this morning, but let's set something up the next time you're in town."

"Sounds good."

Wayne whipped out his cellphone and tapped out something on his screen.

"I know Shanahan is still going over it, but does everything look good on your contract so far?"

And then some, Piper thought. Aloud, she said, "I haven't really gotten too far into it, but so far, so good."

"Great. Feel free to give me a call if you have any questions, okay?" She started edging away. "I'm sorry—I have a conference call in a minute, so I can't stay. Wayne, will you make sure Piper has my card?"

Wayne, Piper was coming to realize, was usually prepared for anything. With a flourish, he extracted the necessary business card from within his leather portfolio and handed it over. Anika gave them a brief wave and disappeared around the corner at a rapid clip.

"I'll hit up Anika's assistant later, and figure out when you two can meet up," Wayne told her as they headed back to the elevators. "Do you like Thai food? It's her favorite."

His phone pinged, and he glanced down—then grinned broadly.

"Anika says to tell you she's also a big fan of your aristocratic amnesiac."

Piper laughed, "Now where have I heard that before?"

"Mr. MacLellan wanted her to read all your books, too, but she has even less time than I do. She cornered me a few months ago and made me tell her which one was the best one, so naturally, that's where I steered her."

"Naturally."

"He really was something," Wayne sighed.

"I commend you on your good—"

They exited the elevator again, this time into what appeared to be a heated argument.

"—taste," Piper finished weakly.

Wayne frowned, taking in the two clusters of people gathered at the side of the large open area. Piper recognized a few familiar faces, looking decidedly put out, and noted the preponderance of new employees.

It looked like PKM had done some house-cleaning here in the design department already.

It took Wayne a couple of tries before he could get someone's attention. Finally, Carol, the woman who'd done most of the work on Piper's last few book covers, trotted over.

"Sorry guys," she breathed, shooting a look behind her. "Not a great time."

Wayne stood straight and was as stiff as Piper had yet seen him. "I have Piper Fulham here for her 11 o'clock with the new design team."

Carol looked back and forth between them, confused. "You…what?"

Another woman Piper had seen before came over then. Piper had never worked with her but knew she was chummy with one of Trident's other authors, one she'd never liked at all.

"I've got this, Carol. Wayne, we're all ready for you and Piper in the conference room. Why don't you guys head in there, and I'll round up the others."

Wayne's chin notched up a fraction at the woman's imperious tone, but he didn't comment. He didn't need to—his stony expression spoke volumes.

Piper shrugged at Carol and followed him away.

THE MEETING WAS a fender bender from the get-go. Trident's designer—Sue, she learned—was utterly determined to stake her claim on Piper's new series. She made a handful of sweeping pronouncements about industry standards and declared firmly that it would be "sexy shirtless men" or nothing for the covers.

PKM's new people were more circumspect. They asked Piper where she saw her new series going, what she thought the general feel of them would be, and which covers she'd liked the look of recently. They listened carefully to her responses and took meticulous notes.

Piper liked them. Sue was incensed.

"With all due respect, Piper's skill set is coming up with the words to fill the books. We're the ones in the business of packaging what she writes. As long as we're conveying the right smut level, I should think—"

Piper held up a hand. "I'm sorry, what did you say?"

"Well, it's hardly like it's rocket science. Sex sells, Piper. You, of all people, ought to know that."

Wayne's eyes narrowed. Piper took a long sip of her water and tried to collect herself.

One of the new designers said hesitantly, "We've seen some new types of covers do very well in this market recently. An author of Ms. Fulham's caliber definitely has the wiggle room to bend the rules a bit. I think if she—"

"Well, she's hardly the next Nora Roberts," Sue sniped. "And besides, I'm sure even *La Nora* knows her place when it comes to these things."

Piper sputtered, "Without me, you won't have anything to sell here!"

Wayne shot to his feet abruptly and pointed at one of PKM's people. "You got what you need for right now?"

The man darted a quick glance at Sue and nodded.

"Great," Wayne said. He pulled on Piper's arm, tugging her to her feet. "We have to boogie. Piper has a lunch meeting she can't miss, but I can bring her back here later to hash out some more particulars if you need her."

Sue looked furious and suspicious. "That would be marvelous. Thank you so much, Wayne."

He smiled thinly and hauled Piper away. In their wake, the conference room erupted into another testy fracas.

"Christ," Wayne muttered, stabbing at the elevator button. "What a shrew."

"Thanks for the bailout," Piper tried, after they'd stood in tense silence for a while.

Wayne frowned mightily and asked her, "Is it always like that?"

"It's not usually that contentious."

"Have you ever worked with Sue before?"

"No. Usually, I had Carol, and some of the other Trident originals."

"Well, this shit ain't gonna work," he told her. "Not by a long shot. Mr. MacLellan would've had a cow if he'd seen that."

He whipped out his phone and texted for a few moments, then slipped it back into his pocket as they hit the street. Wayne looked around expectantly and made a visible effort to shake off his irritation.

"All right, lady. What's good around here? Time to feed the beast."

"There's a good place about a block that way," Piper told him. "Do you like—"

Wayne's pocket burst into a blaring reggae ringtone, making him wince. He clawed at his blazer, freed the device, and stabbed wildly at it.

"Wayne Thompson."

Several frantic sentences later, he hung up with an apologetic grimace.

"Piper, I am so sorry. I have to run back to PKM and put out a little fire." He strode to the curb and threw out his arm to hail an approaching cab. "You grab some lunch. Text me the name of the place and I'll meet you there in time for the rest of that design meeting, I promise."

The cab came to a screeching stop next to him.

Piper called out, "Want me to get you something to eat?"

Wayne leaned out the open window. "Yes! Something with cheese! And mushrooms!" he shouted as the yellow car careened away.

She smiled as she watched him go, relieved that PKM had seen fit to assign her such a relatable chaperone for the day. She turned and headed down the sidewalk, wondering if Red had been behind it.

Six

ROB ARRIVED FOR his weekly meeting with Red bearing his usual punch-list of action items. The head of Trident's transition team also wore the expression he normally saved for when they discussed which troublesome employees had to be cut loose.

It was hardly Red's favorite part either, but it needed to be done if this acquisition was going to proceed the way it was supposed to. The Dentons hadn't exactly been running a tight ship, and it was up to PKM to undo all their years of mismanagement.

"All right, Rob. I know why you're here. Let me have it," Red said.

The man nodded and leaned forward. "Here's the list of the authors we're going to cull. Most of them aren't producing squat and haven't sold a book in years."

"Fine."

Rob sat in silence, staring grimly down at the paper.

Red sighed—he ought to have known it wouldn't be so easy. "Okay, what's the problem?"

"Well, there are a couple of potential issues. This guy, Phil Miller—"

"That's a pen name," Red cut in. "His real name is Jim Denton."

"No shit. He's the son, right?"

"Yep. Their only kid. Get it? *Tri*-Dent?"

"I…wow. Never once put that together."

Red smiled. "He wrote a series of crime thrillers, I believe. Set in Sparta."

"From what I can determine, they weren't terribly popular," Rob countered. "They look like they tanked soon after release, and each one sold worse than the last."

"Reach out to his agent," Red told him. "I suspect they're probably already looking for a new home since Mommy and Daddy aren't running the show anymore. Maybe we can call around and help speed up the process for them."

"I'll check with Anika," Rob said. "But that should work fine with his contract."

Red nodded. "Who else?"

"Rachel Wilbon, here. She had a title that got some attention about three years ago. Won a small literary award, that kind of thing."

"And what has she done for me lately?"

"Jack shit," Rob admitted. "She and her agent both insist she's working on a fabulous new project, but…" He shrugged, making his disbelief clear.

"Do you have her sales numbers anywhere?"

Rob handed him a file. Red paged through it, scrutinizing each sheet. Finally, he looked up.

"Flash in the pan," he decided. "Can her."

Rob winced. "She and her agent are both somewhat…high strung. That is not going to be fun."

"When is it ever?"

Robert scraped at his chin. Red had come to learn through their monthly poker games that it was the man's worst tell—and evidently, his cards sucked right now.

"I've got to get off this goddamn planet," Rob groaned.

Red had to laugh. "Fine, you little pussy. Send the dragon ladies to me. I'll slay them for you while you go have some milk and cookies."

His transition chief popped out of his chair and grabbed for his papers and files. His face was wreathed in relief.

"Thank you, master," he said.

Red spotted a file with Piper's pen name scrawled across the tab and laid a hand on it before Rob could snatch it. He stared the other man down and set all joking aside.

"This one stays on board, Robert. No fucking around with her."

"Fire the breadwinner? What do I look like to you? Some kind of imbecile?"

"Just checking. She's crucial to pulling this off."

"I get it."

"See you next week."

"Not if I take up drinking first."

Red watched him go then ran a hand across the top of Piper's file. That kiss last night…he snorted. Hell, forget the kiss. The whole night with her had been unforgettable. She was gorgeous and smart and funny. Sharp and interesting. Mouthwatering.

Red wondered what Piper was up to right now. If he remembered her schedule correctly, she and Wayne should be getting ready to grab some lunch any minute.

It had been a split-second impulse to send his assistant to Trident that morning to meet her. But Red knew the man could charm the pants off nearly anyone, and he'd wanted Piper to have a buddy as she met all the new people up there. He wanted to give her someone she could lean on. Someone he trusted, who would report back to him if stuff got out of hand.

A crash sounded outside Red's office. He got to his feet to investigate. When he poked his head out his door, Wayne—who was supposed to be minding Red's new favorite author—was crouched in front of his credenza, opening and slamming doors as he muttered and cursed. Piper was nowhere to be found.

"Looking for something?"

Wayne jumped and cracked his knee on the solid mahogany cabinet, then took in an exceptionally long breath as his face turned crimson. At last, he uttered calmly, "Anika needs some paperwork from our presentation to the board. I was sure I filed it in here, but I can't seem to put my hands on it."

"Ah. I talked to her about that earlier. I have it on my desk, sorry."

His assistant's shoulders relaxed markedly. "Oh, thank God."

Red watched him sit on the office carpet for a minute or two, then inquired, "Have you misplaced your charge, Master Wayne?"

"You mean Piper? No, I sent her to get some lunch. I'll pull that stuff together for Anika, then head back to Trident and drop it off. After that, I'll get Piper and bring her back to tangle with the design folks."

"Tangle?"

"Yeah, so…it looks like the old guard and the newcomers aren't exactly playing nice. Piper kind of got caught in the middle of it this morning."

"Wayne," Red warned.

"I know, I know. I'll get them under control when we go back in there." He pushed to his feet and dusted himself off. "But I have to get Anika's stuff, first."

That left Piper sitting alone somewhere, eating lunch all by herself. Abruptly, the idea of stealing another few minutes with her was too tantalizing to resist.

"Where'd Piper go, anyway?" Red asked.

Wayne extracted his cell from his jacket and peered at it. "Someplace called Mama Maisie's. She texted me a picture of the menu. There's a long wait, I guess, but I told her she had time."

Red knew the place. It was only a few blocks from Trident and a pretty decent run from PKM's headquarters. If he hurried, he could probably change and trot over there before Piper even finished her sandwich.

The exercise might help him shake off the restlessness that still lingered after his unexpectedly intriguing date with Ms. Fulham. Seeing her again might put to rest whether last night was some kind of strange fluke.

It might also settle the annoyance Red felt about having to handle Rachel Wilbon later that day. He could already tell she was going to be a handful and a half.

ALL THE BALLS up in the air were making him antsy. It bugged him. As Red's long stride ate up block after block, the allegory wasn't lost on him. There were days when he'd like to leave more than just PKM headaches in his wake.

After the first mile, though, he no longer cared. And after a few more, he felt mostly like himself again. Red was even reasonably confident in his ability to interact with other humans without biting anyone's head off.

Soon, he found the funky cafe down the block from Trident and pushed his way inside. The weather was reasonably cool that day, so at least Red wasn't a stinking, sweaty mess. Still, he ducked into the men's room after he ordered and tried to clean up a bit more.

Red lounged at a table near the window to wait for his food. When he finally spotted Piper, she was tucked in the back corner, alternating between scribbling furiously in a notebook and watching the other customers. Her eyes were a little glazed over, a little unfocused, like she was listening to something important inside her head.

Red realized…she must be writing. Before his very eyes, Piper was creating something out of nothing—new people that didn't exist yet, with thoughts and feelings, histories and futures. *Passions.* Piper would create whole towns for them to live in, too, places with pasts that sometimes acted as much like characters as the people did.

The act of magic she was performing impressed him. Red had a lot of skills, but he knew he couldn't do that. He didn't think he'd even be able to concoct an intelligible bedtime story for a child. He simply wasn't wired that way.

It didn't stop him from enjoying the efforts of others, though. Even as a kid, he'd read incessantly. Red had always relished the sensation of subsuming himself within the parallel universes of books. Escaping his strict reality, even for a few minutes.

And Piper's books had been *quite* an escape. He'd take her version of the world over space adventures or mutiny on the high seas any day. Who wouldn't? To want and be wanted like one of her characters fulfilled every testosterone-laden cell in his body.

Red wracked his brain, trying to remember who Piper had met at Trident that morning. If Piper had been meeting with *him* again, maybe Red could indulge himself into thinking that he'd inspired her current literary efforts.

Though maybe it wasn't someone or something from her morning. Maybe it was their little interaction last night that had tickled Piper's fancy. Did her muse even work that way?

A man could hope.

Red noticed the troubling patchouli-scented cloud that enveloped him one moment before he registered its source, hovering at his shoulder. He turned to find the young woman who'd taken his order standing there studying him, plate in hand. Her name tag read *Eight*.

He puzzled over that while she purred, "Hey, Daddy. Your sandwich is ready. I made it myself."

She placed it in front of him with an expert twist. If Red was inclined, he could admire her scent or even steal a peek down her shirt.

"Thanks," he murmured, looking away.

Since when did they deliver tableside at this joint? In the past, he'd had to retrieve his food from the counter once the cook belted out his number. Mostly, Red had an underling at Trident pick up the food, so he could keep working at whatever desk he was borrowing that day.

The waitress swiveled to present him with an unobstructed view of her ass, then set his drink on the table, too. When she didn't move away immediately, Red peered up at her face. Dark, wavy hair. Olive skin and large, heavily-lined eyes. Eight held his gaze and smiled slowly.

Red suppressed a wince. It was impossible to tell what her face might look like under all the cosmetics. Was so much makeup necessary to sling corned beef, or was she headed somewhere more interesting afterward?

And what on earth did *Eight* mean, anyway? Eight kids? Eight personalities?

The waitress misunderstood Red's focus, of course. "Is there *anything* else I can get for you?" she inquired. "My number, perhaps?" She preened a little, too, stretching to reveal a sliver of skin between the hem of her shirt and the low-slung waist of her painted-on jeans.

She looked like she'd be…demanding. Loud. Emotionally, physically, and financially needy. And Red had fucking been there and done that, too many times to count.

He shook his head, muttered, "No thanks," and then fiddled with the frilly toothpick jammed in his pickle until he felt Eight depart.

He rested his hands beside his plate and wondered what had given him away this time. He was wearing nothing-special running clothes, a bit too damp around the collar to be strictly polite. Red wasn't wearing a fancy watch and hadn't arrived in a late-model sports car. He didn't even bother kidding himself that his face was the showstopper.

And yet, girls like Eight always seemed to sniff out his money from a mile away. Didn't seem to matter what Red wore, where Red went…they found him. They knew him. They were ready for him, and his fat wallet. It was damned exhausting. He couldn't imagine how much more it might suck to actually be famous—an actor or a rock star or something. He'd probably have to become a hermit.

Eventually, he decided it must have been his sneakers, this time. They were a little too new, a little too flashy. Red had allowed the sales guy to talk him into them, but only because they were comfortable, and he'd already grown impatient with the process. Just his luck that Waitress Eight knew her high-end footwear.

Feeling deflated, Red picked up half his turkey club and took a bite. While he chewed, he peeked over at Piper. Just to check on her—not because he wanted to confirm that she was, in fact, far prettier than Eight.

She'd clearly already spotted him, and even more obviously had witnessed his exchange with the waitress. Rather than rolling her eyes at the presumptuous girl, though—or even looking disgusted with him—Piper merely seemed perplexed, like she thought she'd missed something.

Whatever spell Piper had been under before had been broken. Apparently, re-entry to the real world was a bitch. She wasn't watching the other customers any longer or rapidly setting words to the page. She merely stared down at her notebook like her work profoundly disappointed her, then snapped it closed and slipped it into her large leather bag.

Piper fussed with her hair, taking it down, twisting it behind her head, and tying it back up again. Her lovely face was now marred by an expression of dismay. She glanced directly at him as she gathered up the remains of her lunch, and Red knew with a jolt that he couldn't let her leave before he'd spoken to her.

Without thinking too much about that, he bolted upright, tray in hand. Piper's expression mutated into alarm as he marched toward her, but before she could make her excuses and her escape, Red plunked down his lunch and took the seat opposite her.

"Why, Ms. Fulham," he grinned. "What a pleasant surprise. Mind if I join you?"

Indecision was written all over her face, but there'd be no evading him now. Red sprawled just a little, extending knees and elbows to discourage her easy exit from her sheltered little nook. Piper sure looked like she might try to make a break for it. The question was, *why?*

"Be my guest," she said, her cordial words totally at odds with her jumpy demeanor. She eyed Red narrowly as he dug into his sandwich.

He winked at her. Piper's posture relaxed not at all—but she did slide back into her chair the tiniest fraction.

"Thanks," he told her, once he'd swallowed. "I owe you one."

Red would have to be careful not to miss any steps in this dance, he thought. His body wanted to skip a bit farther ahead than was sensible, now that he was close to her again.

"I…" Her brow wrinkled. "For what?"

She smiled, though, the soul of propriety despite her evident confusion. Even though he'd sucked face with her last night, Piper was back to treating him like her boss. And, while the idea did hold a certain sordid appeal, Red wanted her mind in a very different place with him.

"For giving me a safe harbor," he explained. He jerked his chin at his former table, where Eight was wiping down the linoleum with a disgruntled scowl. "The vultures were circling."

Piper's eyebrows shot up toward her hairline when she squinted over his shoulder.

"I doubt that woman has ever been called a vulture before in her life."

He shrugged. "If the shoe fits."

Piper was studying the waitress with a bit more intensity than he'd prefer, so he added, "Don't make eye contact."

Startled, she looked back at him. That was better.

"Why not?"

He wiped his mouth with his napkin and risked his own look at the other woman. "What do you suppose she sees when she looks at me? A random guy out for a run on his lunch break, or a meal ticket?"

Piper's brows darted upward again. "Do you really want me to answer that?"

"No need. I'll tell you. She's not interested in my devastating wit or my sparkling personality." That elicited a cute smirk out of his little author. *Good.*

"No?"

"She is, however, quite interested in my bank account."

"You talked to her for about two minutes. Was it that obvious?"

"Sadly, yes."

"Ew."

"My sentiments exactly," Red agreed.

Piper examined Eight again, this time like she would a bug under a microscope.

"Maybe she thought you were cute," she mused, darting a glance at him.

"Possibly," he conceded, "Though I kind of doubt it. How old must she be? Nineteen?"

Piper studied the waitress as she stomped past, heading behind the counter and back into the depths of the kitchen.

"Yeah, probably. Give or take a few years—it's a little hard to tell, with all that..." she trailed off, waving a hand around her own mostly-unadorned face.

Red was more than happy to finish her thought. "Makeup. Right. There was an awful lot of it, wasn't there? It's certainly her prerogative to look however she wants, but I can't help thinking she'd look healthier without it." He polished off his sandwich and went to work on his protein shake. "Besides, I'm old enough to be her father."

"Oh, I doubt that."

God, it was just too easy. "You didn't know me when I was twenty," he remarked.

That surprised a laugh out of her. Now, Red figured it was time for the *coup de grace.*

"Have dinner with me again." He wanted to be both casual and impossible to refuse. Tricky, that.

Piper flushed a delicious shade of pink and tensed all over. "Oh, you don't have to do that."

"But I want to." Red scrambled to come up with something to convince her. "Listen, you have an early flight out tomorrow, right? I can pick you up at five and have you back to the hotel before you know it." At least, he probably could. As long as he didn't end up banging her in the back of a town car or something.

Red willed Piper to say yes. It was suddenly imperative that she agree—he could taste his need for her acquiescence on his tongue like a wine that had turned sour.

Piper fiddled with her pen, delaying. In all the attention Red had been paying to her face, her hair—her freaking collarbones, for crying out loud—he hadn't noticed that she was still gripping it. When she registered that he was watching her, her hands froze.

"Okay," she said, and Red exhaled the breath he hadn't realized he was holding.

"I'm at the St. Regis," she added. Unnecessarily, in his opinion, given that he'd already tangled tongues with her in that exact location.

Red's grin stretched across his face and he hoped it didn't come off as too fucking feral. "Yes, I remember. I'll meet you out front. Five o'clock, if that works."

Piper swallowed. "Sounds good," she told him.

"I agree."

She jammed her pen deep into her bag and looked around a little wildly. "Okay. Well. I should—"

Red should...whatever...as well. He still had to shower and change before his next meeting.

"One more cup of coffee," he blurted quickly.

Piper looked taken aback. *Damn.* He had to be more careful with her. Charging around like a bull in a china shop was not the way to approach this.

"Please," Red added, forcing himself to say it gently.

"Okay," she said once more. "Thanks."

He gestured toward the front of the shop, relieved that Eight was not working the register anymore. "I'll go order. How do you take it?"

Piper ran her palms over the scuffed wood table and took a deep breath. "Half-caff medium roast, with about a quarter cup of two-percent milk," she instructed him.

Red studied her. For someone who liked to look askance at his demanding mannerisms, Piper sure had her moments.

"That's oddly…specific," he told her.

She shrugged. "I know what I like."

He'd had her pegged as the fancy coffee type. Red would have bet that Piper liked it sweet and weird, with soy milk or caramel foam or some other nonsense. He supposed that fit his admittedly ass-backward notion of a romance writer, better than the reality of Piper Fulham did.

To be sure he hadn't missed anything, he asked, "You sure you don't want to spice it up a bit?"

"No. Why would I?" At his quizzical expression, Piper confided, "Sometimes, I'll get the medium, instead of the small. You know, if it's an especially rough morning. But I'm pretty good today."

Red snorted. Piper took umbrage and dropped the social niceties for once.

"Okay, big shot. What about you? What's so special about your coffee order, huh?"

"Nothing," he admitted. "Full octane dark roast, brewed at home, sometimes with half-and-half. I don't even grind my own beans," he added, in case she got any ideas from him knowing it was dark roast. Red had simply spent many dejected, under-caffeinated mornings staring at the label over the years, waiting for his coffee machine to whir into life.

Piper tilted her pretty head and regarded him with a frown, something in what he'd said stoking her inveterate curiosity. "What's the deciding factor?"

Red was busy repeating her coffee order to himself in his head, over and over. He didn't want to forget it when he finally reached the counter, but he especially didn't want to forget it if he ever managed to get this woman to spend a night in his bed.

Not if—*when*. That was something that absolutely had to happen. This woman had his jaded, shriveled heart beating like no one else had in years. Red stared into space, calculating his odds of success.

Absently, he replied, "What do you mean?"

Piper rolled her eyes. "I mean, what determines whether or not you take cream in it?"

Was there something wrong with him? When Piper got all exasperated, everything she said came out sounding a little dirty. Red looked back at her and gave her what he hoped was a seductive smirk.

"That's easy. If the half-and-half in my fridge is still good, I put some in my coffee. If it isn't, I don't. I am *very* easy to please."

She popped up out of her chair and turned toward the counter, plainly deciding it was safer to order her own coffee. "Oh my God," she groaned as she edged away. "That was such a guy thing to say."

Red rose and slipped his hand around Piper's arm before she could get too far and wished he could press her back against his chest—and other interested parts of him. He wanted to hear Piper let out that little sigh again, like she had when she melted into his embrace in her hotel hallway.

Red dipped his head and breathed next to the delicate shell of her ear, "In case you haven't noticed, I am very much a guy."

She gasped.

Sadly, that was the moment Wayne chose to come flying into the café like his hair was on fire.

"Oh, cool," his assistant said, looking between them. "You found her."

"Excuse me?" Piper said.

"Oh. Busted," Wayne muttered.

Piper squinted up at Red, looking like she was making all sorts of feminine calculations behind those amber eyes. "I was under the impression this was a lucky coincidence," she said.

Wayne opened his mouth, but Red held up his hand before his assistant could say anything dimwitted. Piper's gaze dropped to his fingers and hitched there.

"It was, and it wasn't," he told her.

Piper rolled her eyes and groaned.

"Still want that coffee?"

She looked at Wayne. "Do we have time?"

"Yeah, sure. This meeting wasn't supposed to be anything formal. I'll just call and tell them we'll be late."

"Okay, good," Piper chirped. "Then you can eat the portobello melt I got you."

Red arched an eyebrow at his right-hand man. "That bad?" he wondered. The minute shit got critical, his assistant, without fail, began craving cheese. It didn't matter what form it came in—Wayne's urge was as reliable as death and taxes.

"Um, yes. Are you surprised?"

Red shook his head. "You guys have a seat," he said. "I'll be right back. Wayne, you want something to drink?"

"Just some water."

Red watched the two of them cozy up at the table and battled back the annoyance that had sizzled to the surface with Wayne's arrival. It didn't matter that he had to share Piper, now. Red had secured an even bigger prize for later, in the form of a second dinner date.

While he stood in the line at the register, he refocused and began plotting their evening.

Seven

MR. MACLELLAN, I hardly need to remind you that my client won the Goldstein award for *Come Hither, Moon*. It's very prestigious. And I should think PKM would want that kind of cachet as it moves forward with the Trident transition," Samantha Copeland said.

"Nevertheless," Red pointed out, "Ms. Wilbon has been promising us a new title for the last two years, and she has yet to deliver."

Rachel sniffed and tossed her hair, though the intended effect was marred somewhat by the fact that she'd shellacked her yellow curls into near-total immobility.

"The Dentons understood that the literary arts can't be forced to bend according to some…" Rachel paused and scowled in evident distaste, "…bottom *line*."

Red reminded her, "Trident's bottom line is what ensures you get paid, Ms. Wilbon."

Samantha cleared her throat and tried a placating smile on for size. "Rachel still has four months left on her contract," she said. "And she's so close to finishing her manuscript. You can't cut her loose before you even see it. That would be madness."

"And not the kind of madness that gets a man's blood pumping. Red, you have to trust me. This book will be worth the wait and then some," Rachel purred.

Speaking of crazy, Red was totally fed up with these two women's efforts to alternately bully him and seduce him into submission. He had a dinner with Piper to get to, and he did not intend to be even one second late to it.

He flipped Wilbon's file closed and folded his hands on top. "You have four months. If your book is not complete and in the hands of Trident's editors by then, you're done. No more extensions. No more exceptions. Understood?"

Rachel's cherry-red lips popped open, but her agent was quicker. "I knew you'd see reason," Samantha said, then pulled her client out of her seat and dragged her away.

Red gritted his teeth and watched them go, resentment simmering. He had no doubt the battle had not been won—merely delayed somewhat. Robert was going to have an absolute field day when he found out.

THE IRRITATION THAT Rachel Wilbon and her agent had left festering in their self-important wakes simply wouldn't dissipate. Red knew he'd been handled, but it had been a necessary concession in pursuit of a larger goal.

After they left, he gave up on getting anything else accomplished for the day and made the trip over to Piper's hotel earlier than necessary. Red ordered a stiff drink, parked himself in an armchair near the doorway of the hotel bar, and settled in to wait.

Piper had gotten out of her last meeting an hour before. As instructed, Wayne had called him the minute they'd finished up. For all their sakes, Red hoped the second conference had gone more smoothly than the first, but Wayne would fill him in on that in the morning.

For now, Red was simply looking forward to seeing Piper. He was jonesing for their dinner, so he could watch her across the table, unfettered, like a lovestruck puppy.

When she finally appeared, he admired her outfit once more. She was still wearing the black sleeveless dress she'd had on earlier, with a small flared ruffle that brushed the tops of her knees. Feminine, yet professional. It hugged her curves like…like Red wanted to.

There was almost no one else in the place, but she didn't notice him when she came in. Red didn't make his presence known. Call it research—he wanted to see what she'd do.

Piper paced directly to the bar, back straight, head high. She slipped onto a bar stool and a scant minute later had two fingers of MacLellan Black in front of her. Once she'd taken her first sip, her shoulders relaxed fractionally. Hard day, he guessed.

Red frowned, wondering what specifically had driven Piper to drink. Anika was only supposed to briefly outline the terms that had changed in the new contract, then let her go. Piper didn't even need to sign the thing for another couple weeks. And it was hardly like they were shafting her—Red had sweetened Piper's deal considerably, to underline how committed they were to keeping her in the fold.

There were two other possibilities. Her second meeting with the design people could've devolved into a worse mess than before, but Red expected Wayne would've warned him if that was the case.

Or maybe it was the notion that she had to meet *him* again that had Piper looking for some liquid courage. He couldn't imagine why that might be—Piper didn't even know about his raunchier impulses yet. Red had been on his best behavior so far. Mostly.

Perhaps this was simply what Piper did with her evenings. Maybe he was kidding himself and she was just a drunk. Watching her, Red doubted it, though. Sure, she was putting on a good show of being sophisticated, but she looked a little too stiff to be at ease with the whole solo barfly routine. This was something else.

Before long, Piper had polished off her glass and stood to leave. Red straightened his tie and cuffs, then cleared his throat when she passed his table. Piper jolted in surprise.

He liked the way her eyes went wide at the sight of him and loved the bronze sheen of her hair in the low lighting.

Red pasted what he hoped was a non-threatening smile on his face. "Leaving so soon?"

Piper sighed. "Well, that was my intention." She studied him, curiosity flickering in her gaze.

"I'd like the chance to change your intention," he told her.

Her eyebrows ticked up. "Would you."

Red gestured to the chair next to him. "Join me?"

Piper hesitated. Her mouth twisted to the side as she thought about it, and he watched her chest rise and fall a couple of times. *Yes. Deep breaths*, he thought in amusement. *I won't bite*. Right away, at least.

"All right," Piper agreed finally. "Just for a minute. I want to run upstairs and change before we go out."

She perched on the edge of the chair and desire flared through him. Red still wanted her like he wanted his next breath, it seemed. Yesterday was not an anomaly. Neither was this morning.

"Only a minute? Then I'll have to work quickly." Red stuck out his palm, mentally begging her to touch him, even if it was brief. "Red MacLellan," he said. "Pleasure to meet you."

Piper rolled her eyes at his clunky gambit. "Piper," she retorted. "And we've met." She shook his proffered hand firmly, then graciously let him hold on to it a moment longer. Red caved and brushed a light kiss across her knuckles.

"Your name," she mused. "It's funny, I just…" She fell silent, brow crinkling.

"What?" Red prodded. Damn, she was quick. He'd bet his company that Piper had already made the connection.

She peered at him, perhaps weighing the odds. "It's *quite* a coincidence, but I just drank a glass of MacLellan bourbon."

Red grinned at her. "Did you, now? Imagine that." He indicated his own glass, sitting glittering on its paper coaster. "Same here," he said.

"Hmm."

Suspicious little thing, wasn't she? "May I order you another?" he tried.

"No thank you," she fired back. No pause there. Maybe she hadn't liked it.

"Really?"

"Yes, really," Piper said. "I'm quite aware of how much liquor I can drink and still retain my dignity. I have an entire meal to get through with you—I need to keep my wits about me," she laughed.

Red did, too. There was absolutely nothing about this woman that was predictable. He'd like a few hours to unravel her prim librarian act and turn her into one of her own uninhibited characters. Hell, Piper had written how many scorching books, now? The pages nearly steamed with the heat they put off. The seeds had to be in her somewhere.

Drily, he said, "That's important to you, I suppose?" As far as Red was concerned, her dignity could take a hike if it meant Piper would come for him like her world was cracking apart.

Proper Miss Fulham quirked an eyebrow at him.

"Retaining your dignity," he clarified. Red did love how impervious to him she seemed.

"Of course, it is. Isn't it for you?" Piper demanded.

Something was irritating her. He wanted to know what. He wanted to know everything.

"Well, I imagine that would depend on the circumstance. And possibly the company."

She glanced down at his glass, then back up at him. "I see."

Did she think he was drunk? Might be time to move things along. "So, if I can't interest you in another, maybe you can tell me what you thought of the first glass."

Her eyes followed the amber liquid as he raised his bourbon and took a long sip, then drifted down to his neck when Red swallowed.

Piper might want to pretend she was unaffected by him, but she wasn't. Not by a long shot. Which made them even, he supposed.

"It was…hmm," she murmured silkily. "Exquisite, I'd say." She *knew*. She had to know.

"Ah. You enjoyed it then."

"Very much."

"I'm delighted to hear it."

When she smiled, he grinned lazily back.

She rolled her eyes, adorable thing that she was. "Let me guess. MacLellan bourbon is somehow part of your exalted portfolio?"

When Red nodded, she went on, "How does one end up with boats, booze, and books—all under the same umbrella?"

"Don't forget biotech," he added. "And you do have a way with words."

Piper shook her head, her soft brown hair shimmering. "That's some crazy diversification, right there. Fingers in a lot of pies."

He grinned wider.

"What came first?" she asked hastily, blushing a bit. "The signature bourbon? I know it wasn't the books."

"No," Red laughed, then. "It was the boats. My grandfather was in shipping."

"Of course, he was."

There was that phrase again. *Of course*. Every time she said it, Piper managed to infuse the words with a special irony. He wondered at the breadth of things that Piper shrugged off as comical about him. He didn't feel comical. He felt…hungry. Red wanted Piper Mae Fulham liked he hadn't wanted a woman in years. He downed the rest of his drink and caught her assessing eye again.

"Red. Why are you here so early?" There it was. She'd let him have his fun for a while, at least.

He shrugged, "Wayne told me when your meeting let out. I thought I might run into you."

Piper nodded. "And you wanted to run into me, because…"

"I wanted to see you again." No need to tip-toe around it—it was the truth, and then some.

"You saw me yesterday, for hours. And you saw me today at lunch."

"Yes, and it was great. I wanted to see more of you tonight." *A lot more.*

"You were going to." She glanced at her watch. "In half an hour, I might add."

"That seemed like an awfully long time."

"You might have called ahead," she suggested.

"True." Why hadn't he? Did he expect to trip her up, somehow? Prove she wasn't as beguiling as she seemed?

"I'm not going to invite you up, Red." She said it firmly and calmly. *Good girl.*

Red shrugged. "I know. I didn't expect you to."

"Then what is this?"

"Can't we just…sit and talk?" he asked. "For a little while longer?"

Piper shifted and made a show of checking her watch again, though the gesture was obviously a stalling tactic.

"Okay. Fine," Piper agreed. "Let's talk."

"You don't have to change, anyway. As long as you're comfortable, you look perfect for where we're going."

Piper smoothed her hands down her thighs, and primly crossed her ankles to the side.

"Thank you."

Red took a deep breath. Now that he had her, what was he going to do with her?

She had an early flight, he reminded himself. He was not going to do anything with her. What the fuck good was it to have control if he never planned to exercise it over himself?

PIPER WAS HAVING a very difficult time maintaining her belief that Red was buttering her up for the sake of the company. Everything he'd done that night had spoken to an actual romantic interest in her—from the way his large hand rested on her lower back as he guided her to the waiting town car, to the way that same hand had enveloped hers to lead her through the restaurant.

Red had hung on her every word, then fed her a bite of his crème brûlée. If he was acting, Piper was hard-pressed to see through it. He probably deserved a trophy for his efforts. Above and beyond the call of duty, and all that.

Now, they found themselves back in the hotel hallway outside her room. Red held himself back while the elderly woman who'd shared their elevator passed them by, laden with shopping bags. He winked at Piper in amusement when the woman took her time unlocking her door, peering at them warily the whole time.

Piper made a show of digging through her purse, hoping it looked convincing. The last thing she needed was for that woman to recognize her, or worse, ask why Piper was so obviously stalling in the hopes of another mind-melting kiss.

Once Piper heard the other door slam shut, she looked up at Red. His hands cupped her face instantly, and then his mouth hit hers. His tongue parted her lips with the same kind of urgency that gnawed at her.

Piper dropped her handbag and hung on to his arms while heat and want arrowed through her veins. By the time Red broke away, they were both breathing hard.

She laughed unsteadily. "You know you don't have to do this, right?"

His heavy brows knit together. "Do what?"

"Kiss up to me, so I'll sign that contract."

Red's mouth fell open for a moment before he snapped it shut. "Is that what you think I'm doing?"

"Isn't it?"

"I am obviously not doing this kissing thing correctly."

"Well, I wouldn't go that far."

He looked around in consternation, before staring down at her again. "Piper, open that door."

Oh, sure. She'd already tried that last time, and they'd both seen how well that had worked.

"You do know that my suite still has the same layout as it did yesterday?" she asked tartly. "Still has a bed. You may recall your opposition to its existence."

"Oh, I recall, little dove. Let's just say I've made my peace with it."

"Is that so?"

"Open the goddamn door, sweetheart."

When Piper smiled and told him, "Your wish is my command," Red's growl was everything she'd ever longed for.

She didn't know what had gotten into her. Red made her feel like she'd stepped inside one of her books, and for some crazy reason, she wanted to go along on the ride. For once, she didn't want the real Piper to fall short of Antoinette Corelli's considerable mystique. She wanted to live up to the hype, and Red—Red looked at her like that might actually be possible. How could she turn him down?

Piper's body snapped to attention, even though her lust-drunk brain still trailed sluggishly behind. She fumbled for her room key, took a few tries to jam it into the slot, and waited for the green light to appear. While they stood there, Red leaned down to kiss the bare skin of her shoulder.

As on edge as Piper was, the click of the lock disengaging sounded as loud as a dropped encyclopedia in the empty hallway. She pushed quickly into her room, expecting Red to be hot on her heels. Instead, he lingered on the threshold with one arm holding open the door, waiting for permission like a damn boy scout.

Piper grabbed him and yanked him inside. Belatedly, she remembered to say, "Please come in."

Red stalked toward her, one steady step at a time. "This has nothing to do with you working for Trident, Piper," he rumbled. "And it has zero to do with my company buying yours."

"Okay, then what does it—"

He reached her, and his gentle touch belied the strength behind his words. "It has everything to do with the unholy things your heels do to your legs, and the way all your nervous little laughs make my dick come alive. It's about your skin and your hair, your mouth and most of all, your mind."

Red loomed over her and ran a thumb across her lower lip. "I want to taste the moans in your mouth, Piper. You make me feel like a starving man that someone's put a juicy steak in front of."

"I see."

"How do you feel about that?"

Easy question. "I want that, too. So much."

"Because I'm your boss?"

"No. For every reason except that one."

"Including the money?"

"What money?"

Red kissed her again. His apparent fascination with Piper had to be because of the books she wrote. But so far, he'd been too much of a gentleman to mention them, and Piper certainly wasn't going to bring them up. Still, for the first time in recent memory, she didn't mind quite so much. She wanted to play the role for Red.

So, she smiled and stepped out of her heels, then edged toward the bedroom door.

"Piper, if we go in there…" he warned.

She'd already made her decision, though. With the way this man kissed, the choice hadn't been difficult.

"Yes," she said. "This is my clear and unequivocal yes to all of it."

"I do like the sound of that." Red advanced on her, yanking his tie loose and tossing it aside.

"The jacket, too," Piper instructed, getting into the spirit of things.

He paused a moment before complying, his gaze growing more intent. Piper wanted to experience all that intensity *everywhere*.

Red shrugged out of his blazer and handed it to her with a smirk. She hung it on the nearest doorknob and backed a couple more steps toward the bedroom. He followed her, crowding close enough to hook his fingertips under the hem of her dress.

As a delicious shiver ran through her, Piper was abruptly glad that she'd run her last pair of stockings in her rush to get ready that morning. She'd gone with bare legs all day, figuring that the artsy types on Trident's design floor wouldn't care one way or the other.

She hadn't counted on Red MacLellan, though. Those long fingers were skating right up her thigh, like a heat-seeking missile on a collision course with home base.

"Not yet, Mister," she breathed, and pressed a restraining hand against his stomach. Beneath the starched white cotton, Red felt firm and taut.

He moved back easily. "You seem to be the one with all the bright ideas," he teased. "Lead the way."

"Lose the shirt," Piper told him. "And whatever's under it."

His fingers flew down the placket, deftly releasing buttons and yanking the material free of his waistband. His pristine undershirt followed half a second later, and then he was standing there bare-chested and as beautiful as a Roman statue.

Piper caught her breath. Unlike a lot of guys with his kind of height, Red wasn't slim or reedy in the least. His torso was a sight to behold—with wide shoulders and a chest and stomach packed with lean muscle. A large tattoo wrapped around one bicep, intricate and colorful.

He looked more like a superhero than a denizen of the boardroom. Piper managed to resist the urge to bend forward and lick him all over—but only barely.

Red took her by the hands, pulling them up and placing them against his chest. He slid them up over his heart—jackhammering under his skin—and then brought one to his mouth. He slipped two of her fingers into his warm, wet mouth, and sucked hard.

Piper couldn't help it. She moaned.

"That's my girl," he murmured. "Come here, you."

Red wrapped her in his arms and lifted her until their faces were level, then carried her the rest of the way into the bedroom. The faint lingering fragrance of Piper's shampoo still lingered in the air. His kiss was deep and hungry—incendiary. Red still tasted like the after-dinner mint he'd eaten at the restaurant.

He dropped Piper in the center of the hotel mattress, pushed her hairdryer and cosmetic bag off the side with an impatient swipe of his arm, then propped himself over her and resumed kissing her silly.

His hands were everywhere. Before long, he'd managed to hike her dress up over her hips and dispense entirely with her panties. Piper shuddered again when Red dragged his fingers through the slick heat between her legs—and that was before he brought them to his mouth so he could taste her. His eyes rolled toward the ceiling, and he let out a deep groan.

She whimpered, the sound rapidly grabbing his attention again.

"Forgive me, Ms. Fulham. Was there something you wished to add?"

She shook her head. "I'm confident in your ability to take it from here," Piper told him.

"Oh, good." Red reached for the wallet in his back pocket and dropped it beside them, flipping it open with one hand to find the condom tucked inside. "Because I am dying to be inside you."

Piper clung to his ribcage and stretched up to kiss his neck, breathing in the warm cedar scent of Red's cologne while he kicked off the rest of his clothes. Even from close range, she could tell that the rest of him definitely lived up to the hype of her first impression.

"Piper?"

She looked back at Red's face to find him studying her, waiting for her assent.

"Please," she managed. "Please, yes."

He nodded. "Then let's get this dress off you."

Red pulled her into a sitting position, then reached around her back to unzip her. Piper lifted her arms so he could tug the dress over her head, then unhooked her bra herself and tossed it somewhere stage right.

Red's mouth was on her breasts in the blink of an eye, kissing and licking her fervently. Soon, he guided her to lay back again. He sat back on his heels and ran one fingertip straight down the center of her body, from her chin to her belly button.

"Look at you, sweetheart. You're a goddess."

Piper flinched. Had she written that exact line on one of her books? She thought she might have.

This was no time to dwell on it, though, because Red had grabbed the condom and was tearing it open determinedly. He took himself in hand to roll it over his length, gazing at her with laser focus all the while. Damn, he was big.

If Red was acting out a fantasy he'd pulled from one of her own stories, Piper was totally going along for the ride.

Red set his hands beside her head, stretched over her, and pushed a scant few inches into her. Too soon, he pulled out again. His biceps bulged and flexed. Piper didn't think she'd ever been so aroused in all her life.

"Hurry," she begged.

Red entered her once more, going only a fraction deeper than before. "I can't, dove," he muttered. "I don't want to hurt you." His expression was tight with strain.

"You won't. I'm—"

He pushed in deeper that time, stealing her breath away.

Piper let out a shaky laugh, and assured him, "See? We're fine."

Red shook his head, withdrew almost completely, and thrust impossibly deeper—until he was seated completely inside her body. Piper gasped.

He held himself still while she tried to relax and adjust to his size. *Oh, God.* She really had to learn to be careful what she wished for.

Red's lips were hot against the shell of her ear. "Now we're fine," he said.

Piper opened her mouth, but her vaunted eloquence failed her utterly. Red didn't appear to mind—he simply put his tongue where her reply should've been, and teased hers into a dance.

He set a slow pace at first, moving in long, careful, maddening strokes that wound her desire into a tight, needy coil within her.

"Doing okay?" he wondered eventually.

"I need—" Piper tried. "I need…"

He knew. Oh, yes, Red knew what she needed. His pace quickened then, the flexing of his hips coming faster and stronger.

"…that. Yes, that," she moaned.

Red chuckled, smug and satisfied above her.

"Come on, honey," he urged. "Come for me."

The command in his voice was a dark seductive thrill. She wanted to do what he requested. Piper wanted to satisfy his every bossy demand—and then do it all over again.

She wrapped her legs around Red's hips, kissed him back with a desperation she wouldn't have thought possible, and shattered apart in his arms.

Her real life seemed to have gotten mixed up with the imaginary, panting products of her creative mind. Piper couldn't say she minded. When Red's thrusts grew erratic, when he arched up, threw his head back, and climaxed with a long, tortured groan—she decided reality could take a hike. She was staying right where she was, thank you very much.

Eight

P IPER WOKE TO the sound of Red's phone alarm chiming on the nightstand. Her hotel room was very dark, only one shaft of light from the bathroom keeping it from complete blackness. Red's heavy arm was slung across her middle, and his warm breath stirred the hair on top of her head.

Piper stroked his forearm lightly. He made a deep sound of contentment in response, then pressed the hot, bare length of his body along her back—some parts of which were more interesting than others.

Outside her room, a housekeeping cart squeaked down the hallway and was followed by the hum of an industrial vacuum moving over the carpet. Red turned off his phone and groaned, hunching closer.

"I don't suppose we could convince them to bring us coffee?" His voice sounded rough in her ear. Sexy.

"Doubtful," Piper said. "Besides, they probably need it even more than we do."

His large hand traveled up and down her flank, then began tracing feather-light patterns around her navel.

"Coffee may have to wait," he murmured, gripping her hip and flexing his body against hers.

"Said no one ever."

But then Red rolled Piper onto her back and his talented fingers continued their distracting ministrations. His even more talented tongue joined the party. She had no clue how much time passed before either of them spoke after that—it could have been five minutes or five hours. Who cared?

"All those in favor of caffeine, say *aye*," he eventually rumbled near her ear, startling her out of the blissful doze she was drifting in.

"Oh! Aye!" Piper pried her eyes open and shot one shaky arm straight up in the air, and then the other. "Me, me!"

"No, no," Red admonished. "No double voting. We run an honest operation here." He pried himself away from her and stood with purpose, despite his total lack of clothing. He looked around.

"Now then. There doesn't seem to be a coffee maker in here. So, point me toward the lobby and I will return bearing gifts."

"*Gah.* I'm a terrible hostess," Piper muttered into her pillow. When Red laughed at her, she burrowed deeper under the cozy covers. Let him find his own chipper way to the lobby.

"Really? I thought you were very accommodating. But I was rude and exhausted you, didn't I? Poor baby. That probably wasn't very sporting of me." Red fished around on the floor. When he found his pants, he pulled them on. Piper peeked out from behind her arm, admiring the fine display of his rear end and muscled back.

"You don't have to sound so proud of yourself."

"I beg your pardon. I exerted a lot of effort just now. I'm very proud."

Piper poked her arm out and swiped at him, but Red danced handily backward. How in the hell could he be so damn cheerful? She was certain they hadn't slept for more than four hours, at the most.

She growled in annoyance.

"I'll be back before you know it," Red laughed, threw on his shirt, and headed for the door. "Get dressed, or you'll miss your flight."

"Please inform your evil assistant that I despise him and his crack-of-dawn travel arrangements."

"I'll do no such thing. I like my henchmen good and mean, and finding Wayne was like hitting the lottery."

She sighed dejectedly. "You two are probably perfect for each other."

"Get your sweet ass out of that bed, Piper, or I'll drink all your coffee before I get back."

"Oh, my God. Why don't you go kick some puppies while you're at it? It's your freaking fault I have to rush, now!"

Red just grinned and waltzed out the door.

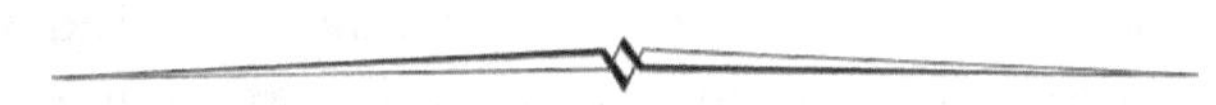

THE ONLY REASON he'd gotten Piper to the airport in time for her flight was that most of the city—along with the sun—was still asleep. The streets had been as empty as they ever got, though Red wouldn't have complained if they'd gotten stuck in some gridlock and Piper had to stay longer.

Piper was not a morning person. She was groggy and grouchy the entire way, only relenting once Red bent down to brand her with another searing kiss beside the security line. Then, Piper turned sweetly, cutely loopy, and that look on her face was still making him smile by the time he got home. Red scrapped playing it cool and texted her. *Have a safe trip.*

Piper responded immediately with a kiss-blowing emoji, and Red went about his business, more satisfied than he'd been in ages.

But later that afternoon, once he judged enough time had passed, he was ready for another fix. *Did you get home okay?*

She sent him a thumbs-up, and then Piper went dark again.

Red gave her twenty-four hours to get settled in and take care of whatever she needed to back home. He tried not to get frustrated that Piper wasn't striking up a rousing thread of sexting with him, or even calling to chat. When had he become such a needy prick, anyway? There were probably women all over this island who would gloat like crazy about it.

On Monday morning, Red managed to sit through his usual round of meetings about the week ahead, before he finally surrendered and pulled out his phone. *I really enjoyed our dinners.*

Same! Piper fired back with a smiley face.

Nothing prevented him from kicking off the sexting. *Almost as much as I enjoyed what came after.*

Those crappy blinking dots popped up while she typed, stopped, and typed again. *Now* the fun would start, Red was sure of it. But all that came through was another grinning emoji and two short words. *Also same.*

Red studied that for a bit, sent Piper a gif of a puppy licking a cat (perhaps a bit too enthusiastically), and decided to leave her be.

He lasted one day. *One.* On Tuesday, Red conjured up some completely unnecessary meetings in D.C., which was supposedly close to Piper's home, and arranged for the jet to take him down there in a couple of days.

So far, so good. He only ran into a snag when every hotel northwest of the city turned out to be booked for the weekend. But no matter—Piper might have an idea of what to do. *ETA Thurs pm. Staying in DC that nite. More mtgs early Fri. *Need rec 4 hotel near u for Fri + Sat nites**

Great! she replied, about an hour later. *I'll look around and get back to you!*

Except then she didn't. When Red hadn't heard back by Wednesday, he decided Piper might need a little reminder. He thought about calling, but…damn it, it felt like this was turning into some kind of weird power play.

Is this the longest week ever? Can't wait to see you, he typed. He stared at the words for a bit, considering them. Finally, Red deleted the second sentence, then hit send.

Piper replied with a large red "*XO*", but no hotel information. Red had to wonder if he had somehow misinterpreted their dates—or their subsequent fucking.

The next morning at the hangar, he pondered whether he was about to make a huge mistake. Maybe Piper was simply busy, though. She had a new series to write, and a new contract to sift through. She probably had other things to do, as well.

She might have friends she needed to catch up with, or a family member to care for. Maybe she had a dog who needed surgery or short-term memory loss. Perhaps Piper just wasn't tied to her phone, like so many other people Red knew.

Maybe he'd botched everything, and she was not into him in the least. *Landed at Dulles. Here goes nothing*, he texted later that morning.

Shoot. Piper replied. *Nearby hotel is being renovated!* Information that might have been useful days ago. Red made a quick call to the place he was staying in town but came up empty. *Current hotel booked for a conference,* he wrote.

Piper said, *Okay, let me think.* She came back ten minutes later. *So...you know that adage about early birds and worms?*

Red rolled his eyes. *<groan>*

It's ok! I have a solution! Piper told him.

He regarded his screen, mulling that over. So far, he'd been underwhelmed by her excitement at seeing him again, as well as her planning skills.

He tapped out, *???*

Stay with me, came quickly back. Now that was something Red hadn't expected. No way would Piper offer it if she weren't into him.

Still, just to be sure, he typed, *Seriously??*

Piper asked, *Too weird?*

No. Sounds perfect. If ur sure ur ok with it. Red could almost hear Piper's exasperation from the back of the airport limo ferrying him to his first meeting.

Well, r u planning on killing me and sticking me in my freezer? she demanded.

Red felt lighter than he had in days. *As it turns out, I've never enjoyed popsicles.*

Piper was as tart as ever. *That's not a no.*

Yes, it is, Red grinned. Then, *Text me your address. I'll drive out tomorrow afternoon.*

He left Piper to her own devices then, but allowed himself one more message during a break between meetings the following day. *WILL THESE PEOPLE NEVER STOP TALKING?*

Piper sent back a laughing face and the words, *Take your time, big guy. I'll be here.*

RED ARRIVED AT Piper's later than he intended that evening—and much later than he'd wanted. His meetings had run long and then the rush hour heading out of D.C. was ghastly, but that was possibly because he'd been working under the presumption that nothing could be as bad as the traffic he was used to in Manhattan.

When he finally pulled into the driveway of her pretty farmhouse, set on a nice piece of property far out in the 'burbs, Red only had a few minutes to get out, stretch his legs, and pull his briefcase out of the back of his rental before Piper was opening her front door and stepping onto the porch.

He drank in his first sight of her in casual clothes—jeans, bare feet, and a loose black top drifting off one shoulder. Her yard was mostly quiet, with only the sounds of cicadas buzzing in the grass, and a lone bird chirping in a tree.

The sun was almost down. Piper's smile lit up the twilight.

Red popped the trunk and pulled out his overnight bag, then stepped toward her. How had he lasted the whole week with almost no contact? All his pent-up frustration and want swirled around in his chest and threatened to consume him.

"You made it!" she exclaimed.

"Barely," he said. "Sorry I'm so late." Red forced himself to take the stairs at a normal pace. Otherwise, he'd be leaping up them and pulling her right into a soul-stealing lip-lock…which Piper was likely to find a touch overeager.

"I hope everything went okay?"

"It was fine. Just the usual back and forth. Everything took twice as long as it should have, including the drive out here."

An unbelievable scent was drifting from the front door behind her. Red wasn't entirely sure whether he'd rather stare more at Piper or follow his nose to her kitchen.

"Come on in," she instructed, stepping aside.

Before she could say anything else, though, he blurted, "God, did you cook? It smells incredible in there."

"I thought you might be hungry. It seemed like you were having a long day."

"You have no idea. And…" Red thought hard but came up blank. "I don't think I've had anything since coffee in my room about twelve hours ago."

Piper gaped at him.

"Seems worth it though, since now I've stepped into heaven. Gorgeous woman bearing food? How lucky am I right now?"

"Ha," she deflected. And then, very efficiently, she added, "Let me show you where to drop your things. Do you want a few minutes to get settled before we eat?" No hug. No kiss. Not even a goddamn handshake.

Red narrowed his eyes. Piper was doing an extremely good job of acting like he was her buddy—and not the man who'd had her panting his name mere days before.

That was not going to work. Not one bit.

SHE POURED HIM a drink while she finished cooking dinner. Much like their first meeting, she'd managed to work one small, sexy flourish into her appearance—this time in the form of short, perfectly-practical nails done up in a glittering gold polish. Red tried not to imagine the way they'd look against his cock and failed miserably. *Solid gold, baby.*

She wrested him from his daydream with a sudden question.

"Hey, can you eat things made in the same facility as peanuts?" she inquired, frowning down at a box of croutons in her hand.

The fact that she'd not only remembered his allergy but appeared to know what to do about it, twisted something even tighter inside Red's chest.

"Nope," he replied, watching to see what she did next.

Piper dropped the croutons in the trash. "Then we should be good to go," she smiled. "Not even a glimmer of a nut in sight."

Besides the ones attached to his body, Red amended silently, and those very much wanted a viewing.

Piper handed him the salad bowl, then led him into the adjoining dining room, where the table was already set. She was chatting amiably about the miserable traffic in the area and how nice the weather was supposed to be that weekend.

Traffic. And the *weather*, for Christ's sake. Red might as well be visiting his grandmother.

He couldn't be positive, but Red suspected he was witnessing one heck of a smokescreen. Piper was putting up an excellent front, and if Red hadn't already slept with her, he might have even believed it. But the more Piper rambled, the more convinced he became that the woman serving him dinner was nervous as fuck.

And only a woman who cared very much about how this visit was going to go would bother with that emotion.

The moment Red's ass hit his chair, he noticed the background music. Quiet, sexy jazz snaked around them. He itched to ditch the food—delicious, though it was—and grab Piper so they could slow dance in the middle of her living room. He wondered if the effect was intentional.

The track changed, and he froze with his fork halfway to his mouth, glancing up at her. Raising her eyebrows, Piper smiled back at him.

"Marvin Gaye?" he inquired.

"Mm-hm!" she nodded cheerfully, pleased with his musical acumen.

Ah. Definitely intentional, then. Red doubted it was dancing Piper was angling for, though. The question was, what was he going to do about it? She'd basically ignored him for the last few days.

The fork continued its journey to his mouth, and Red studied his plate while he chewed. He felt Piper's eyes studying *him*.

After a few minutes, her natural curiosity won out. "Do you like it?"

He swallowed and forced his gaze back to her, already knowing what he'd see. That boxy, loose-fitting black shirt she wore, made from some insidiously filmy, silky kind of material. It had short sleeves and a wide neck and kept slipping off one of her shoulders—and the skin revealed there was scattered with the kind of freckles she'd probably gotten from being in the sun. They were driving Red berserk with *lust*.

He swallowed again, but it didn't clear the tightness in his throat. "Which one?" he croaked. "The music or the food?"

Piper looked puzzled, and then uncertain.

"Either?"

Red pressed his palms to the table beside his plate, willing himself to stay put. It didn't work.

"Fuck it," he muttered and pushed to his feet. His chair squeaked across the wood floor, and Piper jumped.

In two steps, he reached her, grabbed her hand, and yanked her up into his embrace. Her arms wound around his waist willingly, and her hands came to rest on his lower back, warming his skin through his dress shirt. Red gripped Piper close, threading his fingers into her hair.

He growled against her lips, "Yes." One light kiss, then a second. "I love the food." A third, harder kiss, because she tasted salty and delicious. "And I love the music." Red swayed a little with her, faintly approximating dancing. But who was he kidding? He just wanted to hold the woman.

"Then what's wrong?" Piper whispered.

Red cupped her face with one hand, and molded the other around her perfect ass, pressing her body even closer.

"You were too damn far away," was about the most coherent he could get.

Piper blinked faster, assimilating that. "Not anymore." She was melting against him, a soft, feminine armful of sweetness.

"Yes," he grumbled. "Still." He'd intended another light, restrained kiss. But Piper tried to say something else, and when his lips reached her mouth, it was open for him.

All hell broke loose. Red didn't know whose tongue got there first, but instantly they were sliding against each other and there wasn't anything restrained about the way he wanted to inhale the woman. So much for manners.

Eventually, they managed to come up for air. Piper seemed like herself again.

"Hi," Red murmured softly.

"Hi."

Piper was flushed and demure, and he wanted to dive right back in again. There was something he needed to know, though.

"What was all that hostessy business before? I barely recognized you."

"I don't know!" she moaned. "I wasn't sure how to approach this whole thing. When you said you might come down here, I thought it was just blustering! I never expected you to actually do it. I guess I kind of freaked out."

"I told you I wanted to. Hell, I've been texting you all week. What did you think that meant?"

"I don't *know*," she groaned again. "I worried you might regret it. Or that this was going to be weird."

"The only thing that was weird was you acting like we haven't already been in each other's pants. What the hell, woman."

"I'm sorry. It wasn't easy to pull off, if that makes it any better."

Red snorted. "It wasn't easy to sit through, either. I'm pretty happy it's over."

"Me too. Come on, come sit down and finish eating. You must be famished."

"On so many levels, sweetheart."

AFTER DINNER, PIPER leaned against her kitchen counter and sipped her wine, reluctantly allowing Red to handle the dishes. Then she pulled him into the living room and tried to get him to play cards with her. He'd known that whole hobby conversation would come back to bite him.

Red tried to pay attention to the game, he really did. But he couldn't help staring at her.

"*What?*" she finally cried.

No reason to lie. "Just wondering what exactly it will take to light your spark."

"What do you mean?"

"You're very controlled right now," Red said. "No, don't make that face. I don't mean awkward, only…restrained. Keeping yourself on a pretty short leash. You know what I mean."

"Red, as I've noted before, you're kind of my boss. We probably shouldn't be doing this. *Any* of this."

"Will you cut that out? Besides, what if I weren't?"

"Firing me already? It was the pasta, wasn't it? I knew it was too salty."

"The pasta was incredible. And I can't fire you now, little dove. That contract you signed is ironclad. You've got a great lawyer." Shanahan was dotty, but competent, at least. He'd negotiated more money and marketing for his client, and Anika wasn't even that piqued about it.

"Damn straight, I do."

"Besides, you don't even report directly to me. You know that. I don't think that's why you're holding back."

"Let me guess. You have a theory," Piper said drily.

"Sure do. But that's beside the point. What I really need to figure out is how to let loose the woman who writes all those steamy books of yours." Well, that got her attention.

"What did you have in mind?" Piper wondered, but her expression shuttered.

"Are you sure?" Maybe he'd gone too far.

Piper nodded, but it was tentative. Red forced himself to take it slow and kissed her. For a long, long time, all he did was kiss her. It was still incredible—hot and sweet and better than any homemade dessert she could've come up with.

When he was certain they'd both had enough, Red leaned Piper back on her couch. Painfully slowly, he pushed up her top and kissed the upper swell of each breast, giving her tons of time to object if she was going to. She didn't, and that was fortunate. The scent and the heat of her velvety skin were working a bewitching kind of magic on him.

Red scooped her breasts out of their lacy black confines and sucked the tip of one into his mouth. That worked well, so he moved on to the other. Piper's gasp was loud in his ears.

Red pulled back to look straight into her glazed-over eyes, and let her shirt fall back into place.

"That's where I'd start," he told her. He had an even better idea of where he'd like to finish.

"Seems legit," she breathed, in a shaky, sexy little voice. "Tell me more."

Red reached out and traced the neckline of her tissue-thin top with one finger. As it had been doing all evening—as it was probably intended to do—it slipped off her shoulder.

"This shirt of yours has been driving me crazy all night," he muttered. "It's preposterous how something so simple could be so devastating."

"Trust me, I don't usually look like this," Piper snorted, as self-deprecating as ever.

"You dressed up for me? You didn't have to do that, but I'm honored."

Red wondered if she'd thought about it quite that way—about choosing her outfit *for* him. Maybe Piper had only been trying to look nice, going for casual and pretty instead of over-the-top "kiss me again, please." Either way, it was a win.

His eyes roved hungrily over her lovely face, over her neck and her hair.

"You're beautiful," he murmured.

At her blush and her shrug, though, Red frowned. Her mouth opened, and he would've sworn she was getting ready to minimize herself yet again. Piper snapped her mouth shut and managed, only just, to keep silent.

It was awkward, but he jumped into the breach. "Tell me what you would usually wear."

She laughed and didn't attempt anything seductive. Piper merely told the truth, maybe because she felt too unbalanced to come up with anything racier. Red understood that sensation, for sure.

"I mean—you know. Probably running shorts and a t-shirt. Hair up, no makeup, and my glasses," she elaborated.

Red wasn't the least bit deterred, but he did want more details. He asked, "What kind of t-shirt?"

Piper shrugged. "Um, loose with a logo? From places I like, or concerts I enjoyed, that sort of thing."

Evidently, she assumed there couldn't be anything nerdier. She was obviously perplexed by Red's interest. After a protracted moment of Piper squirming under his microscope, Red had to relent.

"You don't need makeup. As I recall, you look beautiful without it."

He let his eyes travel leisurely down her frame before meeting her gaze again. "And running shorts are really short. I am very much in favor of how much leg they expose."

Piper rolled her eyes and demanded, "What about the dorky t-shirts? Or the glasses?"

"The shirts sound like insight into the things you enjoy and admire." At her dubious expression, Red held up a stalling hand. "Things I very much want to know. As for the glasses—you're a *romance* writer. Please tell me I don't have to explain the sexy librarian fantasy to you."

Piper contemplated him. She looked almost afraid to ask, "The hair?"

"I want to take it down," he rejoined, without pausing for breath. "I'd love to take down your hair, right before I messed it all up. You should know that about men, too."

Piper had no answer to that. Not a one. God, she was cute.

An evil smirk tickled the corner of his mouth. "Maybe you can rustle up a corset for me to unlace. Or some garters for me to unsnap. I like sparkling, dangling earrings that will make me stare at your neck, and backless dresses drive me insane. Hell, I would even rip a bodice if you had one handy," he said.

Piper swallowed thickly and shook her head.

"Something to shoot for, I guess. In the meantime, I'll keep enjoying you as you actually are."

Red could care less what Piper wore, as long as she was comfortable—it was obvious that she'd look good in pretty much anything. No, the thing that sparked a thread of annoyance in him was the way Piper kept trying to cut herself down. Like he wasn't lucky to be breathing the same air as her.

Red was definitely going to have to do something about that. Next time, though. All that could wait for next time.

"You know, you're not what I expected," she said shakily.

"Neither are you, but if you think that's going to deter me, you're wrong."

Piper's eyebrows shot up. Red knew she was concerned about how bad it might look if they were found out. She would be the author sleeping her way into a plum contract. And he would be the dirtbag dallying with his employees. On the surface, maybe it did seem sordid.

Except—her new contract had been drafted before Red had even met her, and thanks to their lawyers it was a done deal now.

This thing between them was something else, something other than tawdry. It was rare and electric, and neither one of them seemed to have the power to ignore it.

"I'd like to kiss you again," he said.

Piper nodded, giving him the go-ahead, thank fuck.

So, Red leaned in and placed his lips carefully on hers. Within seconds—at the very first sign of her responding—it turned urgent. His lips and tongue searched hers, exploring and learning, demanding answers she was happy to give.

His hands crept forward, one curling lightly around her upper arm, the other sliding up under her hair. Piper was molten in his arms, and they had all weekend to wallow in one another.

Red had almost stayed in New York. What a travesty that would've been.

Nine

PROPPED ON AN elbow, with the morning sun streaming through the blinds in bright white stripes, Red watched Piper sleep. Maybe that was silly.

She had girly yellow sheets printed all over with tiny flower buds. Damp strands of hair stuck to her flushed cheek. Her arms and legs were flung every which way, only half-covered by the bedding. She was so fucking normal compared to the other women he'd dated recently. Piper seemed so…accessible.

Not very innocent, however. She looked exactly like someone who had spent the night going at it and Red was willing to bet that she'd be happy about that fact once her eyes finally opened.

Something loosened in his chest at the sight of her, and the initial discomfort Red felt when he woke up dissipated. For once, he'd stayed the entire night in a woman's bed, but it was Piper's, and that made it strangely all right. It was a shame the experience was such a novelty for him.

Red lowered himself back down and relaxed into the pillow, matching her breaths until he nodded off again.

When he wandered downstairs later, Piper was sitting at her kitchen table, scribbling intently. She smiled distractedly at him and held up a finger, so Red kept quiet and let her work out the rest of her thought.

He poured himself a cup of coffee, admired her big backyard through the window over the sink, then grabbed a sponge and wiped up a puddle of water leaking from around the base of her faucet. He'd noticed the same thing in her bathroom upstairs and wondered if he ought to mention it.

He decided against it. Piper was the kind of woman who would know what needed to be done. Hell, she probably had it all in a bullet-list with cutesy stickers.

Red checked on her progress, caught her peeking at him, and figured it was safe to stroll over. Piper snapped her notebook closed before he could get a look at what she was working on and sat there toying with her pen.

He'd noticed that every pen in the house, in her purse, and in her briefcase were all the same model. The girl certainly knew what she liked. Luckily, he was one of them.

"Writing in longhand, huh?" he nodded toward her notebook.

She smiled. "Nothing like a pen in hand when I get stuck on something. It works like a charm."

"That's an interesting pen you have there." Red made a show of peering closer. "May I see it?"

Piper clutched it to her chest. "No, you may not. You may not hold, borrow, or otherwise use this pen under any circumstances."

Red blinked. "I…*really?*"

"It's special," she said, before tucking it primly under her notebook, safely out of sight.

"Why?"

"Because it's a ballpoint that writes like a fountain pen. They are very hard to find, and I have to buy cases of them, so I won't run out."

She was so serious, Red couldn't resist teasing her. "It sounds like you have plenty. Share one with me."

"I can't! What if they stop selling them? What if they stop *making* them? I'll be screwed. I need these pens, Red. You don't."

"Well, what if I need to leave you an important note?" He eyed her notebook, and Piper edged that away from him, too.

A challenging glint came into her gaze. "Try blood. I hear that works."

He laughed. Piper was too perfect for words. "Okay, you win." He jerked his chin at the chair across from her and inquired, "Is this seat taken?"

She turned sweet again. "Nope."

Once he'd settled in and taken another long, bracing sip of coffee, Red broached the subject that was at the forefront of his mind. It wasn't whether Piper knew a good plumber to fix the leaks he'd noticed or if she had a paver who could fix the cracks in her driveway.

It was not what he had waiting for him this week back at work, either, or the fact that he appeared to be tumbling head-first into a long-distance relationship with an author that was critical to the success of his latest business venture. No, the thing at the top of Red's list was…

"So, when can I see you again?"

"Why on earth would you want to do that?" It was a preposterous question, but at least she had the sense to laugh when she asked it.

"Oh, I don't know. You're smart and funny, and sweet and gorgeous. For starters."

"Is that all?"

"No, it's not. Your hair feels soft and silky and smells great, too. You have a thousand-watt smile, a very sexy laugh, and unfairly cute dimples. You have extremely expressive eyes, legs that could stop a man's heart, and—if we're keeping it clean—I'd better not to elaborate on your mouth."

Piper choked on her coffee. *Good.* Let her be as wrong-footed as he was. Red hadn't thought he had that kind of litany of praise in him, and he was fairly sure any number of his ex-girlfriends would agree.

His hostess asked, "My mouth gives you unclean thoughts?"

"Hell, yes," he assured her. "And if we are going to go there, you may as well know I've taken a fancy to some other body parts, as well."

"You mean, besides my legs."

"Naturally. I already mentioned those."

She looked at him calmly across her kitchen table. He could almost see the gears turning in her head. And then Piper roused herself with a sudden, dismissive shake of her head.

"I've got to hand it to you, Red. As come-ons go, that one was a doozy."

"Excellent. So, you'll come up to see me?" He pretended to check the watch he was not currently wearing. "How about next week?"

"Careful. I might get the idea that you're eager."

"I think it's too late for that." *And then some.*

She let loose a sigh, but he chose to think of it as an indulgent one. "Never let it be said that I'm a coward. As it happens, I'm supposed to take the train up on Thursday to meet with Trident's design people again. They wanted me to meet some of the models they found for the new covers."

Those geniuses. Red knew he liked them for a reason.

"Forget the train," he told Piper. "I'll send the jet."

PIPER FELT HERSELF falling into the moment, into Red's arms, and—if his expression was any indicator—probably into her bed before long. Once that dizzying sensation began to take root, panic followed quickly on its heels. It was inconvenient timing, to say the least. Her body went rigid and even her face felt like it had turned to stone.

What was she doing? Other than biblically, Piper hardly knew the man. She'd made an uncharacteristic leap by inviting him to stay with her after only a couple whirlwind dates, and even though

Red had been nothing short of wonderful, that didn't mean she should trust him completely.

Things went wrong when Piper let her guard down—she *knew* that. Besides, wasn't there some adage about psychopaths always being the charismatic ones? Piper lived alone. Anything could happen. It could be days before a soul even thought to look for her. A true degenerate would no doubt have figured that out already.

Looking at Red across her table, serenely sipping coffee out of a cat mug, Piper knew she was overreacting. She took a deep breath. Red was definitely not a serial killer.

No, the real danger here was how neatly Piper could slip under his spell. She had to fight against the instinct to let him run the show. To allow Red to take whatever he wanted—to *take*, period.

Red wielded his authority like it was second nature to him, so much so that she'd barely noticed falling so cleanly into line.

Piper couldn't decide what she should do about it, though. Should she insist that they return to a strictly professional relationship? After all, the days of blowing off sex as casual or meaningless were behind her now. After Kyle, she'd nailed them into a coffin and buried them deep. No more fuck buddies or friends with benefits. No more flings with commitment-phobes. Piper needed—and deserved—better than that.

She'd made a conscious decision to invite Red to her bed, though—she wasn't a total doofus. The real surprise was that she hadn't expected him to want more.

Now that he did, Piper had stepped right into uncharted lands. Letting Red into her heart so quickly would be dunderheaded in the extreme. But continuing to get to know him, in and out of the bedroom, would make staying uninvested nearly impossible.

Red MacLellan, Piper had learned, was one deliciously dreamy hunk of a man. He was irresistible.

And, as usual, he noticed everything. "What happened?" he wondered, drawing back slightly in his chair. "What did I do?"

Two deep furrows etched themselves into the space between his eyebrows as he frowned in concern.

Piper shook her head. "Nothing," she told him. *#Lies.*

His expression said he wasn't buying it. Smart man.

She tried again. "I just got a weird case of nerves, that's all."

"Because I want to see you again?"

"Because this suddenly feels a little fast," she admitted. "I have no idea why."

That wasn't entirely true, and Piper hated herself for the waffling. Red probably thought she was a total nut, pulling such an abrupt 180 after basically throwing herself at him every time he stuck his tongue in her mouth. She felt crazy. But she just couldn't let a guy get the best of her again, even one as stunning as Red.

Piper watched his face, waiting to see if he'd be irritated, or just redouble his efforts. Maybe Red would try to force her to capitulate—and that would make this easier. It would give Piper something tangible to fight against, instead of just this flailing around with the amorphous feeling that she should be stronger. Different. More exciting, somehow.

If she wasn't a disappointment, then maybe he wouldn't dick around with her feelings.

Red's face was hard to read, though. There was concern, certainly, but also something else that was harder to define.

He said, "Piper, you aren't in danger from me. You understand that, right? I know I'm overbearing, but you're the one in charge here. Okay? You say stop, we stop. You don't feel comfortable seeing me when you come to New York? That's fine, too."

Oddly, she believed him. Piper bit her lip, the decision whether to pursue this made harder by his refusal to force the issue.

Red looked away, giving her some emotional space. He picked up his coffee and took a sip. When his intense eyes finally returned to snare hers, he even smiled, trying to reassure her.

"I know it's weird, me staying here like this so soon. I promised myself I wouldn't take advantage." He didn't add that it was her own fault he was here, since she'd been the dumbass who'd invited him in the first place.

"Maybe I have, though. Should I be apologizing? Did I take things too far?"

"No, I'm the one who should apologize." Piper tried to salvage things in her usual haphazard way, "I know I'm all over the map right now. I'm sorry. I'm confused, and when that happens, I say the wrong things. I ask too many questions, and then I still can't make up my mind."

"You do ask…*unusual*…questions." His eyes were soft, not accusatory.

"It's just that you have this carefully-crafted persona that's grown up around you—this mythology that everyone knows, and it grows and evolves with every interview you give and every story that's written about you. Obviously, I'm into you, but I'm curious about the real person who lives inside all that. I can't help looking for hints about who you really are—" Piper gestured erratically, "—in there. It's hard to know what to do, when I'm not positive who I'm dealing with right now. I'm completely baffled about what Red MacLellan could possibly see in someone like me. It's…it's wigging me out."

"Ah." Red sank back in his chair, tilting his head to study her. "I'm not sure what to say. Here I thought we had something pretty hot and sweet going on, and you were busily doing a character study on me. Or whatever that was."

"I wouldn't go that far. We've been having a great time together. But the real Red is definitely hunkering down behind some solid fortifications." Piper tried to smile to lessen the sting, which was sort of hilarious given the glass house she was sitting in.

Red was silent so long, she thought he might not respond. Finally, though, he relaxed slightly and said, "That obvious, huh?"

"Glaringly."

Now Red leveled his own devasting smile on her. "And yet, you are the only woman in the last ten years who's noticed it. Didn't take you very long, either, Piper Mae."

"I'd put that down to indelicacy, more than any particular insight on my part."

He picked up her hand and circled her wrist easily with his thumb and index finger. "On the contrary, I think you're very delicate." He stared down at the sight, moving his hand so that her palm rested on top of his, emphasizing the difference in sizes.

Piper huffed, "That's because you're huge."

His eyes flicked up and held her gaze. *Oh.* Look who was making an appearance.

"I suspect you are insightful, in addition to being delicate," he murmured, setting aside the flash of sexual challenge and studying her anew. "What else you got? Hit me hard, Piper. I can take it. Why are you so worried about seeing me again?"

Red's face was so utterly sincere, so open and curious, that Piper said the words she never would've expected she'd admit.

"Honestly? I don't think I have a casual fling in me right now. I mean, I'm over the guy I was with a few years ago, but now…I don't want a relationship that's not headed anywhere. You know?"

"I understand."

"That's not to put pressure on you or anything. I like you a lot. But you're hardly the settling-down type."

"And you know this how?"

"Everyone knows it."

"Yeah, I must have missed that memo. Besides, didn't we *just* have the conversation that the whole Padraig MacLellan mythology might not bear much of a resemblance to the actual human being that inspires it?"

Oh God, he was so right. She'd really gone and done it now. Piper was so busy trying to slink away from her own stupid insecurities, that she hadn't even realized she was trying to do it by making everything his fault.

She groaned, dropping her head into her hands. Red chuckled. "Sorry," she muttered, but it was muffled.

He laughed harder. "What do you say we agree to take this one step at a time? I'll try not to push too hard or too fast, and you try not to make assumptions about what I might or might not want from you."

Piper peeked up at him.

"Deal?" he asked, raising his brows at her.

She didn't deserve him, but man did she want him. "Deal."

SHE MIGHT HAVE known Red would be the mighty overlord of BigTalker.com. After he'd left, Piper hadn't heard from the jerk in four freaking days. No jet to fly her to the moon. No phone calls. Not even a single texted emoticon, despite all his protests that he wanted to see where their relationship would lead.

Well, she wasn't going to go panting after him. Red could trip into the sewer for all she cared.

But, as luck would have it, Red's driver dropped him at the curb just as Piper was hoofing it up the block to the Trident building on Thursday morning. He stepped from the car looking fresh and pressed and ready for world domination.

Piper was running too late to care. She kept her head down and marched right past him. She should have expected he wouldn't let her get far.

"Good Morning, Piper Mae," he drawled, quickening his step to keep up with her. What was he doing in Midtown anyway? Shouldn't he be behind his desk at PKM by now, conquering minions and counting his assets?

Maybe Red had only meant to tease her with her full name. But when Piper didn't acknowledge him—when she didn't stop to fall at his stupidly good-looking feet—his irritation broke through.

"Piper Mae," he barked, like a scolding schoolmarm. Why had her parents named her that, anyway? On his lips, it sounded like a cartoon character, for crying out loud.

She shook off her pique, and muttered, "Morning."

Piper even offered Red a half-hearted wave, but otherwise saw no need to break stride. Screw him and his love-em-and-leave-em ways.

While she wended through the glass revolving door, she caught sight of him on the sidewalk, gaping at her as she was swallowed up by the office building.

Oh, poor baby. The little woman hadn't stopped in her tracks to talk to him, huh? Her face hadn't lit up when she gazed upon his magnificence? *Tough.* Red could rot out there on the pavement like the inconsequential gnat that he was. Piper had a meeting to get to.

Once inside, she turned her attention to the lobby. It had been redecorated in the last week, and now sported spare, ultra-modern décor. It looked rich, as she'd expect from PKM, but it felt cold now. Antiseptic. Piper decided she was not impressed.

Red barreled in, catching up with her a few feet in front of the guard station.

"I thought you'd at least let me know when you got to town," he growled.

"And I thought I'd actually hear from you sometime in the past four days."

Maybe the rest of the employees had already arrived, but for such a large lobby, it was disconcertingly empty. Red only had to jerk his chin at the curious guard, who rose without a word and slipped into the office behind his station, and they were alone.

Then Red grabbed Piper's arm and hustled her into the open janitor closet off to the side, slamming the door closed behind them. It was dark, but at least there probably wasn't a security camera—and no audience for when the boss man lost his shit.

Piper sighed and groped along the wall next to the door, searching for a light switch, but his hand clamped onto her wrist and held her firm. When she whacked him in the arm with her other hand, he grabbed that one, too.

Of course, he did. Freaking apex predator. He probably got a charge out of it.

"Damn it, Red. What are you doing?" she hissed, furious.

Infinitely slowly, the infernal man crowded her back against the wall and pinned her hands beside her. His nose tickled the sensitive skin beneath her ear, breathing deep, and Piper was suddenly thankful she'd remembered to wear a little perfume that morning.

Then Red tilted his head and took her mouth.

Her upright intentions—as they always seemed to do around to him—took a hike. Rather than allowing him a grudging buss on the lips, Piper's kiss devolved into something hot and deep. Something desperate and feral.

It went on for a long while. Too long for comfort.

When they broke apart she was breathing as hard as a racehorse. Red sounded casual, like they'd just met over a brunch buffet. "Good Morning, Ms. Fulham," he murmured.

This time, she was ready for her cue. "Good Morning, Mr. MacLellan," she replied politely. At least, as politely as she could manage, while trapped by a hulking piece of testosterone in a broom closet. He was lucky his tongue knew its way around hers—otherwise, Piper might've bitten it clean off.

"Why didn't you call?" he wondered, only a bit less friendly.

"And look pathetic?" she inquired starchily. "I think not."

"How on earth does that make you pathetic? If anyone looks pathetic here, it's me."

"Might I point out that you didn't call first? Or email. Or text. Or *anything at all*. Asshole."

"I called every day and went straight to voicemail. Then I texted you. Twelve damn times. Check your goddamn phone, Piper."

Next to her head, his breath sawed in and out in a somewhat normal rhythm. Hers, however, felt ragged in her lungs. Her chest rose and fell too fast, brushing against the front of his pristine suit each time. Piper pressed back against the wall but couldn't escape the way Red pushed every one of her buttons without even trying.

Why did he have to smell so good, anyway? Why couldn't he be a total washout in the sack? He wasn't, though. Red felt and tasted so utterly perfect that she transformed into a pea-brained fangirl whenever he got close.

When Piper could manage to speak again, she didn't mention the texts, or the lack thereof. Her voice sounded too husky in the little room.

"I think we need to hash out how soon we can sleep together again."

"Oh?" Bastard managed to sound cool as a cucumber, but every muscle in his body had tensed. She knew—she could feel them all. Hell, Piper could *picture* them all.

"And why is that?" he asked.

"I don't know. Maybe because you have me pinned against the wall of a dark janitor closet at eight in the morning. In an office building. Making me even later than I already was to begin with."

He contemplated that piece of information in silence for a few moments but didn't release her quite yet.

"It's been nearly a week with no word from you," Red finally complained. "If you'd made me wait much longer, who knows what could've happened? I might've combusted."

"It was barely four days. Don't be dramatic."

"They were very long days."

"Point taken," she conceded.

Red nuzzled her hair in the dark, and his voice went softer. "Does Wayne know where you're staying?"

"Yes." Piper had enthused about her prior hotel just enough, that Wayne had booked her at the same place again.

"Then I'll pick you up for dinner tonight at seven. Be ready, little dove."

With that edict delivered, Red released her wrists, hit the light switch, and let himself out of the closet. He squared his shoulders and strode across the lobby toward the elevators at the back. Piper could almost hear his thoughts: *Handled the hell out of that.*

What a knucklehead. Mr. Red "Too Big For His Britches" MacLellan was going to drive her insane with his antics.

Who did he think he was? For days, she'd heroically fought back every slavering impulse she'd had—to not call him at all hours, to not whine about him ignoring her, to not simply show up on his doorstep begging for another one of the thermonuclear assaults he called kisses.

And he had the nerve to be pissed that she hadn't called? She knew what century it was, thank you very much. Red should have at least thanked her for putting him up last weekend. For fawning over him like houseguest royalty.

Piper slipped into the lobby and waited for him to disappear inside one of the elevators, then stomped over to hit the button for another one. Inside the next car, she jabbed at the button for the design floor.

Then she slipped her cell from her purse and eyed the screen dubiously. Red hadn't *really* called and texted all those times, had he? It was one thing to jockey for position with him, bossy as he was, but she never would've been so rude as to ignore that many attempts to contact her.

Piper considered the dark screen. She was getting close to the time she was supposed to upgrade, and her phone *had* been acting sort of temperamental lately. And, come to think of it, other people had also mentioned texts she'd never received.

She'd assumed they were fudging to cover their own asses, but what if they weren't? Swallowing hard, she held down the power button, shut the phone down, and tucked it back into her purse.

Once she was settled at a conference table in the design department, a hot cup of coffee and several pages of cover model headshots spread before her, Piper took the phone out again. Setting it on the table, she powered it up and waited nervously. Any minute, several of the models would be coming in to meet her. She didn't have a ton of time.

No more than two minutes later, the accursed thing started making its classic whooshing sound, sending out message after message she'd thought had been delivered days ago. *Weeks* ago. Piper winced, fearing what was coming next.

After a pause that stretched for an eternity, the missed calls and incoming texts began arriving. Two from her mom. Five from her best friend. One from her brother. Piper pulled the device closer and stared, holding her breath.

One text from Red. Then two. *Three.* And on and on, with increasing urgency, all the way up to twelve texts from His Highness. Piper blew out a long, agonized breath. *Crap.* She was a writer, not a techie. She really shouldn't be allowed to handle electronics.

With one last, meek-sounding tone, her faithless phone sent out the last text she'd forgotten she sent, letting Red know she'd had a great time and hoping he got home safe and sound.

Four bloody days ago.

Piper hung her head and groaned. Things like this just did not happen to other people.

Before she had a chance to call Red and apologize, the conference room door swung open, admitting two of the new designers. Piper vaguely recognized them from her last meeting.

They, in turn, ushered in a handful of exceptionally beautiful young men bearing unseasonable tans and gleaming white smiles.

Piper stood up. Their headshots had not done them justice.

The cover designers looked excited. The first said, "The ladies will join us in a few. For now, just take a look at these guy's faces."

Piper smiled at the models. "They are very nice faces," she told them. Based on what she was seeing, they probably looked nice all over. But were they a good fit for her new series? That remained to be seen.

"Have a seat," the second designer said, "And let us tell you what we have in mind."

Ten

THE SOMMELIER TOOK forever to approach their table at the restaurant that night. Red reigned in his annoyance as he perused the wine list, only half listening to Piper's small talk while he tried to pick the perfect bottle to go with their dinners.

Once he finally got to order, the sommelier only said, "Very good, sir." To be fair, the man never said anything else, but Red could tell he was impressed.

Piper didn't notice. She was too busy looking around the cozy room with a tiny smile, her pleasure obvious. Red silently congratulated himself—he'd chosen well tonight. A good thing, too, since he only deliberated for half the damn morning, trying to decide what she'd like in her current frame of mind. At least he'd gotten it right.

Once Wayne had assured him that Piper had arrived in New York that morning as planned, and clued him in on her schedule, Red had headed over to Trident hoping to run into her—and he had. He just hadn't realized quite how desperate he'd been. Not until they found themselves lip-locking in a broom closet, that was.

Whatever. He and Piper had ironed out their misunderstanding and were back on track now. That was what was important.

The wine arrived, and the sommelier opened it with a bit of an understated flourish. Red tasted it, gave his customary nod, then watched as the man filled their glasses and melted away. Piper and took her first sip, then another longer one.

"Wow. This is really nice," she told him. Her lips were painted a vibrant red tonight and left a small smudge on the rim of her wine glass.

For a long minute, Red entertained himself with the cascade of images that the combination of those lips and the wine engendered. Eventually, Piper started to fidget a bit. He shook off the daydream and glanced at the bottle.

The wine had better be nice. He'd just dropped a small fortune on it—overcompensating for the frustration of the last few days, he supposed. Though why he thought Piper might be mesmerized by his posturing, he couldn't begin to guess.

"Oh good," he replied, somewhat lamely. Red surveyed her as she took another swallow, enjoying the movement of her pale throat as she drank. "It's a…"

He paused. Glanced down at the label once more. Piper wouldn't care one whit what the vineyard was, or the vintage year. She might care what he'd paid for it, but probably only so she could squawk about it.

She would care whether she actually liked it, though, and she did. She'd said so.

"It's a—?" Piper prompted him. Her expressive eyebrows drifted upward. *Right.* Red was supposed to be speaking.

"It's a pinot noir," he smiled. "I'm glad you like it."

This woman. Everything felt so much simpler with her. Consequently, that made this fling of theirs much more complicated. She was destined to make him crazy. Red already adored her.

"I do," Piper replied. She eyed his glass quizzically. "Don't you?"

He looked down and realized that he hadn't touched his glass since he'd taken that first exploratory sip. Red had been too preoccupied with his own rioting thoughts and too transfixed by the vision of Piper savoring the taste of the drink. He hadn't even remembered to toast her, much less join in.

Red raised his glass now, inhaling the scent of the wine within, taking in its color, cataloging the various flavor notes as they washed across his tongue. And then—then, he allowed all those details to dissipate, like smoke in his mouth. He just tasted and enjoyed.

He smiled wider at the sorceress across the table. "I do," he answered. "I like it a lot."

Easy.

Piper clinked her goblet against his, beaming right back at him. "To technology that works as advertised," she said.

Red laughed. "To seeing where things go," he fired back. He really, really hoped it would be toward a bed.

AFTER DINNER, THEY didn't pile into his car right away. Instead, they strolled lazily up the block, holding hands and enjoying being together again. They came to a large bookstore first.

"Want to go book shopping?" Red asked her.

"Always. But not in there."

"Why? It's nice. And, they have coffee."

"But they don't have a romance section," Piper explained. "And for your information, they aren't very nice, either. The jerks at Millhouse & Rock are high and mighty snobs, and I wouldn't buy a book from them if it was the last book on earth."

"That sounds serious. I had no idea." Red examined the façade of the store again, trying to find evidence of Piper's assertion. "They look so elegant."

"It's okay," she said, tugging him along. "They fooled you with all the brass and the wood paneling. That's how they get everyone."

At the next storefront, Piper's interest picked up significantly. It was hard to miss the way she did a longing double-take on a sexy pair of cheetah-print heels in the window. She tried to keep walking, though, her hand tucked sweetly into the bend of Red's elbow. She seemed surprised when he tugged her to a stop.

Red nodded toward the shoes. "You would look terrific in them."

Piper smiled faintly. Her eyes roved over the street, the window display, and the name of the store. There was a tiny flicker of apprehension, maybe, or discomfort—but it was gone in an instant, and then Piper was back to looking happy.

"Thank you. But maybe this isn't the best time to drool over them."

"Nonsense." Red pulled the shop door open and gestured her in. "No time like the present. Maybe there will be others inside that you like even more." Hell, based on what he was seeing, he was fairly certain there'd be more that he liked, too.

Piper stepped in reluctantly, then froze about two feet later to stare around like a deer caught in headlights. Red leaned over the waist-high wall to lift the object of her affection from the window display, then handed it to her.

Piper accepted the shoe reverently, cradling it in her hands with wide eyes.

When she spoke, her voice was forlorn, however. "I really should try to fight my love of animal prints a bit harder. It seems very trashy of me to be so fixated on them."

"Nah, they're fine if they're done right. Those leopard ones you wore to our meeting were perfect. Besides, if something this innocuous makes you happy, then who cares what other people think?" Look at him, acting all open-minded.

Before Red could dwell on the deeper ramifications of that mental oddity, he grabbed Piper's arm and led her deeper into the store.

She sighed, "You live in a very rarified world, don't you?"

Red shrugged. It was what it was. He moved away to peruse the displays scattered around, strolling slowly until Piper finally allowed herself to look around. Once she did, he observed her, instead.

She didn't look at prices, at least not that he saw. That was probably wise—these babies undoubtedly cost as much as some people's first car, and Piper would give herself a heart attack if she saw that.

"So rarified," he told her, "That I don't believe I have ever felt compelled to take a woman shoe shopping."

Just then, Red's attention was snagged by a display he hadn't inspected yet. Piper followed his line of sight, searching for what had diverted him. In two steps he was there, hooking his finger under the strap of a dark crimson, patent leather heel. He turned and extended it.

"Try these, too," he instructed. The heated look Piper gave Red in return had all the blood in his skull abruptly decamping for points south.

An employee had glided up, so Red handed her the shoe he held instead. Then he grabbed Piper's cheetah-printed number and passed that off, too.

"She'll try these in a size…?"

"Eight," Piper supplied weakly. She shuffled over to the low, padded leather bench the other woman indicated and sank down.

A second employee approached, this one a man with slicked-back hair, heavy cologne, and a slight potbelly. His expression was avid as he made to kneel in front of Piper. He'd greeted her too warmly, oozing obsequiousness.

Red's gut-level reaction was instantaneous. "No," he barked, waving the man off.

The guy straightened quickly and backed up, no doubt used to the peccadilloes of the customers who usually shopped there. Red stepped into the breach, lest there be any further confusion.

"I'll do it," he told him, demanding the man's departure with his most commanding glare.

Once he'd gotten his way, Red knelt at Piper's feet. As he had at the Japanese restaurant a few weeks back, he removed her shoes carefully. The short brown boots looked downright sensible next to the two sexy samples on the bench next to her. It was almost laughable the way Piper could move between the two extremes so effortlessly.

Red caressed her ankles lightly while they waited for the first woman to return. Piper sighed and ran a hand into his hair. He had to look away, so he wouldn't be tempted to spread her knees and dive between them, right then and there.

Once the female employee reappeared, Red slipped the cheetah pumps on Piper first, securing each tiny buckle on the row of straps with his too-large fingers. Seemed like a perfect fit to him, but she was the one who had to walk in them.

"How are they?" he asked, shifting back.

Piper was already so in love, she may as well have melted onto the floor. But she dutifully stood and took a few steps, transfixed by her own feet.

"Oh. Wow," she marveled breathlessly. "They're a lot more comfortable than they look."

"And they look hot, hot, *hot*," enthused the oily shoe salesman, sidling up once more.

Hadn't Red already run this one off? He scowled a bit more ferociously this time, which immediately had the guy's cohort clamping her lips together and shooing him into the back.

Red turned back to Piper. "Fine Italian design," he told her, leading her back to the bench. "Now try mine." He crouched and switched the cheetah heels out for the dark red ones.

Piper rose and walked away again, watching her feet in the mirrors that lined the walls. Red devoured the long lines of her legs, the sway of her hips, the arch of her spine. Much more of those wanton shoes and he was going to need to get Piper alone—and soon. They looked even better on her than he'd expected, and that was really saying something.

When she sat again, Piper looked a little shell-shocked. Red could empathize.

He told her, "You walk differently in these."

Piper stared at him, and he willed her to read his mind. He'd pay any price if it meant she left this store with those shoes in her possession. He'd do anything if she'd wear them for him later.

The employee broke the mood simmering between them with a polite little cough.

"I'm not sure what you'll think of these, but I spotted them in the back earlier. Do you want to try them, too?" She extended the open box carefully, revealing a strappy pair of heeled sandals nestled in tissue paper.

Piper hissed between her teeth and grabbed for them, slipping off the crimson shoes and quickly setting them aside.

"Do you mind?" she begged. She looked a little guilty, poor thing.

But Red could be magnanimous when the situation warranted it. "By all means."

He let the women handle the donning of this pair themselves, standing back and smirking at how smitten Piper already looked. Thin cords crisscrossed the top of each foot, then wound around her ankles. Her pale skin contrasted beautifully with the narrow straps of black suede. Tiny tassels dangled from the loose ends of each bow.

Once Piper was ready to stand, Red laced his fingers through hers and helped her up.

"I'm beginning to think you'll look gorgeous in every pair in here," he told her.

She sauntered away, did a runway-worthy spin, then came back. Those fiendish tassels danced around her ankles with every step. "We don't have that kind of time," she joked.

Red disagreed. If it meant watching Piper sashay around the boutique in increasingly stimulating pairs of heels, then he had all the time in the world.

Sadly, she sat down too soon, then clapped her hands together.

"Okay!" she chirped brightly. Red didn't like the note of finality in her voice. Piper didn't actually think she was leaving those shoes *here*, did she?

"Woman, you're going to break hearts all over town, when people get a load of you." They were shoes that could tempt a saint, and Red was clearly not one of those.

"Don't be ridiculous." Piper rolled her eyes, and then finally did what he'd hoped she wouldn't—she peeked at the price tag. Then she blanched, paralyzed in the act of untying that second erotic bow at her ankle.

Before the moment could get away from him, Red turned to the tidy woman beside him and declared, "We'll take all three." He turned back to Piper and asked, "Do you want to wear those out?"

"What!" she screeched. "Red!"

He nodded at the employee, who ducked her head and began packing up the loose shoes. She tucked Piper's boots into the last empty box and stood, waiting expectantly.

Piper stammered, "Oh—oh my God. Red, you can't do this."

He could so. Red handed his credit card to the saleswoman, and she took off for the register at the back of the store. Probably didn't want to hang around too long, in case Piper was successful in robbing her of her commission.

"I cannot accept these from you," Piper protested again, in a slightly firmer voice.

Red grinned. "Up we go," he instructed, holding out his hand.

"Wait," she wailed, bending to re-tie both bows quickly.

The employee returned with a large bag and a sales slip for Red to sign, and then, miraculously, he was able to hustle Piper toward the door.

"Please," she pleaded. "Will you listen to me?"

"I listen to every word you say," Red told her, "And even some you don't." He tucked his card and receipt inside his breast pocket, then towed Piper by the hand out to the sidewalk.

His driver was still idling by the curb where they'd left him. When Felix spotted them, he threw the car into park and trotted over. Red handed him the bag to put in the trunk, then returned to Piper's side before she could budge.

"You're insane," she muttered.

"Why fight it? You adored those shoes, and so did I."

"I hate to break it to you, big guy, but you might be in the throes of a full-on shoe fetish."

Oh, she had no idea.

Red said, "Why don't we agree it's a 'you' fetish and call it a day."

Piper scowled. It made him a little testy.

"Jesus. There's no catch, woman. All you have to do is enjoy the gift and move on. Wear them for me sometime, if you want."

If he'd hoped to chasten her, it didn't work. "Still, you didn't have to do that," she insisted.

"No, I didn't. But I wanted to. Is that really so bad?"

Piper peeked at her feet. "I guess not," she murmured. "So…thank you."

"My pleasure, believe me." Red pecked her lightly on the cheek. "There's not much else up this way, and those new kicks of yours really ought to be debuted properly." At her look of inquiry, he admitted, "Okay, fine. I'm not ready to relinquish you, yet. I want to show you off, like the caveman I am. Happy now?"

Piper finally smiled and nodded. "As a matter of fact, I am."

"Good, then we have one more stop."

Eleven

A S WITH MOST things in the city, getting wherever they were going was a long, slow slog across town. Piper finally buckled and had to ask Red if they could pull over somewhere for a potty break. The look he gave her made it clear he thought she'd been rusticating in the suburbs for far too long.

As luck would have it, though, the nearest bathroom turned out to be the one at his place. In the dark, the neighborhood seemed edgier than it probably was. The streets made Piper a little nervous as the car rolled along them, and that didn't dissipate once his driver let them off at the curb. It was eerily quiet on his block. She'd clearly lived in the suburbs too long.

"Nice place," she tried. The elevator ride up to Red's floor wasn't helping.

He chuckled. "Wait until you've seen it. Then decide."

Piper steeled herself for what Red's apartment might look like. Given his wealth, she would've expected some old-money townhouse replete with monograms and estate silver. Maybe some paintings of hunting dogs, expensive urns on pedestals, the lingering essence of stuck-up ancestors in the air. Based on what she'd seen so far, though, that idea was dissolving pretty quickly.

Even with Piper's shaky understanding of city real estate, she was aware it could cost an arm and a leg. Despite all his success, maybe the best Red could manage was some setup in a hip, gentrifying neighborhood, with a decent amount of space and a large threat of mugging.

Judging by the no-frills lobby and the clanking elevator, Piper was now betting that Red's apartment would have an industrial vibe, something with exposed pipes and bare light bulbs. There would probably be old movie posters on the walls, but they'd be framed nicely.

Piper peeked at Red out of the corner of her eye while he studied the flickering floor numbers over the metal elevator gate. No, not movies, she decided. Red would have concert posters, but they'd be for bands she'd never heard of.

Still, Piper suspected this little detour was going to be a challenge. So far, she'd tried to take the elegant dinners in stride. The whole shoe-shopping thing Red dropped on her tonight had been kind of preposterous—but it had also been heavy with eroticism, and somehow that softened the edges.

But Piper had the feeling she was about to be hit over the head with exactly how different she and Red really were. He probably had all sorts of savings and investments, the sort of debt that was calculated for leverage only, and no financial worries whatsoever. She expected that if this man wanted something, he bought it. If something was broken, he hired someone to fix it. Simple as that.

It wasn't like Piper was hurting for cash herself these days, but she still budgeted and spent what she had carefully. It was part of why she was doing okay—part of why she didn't have to agonize over every cent like she'd once done. At least her parents had taught her that much.

It was a skill that was coming in awfully handy now that she'd taken over her grandparents' old house, and especially now that the royalties from her backlist were beginning to drop off so much. It would be a welcome relief if PKM could launch her new series into success.

The elevator slowed as it neared the top, and Piper resolved not to judge Red. She wasn't going to envy the man for his good fortune, knowing how hard he probably worked for it. Besides, success like his came with a price, didn't it? Red had said as much.

All she really wanted was the chance to understand him as a person, without the interfering static of his wealth, his reputation, and his notoriety. Maybe that was possible, and maybe it wasn't. Only time would tell.

He was quiet. Piper wondered if he'd picked up on her unease, or if he was nervous himself, for some reason. The thought was unexpectedly endearing.

"So," Piper said, "You're in the penthouse, huh?"

Red's voice was wry. "Yeah, well, I wanted to make sure I got one with a bathroom. Just in case."

"The other apartments don't have bathrooms? Do they, like, share one at the end of the hall or something?" She grimaced, not even wanting to contemplate the germs involved. Too many shades of youth hostel for her.

"It was a joke, little dove." He shook his head. "Come on."

The elevator gave a sickening lurch, then stopped. Red pushed back the metal gate and led Piper out. The outer hallway wasn't much to look at—it could've been in a factory or a mental hospital, for all its aesthetic appeal. But then, Red unlocked his door and casually swung it wide.

"Brace yourself. Here it is," he said.

The loft's interior was cavernous. Piper stepped inside, and in one sweeping glance took in the three-story ceilings, the wide-open floor plan, and the elementary-school color scheme. Everywhere she looked, there was stark white or glossy black, punctuated by small bursts of primary colors.

A curving set of black metal stairs rose from the center of the space, leading to a shadowy upper level hovering over a portion of the room. The living area sported clear tables and white leather couches. Piper spotted a round red lamp and a huge, mostly-white canvas spattered with blue and black paint.

She took a deep breath, then let it out slowly. "Wow," she told him.

It all looked spectacularly uncomfortable, stark and cold enough to be an ultramodern art museum instead of someone's home. It must have cost Red a bloody fortune.

Piper's shoulders relaxed a fraction, and she forced a smile to her face. Her problem was suddenly a very different one than she'd anticipated. She wasn't jealous of him—but she would have to pretend to like his taste. There was no way he wouldn't be proud of this ghastly mess.

After the nice night they'd had, it seemed rude to hurt his feelings. Piper wasn't entirely certain she could respect him after seeing this, however. The place just screamed "pretentious ass."

Piper was saved from having to make immediate eye contact when Red eased her coat from her shoulders and placed it on a nearby chair, along with her purse.

"Bathroom is right in there," he said, indicating a cracked door off to the side.

Piper marched over, happy to have a minute alone to compose herself. Sadly, once inside, she was faced with four walls papered in a design that evoked nothing so much as the demented scribbles of a truly deranged mind. She squeezed her eyes shut and peed as fast as she could, then washed her hands and bolted out of there like her pants were on fire. *Ugh*.

Red still stood where she'd left him. He turned to her with an expectant expression, and Piper couldn't hide anymore.

"There you are. So, what do you—" Red regarded her and the corners of his mouth ticked up. "Oh my God," he said.

Piper swallowed. Shit—she was busted. "What?"

Red's brows veered together as he studied her face. "You actually hate it, don't you?"

There was no fudging it. Piper really ought to look into some acting lessons or something.

"No. Really," she tried. "It's very nice."

Red laughed outright at that. "Now I know you despise it."

"Well, it's not *my* taste, exactly, but…"

"But what?" He gazed steadily at her, amused by her fumbling. He didn't seem hurt or angry, so at least there was that.

"Let's just say, you'd better hope my parents never see this place," Piper hedged. She might as well roll them under the bus. It wasn't like they'd ever meet Red, and it would save her from having to tell him she thought his taste was atrocious.

Her comment merely piqued his curiosity, though. "Oh, really? And why is that?"

"My dad is ex-Army and my mom is a bit of a nervous nelly. What do you think?"

Piper could see her father's dour face like it was right there, silently condemning all the ostentatious ugliness surrounding them. God forbid anyone asked him what to do about it, though—he'd only instruct them to *figure it out.*

And Piper knew that any attempts her mother might make to help would only hit left of center. Like the time Piper had decided to get fit so she would have a better chance of making her school soccer team, only to have her mother take up baking with a vengeance. Or the times she tried to cram for big tests, and her mom suddenly wanted to take her shopping all afternoon to de-stress her.

"I would think that with a daughter like you, they might be more receptive to creativity in *all* its forms," Red smiled.

His eyes skated over Piper's face, meticulously cataloging her expression and body language. He probably wasn't even aware he was doing it. She'd bet he did that with everyone.

"That's a laugh," she fired back. "When I landed my first deal with Trident, my dad told me that if I was going to insist on being artsy-fartsy all my life, the least I could do was write a real book."

That set Red back on his heels, all right. Piper couldn't think of too many men who might give Padraig MacLellan a run for his money, but her father was definitely one of them.

"Just out of curiosity, what would constitute a 'real' book?"

"A comprehensive history of trench warfare. Naturally."

"Of course," he said. "How foolish of me."

There was a long pause, in which Piper attempted to look around again without being too obvious or letting her eyes linger on any one hideous thing too long.

"Do your parents have *any* conception of how popular your books are?" Red inquired.

"They think I'm faking." Piper blew out a long breath, remembering *those* excruciating conversations.

"Fascinating."

Not even close. She cast around for a change in subject, but there was only one real direction for her to head in.

"So, did you pick all this out yourself?" Piper managed weakly.

"Almost none of it." Red beamed, looking around. "My parents chose the apartment and gave it to me when I finished grad school. They said it would be good for a bachelor pad."

"And the—" Piper cleared her throat and pushed on, "—the furniture and everything?"

"A decorator, obviously. My mother got restless when I didn't buy much more than a mattress in the first few months I was here. She hired some friend of hers, and every day after work there'd be new stuff here. It went on for months."

"And this is what happened."

"Yup," he said cheerfully. Red jammed his hands in his pockets and bounced on his toes a little as he looked around.

Piper spun away, trying to hold it together, but her eyes landed right on an enormous canvas on the brick wall beside her. She couldn't help her astonished gasp. *The horror.*

"It's gruesome, isn't it?" Red laughed.

"Little bit. Yeah."

"I've always thought it looked a lot like a crime scene," he mused.

Piper stared upward. "Oh, God. You're right. How do you even live with that atrocity every day?"

Red steered her deeper into the loft. "It's no big deal. I just try to ignore it."

Piper frowned, more troubled than before.

"What now?" he laughed, when he caught sight of her face. She had no idea why he might find her distress charming.

"Doesn't it bother you?" she demanded.

"Why? Because it's revolting?"

"No. Because it's…it's soulless. You didn't choose *any* of this." A broad sweep of her arm encompassed it all. "But you still have to live here, surrounded by an environment you don't like, every single day."

Red examined the huge factory windows set in the outer wall, and the grimy rooftops visible beyond. "I think you may be the first woman I've ever brought here who didn't gush over it," he mused, smirking back down at her again. "Or at a minimum, the first who admitted to not liking it. It's amazing, frankly."

Piper liked that Red was counting it as a point in her favor, but she couldn't help ribbing him. She arched her eyebrows and prodded, "How many hordes of female visitors are we talking, exactly?"

Red snorted but didn't bother answering. Instead, he explained, "Since I'm not here much, it never seemed worth the trouble to change everything. Why would I? Everyone else loved it."

"Like that matters. Doesn't *your* opinion rate at all?"

Red shrugged.

"Well, honestly," Piper replied tartly, "If you're going to base major decisions on what other people think, you really shouldn't surround yourself with sycophants."

"Syco—" Red burst out laughing. His eyes watered, and he chortled so much he couldn't even finish the word. Before he recovered completely, he muttered something that sounded an awful lot like, "I ought to spank you for that little gem."

Piper crossed her arms over her chest. He wouldn't dare.

At last he pulled himself together, but mirth still creased the corners of his eyes. "Tell me, Miss Fulham—if you lived here, what would you pick instead?"

Piper's first thought was that she'd never be able to afford the kind of place she'd seen in the movies, especially if her sales numbers continued to decline. But she decided it was all speculation anyway. Why not run with it?

Her mind wandered a bit before she murmured, "Hmm, probably one of those big, airy places that's always in architecture magazines, with all the arched windows and crown molding." As she warmed to the topic and Red's curious expression, she added, "Parquet floors. Overlooking the park. And one of those long terraces with boxwood bushes and trees in big stone planters." Piper couldn't help appending, "And a friendly doorman."

Red's gaze went soft. He said quietly, "I could see that." Then he cleared his throat. "In my defense, I did pick out a few things in this place."

"Oh really?"

"Can I show you my favorite?"

"Definitely. Where is it?" Piper peeked around, desperately hoping it wasn't one of the lurid sculptures scattered around.

"Upstairs in the bedroom. It's a painting," he explained.

Of course. "Not a scandalous etching?" Piper inquired, saccharine-sweet.

Red smirked again and took her elbow, leading her toward the staircase. "Unfortunately, not. But you can bet that's an oversight I'll be rectifying as soon as possible."

Piper grinned as she climbed the curving stairs, then paused at the top, waiting for Red to direct her.

He flicked a light switch, dimly illuminating a larger area than she'd expected to see. His lair turned out to be a study in dark browns, moody and masculine. It wasn't quite neat as a pin, not like the downstairs. Piper could almost believe the virile, seductive man next to her lived here. Slept here—fucked here.

She coughed and turned quickly around. Red was standing near the far wall, next to a painting that hung facing his bed, where he could see it when he woke up every morning. He gestured to it like a game show host, then moved away to turn on more lamps. Piper tried not to imagine him laying on that huge bed.

Red returned to stand easily next to her and studied the oil with an appraising eye. Piper could feel the heat coming off him. With his burnished auburn hair, towering frame, and sinfully-seductive face, Red was like a blaze burning at the center of the chocolate-brown room. She wanted to melt for him.

The painting he was perusing was an abstract, but unlike the others downstairs, this one was soft and muted. As she examined it, too, Piper decided it reminded her of a forest, cold and barren at the end of winter. White sky, gray and black tree trunks, brown mulch blanketing the ground. She thought there might be the faintest suggestion of tiny green buds, beginning to emerge on some branches.

Despite the lack of definition in the brushstrokes, Piper could almost feel the brisk bite of the air on her face. Smell the rotted leaves and icy frost. It was the diametric opposite of the city that surrounded Red's apartment. It beckoned you in, and if it were a real place, Piper would want to walk there with Red, bundled up and hand in hand.

She pulled back and refocused on his face. What did he see when he looked at it? Maybe not a forest, but a worn stone wall, streaked with mold or algae? Or maybe Red simply saw more dripping paint.

He turned to her, and his hazy brown eyes gradually cleared. "You can hear the twigs snapping underfoot, can't you?" he asked, looking almost sheepish.

Piper nodded eagerly, delighted that they saw it the same way, after all. Red's eyes flicked over her shoulder to his bed, then quickly back to her face. "I won it at an auction one time," he said quickly.

"Lucky you."

He peeked at his bed once more, and Piper began to wonder if she was finally going to get kissed again. Instead, Red squared his shoulders. "Dessert," he announced. "Before we go. I got tiramisu at the Italian market."

No make-out session, then. Piper sighed and trooped after him to the stairs. "Yum," was about the best she could muster.

Down in the kitchen, Red parked her on a tall metal barstool while he pulled out some plates and forks. "Would you like some coffee?"

"No thanks."

Red plunked a slice of the dessert in front of Piper, then settled on the next stool to dig into his own piece.

Her first bite melted on her tongue in a miasma of espresso, custard, and liquor-soaked cake. Piper groaned. "Oh my God. This is so good."

His eyes drifted briefly to her mouth before he nodded. "It's my favorite."

"If I could find it this good at home, it would be mine too."

Red finished off his portion in about five bites, then turned and watched Piper work her way through hers. "Are you tired?" he asked at last. "Or do you think you still have that extra stop in you?"

"This wasn't it?"

"If you recall, this was the unscheduled potty break."

"Ah. Right. Well, what did you have in mind?"

"I have a club about ten minutes from here. If you want, we can go have a quick drink and listen to some music. I'll show you around, and then I promise I'll let you go."

Piper didn't expect Red had ever let something go without a fight, but if the object in question was her, who was she to complain? Besides, there were bigger issues at play—because it had sounded an awful lot like he'd just said, *I have a club*. She definitely needed to see that.

"I'm down," she told him, unhooking her heel from the rung of the barstool and letting her foot swing free. Red's eyes tracked the movement immediately, turning hot and hungry.

"Good. Much as I'd like to be the only one who gets to see those damn shoes," he muttered, "They probably deserve a wider audience."

"You got that right," Piper told him, leaning closer.

She was only a breath away by the time Red realized what she was doing. He ripped his gaze from her shoes, met her challenging stare with one of his own, and set her heart galloping in her chest.

Piper glanced at his impossibly sexy mouth and her breath hitched. Red made a low, sexy sound deep in his throat, and then, finally, his mouth was meeting hers. Her lips parted, his tongue swept in, and all the grotesque décor around them spun away in a fog of cocoa-flavored lust.

Twelve

R ED HAD NO idea how he'd managed to let Piper go. It felt like an insurmountable task when she was standing two feet from his bed, and positively Herculean once she'd basically invited him to taste her in his kitchen.

Tiramisu-flavored Piper. Fucking hell, Red wasn't likely to forget *that* anytime soon.

Somehow, he'd gotten them back out of his apartment without tumbling Piper onto the nearest horizontal surface, but that was mainly because she'd seemed a little skittish when they were there. Her mood hadn't been screaming *Take me now*, so much as *Dear God, I think that art wants to kill me*.

It really was past time for Red to make some adjustments to the décor in his loft. He'd been ignoring it for too long, but maybe Miss Piper could help rectify the situation.

He couldn't fault her taste, after all. After a brief spell of agonizing in the back of his car, she'd decided to don her new red fuck-me heels for their stop at the club—and Red couldn't take his eyes off them.

Unfortunately, neither could Piper. In between watching the dancers, she kept stealing glances at her feet, obviously smitten beyond all reason. Hell, even Red's dick wanted to get in on the action, flexing like a Jersey shore bodybuilder behind his zipper, hoping for its own look-see.

He winced and readjusted himself on the leather loveseat for the umpteenth time. Security had commandeered the upstairs VIP area for him and Piper the moment they'd arrived, and fortunately, they'd been left alone after that. If Red was forced to get up and walk around right then, people would be in for quite a show.

"If I had known how much I would have to compete with those shoes for your attention," he told Piper drily, "I'm not sure I would have been so eager to get them for you."

She pulled her gaze from the mass of gyrating bodies below the balcony and giggled. "They're a little like wingtips on ecstasy, aren't they?" Piper took another happy slurp of her second whiskey and ginger ale, and Red wondered if she was getting tipsy. *That* would be something.

He draped an arm around her shoulders, unable to resist getting closer. "I'll give you this," he said. "Your facility with words is not limited to the printed page."

Piper sighed and snuggled into his side, and Red wanted to thump his chest like a fucking gorilla. He inhaled the light scent of her perfume and the warm fragrance that was simply *her.*

"If you say so." She turned her head to look up at him and her eyes went seductively hazy. "Guess what? My wingtips are better than your wingtips," she teased, drawing out the syllables and making him burn even hotter.

The sass of her. Piper was lucky Red didn't yank her onto his lap and take her right there in front of all and sundry. The lights were low, the bass was thumping in time with the insistent pulse of his blood, and Piper was caged securely in his arms. As plan Bs went, this was nearly as good as having her back at his house was.

Red had just bent to have another taste of that tempting, whiskey-laced mouth when a sudden camera flash exploded in his peripheral vision.

"*Fuck,*" he growled, leaping up and blocking Piper with his body. That sure hadn't taken long.

He threw his hand out, reaching through the spots dancing across his vision to clamp onto the paparazzo's arm before the little weasel managed to dart away. The guy looked indignant, like he was getting ready to work himself into an epic tantrum. Too bad.

Red searched for Mutt and Bill, the two bulky bouncers usually parked in the corner of the VIP lounge, but they were already on their way over. When the cameraman caught sight of *them*, he really began to struggle in earnest. He flailed around, catching the edge of a table with his hip and sending a couple of glasses crashing to the floor near Piper's feet.

She gasped and shrank back. Mutt took one look at the mess, hauled back, and clocked the vermin dead in the face.

Red released the guy's arm and let him slump to the floor. Bill nudged him onto his back with his enormous combat boot, then leaned down and carefully slipped the camera strap over the paparazzo's head. He took one look at the display screen and handed the camera right to Red.

Behind him, Piper sat frozen on the sofa, wide-eyed and not saying a word. "You okay, sweetheart?" Red asked.

She gripped her hands together in her lap and gave him a quick nod, then peeped around Red's legs to check out the dude on the carpet, now beginning to whine and clutch at his nose.

Red turned his attention back to the camera. The jerk had been taking pictures of him and Piper for a while. Red arrowed back through the array of photos, deleting them one by one until he came to some fuzzier images at the beginning of the set.

The dark alley behind the club, where the employee entrance was. Piper leaning against the grimy brick wall, Red's hands on her ass and tongue down her throat. Even though he could hardly make out their features in the unfocused frames, it still looked bad—illicit and sleazy. It hadn't been, though. They'd only stopped for one hot-and-heavy minute between leaving the car and ducking into the club.

Red deleted those shots, too, then scanned through the camera's other screens and settings to make sure the photos weren't sitting in some digital trash bin somewhere, waiting to be restored. He hoped to hell the man hadn't managed to upload anything yet.

Poor Piper would be mortified if any of those pictures made it into the gossip pages, and Red's Trident investors would feel even worse. They were a squirrelly bunch—okay with funding some lifestyle brands here and there, but warier than expected about Red's decision to move into the arts last year.

Terry, his head of security, trotted up, holding his headset in place at one ear. "Take that asshole out front to wait for the police," he ordered his guys.

"How did he get in here?" Red demanded. He glanced quickly at Piper again, but she was still sitting behind him, untouched and unharmed. He forced himself to calm down before he ripped someone's head off right in front of her.

Terry looked to Mutt, asking, "Who's on the door right now?" while Bill smacked the paparazzo into complaisance and hauled him to his feet.

Mutt said, "The new guy, Collin. We'll talk to him on our way out." Then the bouncers dragged the interloper unceremoniously away.

"I'll check the tapes," Terry told Red, "But I don't think he came in the front. Any one of us would've spotted that lens in a second. Even Collin."

"All right. Have the other guys do a sweep to find out how he did get in."

"Where was he hiding? Could you tell?"

"I'm not sure. Maybe the stairwell over there." Red slung the camera over his shoulder and blew out a long breath. "Do me a favor. Take Ms. Fulham to the office to wait for me, in case there are any others still inside."

Red pushed away his disappointment at the unwelcome turn of events and reached a hand toward Piper. "That's our cue, I'm afraid."

Piper pouted prettily at his weak joke, but underneath it she was clearly shaken. She sucked down the last of her drink through the little plastic stirrer, then let Red help her to her feet.

"I guess I'm bad luck tonight, huh?" she said.

Red really needed her to lay off that self-deprecating crap. And he thought that maybe—just maybe—it was an instance in which his particular interests might come in handy. The next time he found himself in a bed with her, perhaps he could teach Piper a thing or two about her own worth.

He gave himself half a minute to play out the fantasy. With Piper acting as his submissive, Red would have her confidence where it ought to be in no time. And hell—he'd probably be feeling pretty good about himself, too.

There was no time for that train of thought right now, though. "Forget that," he said. "Terry is going to take you to the club's office. Hang tight there and wait for me, okay? So I know you're safe?"

She nodded, innocent and dutiful. Coupled with the shoes, it was like catnip for his degenerate soul. "Where are you going?" she wondered.

To hell, probably. "I'm going to go down and talk to the cops, but I'll be back to get you as soon as I possibly can."

"Okay."

"I'm really sorry, sweetheart. This is obviously not how I wanted to end the night."

Piper swayed an inch toward him, so Red wrapped an arm around her and kissed the top of her head to comfort her. Then he released her to Terry with a speaking glare.

The man jerked his chin in acknowledgment and whisked Piper away. Red watched them until they disappeared behind the hidden door leading into the back hall and the offices beyond, then hit the employee elevator to go clean up this mess.

THE POLICE OFFICERS had arrived by the time Red strode into the chilly night air. Their black-and-white was pulled onto the sidewalk, its flashing lights making it seem like the party was outside rather than in.

The paparazzo had regained his wits and was bitching loudly about assault, theft, and property destruction. He had an interested audience in the people waiting in line, many of them standing with their cellphones out and ready to record, in case things went sideways.

The dude had a less-interested audience in the cops, however. Red introduced himself and drew them aside, so he could be heard over the din.

The older man in the pair wasted no time. "How'd his nose get broken?"

"Security had to neutralize him before he hurt himself or someone else," Red said.

"Acting like this inside?"

"And then some. You know my guys don't like to get rough when they have to toss people. But if dropping someone quickly means that they won't cause a bigger scuffle, then that's what they do. Besides, I have a guest with me tonight. She's a petite woman, and this guy was right up in our faces. Security didn't want her to get caught in the middle of something."

Terry walked up. Red didn't need to introduce him; the officers who worked this district knew his team well—and knew they ran a tight ship. A clean club. Red wasn't going to worry, not yet.

"We found a broken window on the third floor," Terry explained. "Fucker scaled the fire escape, cut the alarm, and came in through the women's locker room."

The officer sighed, "No photography allowed on the premises, I presume?"

"Private property," Red smiled. "He did not have permission from the management to take photos tonight."

"All right, MacLellan. Look, this character's got a rap sheet a mile long and our shift is over in forty-five minutes. Let's wrap this up."

The cop nodded at his partner, who shut down the paparazzo's antics with a decisive yank on his arm. A moment later, the officer was guiding the idiot's head past the cruiser's doorframe and stuffing him into the back.

The cameraman twitched on the seat, trying to get comfortable with his hands cuffed behind him. Red stared him down, willing the bastard to read the murderous thoughts churning through his mind.

"You and your goons available to come down to the station tomorrow to give statements?" Cop One asked.

"Of course. The club's open for three more hours, or they'd come tonight."

"What about your lady friend?"

Red paused. *Shit.* In all his fury, he hadn't thought this far ahead. If word got out, it might do worse than merely embarrass her—it could seriously dent Piper's squeaky-clean reputation. With Trident's transition on shaky ground already, Red couldn't risk anything that took away from her sterling public persona.

"She's upstairs, but—"

The officer frowned.

"Here's the thing," Red told him. "She's in town for meetings with my company this week. She's an author—a well-known one. She's only a bystander, and I'd hate for her name to be tainted in any way if this were to make the news."

"Understood. Who is it?"

Red decided to go for name recognition, rather than legality. "Her name is Antoinette Corelli. She's a—"

"No shit? My wife inhales everything that woman puts out. Can't say I mind, either." He raised his eyebrows and waggled them meaningfully.

"Your wife is in very good company," Red said.

"Okay, chief. I'm gonna need to talk to her, but I'll keep it brief. Lead the way."

RED WAITED OUTSIDE the office for what felt like an eternity, watching the dancers below while Piper gave her statement. In truth, less than an hour passed before he was ushering the cop back outside and rejoining Piper upstairs.

With the photographer mess out of the way, though, Red could finally fold her into his arms and get another taste of the sweetness he'd been hungering for. He lingered over the kiss, slow and lazy, letting it calm his frayed nerves and settle his black mood.

When they finally broke apart, Piper grinned and whisked an unsteady hand across her brow. "Whew," she said. "I wasn't expecting that. Getting warm in here, no?"

Jesus. Her moves—such as they were—were awkward and ridiculous, and Red loved them all. "Come on, hot stuff," he told her. "It's been a long night. Bring your kinky wingtips and let's get you back to your hotel."

"I'll have you know these babies are all business," she retorted, following him down the back stairs, and out to the alley where Felix was waiting with the car.

"They fit right in," he murmured.

He held Piper's hand and settled into his seat, tracking the late-night sights of the city rushing past the tinted windows. Stumbling drunks. Homeless folks with their loaded shopping carts. Flickering streetlights and darkened ground-floor shop windows.

Piper had been amazing tonight, rolling with every change of direction with unwavering aplomb. Red could probably learn a thing or two from her, too.

Piper squeezed his hand. "You aren't unhappy with me, are you?" she asked.

Red was startled. He'd been mentally singing her praises, then dwelling on the untimely interruption of their evening, and on what needed to get rescheduled the next morning so he could go down to the station. But Piper was blameless.

"Of course not. Why would you think that?"

"You're pretty grim. Haven't said three words to me since we left the club."

Red brooded for a few more minutes, thinking. "You know, I've had to deal with jerks like that for a while now. They're relentless, but my team has a protocol and for the most part, it works pretty well. I get to maintain a little privacy, at least. I guess I'm just furious that things went wrong tonight, and that you got pulled into it."

"It seems like it will be okay, though, right? That cop acted like he believed us."

"Yeah, he seemed to. But it's still an invasion. A violation of our time, our space…it's not okay. I'm pissed, Piper, but not at you. I'm sorry if it seemed that way."

She studied him, blocks of light and shadow moving across her face as the car maneuvered through the city streets toward her hotel.

"You must have to be on guard constantly," she mused. "Careful where you're seen, careful who you're seen with. You're the brand, aren't you? The famous Red MacLellan, head of PKM—not allowed to be anonymous. Not allowed to live your life without public interference."

Red swallowed. Piper was uncomfortably close to his reality and he didn't want it to put her off. "I'm not sure it's quite as bad as all that," he demurred. "But those tabloid guys love a juicy story, and they don't mind if they have to make one up along the way. They're more than happy to spin the innocuous into the sordid, and they don't care who they hurt in the process."

Her forehead crinkled in thought. "You're angrier that they're dishonest, aren't you? To you, it's worse than the fact that they don't respect personal boundaries, isn't it?"

"I'm…" Red struggled for the words, to reign in his temper and respond to the simple curiosity in her face rather than to his disquiet at her probing. "I'm furious at him for ruining our great evening," he managed eventually.

"Well," Piper spoke softly, her eyes still scrutinizing him. Seeing too much. "He didn't ruin everything. And the night isn't quite over yet. Maybe we still have time to salvage it."

Red's mood perked up and so did his dick. This woman never ceased to amaze him.

"I would've thought you'd be appalled by all this."

"Oh, I'm appalled all right—but with that photographer, not you. You managed to remain cool under pressure, which is easier said than done. And, you managed to avoid posturing, so…way to go, Stud."

The anxiety Red felt abruptly let go, so he laughed. "I don't think I said, *'Do you know who I am?'* even once tonight."

"See? What'd I tell you?"

"Were you shocked, though?" He stroked Piper's fingers with his free hand. "That asshole kind of popped up out of nowhere."

"Maybe a little," she admitted. "But given that my day pretty much jumped the shark several hours before that, I'd hardly call it traumatizing."

Red was perplexed, and it must have been obvious. Piper rushed to explain, "Seriously. Anything beyond me ordering room service and turning in early out of sheer boredom would've counted as a win today."

"Jumped the shark?" Red murmured, lacing his fingers tightly with hers again. Holding hands—it was the simplest of gestures, and yet… "Is there any way at all I can interpret that as something dirty?"

"There is nothing dirty about the Fonz," Piper laughed.

He leaned in to kiss the side of her neck, just as Felix pulled off the avenue and into her hotel's turnaround. The car slid slowly to a stop. His driver took his time exiting, then ambled around the hood toward Piper's door.

She watched his progress through the windshield. "There is, however, something very sexy about elevators," she whispered.

Her door swung open, Piper swiveled to set her feet on the pavement, and she gave Felix her hand.

"I'll walk you up," Red announced, his sense of purpose suddenly renewed.

The doorman of the hotel held the entrance wide. Red took the bag containing Piper's new shoes from his driver and told him, "Hang out for a bit. I'll only be a few minutes."

He followed Piper into the lobby, his longer strides quickly shrinking the distance between them. The girl lounging behind the reception desk was watching their progress a bit too avidly. Red scowled at her, feeling thin-skinned after the encounter at the club.

Little things like this were how rumors got started, he knew. Someone recognized either one of them, thought they knew what was happening…and then he and Piper ended up front and center on the gossip pages.

Any other time, the publicity might not bother Red quite so much. But with things so new between him and Piper, and the way the transition was unfolding at Trident, it made sense to lay low for a bit.

Inside the elevator, Red set the shopping bag down and pressed the button for Piper's floor.

Her eyebrows twitched together. "How did you know my floor? I didn't tell you that."

"I asked Wayne. I had him approve the suite they wanted to give you."

"Is that so? Even though we didn't talk all week?"

The doors closed smoothly, and Red grabbed her by the hips, pulling Piper toward him. The kiss rocketed in a heartbeat toward nuclear meltdown territory. Red kept one eye on the floor numbers and the other on Piper, and tried not to grind his suddenly-rampant cock against her like a wayward hound.

When they were close to her floor, he broke things off, but he couldn't bring himself to go far. Lost in thought, he wondered against Piper's lips, "Why were we discussing the Fonz, again?"

"Don't you remember *Happy Days*?"

"Of course. Doesn't mean I have any idea what you were talking about." They exited the elevator and strolled up the hushed hallway, and Red was besieged by the desire to draw out this goodbye as long as humanly possible—especially since he didn't intend to stay the night.

Not after what had happened with the paparazzo earlier. Piper might be trying her hardest to act like she wasn't affected by it, but Red knew she was bothered.

"*Geez*. At least tell me you remember Arthur Fonzarelli. Everyone loved him."

"The Fonz."

"*Yes*, Red. The Fonz."

He'd paused halfway down the hall to revel in how cute she was when she was riled up, but she tugged him along.

"What does he have to do with sharks, though?"

Piper squinted at him. "You seriously don't remember?" she huffed. "Every season, the Fonz found himself in increasingly implausible situations. And then they had the episode where they all went *waterskiing*."

"He jumped a *shark* on water skis?" Red didn't have to feign his incredulity this time.

She grinned. "I'm afraid so."

"I definitely don't remember that one." He shook his head. "So…*jumping the shark* means its nuts and implausible." About as unlikely as him being able to hide the erection in his pants the closer they got to her room—standing at attention and begging for some goddamn person here to acknowledge its presence.

Piper's smile was the height of deliciousness. "Exactly," she said. Red struggled to recall why he'd decided not to hustle her into her room and take her hard and fast against the wall. Something about a run-in with the police…late night…early morning…*yadda yadda yadda*.

He talked fast, lest his filthy yearnings run away with the situation. "Are you telling me that you don't jet off to major cities;

don't dine with dashing heads of multinational companies; and don't buy loads of astronomically expensive footwear on a regular basis? Next, you'll tell me that you don't get accosted by paparazzi at scintillating nightclubs or have to give statements to police detectives in the wee hours of the morning."

Piper shrugged cheerfully.

"You expect me to believe that these sorts of things do not happen to you all the time?"

"No, they do not. My real life is exceptionally dull."

Red pressed closer, though that exponentially ratcheted up the danger of him tackling her. "Poor little dove. And so, you channel your hopes and dreams into your dirty stories, is that it?" Shockingly, he'd managed to keep a straight face for that last salvo, but only just.

Piper's answering grin brought out her dimples, even cuter in good lighting than they'd been in all the dim locations he'd admired them in before.

"It's a tragedy of Havisham proportions," she told him.

Her cheekiness faded when Red pinned her against the wall with his body. She wrapped her arms around his waist and stole a look down the hall, presumably to make sure they were still alone. He dipped his head and kissed her cheek, ever so gently.

"Wanna come in?" she asked breathlessly.

Yes. Red kissed her again, long and lingeringly. "Thank you for asking, but I don't dare. If I go into that room with you, I won't be leaving again until tomorrow."

"That doesn't sound so bad."

"Agreed. But I need to drop by the station first thing tomorrow, and I should make sure Terry and the other guys are all squared away tonight."

"It's hard out there for the mighty, isn't it?" Piper asked, stroking his back through his shirt.

Red fought back against the memory of her doing that when he'd been buried deep inside her. "You have no idea," he groaned.

Thirteen

P IPER SPENT FRIDAY morning back at Trident, then lingered over a long and friendly lunch with two of the new PKM designers assigned to her series. By early afternoon, she returned to her hotel, overfed and cheerful, to write for a few hours before meeting Red.

He'd asked her to join him at his loft for dinner, so they could enjoy a quiet night together after the fiasco at his club. Piper wasn't looking forward to an extended exposure to his home's horrible décor, but it would be nice to relax with the lion in his den.

Red had been so easygoing and charming when he'd visited her in Maryland. She hoped he'd be the same tonight—it was a lot less intimidating than the Most Eligible Bachelor routine he worked here.

Still, his dashing way with a three-piece suit was in the front of her mind as Piper worked. And Red's excellent out-of-suit skill set kept her plenty focused as she got ready that evening.

At six on the nose, she stepped from her cab and found Red waiting for her—tie loosened and takeout bag in hand—on the sidewalk in front of his building.

"I do love a punctual woman," he grinned, shaking his head.

"I would have been early," she told him, "But there was an accident on 7th Avenue. We had to go around."

Red led her through the lobby and into a waiting elevator. "Hungry?"

It really was unfair the way his eyes crinkled at the corners, and the way his sexy mouth twitched up just a little at the sides. It made everything he said sound like a dirty little tease.

Piper plastered on her best happy face. "You know it," she said.

She reminded herself that she was a grown woman and she could hold a normal conversation without obsessing over whether they'd end up in bed again. Either they would, or they wouldn't. Red might have invited her over for that express purpose, or he might simply want to talk. She could function though. *She could.*

Piper couldn't. She absolutely could not concentrate on eating, talking, or pretending like her brain was not racing headlong down one filthy straightaway, all at the same time. It was too much to ask.

She needed a distraction. So, after fumbling her way through dinner, Piper looked around Red's living area a little desperately. When she spotted a backgammon board displayed on one of his bookshelves, she breathed a sigh of relief and carried it over to the couch.

"Do you play?" he asked her.

"Sure. My dad taught me when I was little."

Red smiled. "I played with my grandfather, mostly. But I should warn you—I never lose."

"Funny," Piper drawled. "Neither do I."

He was competitive, she'd give him that, but Piper still beat him three times in a row. His glower was a sight to behold. Red clearly didn't like to lose, but who did?

"Maybe we ought to switch to cards," he groused. "Or Scrabble. Surely I have a different board game in this place somewhere."

"Bring it on, sore loser," Piper taunted. "I could go like this all night long,"

Red gave up his sulk and laughed at her bravado, then leaned forward to kiss her soundly. When he pulled back, he nudged their wine glasses a few more inches away.

"Maybe I need to cut you off. You get ballsy when you drink."

"Ha, ha," Piper sneered. "I am stone cold sober, and you know it. Cast aspersions all you like, but it won't change how many times I just won." She stood and grabbed the nearly-empty bottle and their glasses, then strutted toward Red's kitchen to leave them by the sink.

He chuckled louder, watching her go.

Piper looked at him over her shoulder. "What now?"

"That ass of yours ought to come with a warning label, sweetheart. Especially in those jeans."

His laser-like focus made her a bit self-conscious. Piper frowned down at herself. "Is that a good thing or a bad thing?"

"Good. Definitely good. You should wear those jeans every day for the rest of your life. True, you'll probably have to beat dudes off with a stick, but it seems like a small price to pay."

"Oh, come on." She set the bottle and glasses on his counter and turned back.

Red said, "Honestly, I'm not sure whether I want to spank it, kiss it, or take a bite out of it."

Piper stopped, eyeing him curiously. "I'm sorry. Did you say 'spank'?"

"God, yes," he breathed in reverence. He twirled his finger so she'd turn for him, and his eyes studied her backside appreciatively once more.

When he met her stare again, her expression must have communicated her surprise pretty effectively. Red smiled a little sheepishly and shrugged, a faint pink tinging his cheekbones.

"Is that, uh, something you do a lot? Something you like, I mean?" Piper had written spanking scenes before, of course. Her readers loved that kind of play. But—as with so much in her books—she'd always had to make things up as she went along. Now, though…

Red pushed to his feet and walked slowly over. He brushed Piper's hair behind her shoulders with very gentle hands, like he was afraid of spooking her.

"Not all the time," he said softly. "But sometimes, with the right person, yeah—it can be a turn-on."

"Oh." Her voice was barely audible in the large wide-open space. "Am I the right kind of person?"

"Piper, you are as right as right can be." Red cupped her head and brushed his lips softly against hers. "Have you ever—?"

He trailed off when she shook her head quickly.

His hands glided lightly down her arms, and then Red laced his fingers through hers. "Do you think you might want to try?"

Something tight and scared inside Piper unraveled all at once at his tone. She hoped her inexperience wouldn't ruin everything between them, but she really couldn't let a chance like this pass her by.

"Yeah, I think I do," Piper said.

Red studied her face, then gathered her close and held her for a long moment, stroking her hair. Piper laid her cheek against his chest and tried to gather her wits.

She needed to brace herself for however this might unfold. It might be interesting, and it might be fun, but it might not be, too. Piper had learned to prepare for the way that reality often turned out far differently than she ever imagined it would.

Red pulled back to look into her eyes. "Listen. I won't hurt you. I swear. I won't lose control, and I won't let it get out of hand. Okay?"

"Okay." He certainly seemed to know what to say. Piper wondered how often, exactly, he'd had this conversation.

"If you want me to stop, tell me right away. If you don't like it, I don't want you to suffer through, in some misguided attempt to please me. That's not what I want," he insisted. Red studied her face. "Promise me."

"I promise." Piper swallowed, unnerved by how serious he'd gotten. What exactly was she getting herself into?

"Then, come here." Red made a sexy, animal sound deep in his throat and kissed her hard.

He lifted Piper into his arms like she didn't weigh a thing and carried her up the twisting iron staircase. In his bedroom, he kicked aside a pair of running shoes on the floor and set Piper on her feet.

"Last chance," he murmured.

"I'm in," Piper told him.

Red grinned, then went for the button of her jeans. Biting his lip, he slid down the zipper, pushed the snug denim over her hips, and dragged it down her legs. Piper shimmied the rest of the way out of it, and he led her toward the bed.

He sat on the side of the mattress. Pulling Piper between his knees, Red ran his large hands over her hips, whistling at her lacy black panties. He touched the tiny satin bows at the sides with tentative fingertips, then concentrating on easing them off her.

Piper shivered. She rested her hands on his shoulders and waited awkwardly, thrown off by the sensation of standing there in her bra and sweater, totally exposed from the waist down.

She had no idea what she was supposed to do next. Kneel? Beg?

She searched Red's face, and the answering heat she saw there was enough to combust every bone in her body. He'd said it was a turn-on, but Piper suspected that was a weak description of what this really was for him. When he leaned forward to press a lingering kiss on the tender skin below her navel, her knees nearly buckled.

Red guided her to stand beside him and instructed, "Lay across my lap."

She tried to do as he asked but had to let him readjust her position into something more comfortable. Well—as comfortable as it could be, under the circumstances.

"Like this?" she wondered. The air was cool against her skin. She gripped the duvet, every nerve-ending alert and wary.

"Oh, Piper. Just like that. You have no idea how beautiful you look right now."

One large hand settled on the small of her back, a steadying warmth, firm and heavy.

Red stroked her over and over with his other palm—across her butt, down her thighs, and back again. She'd had no idea the skin there would be so sensitive, but his touch felt incredible, and the thrill of being so exposed was driving her crazy with longing.

His fingers hesitated, then dipped between her legs, trailing casually through her folds. Piper jerked, startled by the contact. She was wet for him, and Red hadn't even begun. Maybe she should be embarrassed by that, but it was hard to think when anticipation was frying every one of her brain cells.

The stroking hand left her, and Piper heard Red's short intake of breath.

"Five, I think. To start."

Before she could say a word, his palm landed on her rear end with a loud, decisive smack. She gasped, shocked.

Red paused. Her breathing seemed too loud. Her heartbeat was deafening. When she didn't protest, though, he spanked her again. Then again.

That hand on her back held her firmly in place. He smoothed his other lightly across her ass, caressing her blazing skin. Piper flinched when his fingers sought out her cleft again, not expecting him to spread around the slickness he found there, or for him to enter her with one long finger.

Her body contracted around him instantly. Red murmured something unintelligible, but his approval was clear. He withdrew, then pushed two fingers inside her again, pressing deep. Piper pushed back against his hand, desperate for the release she felt building—but Red pulled his hand quickly away and spanked her again. Once. Twice.

And then, exactly like he'd said he would, he stopped. Red held still, one hand on her back, the other cupping her butt possessively. His palms were warm, but not as hot as her flaming skin.

Piper whimpered and shifted, needing more.

"That's it," he breathed, but still he didn't move. His erection was an insistent, rigid bar against her side. She leaned into it, wanting him to feel as agitated as she did.

Red was waiting, she supposed, for some comment from her. When she finally spoke, Piper surprised them both.

"More," she said. Then, louder, "Please, just a little more."

The wait for him to respond was interminable.

Finally, he asked, "Are you sure?"

"Very sure." And, shockingly, she was.

Red spanked her five more times. After that, he was done waiting. He shoved his pants down only far enough to free himself and roll on a condom, and then Red was pulling Piper astride him and sinking into her heat with a loud, unholy groan.

She didn't think about the whats or the whys of what they'd done. She just rode him for all she was worth, until they came together in the kind of heady, shuddering release that defied all her previous experiences.

The real ones, at least. Piper was so ensconced in the moment, it didn't even occur to her to catalog sensations. If she ever decided to use this experience in a book someday, she'd have to think up the descriptions later.

Red held her cradled against his chest while their breathing slowly returned to normal. Piper snuggled her cheek against his neck, soaking up his warmth. He trailed light fingers up and down the column of her spine.

"Doing okay?" Red whispered eventually.

"Mmmm."

"You're magnificent, you know."

"If you say so."

"Piper." He lifted her head so he could see her face. "I loved that. With you."

"Me, too," she admitted, probably unnecessarily. "More than I expected."

"Thank you for trusting me."

And she did, Piper realized. Also, more than she'd expected.

PIPER BLINKED AWAKE the next morning, disoriented and trying to place where she was. She stared at the wall in front of her. Wallpaper, its seams nearly imperceptible, its calm taupe design mimicking the look of ancient European stone. Travertine perhaps, or limestone. Something a handsome, burly gladiator might make his servant girl kneel on while she serviced him.

Piper swallowed. *Wait.* This was Red's room.

Even though she almost always awoke with new scenes in her head, she couldn't afford to play one out now. For one thing, she wasn't at home and therefore didn't have a notebook and pen within easy reach to jot the ideas down before she lost them.

For another, following the images to their natural conclusion would inevitably lead to her getting a little bit hot-and-bothered, and Piper had seen last night how *that* turned out. Acting like one of her characters required more bravery than she was currently in possession of.

Behind her, Red shifted, yawning and stretching his large, long body. Piper had a sudden, unwelcome flash of those infrequent mornings at Kyle's house. She steeled herself for what would happen next—the distance Red would inevitably want to put between them once he woke up.

Maybe he'd lock himself in the bathroom to scrub off any lingering vestiges of their night together, while Piper got dressed and slipped out. Or perhaps Red would lever himself off the wide mattress and head downstairs, to brew the coffee that would signal to her, loud and clear, that the party was over, and it was time for her to leave.

Last night had been amazing, though. Piper had taken a chance and let Red teach her something she'd always wondered about, and for once in her life, it had been everything she'd hoped for. She could barely believe it. He was incredible.

And he clearly knew his way around a spanking. Practice made perfect, she supposed.

Red MacLellan was absolutely nothing like Piper had expected him to be, and she…she *liked* him. More than she ought to—this wasn't one of her books, after all. This was real life, and in real life, even fantasy nights came to an end.

There was a sudden jolt behind her, then some rustling of the sheets as Red remembered her presence and acclimated to it. And then, inexplicably, his size and heat were invading the air along her spine, and molding to her body like they were made to fit together.

Red folded his heavy, muscled arm around Piper's chest, tucking her close against him. His long, strong leg nudged between hers, his ankle wedging between her feet and finding purchase. Piper felt Red's face nuzzling the top of her head, a gruff, satisfied sound rumbled in his throat—and then Red's limbs were relaxing again, falling back into sleep tangled with hers.

Piper held her breath in shock. Red was hard against her back, his hot breath stirring the fine hairs on her head, his thigh between hers making her all kinds of horny.

She'd been so sure she was about to be sent on her way, but once again Red had proved her wrong. This was no morning-after dismissal—this was intimate and unwavering want. And Piper was shaken by the power of it.

Want came with expectations, with costs, and she had no idea if she could fulfill them.

In moments Red jerked awake again, but not by anything she'd done, this time. His cell phone had started chiming from the nightstand on the other side of the bed, and he rolled away to answer it with a resigned groan.

It seemed to be someone from PKM, asking Red to come into the office for an emergency meeting. Well, there it was, Piper thought. He'd known he didn't need to kick her out himself. Red had planned ahead and employed the ever-popular phone-a-friend strategy. Hell, he'd probably had his exit planned before she'd ever crossed his threshold last night.

Piper took another careful look at that wallpaper. If she could get back to her hotel room quickly enough, maybe she could still salvage the threads of that gladiator scene she'd envisioned, and the morning wouldn't be a total loss.

There. No reason for disappointment. Red might not want Piper to stick around too long in his bed, but she'd bet good money he'd enjoy selling the words she'd cooked up here. Win-win, if you asked her.

Now all she had to do was figure out where her pants were.

Fourteen

W HEN RED WOKE up, he was thoroughly prepared to feel disgruntled—at least, he was until he discovered that he had his arms full of Piper. His usual irritation at morning in general turned pretty quickly into pervasive joy at being the luckiest bastard in the city.

That joy rapidly notched upward into elation once he remembered that she'd let him spank that sweet, tantalizing ass of hers the night before, and then begged him for more.

God, she'd been perfection. They'd fucked each other into oblivion, drifted off for a couple of hours, and then come together again in the dead of night—making the sort of quiet, slow love Red didn't think he'd ever enjoyed before.

It seemed too good to be true. He had half-expected Piper to make a break for it—to slip out sometime during the night so she wouldn't have to face him come morning. The fact that she'd stayed instead warmed him from the inside out.

Red couldn't wait to see what came next. He hoped it would be her. And then him.

He remembered spotting the tattoo on her side last night when she'd been draped across his lap. It meandered provocatively over her hip and up toward her ribcage, and Red couldn't imagine how he hadn't investigated it before.

Perhaps it was too dark every other time they'd been together. Or too rushed? Either way, he remembered their conversation about it and looked forward to taking a closer peek in the light of day.

Just then, his phone went off, vibrating across the nightstand with agonizingly awful timing. Red was torn between the warm promise of the woman in his arms, and the easily recognizable ringtone signaling the head of his transition team at Trident.

He wanted to roar with frustration but figured that would only spook Piper. He could tell she wasn't asleep anymore, but she hadn't said a word yet. Red kissed her hair, disentangled himself as gently as he could, and reluctantly answered the goddamn call.

Maybe it was about something simple. Maybe he could talk Rob through whatever this was and get back to the sexy angel beside him.

However, when Rob called at the ass-crack of dawn on a Saturday morning and asked for an emergency meeting, the man wasn't just dicking around. Before he'd even had a decent amount of caffeine, Red was dressed and saying goodbye to Piper and then heading downtown.

She was too quiet, and Red didn't like the way Piper's eyes kept sliding away from his. There wasn't time to decide if it was embarrassment, or shame, or simple morning grouchiness, though. It gnawed at him, but it would have to wait.

Rob was already waiting outside Red's office when he got off the elevator at PKM. The man wasted no time—he just dropped into a chair, gripped his stack of folders like a schoolgirl holding her textbooks, and fidgeted while Red got settled behind his desk.

Red sighed. Nothing was ever easy.

"We have a situation," Rob announced. The words were blunt enough, but the man's knee was bobbing up and down in agitation.

"Wayne!" Red barked, as loud as he dared. His assistant wasn't exactly friendly in the mornings anymore—not since he'd started taking law school classes at night. That went double for weekends.

But no way could Red tackle whatever this was going to be without some more coffee. Thankfully, Wayne was on the case already, stomping over with a towering latte and Monday's schedule in his hands. He set them beside Red and turned to their guest.

"Can I get you anything?"

"I'm good. Thanks."

Red took in Rob's greenish complexion and told Wayne, "Close the door on your way out."

He was going to have a hell of a time trying to replace his assistant when he graduated someday. The thought was nearly as depressing as putting Piper in a cab this morning had been.

He asked Rob, "All right, what have we got?"

"You know that guy we had to let go last week? Brian?"

Red nodded. Brian had been a lazy, whining son-of-a-bitch. Red had been thrilled to cut him loose.

"The auditors found some stuff on his computer."

"Porn?" He'd seemed like the type.

"Worse," Rob said. "Anomalies." And then he sat there, looking wan.

"You're killing me, Robert," Red told him. "Just spit it out."

"We're still trying to unravel it all, but it looks like the Dentons were diverting money from the normal lines of business."

"Fuck." Red scrubbed his hands over his face. "Where did it go?"

"It *seems* like it was mostly to themselves and Brian, but maybe to some others, too. It's possible they were propping up a couple of the low-performing authors. I'm still tracking down all the players, but I didn't think this should wait."

"You're right. How much are we talking?"

Rob glared down at his folders but didn't open any of them. "Best guess? Too much to make this easy."

"Shit." Red sucked down some more coffee and tapped his desk, willing his brain to start functioning at its normal capacity. All he could seem to see was Piper, though, head thrown back and telling him, *don't stop.*

"Can we bring in some money from the tech division to cover this?" Rob wondered. "Please say yes."

"No," Red fired back, shutting down the hope on his team leader's face without mercy. "Not right now, at least. Their project has to move forward on schedule if we want to keep the board happy."

"That's…not good news."

"This was supposed to be a fairly straightforward turnaround, Robert. Get in, clean house, rake in the returns. How did no one catch this shit earlier?"

Rob shook his head. "I have no flipping idea."

Red dropped his own head back to stare at the ceiling. He really did not need this crap today, but when did he ever? It came with the terrain, though, and he'd simply have to figure it out so they could all get back to business.

Or rather, so Rob could get back to business and Red could get back to Piper Mae.

"You got anything else for me right now?" he asked.

Rob blew out a long, dejected breath. "No. I'll let you know as soon as I find out more."

"All right. No stone unturned, got it?" Red stood up, forcing the other man to do the same. "I don't want any more surprises later," he said, in case that wasn't patently obvious.

"You and me both."

Rob turned on his heel and left. Red watched him go, then frowned at his dark computer screen for a while, trying to decide how to finesse this newest wrinkle in the plan.

IT WAS AN emotional move, setting his cap for Trident. As a family, the MacLellans had always loved books, but this wasn't like writing a few checks to a library or two. Owning an actual publisher was a completely different animal, and when Red came across the opportunity, he just had to take the shot.

Even so, negotiating to buy the company was tricky. The Dentons resisted logic and were cagey about so much, but Red had been focused on the end game—determined to win, no matter what. He'd seen some concerning signs, but he hadn't cared. Red knew what he could do. He knew what he was *going* to do.

When they finally took over the struggling publishing house and got their first deep look at Trident's books, Red knew right away that things were a bit worse than they'd anticipated. Nothing too insurmountable, but certainly a bigger headache than he'd hoped for.

Only one powerhouse author's rock star sales had kept the whole operation from sinking like a stone. One cute little *romance* author, who he'd never even *heard* of until a couple of months ago. Red doubted the Dentons had appreciated the kind of superstar they'd had under their roof, or what she was capable of.

Piper should have been nurtured in her career by the best in the business. It boggled Red's mind what she might have been able to accomplish, given the proper team behind her—the kind of team PKM intended to give her now. He wondered if she was as impatient for the impending level-up as he was.

Regardless, Red needed to keep his ace-in-the-hole happy and on board. If he couldn't, Trident's woes would drag PKM's earnings down for many quarters to come. Then the board might vote to unload it again, and they definitely would not look kindly on the next unusual venture Red decided to dabble in.

That outcome would not work for him at all. Red hated to be gainsaid and he liked his executive freedom. When he identified a project that he knew he could work his magic on, he only wanted to see green lights and open road ahead. So, this had to succeed.

The first step forward was giving Piper a fresh, lucrative contract that she couldn't possibly turn down. Now, Red could only hope that it would keep her occupied long enough for them to unravel this mess before it had a chance to affect her.

His team was good. They would figure out where Trident's errant income went, and how PKM could nurse the publisher along until its ship was righted. With a little luck, they could also keep this shitstorm out of the hands of the media, so Red's investors didn't defect too soon.

If PKM was going to be successful in repositioning Trident within the sagging publishing industry, they couldn't have one word of bad publicity hit the papers. If investors didn't believe Red could work wonders with companies like this, he'd likely never get the chance again.

Red sighed, refusing to go down that road. Borrowing trouble never helped anybody.

It was just that the whole project had taken on a different cast, now that he'd hooked up with Piper. He still wanted it to succeed because he was damned if he was going to fail, but—Red also wanted it to go perfectly because he wanted what it could do for Piper's career. For *Piper*.

He couldn't imagine someone who deserved it more. He wanted her to be happy. He wanted to be the guy who made her happy. That, of course, was the biggest complication.

Piper Mae Fulham was too damn delectable to resist on any level, and Red didn't exactly have the best track record in sedately foregoing the things he wanted. And the better he got to know her, the more he wanted to keep her.

Red wanted Piper's body and he wanted her trust. Hell, at this rate, she might as well throw in her heart, too—and that was definitely something he'd never thought he'd say so easily. Unfortunately, having Piper as his own meant mixing business with pleasure to a degree he'd never contemplated before.

Somehow, Red was going to have to figure out a way to serve both masters. If he kept a level head about Trident and could ensure that both the publisher and PKM's main lines of business stayed sound, then fortune might smile on him and this diverted cash nonsense wouldn't come back and bite him in the ass.

In turn, that would buy Red the time he needed on the female front. Piper was going to need some serious convincing before she'd grant him a real, fighting chance to win her. She clearly didn't believe that he was the real deal, and while Red didn't know why that was yet, he intended to find out. For once, he didn't mind the effort and patience it would take to pull down a woman's walls.

Red might not want Piper to doubt her sparkling new contract or the fact that PKM was behind her one hundred percent, but he especially didn't want Piper doubting *him*. Red had the ability to look out for her and the desire to care for her. He could already see how perfect they would be together if she'd only drop her guard.

In the meantime, Red simply needed to compartmentalize. To the extent that it was possible, any disruptions at Trident had to stay separate from Piper. If he could keep them apart for long enough, Red could arrange everything exactly the way it should be, and no harm would come to either side. *Easy.*

With that sorted out, he picked up his desk phone and called Piper's cell. She answered on the second ring but seemed surprised to hear from him.

"Hey, Beautiful," Red said. "I should be able to get out of here soon. You want to grab some lunch in a bit?"

Piper groaned. "Oh man, I wish I could. But I've got to hang out here and make some calls for a while." He couldn't decide if she was conning him or not.

"You don't sound very happy. Everything okay?"

"Yes," she sighed. And then, "No. I don't know. My cat sitter called and said she found a ton of water on the bathroom floor upstairs last night. She cleaned it up, but I'm trying to decide if I need to get a plumber in there right now, or if it can wait until I get back. I tried to call my folks to see if they could run by, but they're not picking up."

Red frowned. Leaking water was never a good thing. "I noticed the way those pipes groaned when I was there. Seemed a little out of the ordinary."

"Yep," she agreed. "That's one way of putting it."

"Ever had them looked at?"

"Yes. Turns out they're very old," Piper said prosaically. "Trust me, fixing them is on the list. Along with every other damn thing."

Red sat back in his chair, carefully feeling his way. He wanted her to open up, to share this kind of thing with him, but he wasn't sure she'd appreciate him prying. "So…your house needs some work, huh?"

"Are you kidding?" Piper laughed bitterly. "With a place as old as that, it never ends."

"I can imagine."

"My folks tried to warn me. Sort of. But you know how it is— I was so determined to keep the place in the family when they were threatening to sell, that I brushed off the details. I figured I'd take care of things one at a time, and it would all work out in the end."

Red wasn't sure he did know, but that sounded an awful lot like the way he'd approached the Trident deal. He had to admire Piper's can-do spirit, at least.

"How's that going?"

Red could almost hear Piper's shrug through the phone. "Fine," she muttered. "It'll all get done. Eventually."

"Anything I can do to help?"

"Thanks, but no. I just need a couple hours to work this out. I'm sure my dad will go over later and turn off the water. Or whatever. At least the cats were okay."

Red sat up straight as what she said registered: cat sitter. Cats. He'd been there for an entire weekend and was sure he had never laid eyes on a single animal, much less more than one.

"Wait. You have *cats*? As is, plural cats? How did I not know this?"

"Yes, two. Sonny and Fredo. You saw them." A long pause. "Didn't you?"

"No, I most certainly did not. Because if I had, I assure you we would have talked about why you named your pets after mobsters."

She giggled. "First of all, you have no idea how often I get to say, *I know it was you, Fredo,* and I really can't overstate how fun that is. Secondly, wait until you get to know them. If those two galoots aren't mafioso, then I don't know who is."

"That sounds absurd and possibly shady. And it gives me the perfect excuse to visit the great state of Maryland again," Red smiled. "What about later, though? You want to hang out once you wrap up Pipegate?"

"That's *Pipergate*, to you," she sassed. "And, sure—by then, I'll probably be begging you to take my mind off wayward water and pesky pipes."

Red chuckled. "I can probably do that." He let his mind wander for a minute about how he might accomplish it, then added, "How about this? Text me when you're ready, and I'll send the car for you. We can decide what to do once you get here. Sound good?"

"Sounds perfect," Piper agreed. "Are you sure you don't mind waiting around for me?"

Red was pretty confident he would wait for an eternity if it meant he got to be with Piper at the end of it. Come to think of it, he kind of already had—thirty-six interminable fucking years of bachelorhood in the city. It was enough to bury anyone.

"I'm sure," Red assured her. He hung up satisfied that he'd managed to joke her out of her funk. At least she sounded better now, and later he'd work on her mood some more.

Piper was like that candy with the bright, shiny shell and the soft and sweet center. Red hungered for her, inside and out.

It was a shock to realize that the impossible had finally happened to *him*. He wanted all of it—all of life—with her.

Fifteen

THEY WERE HAVING trouble deciding on dinner. That was probably because Piper found herself perched on his kitchen counter roughly two minutes after she walked through Red's front door, kissing him clear into the next county.

There wasn't a whole lot of talking going on. But really, with a tongue like Red's in the mix, did a person need food to survive? Piper thought not.

At least, that was the direction her mind was headed before they heard the front door bang open.

A woman called, "Padraig! Where are you?"

Red buried his face in Piper's neck and emitted a long and tormented groan.

Piper pried him away. "Who is that?" she whispered. She could hear a set of high heels clicking across the floor of the living room, but they apparently hadn't been spotted yet. Maybe they were hidden by one of the support beams or a convenient patch of shadow.

"God damn it. It's my mother," he explained frantically. "She's completely insane and I apologize in advance for whatever awful thing she's about to say to you." Hastily, he tried to straighten out her shirt.

"What!"

Red was dead serious. He clamped an urgent hand over her mouth and begged, "Shh!"

The sound of those heels stopped abruptly, paused, then changed direction and headed right for them. Red seemed inclined to cling to Piper like grim death—she barely had time to pull away and get both feet on the floor before his mom appeared.

Red's heavy arm dropped across Piper's shoulders. "Mom. This is a surprise. I very obviously did not know you were coming."

The woman was trim and polished, dressed in a coordinating outfit of wine-colored wool that set off her sleek white bob nicely. She was also sporting a scowl that could probably turn unwary innocents to stone. Piper guessed that explained where Red had gotten his from.

Mrs. MacLellan's eyes ran quickly over Piper, then just as rapidly dismissed her. "Yes, I see that," she commented.

"This is my friend Piper. Piper, my mother, Gina MacLellan."

Piper gripped the back of Red's shirt and stuck out a hand, "It's a pleasure to meet you."

Mrs. MacLellan smiled thinly and looked like she might be concerned about contamination.

Piper continued nervously, "You must be so proud of Red. He's so smart and—" she stumbled. *Sexy? Commanding?* "—accomplished." Yes, that was an adjective fit to use on his mother.

Red snorted under his breath and muttered, "Seriously?"

Piper pinched his back. "And his work with PKM's foundation must make you proud, too. He's changing so many lives," she enthused. She took a deep breath, preparing to elaborate, when the other woman held up a hand to cut her off.

"As is expected of him. Naturally, he has many other responsibilities, too—to the company, to the community, and to his family as well. Padraig must carefully balance his obligations if we expect him to remain successful."

"Naturally," Piper agreed. She was beginning to see why Red had felt the need to warn her.

His mother continued, "Padraig surrounds himself with excellent advisors, of course. That way, if one part of his life upsets the balance and other areas begin to suffer, those advisors can steer him back on course. It works very well."

Red murmured, "What the fuck?"

Piper opened her mouth to attempt some response to that Machiavellian spiel, but Red squeezed her shoulder, willing her into silence.

"Well, that was very…instructive," he drawled. "I can only assume you include yourself on that list of advisors. Otherwise, why make the effort to explain it to Piper within two seconds of meeting her?" He released Piper and began to advance on the other woman. "Or, maybe you only meant to warn her that you won't let her take over my life. Was that it?"

"Padraig, don't be silly," Gina huffed.

Red had a hand on his mother's back and was steering her firmly toward the door. "Regardless, Piper and I have plans for the evening. So, if there was nothing else…?"

His mother sputtered in indignation, but when Red snatched her purse off the console in the foyer and handed it to her, she accepted it regally. In moments, he had the front door flung wide, his mother hustled over the threshold, and was pressing the elevator's call button.

"Do you need me to walk you downstairs?" he asked. "Or is Dad waiting for you?"

"Well, yes, he is. But I—" she attempted.

"Oh, one more thing."

Piper crept closer, curious about what he'd say.

"What?"

"My key, Mom." Red held out his hand, unwavering and insistent.

"Red." Gina's manicured hand dug lazily around inside her gold leather satchel. "I don't know why you're being like this." She darted a quick, scathing look over his shoulder that said she had a pretty good idea, though, then dropped her angry gaze back to the interior of her purse.

"I'm sure you can figure it out if you think hard enough. Stop stalling," Red grumbled.

"Honestly. You're being ridiculous. What if there was an emergency or you got locked out?"

Red plunged his large hand into his mother's bag and efficiently withdrew her keychain, then worked his house key off the silver ring a moment later. Mrs. MacLellan stood there red-faced, watching him in consternation.

Fury was rolling off the woman like heat waves rising from a summer street. Piper moved further back into Red's apartment, stepping behind the open door and out of sight of his mother.

As first impressions went, she didn't think this had been the slam-dunk she would've wanted. For either of them.

The elevator, like so much else in the world, obeyed Red's command quickly. When Piper heard the metal door clang open, she risked a peek.

Red ushered his mother into the cage, waved farewell, and stepped back toward his apartment before she could even finish her goodbye.

Piper briefly met the woman's eyes—the woman's *glare*—through the accordion-style gate, and then the elevator car began its slow descent. Red came in and swung his door shut without any apparent guilt or mercy.

For lack of a better option, Piper inquired weakly, "We have plans?"

"We do now," he retorted.

RED BROUGHT HER to a tiny dumpling house a few blocks away and launched his campaign over dinner. Red had obviously been ruminating on Piper's house situation all day—long enough to think up all kinds of logical reasons why he should be allowed to take care of things.

But honestly—they'd only known each other a few weeks. He might think that made it okay for him to stick his nose and his wallet into her business, but Piper did not.

Red was as tenacious as a dog with a bone, though. Exasperatingly so.

He explained to her, patiently and calmly, "Listen, I clearly have an excess of money. I might even have a bit of influence. If I can take some things off your plate with the judicious application of either of those things, of course I want to."

"Why *of course*?" Piper prodded. "I'm perfectly capable of handling what has to get done. I told you that. By pushing your offer, you're implying that you don't think I'm up to it."

"I'm not implying that at all," he argued. "I just want to help."

"But why?"

Red sighed, his equanimity faltering in the face of her stubbornness. "Piper, you have to understand—before I met you, I may as well have been on autopilot. I was walking around New York living this two-dimensional, black-and-white life. But meeting you changed that. You brought in life, and air. And…" he set down his chopsticks and threw up his hands. "…if you would just let me take care of some of this stuff for you in return, I'd really, really appreciate it."

"Okay, Sleeping Beauty, look—you know I don't expect payment for accidentally being the one to rip you out of your flat and boring stupor, right?" Piper rolled her eyes.

Red smirked. "What if I paid in kisses?"

"Well…" Damn, he had her there. Red was an excellent kisser. "Maybe a kiss."

"Maybe two. And then let me take care of those pipes for you. Please?"

"You think I don't want to? That I'm not tempted?" Piper demanded. "Believe me, letting someone else take care of this stuff sounds *awesome*. But you told me yourself that women hit on you for your money all the time. So, if I let you do this and it makes you think for even one minute that it's why I care about you, then I'm going to keep turning you down, Red."

His protest was immediate. "I don't think that about you, at all. I won't think that."

"What about other people, then? What about your mother, or the other authors at Trident? The minute they find out you're fixing up my house, people are going to talk. They're going to call me a gold digger and say I'm sleeping my way to the top."

Red snarled, "No. They will think that I am taking good care of my woman."

"Don't be naïve," Piper scoffed.

"You let me buy you shoes." *Like that made any sense.*

"I didn't let you do anything! You steamrolled me!" Piper cried. The cooks behind the counter peered at her through the haze of steam rising from their woks, and she lowered her voice. "Besides, shoes are way different than renovating a freaking *house.*"

Red reached for her hands. "Piper, why do you care what anyone else thinks, anyway?"

"Because once they start saying it often enough, once you start hearing it often enough, maybe you *do* start believing it. Maybe you *will* decide they're right and that I only like you for your spending power."

Red scratched his chin. "Just to clarify—who is 'they' again?"

Piper pressed her lips together. She didn't need to dignify that—it was completely beside the point.

"If I lost everything tomorrow, would you still want me?" he wondered. There was just the tiniest hint of uncertainty in his voice.

Piper's whole being went soft at the rare glimpse of vulnerability. "You know I would. Don't be silly."

He snorted. "Christ. Knowing you, you'd probably want me *more.*"

"Probably. You would certainly be less complicated."

"True." Red leaned across the table and planted a lingering, salty kiss on her lips. "And I would want you," he murmured. "No matter what."

"Why thank you. But let's hope it doesn't come to that."

"Piper, just so you know…I think I'm going to want you permanently someday."

Piper's breath snagged suddenly and uncomfortably in her lungs. Red forestalled her impending panic with a placating hand.

"Not yet," he said. "I get that's it's way too soon to say shit like that. But I hope, when the time does come, that you'll trust me enough to choose me."

"God, Red," was all she could say.

He barreled on, dogged and determined. "Even if you don't, I still want to do this thing for you. Let me."

"I'll think about it," Piper finally sighed, sitting back. She looked him over and shook her head at his triumphant expression. "You're very persistent, you know that?"

"It might have been mentioned a time or two," he grinned. "But I don't see how that's relevant."

Piper nibbled on her last dumpling while she decided whether to bring up the other large elephant in the room.

Red wasn't fooled in the least. "Go ahead," he prodded, crossing his arms sedately across his chest and stretching one long leg out beside her chair. "Say it."

"About your mother," she began.

He chuckled, good-natured despite his earlier frustration with the woman. Because he was in such a good mood, Piper elected to skip over why his mom would barge into his home uninvited, why she would come out swinging with a person she'd only just met, and why she'd be so territorial about her grown-ass son.

Piper went for the low-hanging fruit, instead.

"So…does your mom always call you Padraig, or only when she's pissed?"

Red squeezed his eyes closed and groaned, a drawn-out and deeply-felt sound of suffering.

Piper pressed on. "How'd you get saddled with an unusual name like that, anyway? Why not name you Patrick? Or—I don't know—Bob?"

"*Bob?*" His eyes popped open in disbelief.

"Okay, maybe not Bob."

Red laughed, explaining, "It's a family name. You'll be happy to hear that both my dad and my grandfather are Padraigs, too." He rose and took her hand. They wandered out into the cool night air, where a knot of people stood listening to a lanky boy drumming on an overturned bucket for tips. Red took her hand and headed back toward his building.

"Jesus. On top of everything else, you're a *third*, too?" Piper sputtered.

"No! God, no. That would be insane."

"More insane than three *Padraigs* in a row?"

"Well, we all have different middle names," he clarified. "Grandpa was James, Dad is Michael, and I'm Keith. Plus, my grandfather went by Paddy and my father usually goes by Pat. I can't imagine how I got stuck with Red, though."

On the stone steps of his building, Piper turned to run her fingers reverently through his soft auburn waves. "Such a mystery," she said.

Red leaned into her touch and nearly purred.

"Your grandpa was the one who started PKM, right? Did he name the company after you? Or did you just change the name when you took over?"

"He named it after me. I was the first grandkid." Red led her inside, then leaned a shoulder against the wall of mailboxes while they waited for the elevator. "It's a good thing I went into the family business, though, right? Might've gotten awkward if I'd gone off to be a rock star or something."

"Oh, I don't know," Piper mused. "He could've just told people PKM stood for something else."

He arched a brow. "Like what?"

"How about...*People Keep Meowing?*"

He flashed a devilish grin and backed her into the empty elevator. "I think I like *Please Kiss Me* better."

"Aw. That's sweet. Better than your initials, even."

"Can you refrain from pointing that out to all the people I'm trying to terrify into submission, please?" He took Piper into his arms and ruffled her hair while they soared upward. "As it turns out, *sweet* is not actually very good for business."

"It is if you're a bakery," she retorted.

"*Anyway*. There's a picture of the big event. You want to see it?"

"Are you kidding? Of course, I want to see it."

Red let her into his loft. Then he sauntered over to a long mahogany sideboard, rifled through a drawer, and produced a photo. Piper gazed down at the black-and-white publicity shot of two smiling men in suits, a laughing baby held high between them.

Red pointed, "I'm the handsome devil in the footie pajamas."

"Oh, look at you," she breathed, taking in his flushed round cheeks and big baby eyes. "You should probably wear that outfit to all your meetings. No one would deny you a thing."

He chuckled. "I'll look into. Sizing could be an issue, though."

"Only if you're a quitter." Piper squinted at the older men, noting the similarities to Red in both their faces and stances. "Is your grandfather still alive?"

"No, we lost him a few years back, unfortunately."

"But you still have your Dad?"

"Yes. He is quite alive and very much enjoying his retirement. He's made an art form out of delivering vague, yet benevolent, advice. And he manages to escort my mother to every charity event in town without strangling her, so that's something."

Red tucked the photo back in its drawer, then drew Piper over to the hard, white sofa.

"Tell me something about you, now," he said settling down. "How'd you snag a name like 'Piper Mae'?"

"God only knows," she said. "I sound like a hillbilly, don't I?"

"I like it. It's cute."

Piper groaned.

"Okay, then tell me how you came by a pen name so different from your real name?"

This time her smile came easily. "It sounds like something right out of Romance Marketing, doesn't it?"

"Yes. It's not?"

"Nope. It's my grandma's middle name and maiden name. Too perfect to pass up, right?"

"I'll say. I hope she at least lived long enough to enjoy the notoriety."

"Are you kidding? She's 92 and the most popular woman in her retirement community. I think she milks the name thing every chance she gets, too. Look." Piper got up to retrieve her phone and scroll through her photos, finally brandishing the one she wanted: her glamorous, pint-sized grandma, in large black sunglasses and a gold scarf with six-inch fringe.

"Oh, man. She looks tiny."

"Only in stature."

"What's her first name?"

"Teresa. I almost used that, too, but my mom put her foot down. I guess she wanted to make sure Grandma could stay anonymous if the kissing book thing went south for me."

"Little did she know," he said.

Piper shrugged.

"Does she live near you?" Red looked up and met her eyes. "Maybe I could meet her."

"She's in Florida," she explained. "If you want to meet her, you'll have to bring your appetite, your swim trunks, and a whole lot of sunscreen."

"Done and done."

Sixteen

RED'S ROCK-SOLID PLAN the next day accounted for many things—the crisp autumn weather, the changing leaves in the park, and his girlfriend's healthy morning appetite. His meticulous planning was utterly useless, however, in the face of Piper's unwavering ability to do the unexpected. Consequently, Red's Sunday had really gone from bad to worse.

They'd checked Piper out of her hotel first thing, then moved her stuff to his place. She was completely on board with the brunch plan and the subsequent walk in the park, and even suggested a trip to Chelsea Market once they were done. But then Piper had gotten a surprise call in the car, and before Red knew it, she was apologizing profusely and making different plans.

Some author friend of hers had heard she was in town. So, Red had to fix an understanding smile on his mug and pack Piper off to enjoy a museum with someone else, in place of spending her last day together as he'd planned. Piper was supposed to fly back home the next morning.

Instead of wallowing, Red shopped for their last dinner at the bodega down the street. He threw in a load of laundry, and while he waited for the cycle to finish, he stewed about that horrible run-in they'd had with his mother.

He had to call six locksmiths before he found one that would come out immediately. The asshole took one look around Red's place and informed him that he'd be charging triple time for the weekend work—but that annoyance barely registered once the work was done.

It was the bitter fight with his mother afterward that made the real impression. She'd tried to barge in *again* and been incensed to discover that Red had changed the locks on her so quickly. His mom had truly lost her mind, then—it made her nastiness with Piper look like a fucking tea party.

Tough shit. Dropping in unannounced on your thirty-six-year-old son was a move better left to the soap operas on TV. Red just wished she hadn't been so quick to blame it all on Piper.

Nevertheless, shutting her down had been easy. It was way harder to shed his pissy mood after it was all over. Even though Piper checked in occasionally, it was usually to tell Red that she was staying out with her friend longer.

He googled the friend's name, to see what he was up against. But deep into the third magazine article, he realized with a sudden, creeping discomfort, that he was acting like a jealous prick. So Red grabbed his keys and left for the gym before he could come up with any other bright, stalkery ideas.

WHEN FELIX DROPPED her off late that afternoon, Piper had no trouble picking up on Red's foul mood—probably because he was still acting like a spoiled little bitch.

"Look what the cat dragged in," he drawled, dumping clean laundry onto his couch.

"And look who's turned sullen," she fired back, eyeing him. Piper's eyebrows shot up at the sharp snap of his undershirt when he shook it out and folded it.

God damn it. Red had a housekeeper for this kind of shit. Mrs. Markham was going to think he'd gone around the bend.

Piper didn't take his bad attitude lying down, thank fuck. She held her own, lobbing a few snippy arrows right back at him. They landed disturbingly close to their marks. Good for her.

Red realized they probably needed to get out of there, though, if they didn't want to spend the last evening of Piper's visit slinging testy salvos back and forth like relationship jai alai.

It almost felt like his mother's hideous décor was infecting them as revenge.

Red scrapped his preparations for homemade enchiladas, made some hasty reservations at a high-end gastropub he knew in the Village, and fled with his woman.

The relief he felt with the change of scenery was palpable. In the car, Red felt like he could breathe again. Piper, empathic as always, immediately began sounding like herself, too. And finally, he was able to stand down and apologize for acting like a prick.

He said exactly that. "I'm sorry I've been acting like a prick, little dove. It's been a crappy day. My mom stopped by again." Enough said, right?

"I'm sorry I bailed on you for so long. And I happen to like your prick," she smiled.

True to the day's theme, though, the hostess's face blanched when she saw Red come in.

"Mr. MacLellan, I am so sorry. The party before you is running long. We'll find you another table as soon as we can, I promise."

"No worries," he assured her. "Anyone I know?"

She glanced furtively around before whispering, "It's Senator Hastings. He said it was his 25th anniversary."

"Hmm. That's the silver wedding anniversary, isn't it?" Red arched a brow at Piper. "Good for them."

She made a slightly-impressed face in return. "Not too shabby," she murmured, though she sounded as dubious as he felt. Evidently, Miss Piper had read the same newspaper articles about the senator that Red had.

The hostess wanted in on the action, maybe to smooth over her lack of a free table. "You'd never know it," she confided. She tilted her head across the room, where the jovial senator could be seen schmoozing with a starstruck constituent while his wife poked desultorily at her dessert.

Red scratched the bridge of his nose. Fantastic. All today needed was the visual example of a dirtbag for Piper to focus on and compare him to. That would do wonders for her trust of him.

"Do you see…" Piper began.

"Yup." Abruptly, he told the hostess, "We'll be in the bar."

Red towed Piper behind him into the long narrow space that opened off to the side. The bartender didn't acknowledge them, even when Red greeted him. He was so focused on one of the cocktail waitresses—or rather, the waitress's ample tits—that it apparently affected his hearing.

Red got Piper's drink order, then settled her at a pair of empty stools he found near the front. He trooped over to get the barkeep's attention. The waitress, seeing his expression, grabbed her tray and took off for the kitchen.

Red barely got three words out before there was a raucous cheer from the other end of the bar—the end where three middle-aged men were putting their hands on Piper, acting like she was their long-lost buddy. Hands on her shoulders. Hands on her arms.

Red bristled, watching those wandering hands. The same hands they raised their pints with, the same hands that fiddled with their cell phones and billfolds. Three gold rings on three married men's fingers. If they didn't lay off soon, those rings might be all that was left once Red was done with them.

He hissed out the rest of their order and paced back over. Piper didn't look comfortable or happy, yet the men kept gazing at her with greedy, covetous eyes. Maybe they didn't understand that she was *with* someone.

How did Piper know them? Between the fake smile plastered on her face and her rigid posture, Red could tell they weren't real friends.

Right on cue, she glanced around, searching for him. Time to stake his claim.

The bartender advanced and slid their cocktails across the polished wood, at exactly the moment Red pushed through the scrum and parked himself next to Piper.

"Oh, good," she breathed, her shoulders loosening up a little. "Red, this is Jim Denton. And—" She floundered on the other names.

"Mitch."

"Bill."

Red leaned in. "Red. How do you do?" No need to remind Denton who Red was just yet, since the man hadn't shown the slightest bit of recognition.

Red shook each of their hands in turn, with Denton trying to go hardass on him by squeezing too tight. Red gripped him back even tighter.

Denton balked first, covering his discomfort with some florid bluster. "Who's this bastard think he is, trying to wine and dine our Toni?" he demanded of the others.

Bill muttered, "Lucky prick probably doesn't even know he won the chick lottery."

"Right?" said the third stooge. That one deigned to address Red directly, "If you knew Toni like we do, you'd understand how freaking crazy this is. She doesn't get with *anybody*."

Piper blinked rapidly at Red, mortified.

Red mouthed, *Toni?*

Her eyes squeezed shut in evident pain before she leaned close and put her lips to his ear. "My pen name, remember? Antoinette. *Toni.*"

And then the pieces slid into place. He'd known Denton's name since he was the only son of Trident's former owners. That meant the others must be William Hodges and Mitchell Fleck, two of the bottom-feeder hacks from Trident's thriller division.

The three men watched Piper's every move with calculating eyes, but she and Red were saved from further conversation by the hostess clicking briskly over.

"Mr. MacLellan? Your table is ready now. I'm very sorry about the delay."

Red took Piper's hand and helped her off her stool, drinking in her grateful look. They picked up their untouched cocktails to bring them to their table.

"Gentlemen," he nodded. Denton had grown wan at the announcement of Red's name, but not the others. *Idiots*. Red dearly hoped they were on Rob's pink-slip list.

"Don't stay out too late, Toni," Fleck drawled.

"Yeah," Hodges chuckled boozily. "You're like our hot kid sister. If you miss curfew, we'll probably have to kick this guy's ass."

Red muttered, "I invite you to try," as Piper pulled him away, her hand small and pretty—but determined—in his.

They passed the celebratory senator and his wife—still not enjoying themselves in the center of the dining room—and made their way to a quiet table in the corner. The first thing out of Piper's mouth once the hostess seated them was an apology.

"I am so sorry," she said. "I have no idea why those guys were being such boneheads."

That infuriated Red even more than the jerks themselves. "Sweetheart, you have nothing to be sorry for—it's those asshole pseudo-writers who do."

"Even so," she insisted. "I don't want them to ruin our dinner."

Piper had positioned herself with her back to the room, and she tried to put a good face on things. But her movements were robotic, like she could still sense the men's stares on her. Every gesture was stilted and calculated for effect. Or rather, *lack* of effect.

"Are they always like that?" Red wondered. The men had acted awfully familiar, considering how little interaction they'd likely had with her. Piper lived in a different state, several hours away, and couldn't have been up here too often.

"Mostly," she admitted.

"Is that why they don't even use your real name?"

"Yes. It seemed better that way. Kept some distance, you know?"

The men in question had moved close to the entrance of the bar, so they could keep Red and Piper in their sights. Every time Red glanced over Piper's shoulder and spotted their lazy smirks and assessing gazes, he tensed a bit more.

None of this day was going the way he wanted. Red hated it. He hated how all the forces outside his control seemed to be lining up at once to defy his wishes. He hated the way other irritating people kept invading his last few hours with Piper. And he especially despised the fact that he hadn't been able to do a damn thing to protect her from those dickhead colleagues of hers.

Piper wasn't oblivious, of course. She could tell Red was unhappy again. When the waitress inquired about dessert, Piper politely insisted she didn't want any.

Red didn't even bother tossing out a double entendre about treats he might have for her at home. He doubted Piper was too eager to be alone with him again, not after his snit before. Yet another thing Asshole and Company had wrecked.

Still, when they slid into the car waiting out front for them, Piper laid her hand on the seat and didn't balk when Red covered it with his. His fingers slid easily into the spaces between hers.

Touching her ignited something possessive within him, something that had been simmering beneath the surface for hours already. Red's fingers stroked hers, Piper held her breath and didn't move a muscle—and neither of them could seem to look away from their joined hands.

Too close to home, Red finally broke and hauled her close for an incendiary clash of lips and tongues. In moments, though, the car glided to a stop outside his building and Felix got out. His driver stepped rapidly around to open Piper's door and hold it wide.

A little dazed, Red staggered across the antiseptic lobby with her and straight into the industrial cage of the elevator. Once he pulled the gate shut again and the elevator began climbing, they turned back to each other. Inhaling. Devouring. Holding too tight to even get much groping accomplished.

Red was panting like he'd been running sprints by the time they exited in the little hallway on the top floor, with its unassuming door leading into his loft. He wasn't even aware of dragging Piper inside, only of the overwhelming relief once he had her alone, behind a closed and locked door where no one could bother them.

He knew he was losing it, and he knew none of it was Piper's fault. Still, Red was hungry, and he wanted it rough—wanted to expunge every last frustrating moment of his day in a torrent of sensation with Piper at its crux.

He hoped she wasn't feeling too sensitive after what went down with Denton and his buddies. She was certainly acting as desperate as he felt. Red backed her toward the couch and owned the hell out of her tantalizing mouth. *His.* All his.

Red turned her and bent her over the arm of the couch, hiked up Piper's dress and pushed her panties down. It was the work of a moment to drop his zipper and sheath himself in a condom from his wallet.

And then, gloriously, Red was sinking into Piper's body and thrusting into her blazing heat. He wrapped his hand around her lush inked hip to help keep her steady and reveled in the frenzied sounds she made.

She was so wet for him, and he was so riled up, that it didn't take long. After that elevator ride, they were probably both halfway home anyway. Red loved that Piper was with him like that. That she *got* him, on a level no one ever had.

He pulled her up and spun her around, then bent to kiss her nose. Red's earlier stress and frustration had ebbed away like smoke. Piper smiled seductively up at him, and he was grateful they had this intimacy with each other. This understanding.

He thrilled at being able to have her here, all to himself. Red loved that he could finally be himself, with Piper. He dropped the condom in the kitchen trash, and she giggled and pulled him in the direction of the stairs.

They managed to get rid of most of their clothes stumbling across the living room. They were giddy and tripping on dropped shoes, trying to keep forward momentum while still kissing each other.

Rapidly, the tension cranked hot again. Impatient and determined to have Piper in his bed instead of on the red geometric rug at the base of the stairs, Red picked her up in a big bear hug and carried her the rest of the way.

At the top, he dumped her on his mattress and leaned over. Red plundered Piper's mouth, then backed off so he could kiss her the same way between her thighs. God, she was sweet.

The surprised, breathy little cry she let out when his whiskers chafed against her skin nearly undid him entirely. Caught up in it—in her—and not considering for even a minute what he was doing, Red flipped her onto her stomach.

He planted a fervent kiss between her shoulder blades and pressed himself against her glorious, rounded ass, then straightened up and spanked her.

Piper burst out with a sharper sound at that, but it wasn't a bad one. He spanked her again on the other side, and the way her ivory skin flushed had him even harder than he'd been in the elevator. Piper said something, but it was muffled by the mattress. She squirmed a little too, but she stayed put.

"You want more?" Red growled.

She didn't reply. She didn't move. Last time, she'd wanted more.

"Yeah, I think some more." Red spanked Piper a few more times, fascinated by the lines of her back and legs, enamored with the curve of her spine and her ass, drunk on all that she was, and all that they could be together.

He stopped and smoothed his palms lightly down the lower arc of her rear, down the tops of her thighs, feeling the heat under that velvety-soft skin. It must have tickled—Piper jumped and gripped the edges of his pillow tightly.

Red trailed his fingertips between her legs, longing for her to be ready for him again. His balls drew up tight at the slickness he found, but…something in the air had shifted. Something felt wrong.

He urged Piper onto her back and examined her face, but her expression was hard to decipher. Slowly, so slowly, he levered himself over her and dropped a kiss on her lips. And another.

Only when she began responding again, wrapping her arms around his waist and spreading her legs wide so he could settle between them, did Red release her mouth and move lower. He dwelled on her beautiful breasts, working his way out of his boxer briefs while he sucked and nibbled at her.

When she whimpered, he reached down and carefully stroked her cleft. Now—now Piper was ready again, gripping Red's head and shoulders, digging her nails into his skin. He scrabbled for a condom in the bedside drawer, hissing as he tried to work it over himself.

Finally, though, he was arching back and entering her in one smooth thrust. "Okay, sweetheart?" he asked, holding steady even though it felt like it might kill him.

"Yes. Please, just—"

He watched Piper's face for any sign of discomfort, but she pressed her head back into his pillow, squeezing her eyes shut against his gaze. Her lovely, plush mouth dropped open on a silent inhale.

God, she was a vision. So sweet and soft, Red wished he could kiss Piper everywhere at once. After only a few more delectable thrusts, he needed to get closer. So, he dropped onto his forearms and pressed his chest against hers, then slid into her tight heat again. Piper whimpered like she was getting close. Her legs locked around his hips and her arms clung to his ribcage.

Red tried to capture her mouth with his, but their pace was too rushed to maintain the contact. Before long, all he could do was bury his face in her fragrant hair and cling to the sound of Piper's cries as they spent themselves once more.

THEY LAID LIKE that for a long time afterward, frozen in a tangle of hot, heavy limbs. When he could bear to move again, Red reached toward the lamp. He wanted to appreciate every inch of Piper, spread out next to him like a decadent gift from some underworld god.

Instead, he was taken aback to see the flat look in her eyes, and not the soaring happiness he was feeling. It was resignation, perhaps, but not bliss. *Fuck.*

He'd been certain Piper was enjoying herself as much as he was. All the signs were there. But as Red well knew, sometimes a body and a brain weren't exactly in sync. Add in a heart, and you had the makings of one hell of a wreck.

He brushed a tendril of hair off her cheek. "What's wrong, little dove? What happened?"

Piper's eyes slid away, and she opened her lips to speak.

Red had a very bad feeling about what she was about to say. "I swear to God, honey—don't even try to tell me *nothing.*"

She stayed quiet for several excruciating minutes, during which Red attempted to remain calm and review what they'd done. He hadn't hurt her, had he? He'd been slightly wild, but they'd both been that.

Right?

Or was Red inexpressibly clueless? Had his lack of restraint just deep-sixed the first promising relationship he'd had in years—if ever?

Piper spoke up, "Do you think you might be this way because of the peanut allergy? Or is it something else?"

Red paused, confused by her direction. "What way?"

"You know. Kind of…controlling."

"*Kind of?*" Red snorted.

Piper shrugged. "I was just thinking that maybe because you can't really control what other people do regarding the food thing, maybe it makes you want to control other things more."

"I really don't know," he admitted. "I don't think so, but I suppose I've never really thought about it that way."

"Except, on some level, you're thinking about it every day. Every time you put something in your mouth."

"Well," he winked, "Not all the things I put in my mouth."

Piper scowled and poked him in the arm. "I'm serious."

"Piper, what do you want me to say? It has never once occurred to me to psychoanalyze myself about either my allergy or my bedroom predilections. Some things just are the way they are."

"Huh."

"That's it? *Huh*?"

Another casual shrug. "Yup."

This was absurd. "Piper?" he asked. "Did I hurt you? Before, I mean."

With studied carelessness, she said, "Not really, no." But again, from inches away on his pillow, she wouldn't look him in the eye.

"But maybe a little?" Red prodded.

"Well, you smacked my ass pretty good. So, yeah," Piper admitted. "That's fair to say. Did you intend to?"

Red was dumbfounded. "I…*no*. You liked it that way last time, so I thought…"

"So, it wasn't some kind of twisted punishment for what happened with the guys in the bar earlier?" Now she stared at him, accusation heavy in her expression. Still, Red could tell it took something out of her to say it.

"Of course not," he objected. But when he added, "What those assholes did was not your fault," he had to wonder who he was trying to reassure.

"Figured I ought to check anyway," she countered.

"Just so I'm clear. You're telling me you didn't like the spanking this time."

"Not really, no," Piper reiterated. "It was different than last time. You were different."

Which made Red feel…how, exactly? He was floundering, searching for the solid ground beneath this slippery situation.

"Then why'd you let me do it? Why didn't you say something sooner?"

Piper frowned off into space. "Well…I'm not sure, to be honest. If you'd asked me two weeks ago about any of this, I probably would've thought I knew everything there was to know. But, as it turns out, I don't know shit."

Coming from an erotic romance author, that was fascinating. "You've *truly* never even been spanked before?" Red asked.

Her mouth twisted ruefully to the side. "Only by you. I made up what I wrote in the books, of course."

Red turned his face into the pillow and groaned, but that wasn't going to fix this. He made himself face her again. "Piper, honey, I'm really sorry. I should've…asked you if it was okay this time, too. Or whatever you needed." *Whatever.* Like he was in middle school, and not a grown man with a gorgeous naked woman in his bed.

He was on thin ice here, and not entirely sure of his next move.

"It's okay," Piper murmured. "We both got caught up in the moment."

"That's the truth." Red considered his next words carefully. "Listen, can I ask you something?" He didn't want to, precisely, but he had a feeling if he didn't, he might never be able to repair what had been broken tonight.

"Okay." Piper was still so wary, and it scraped across his nerve endings like sandpaper.

"I know you said I didn't hurt you, and that you didn't love it. But what *did* you feel, just now?"

Piper's brows drew together thoughtfully. "Well. I suppose it…I just felt kind of depressed. Sad, almost."

"Seriously?" Now Red was outright alarmed. *Sad* was probably the last thing he wanted her to feel while she was in bed with him.

"Yeah. You know, like, *if this guy actually cares about me, why on earth would he want to hit me?* Especially, like that. Intimately. When you were grouchy."

Red took a slow breath in and let it out. This was awful. He was, quite possibly, just as bad at relationships as people had always said he was. Unfortunately, his latest victim wasn't done. Not nearly.

"It made me feel like there must be something wrong with me." Piper gestured spastically between them. "Something deficient, if you need to spank me to get motivated. Look, Red—"

Oh, good. She had more.

"I don't often feel like I'm not good enough, you know? But when I do, it always seems to be at the hands of a guy who's supposed to care about me. So, yeah. That saddens and depresses me."

Red was well and truly speechless. Entirely bereft of a single helpful word. But he had to say something, if only so Piper wouldn't continue to believe that she was less than what she was.

"That is not at all what I thought you'd say," he began, scrambling to come up with the rest of it on the fly.

She peered at him. "What did you think I was going to say?"

"I suppose I expected you to wonder what the fuck was wrong with *me* for wanting to spank you. You're over there making connections with my allergy and shit. Why not?"

"There's nothing wrong with you," she soothed automatically.

"Oh, so it must be you?" he scoffed. "You can't tell me you think you're somehow inferior to me."

"I guess. In this, at least. I write about kink all the time, Red. Isn't it kind of lame that I don't actually know what I'm talking about?"

Red had read her books. She knew what she was talking about.

"Piper, please believe me when I say that just because you don't want to be spanked every time we hit the sheets, doesn't mean you're deficient in some way. Honestly, look at you!"

She sniffed, like she was a troll laying there, instead of a goddess.

"Don't give me that," he warned. "You're pretty, soft, and sweet." He ran a hand down her arm, then cupped her jaw. Piper's amber eyes watched him, wide and dubious. "You're kind and smart, funny, open…and you have faith that life will work out the way it's supposed to. That's rare. Also, you're so damn pretty."

"You said that already."

"It's true."

"I'm not sure I'm *that* open. I'm actually a very suspicious person," she told him.

"I don't believe you," he smiled.

Piper smiled, too, and Red relaxed, just a little. "Maybe I just don't get why—when you could clearly have any woman in this town—you would want me. I feel like a fraud, like at any moment you'll discover the real me and run screaming for the hills."

"You've got to be kidding me," he balked. "Have you met any women around here?"

"Some, yeah. They were beautiful, elegant, refined, sophisticated, accomplished…"

Red cut Piper off before she could go much further. "The women I have dated recently were grasping vipers focused wholly on forwarding their own agendas. They couldn't have cared less about me as a human being. Ergo, far bigger frauds than you could ever be."

They had seen him only as a youngish man with a tolerable face and nice, large wallet. Red's forays into domination probably had way more to do with *that* than with any poisonous little legumes.

Piper huffed, "They couldn't have all been like that."

"Trust me. There were enough that I was able to turn repelling the repellant into a pretty legit side hustle."

"And you say I have a way with words." She rolled her eyes.

Red snorted.

"Anyway, what makes you think I'm so different? Maybe I'm just like all the others."

"Seriously?" This part, at least, was easy. "You have fought me literally every time I've tried to do more for you than open a damn door. Besides that, you are a caring, compassionate human being, with the ability to express interesting thoughts and opinions that may or may not coincide with mine." Red stared her down. "You can hold a conversation, Piper. You can cook. And, you have a terrific bedside manner."

"I could say the same for you, aside from the cooking. That's still TBD."

"I have a limited kitchen repertoire that you will quickly tire of. But you truly are the first woman in recent memory who seems to have looked for, or found, any of that other stuff in me. Hence, my clinging to you like the whole ship is going down."

Piper shifted toward him then and pressed a gentle kiss of forgiveness on Red's lips. "If we keep talking about the important stuff, I swear we won't drown."

"Not if I can help it," he told her. Ironically, he even believed it.

Seventeen

LATER, WHEN THEY'D gone back downstairs and Red was trying his hand at making flan from a box, he brought up the men in the bar again. Piper was expecting it, but she wished he hadn't had quite so much time to brood about the subject.

As it turned out, though, he had set aside his anger at Jim and his buddies for the time being. Now, Red had his executive hat on and wanted to question Piper about the general work environment at Trident.

While he mixed a vivid yellow powder with hot water in a bowl, Piper told him how some of the male authors had viewed the romance writers as a trollopy harem—amusing as potential hookups, but not respectable as colleagues.

Because of that, Piper explained that the occasional conferences and holiday parties the Dentons engineered could be uncomfortable.

"I tried to stay as aloof as I could," she told him. "Some of the women went along with their crap, but I didn't want to incite the guys any more than necessary. With Jim especially, nothing I did seemed to help, though."

Red bristled at that, turning from the oven he was attempting to turn on and demanding, "What did HR do?"

Piper pushed off the barstool where she was perched and went over to help him turn on his oven. She liked that Red didn't even bother questioning whether she had pursued the HR angle, and thankfully she didn't have to disappoint him.

"They told me that, since the guys hadn't actually gotten physical with me, I should lighten up and try to laugh it off. That it would be too much trouble to file an official complaint about something so minor."

Red was aghast. "Just because they didn't lay hands on you doesn't mean it wasn't harassment."

Piper took the pan of uncooked custard he was holding before he could spill it. "I realize that," she said, and carefully set the flan onto the counter until the oven heated up.

"So?" Red had stuck his hand in the oven, presumably to make sure it was warming as expected, but now he slammed the door shut with a bit more force than necessary and wheeled to glare at her.

"Well, Perry and I were considering whether we wanted to pursue litigation or just find a different publisher when PKM swooped in and took over."

"I see." That settled him down nicely. He clamped his lips together, grabbed a bright red timer in the shape of a rooster from the counter, and focused on setting it. It was an oddly homey touch amidst the sea of industrial modernism surrounding them.

Piper smirked, "There I was, biding my time, waiting to see what would happen. And, look—a fancy new contract for me, and terminations for half of the jerks. I do love karma."

"Well, I can assure you that a reorganization of the HR department just got added to the transition team's list, too," Red laughed.

"How very gallant of you."

"We at PKM aim to please." He kissed her quickly, but thoroughly, then asked, "Do you know how bad it might have been for the other female writers? Do you think Denton and his buddies crossed the line with anyone else?"

"You'll have to ask to them directly," Piper said, "But as far as I know, the other ladies only had experiences like mine."

"You say *only* like what they did wasn't a big deal. Maybe you've already forgotten that I saw them in action earlier," he growled, bracing his hands on the counter.

"Red…" Piper sighed. "Don't be dense. That kind of shit goes on all the time, for most women, everywhere. It's not that it isn't a big deal—it's that after three decades of it happening pretty pervasively in my life, I've realized that I can't fight every damn battle. No one can. We'd never have time to get anything else done, otherwise." The oven chimed, so she edged past him to slide the flan inside.

He stared at her. "That's sick, Piper. You can't just…not stand up for yourself."

"Don't I know it." Piper walked around the island and parked herself back on her stool. "But sometimes life requires turning the proverbial other cheek."

"Not anymore, it doesn't." He grabbed the small cardboard box the dessert mix had come in and pitched it angrily into the trash bin in the corner of his kitchen.

"Oh, really? And what are you going to do about it?"

He shook his fist in the air. "I shall destroy them all." At least he grinned at her afterward, or she might have wondered at his sanity.

"I'm not sure that's necessary," Piper smiled back.

"Okay, fine. Some of them, then."

"If you insist."

Red came around the counter and leaned against the counter beside her. He ran a finger up her side, pulling up her t-shirt so he could trace the black lines of her tattoo. "Let's change the subject. Is this the tattoo you told me about the first time we went out? The one you added on to later?"

Piper nodded, twisting around to see the gnarled tree that stretched from her hip to her ribs. "It is."

His soft touch, up and down each root and branch, raised goosebumps on her skin. "What did you change?"

"It used to just be a tree from my grandparents' yard, the one where they hung my swing when I was a kid. When I graduated college, I brought a picture of it to the tattoo parlor near campus for the artist to copy. I never thought the real thing would be mine someday."

Red made a pleased sound, studying it.

"Then, a few years ago, I hit a rough patch." Piper paused, startled by her casual description. Could Kyle's infidelities and betrayals really be reduced to such an anemic phrase? It didn't seem possible after what she'd gone through, and yet here she was with those words exiting her mouth.

"What happened?" Red prompted, looking up at her.

Piper had to clear her throat a couple of times before she could be sure her voice wouldn't falter. "I was engaged to this guy, but it didn't work out. I realized after a while that it was for the best but, for a time there, I needed a tangible reminder that I wasn't unique—that everything in the world goes through fallow and fruitful periods. So, I added flowers to the branches."

"You made barren winter into hopeful spring," he said, understanding her imagery immediately.

"Exactly."

"Like you did with me," Red pointed out, lifting his hand to her hair. "You're like a modern-day alchemist, Piper. Turning lead into gold. Desolation into…potential."

Piper winced. "Don't get carried away. It's just a tattoo."

Red shook his head with a smirk. "Agree to disagree."

She knew if she let him think too long about what she'd said, an interrogation about Kyle was sure to follow. To distract him, Piper pointed quickly to Red's own arm and the curling parchment on his bicep, like the flyleaf in an old pirate story.

"What about yours? It's a treasure map, isn't it?"

"Of sorts," he agreed.

She leaned to the side to take a closer look. "Let's see. There's an old ship, some whiskey casks, and…what's that thing? A wine carafe?"

"Nope," Red grinned. "It's a beaker."

Understanding dawned. "Oh, my God—*boats, booze, and biotech*, right?"

"Right." He was proud as could be.

"That's so cute. But I think you probably need to add some books now."

He explained, "I want to. But the guy I use went to a tattoo convention in Amsterdam last month and never came back. I figured I'd give him a little more time to return before I find someone new. I think it'll look better if it's all done by the same artist."

"True." Piper traced the red dotted line that wound through the tiny icons, then sat straight as another thought occurred to her. There was no *X-marks-the-spot*. "What about the personal things?" she wondered.

Red's easy sprawl against the counter turned almost imperceptibly stiff. "What do you mean?"

"Well, you've got all this work-related stuff. Don't you think you ought to add something that's just about you?"

Red stared out the huge factory window over her shoulder. When he asked, "Like what?" his face was a mask she couldn't read.

"I don't know," Piper shrugged. "That's for you to decide."

He nodded, then turned to prop both elbows behind himself on the counter. "I'm sure something will come to me eventually," he said.

Several feet away, the rooster timer began crowing. Red stepped quickly into the kitchen to remove the flan from the oven, then busied himself trying to invert the pan onto a large plate. Piper wanted to go help him, but he seemed to need his space.

She stayed put and was soon rewarded with Red's obvious pride and satisfaction when he finally lifted up the pan to reveal a perfectly-caramelized custard underneath. He dug in a drawer for two spoons, then carried his offering back to her.

Once he and Piper had taken a few bites, he shifted and took her free hand.

"Listen, I had an idea," he said, almost physically shaking off whatever had been bothering him before. "I know you have that water thing going on at home, but do you think you could stay another day or two?"

Piper had known he was disappointed when she left to spend the day with her friend. She should have realized his orderly brain would find some way to rebalance the scales.

"Maybe," she said, thinking about the week ahead. "My dad's probably been over to turn off the water by now. It's too late to call the cat sitter, but I could call her in the morning and see if she's free. My train ticket would be easy enough to change, too. Why?"

"There's somewhere I'd love to show you before you go back. And honestly, I could really use the mental health day," Red said.

"Dreading Monday already?" Piper joked, even though he suddenly seemed exhausted. Before getting to know him, she'd never thought about how hard someone in his position might have to work—or the toll that would take on their personal life.

"I dread all the days when you leave," he fired back, confirming her impression. "So, what do you think? Can you stand me for another day?"

Leaking pipes seemed very far away, and Piper couldn't stand to squash the hope in his voice. "I don't know. What are the chances you can make other weirdly-delicious instant desserts like this flan?"

She shoveled in another embarrassingly large bite and pulled the plate an inch or two closer. At the rate they were going, they would have the entire thing demolished soon.

Red puffed out his chest, victory shining from his gaze. "The bodega down the block has a whole shelf full of these babies. They're, like, a buck apiece. We could eat them for a month if you wanted to."

"Then it looks like we have a date," Piper told him.

"*Yes.*" He pumped his fist, then took off in search of his cell phone.

Not one to miss a dessert-related opportunity, Piper took a few extra bites of flan, then followed his voice up the stairs.

Red was pacing the floor near the foot of his bed, saying, "Thanks buddy," before disconnecting and calling another number.

He winked at her when he saw her come in, setting off a burst of flutters in Piper's chest like a flock of starlings taking flight.

"Mom," he said, then stuck out his tongue when Piper gaped at him.

She could hear the other woman's voice, rapid-fire and strident through the phone.

Red blew out a breath and dropped his head back. "Mother. I realize that. Yes, I know," he began, attempting to keep up with the flow of words accosting him.

Then, after a long lull, Piper watched Red summon what must have been every ounce of restraint he possessed. "You're right," he agreed. "I should not have lost my temper." He flopped back on the bed, stretching in a long, enticing line of delicious male, right next to where Piper was sitting.

"She probably deserved it," Piper whispered.

Red widened his eyes and nodded emphatically in agreement.

"Okay, well that is definitely a conversation for another time," he told his mother. "I was just calling to ask Dad something really quickly. Can you put him on?"

Judging by Red's expression, that set off a whole new onslaught of invective. When his father finally managed to seize the phone, his son's relief was immediate.

"Hey, Dad. Yeah, I just wanted to know if anyone is using the Hampton house right now. I need to get out of here for a couple of days or I'm going to inflict bodily harm on—" Red stopped, listened, and laughed. "Yes. And if you could possibly keep Mom out of my hair for a few days, that would be splendid."

Piper arched a brow at him. It seemed that not only was Red whisking her off for a little field trip to the Hamptons, but he was also making sure his mother wouldn't find a way to pop in unannounced again. That kind of pro-level effort deserved a reward.

She shifted around and straddled Red's hips, narrowing her eyes at him when he immediately spread his legs to force her thighs wider apart. He grinned wickedly and sunk his teeth into his lower lip, clearly not paying the slightest attention to anything his father was saying.

"You be good," Piper murmured, "And maybe I will be too."

"Dad?" Red asked quickly. "I—"

Piper untied the cord of Red's sweatpants as slowly as she could, then dragged one fingernail carefully across his lower stomach, from one side of his waist to the other. His reaction was instantaneous, a shudder rippling through his large frame from top to bottom.

His father was still talking, but Red wasn't hearing a thing. His eyes were glued to the skin Piper was revealing by peeling off her t-shirt, inch by torturous inch.

Once her head cleared the neckline, she tossed it aside. Red lifted one hand to her breast, his palm blazingly hot as he tested the weight in his hand.

"Dad, something's come up," he barked quickly.

Piper raised her eyebrows at him. "I'll say."

Red blurted, "I gotta run," checked twice to make sure he'd really hung up, then lunged for her.

Eighteen

A S EXPECTED, PIPER had no trouble changing her ticket to leave Tuesday at lunchtime. It didn't give them a ton more time but at the moment, Red didn't have a ton of time to give.

Still, twenty-four more hours before he had to get back to reality was better than nothing. To preserve as much of it as he could, he opted to charter a helicopter out to the Hampton house instead of driving.

The truth was, he hadn't actually expected anyone to be at the house—his mother extended invitations to the family's vacation home about as often as she admitted she was in the wrong, and never in the off-season—but his call to his parents did have a purpose.

At least now Red could be sure his mother wouldn't come hunting for him for another day or two. His father would make sure of that. By the time his mom figured out a way around her husband's goal-tending, Red would be back behind his desk and ready for her, and Piper would be safe at home, three states away.

Not yet, though. Red had one more day to bask in all things Piper, and the thing he was currently enjoying the most was the expression on her face. She was perched on her seat in the back of the helicopter like she half expected to be ejected off the PKM roof without warning. Red bent over to latch her in and wondered if she'd ever flown in something quite so small and fast.

"You sure you're okay with this?" he asked her.

Piper's face was grim as she stared at him, her nervousness apparent while he checked and re-checked her straps and buckles. Her hands fluttered around his, trying to help.

"It's only a short hop. We'll be fine. Nothing's going to happen," she said firmly.

Red laughed and shook his head. "Who are you trying to convince?"

"What do you expect?" she demanded testily. "This kind of outing does not go well for people like…well, fancy people."

"Piper, look outside. It's a perfectly calm and clear day. We'll be back on the ground in forty-five minutes."

"Famous last words," she muttered.

Red knew he shouldn't, not after Spanking Round Two had gone south, but he just couldn't resist poking at her. "Don't you think there's something really kinky about this?" he murmured, low enough so the pilot couldn't hear. "All these restraints? Giving me a huge hard-on."

As distractions went, it was an excellent one. Piper's eyes immediately flew south to assess the situation, but Red foiled her by pivoting and settling into his own seat so she couldn't get a good look. He buckled up like he didn't have a care in the world while the pilot ran through his checklist.

"You know," she said narrowly, "I think you might be a bit of a bad seed."

The rotors began spinning, but even over the noise, Piper clearly caught his response. "Oh honey, you have no idea," Red laughed.

Minutes later, they were airborne, and Piper's eyes went wide, taking in the sweeping view of Manhattan as they banked and turned toward Long Island. Red pointed out a landmark or two along the way, but mostly he just took pleasure in the way her expressions shifted when she registered each new detail, cataloging them and filing them away in her fascinating brain.

The helipad closest to his parents' house wasn't much of an airfield—only a tight square of asphalt tucked onto a sandy spit of land between the road and the shore. Red had arranged for the caretaker to leave a car at the small beachside lot for them, and as the helicopter set down, he saw that it was already there. In moments, he and Piper had accepted their bags from the pilot, stepped across the sand and the trampled rushgrass, and slipped into the tan leather seats of the coupe.

The morning air was fresh and crisp but not too cold, so they rolled down the windows for the short drive to the house. It was still early in the off-season, but it was also early on a Monday, so there was barely anyone else around—only the occasional workman's truck, and some bicycles here and there. A handful of people were strolling the beach, and a couple of hardy surfers bobbed out on the water.

The contrast to the hustle and buzz of weekday Manhattan made Red felt like they'd not only left the city but entered another stratosphere altogether.

In the passenger seat, Piper was soaking in the view and the breeze, and looking like she'd shed a huge weight from her shoulders. She clearly hadn't been kidding when she'd told him she enjoyed being out in nature.

Red drove fast, impatient to see her reaction to his parent's summer retreat—especially since it was so patently opposite his own home. However, when Red slowed the car and hit the remote for the gate, Piper shot him a look of panic.

"You can't be serious," she breathed.

"As a heart attack," he grinned.

The property was on the large side, and it took them a minute to work their way up the curved pea gravel driveway. Red watched as the house came into full view and tried to see it through Piper's eyes.

The place was a classic, sprawling shingle-style, covered with broad windows and bright white trim. Vivid fuchsia flowers spilled from the window boxes, still surviving into the autumn since there hadn't been a hard frost to kill them off yet. His mother's beloved hydrangeas were burgeoning, too, dotting the lawn with pale blue blossoms.

The scent of salt water and seaweed hung pungently in the air, blowing in off the water out back. The leaves on the trees had begun to turn, but the rambling lawns and tall privet hedges were still a vibrant, emerald green. Despite all the irritating social events he'd had to suffer through here over the years, it was still one of his favorite places on earth.

"Red," Piper gasped. "This is *incredible*."

He pulled the little sportscar into the turnaround in front of the porch, and barely had time to get her door open before Piper was up and out of the passenger seat. Then she stood stock still beside the car, gaping around in shocked delight.

"Come on." Red grabbed her by the hand and led her up the stairs, then let her into the sunny front hall. "Hang tight here for a minute," he said. "I'll go grab our bags and be right back."

Piper hadn't moved an inch when he returned. Red dumped their stuff at the bottom of the stairs and smiled too. It had been way too long since he'd logged a visit here, and he was glad his first time back was with her.

The décor was still mercifully normal—straight coastal magazine, everything crisp and nautical. Couches slipcovered in marine-blue denim. Seagrass rugs. Shells in pebbled glass jars on the end tables and huge paintings of sailing ships on the walls.

"Oh, Red," she breathed. "How do you ever leave here? It's so beautiful."

He could have made a joke about the hideousness of his loft in town, but instead Red told her, "Not as beautiful as you." He meant it—her happiness was incandescent, lighting up her tawny eyes and shining from her face.

Naturally, Piper snorted at that.

"Let me show you around," he said.

While they walked through the rooms, Red sifted through all the things in the area that they could do today, but knowing Piper, food probably had to come first. He'd woken her and dragged her to their flight too early for her to eat much breakfast.

"Are you hungry?" It was a silly question. She only ever answered it in the affirmative. Frankly, if she said no at this point, Red would probably begin to worry.

"Of course!" Piper chirped, not looking his way, but dancing from window to window, so she could peer out at each new vista.

From the living room, Red glanced into the yard and saw that the pool cover was already on for winter, so he reluctantly crossed skinny-dipping off his mental list. However, from the kitchen, Red noticed that the wooden boardwalk at the back of the yard, which led over low dunes to access the beach, looked like it had been reconstructed recently.

That was good news. Once it warmed up more, he and Piper could go hang out on the sand, maybe take a long walk or play Frisbee.

There had been a nice little restaurant about a half-mile east of there, next to the jetty. Looking in that direction, Red had a sudden, visceral memory of eating steamed clams on their back patio and knew, at minimum, he should take Piper there for dinner. He called up their website on his phone and was relieved to see that they hadn't yet closed for the season.

"Hey, do you like shellfish?" he asked Piper, drawing her attention away from the wide grassy rectangle stretching below the house's back windows. She sighed and wandered over with an ecstatic look on her face. Red congratulated himself on the best idea he'd probably ever had—next to meeting her to begin with, that was.

"I love it," she said, then reconsidered. "Though…maybe not for breakfast."

"No worries." He ducked his head into the fridge and found that the caretaker had stocked the usual array of staples. "We've got bacon and eggs and fruit for breakfast. But I know a great seafood place up the way that we can hit up for dinner if you want."

"Perfect," she grinned.

After they ate and mapped out their plan for the day, they dropped their things in his bedroom upstairs, changed their shoes, and headed out to do some sight-seeing. They wandered the wildlife refuge until hunger struck again, grabbed decadent little gourmet pizzas in Sag Harbor for lunch, then browsed lazily through a couple of antique shops before driving out to Montauk to do a tour of the lighthouse.

It was amazing, really. When Red visited with his parents, there were always new restaurants to try, familiar old haunts at which they had to put in appearances, and charity events to navigate. There was a familiar roster of people that they knew from the city, parading their assorted unmarried daughters in front of him. It didn't often feel like rest, so much as his regular life with a different backdrop.

But now, alone here with Piper, Red had nothing to do but have a good time. They didn't tackle a single Gina MacLellan-approved thing for the entire day, and it was like his brain was drunk on the concept—flooded with ideas of even more they could try, if only he could convince Piper to come back again.

Measuring her indolent smile on the drive back to the house, Red didn't think it would be too difficult a task. He let his mind go sprinting into the future, where there bloomed a joy-filled place of their own, with laughing little kids and dogs running around.

Which was crazy, of course. Red was hardly father material and had no idea whether Piper, the cat person, even *liked* dogs. What was more, she had a full-blown life already in progress somewhere else and entertaining too many fantasies of her pulling up stakes to join his circus was ambitious, even for him.

Still, Red reached across the gearstick and wrapped Piper's hand in his. It was impossible not to touch her. At first, he'd worried it was some jealous, proprietary thing, but eventually realized he wasn't registering other people at all—Red only had eyes for Piper, and his hands were compelled to follow wherever his eyes led.

He simply couldn't keep them to himself. If he looked at Piper's hair, or her slim, tan arms, or her oddly enticing collarbones, his fingers tripped along moments later—like Red couldn't help but feel what he was seeing. What he was studying with such fervent appreciation.

The scenery around them made about as big an impression on him as a stage prop. But was Red trying to commit Piper to memory, since she was leaving again tomorrow? Or was he just doing what came naturally—learning a new terrain with the complete concentration that helped him succeed at nearly everything he attempted?

He didn't know.

At least he could dispense with the thought that maybe he was measuring Piper against that ever-present, unknown paradigm he'd been searching so long for. Women he met had never been able to live up to it, before now—but Red didn't think Piper would even have to try. Somehow, in the short time he'd known her, Piper had *become* the ideal.

What that meant was anyone's guess. Back at home, while they showered and changed for dinner, it occurred to Red that his particular…needs, such as they were, had mostly been laying low with Piper. Sure, they'd tried some spanking, with inconclusive success. But as for all the rest of it, the domination and submission, the restraints and toys and total control—Red felt remarkably indifferent to its absence.

He didn't need it. Not with Piper. It was confusing and odd, but also kind of freeing. He wondered how long it would last.

AT THE END of the day, they conceded defeat and admitted to each other that they were too tired from playing tourist to make the walk up the beach to dinner. Instead, Red tucked Piper into the car and drove the few minutes to the restaurant. She was as fresh as a spring daisy after her primping, and Red almost wanted to skip dinner and feast on her instead.

He'd start at the top of her glossy light brown hair and work his way down, charting a map of every gorgeous inch of her. And then, once he'd made it to the tip of her pretty painted toes, Red would reverse course and wander his way up again.

"Food is for suckers," he muttered, pulling into the small, roped-off parking area.

Piper was, understandably, startled. "What?"

Red shook his head. "Never mind," he said, resolving to tolerate her current, clothed state—for the next hour or two, at least. This had been his brainy idea anyway, and he didn't want to disappoint her.

Now that it was fall, the restaurant was quieter than he was used to—sitting on its rocky outcropping like a little jewel, its nautical brass fittings gleaming and big windows reflecting the sinking sun.

Inside, the bar was mostly empty, the music was soft, and the unhurried staff was attentive. He and Piper sat at a small table on the covered porch in the back, warmed by a nearby heating lamp while they devoured clams and oysters and chowder. It was heaven on earth, watching Piper survey the sailboats drift lazily by.

Something she'd said recently had been nagging at him, though, like a small but sharp thorn in the back of his mind. Without thinking it out, Red blurted, "Tell me about this former fiancé of yours. Who was he?"

Piper turned and leveled a baleful glare his way. "Oh, man," she groaned. "Me and my big mouth. And this day was going so well, too."

"Come on, you knew I'd ask. Besides, the day's still good— we're just talking, that's all."

"Honestly, the less I have to think about Kyle Dwyer, the better."

"Except, if I don't ask, I won't be able to stop thinking about him," Red reasoned.

Piper wrinkled her nose in distaste. "Why do you want to know about him, anyway? I can assure you that I'm not pining for him. The relationship is totally dead and over and has zero chance of ever being resuscitated." She waved her hand beside her in dramatic pantomime of a brush-off.

"Humor me," Red smirked.

"*Really?*" Piper demanded back.

"Yes. Maybe I want to see what I'm up against. Scope out the competition, as it were."

"Trust me, you are not in competition with jerky Kyle. You are not only *not* in the same contest, but you are in totally different weight classes. Different leagues. Different sports, even."

"I'm no expert," he mused, "But you may have just violated a rule about too many analogies in one sentence."

She tipped her glass of prosecco in his direction in challenge. "Who's the writer here? You or me?"

"Nice try, but you aren't going to change this particular subject, little dove."

"Not feeling very peace-like at the moment, if you must know."

"How'd you meet him?" Red tried, steamrolling ahead.

"Through friends."

"Length of relationship?"

"Too long."

Red chuckled. So stubborn. "How recently did the split occur? How about that?"

Piper sighed, long and beleaguered. "About three years ago. I'm over it, I promise you. And...I guess if you really want to know more, I can tell you someday. But can we please not dredge it up tonight?"

"Sure. Just let me know if I need to kill him."

"Please stop."

"Fair enough," Red capitulated, a little bemused by her reticence. "I'll back off. But could you at least advise me on how *not* to make the same mistake he did?"

Piper toyed with the small blown-glass hurricane near her plate, her amber eyes reflecting the flame of the candle as she stared back at him. "In very simple terms," she said haltingly, "Kyle…betrayed my trust. And Red, once that's gone, there's…no going back for me." Piper sniffed in derision. "Not like he wanted to, anyway."

"I totally understand," Red told her. And he thought to himself, *No sweat.*

He knew all about trust, didn't he? At this point, it might as well have been his middle name. And Piper, of all people, had no reason not to trust him because Red only wanted the best for her. He truly intended to take care of her as long as she'd let him.

Hell—he was already looking out for Piper in ways she wasn't even aware of yet. And if keeping her trust was the worst Red had to worry about, this relationship couldn't possibly go wrong. They were too compatible. Too perfect for each other.

Red had no idea what he'd done to deserve her, and he didn't really care. He had Piper now, and no way was he going down like that asshole Kyle.

THE SUN HAD been down for a while by the time they were finally ready to leave. The moon hung big and bright over the water, and Red and Piper stood near the sand, gazing at the stars and the lights of the boats mirrored on the bay. It felt like every one of his nerve-endings was on high-alert, vibrating for any hint of her touch or scent.

As if she could sense his need for her, Piper leaned her head against him and slipped her arm around Red's waist. As she did so, the wind gusted and blew up the edge of his button-down, and her hand landed on the bare skin of his back instead of on pressed cotton.

The unexpected sensation jolted him. Piper stroked his skin gently, calming him like she might a spooked animal. Her hand was a warm and tantalizing contrast to the evening air. Red looked into her upturned face and for the hundredth time that day lost himself in her molten, decadent mouth.

The drive back home was marked by small vivid slices in the dark. Piper's hand on his thigh. Her light, barely-there scent teasing the air. The occasional streetlamp casting polygons of light across her face and throat.

Red grabbed Piper's hand in the driveway, pulled her straight down the brick path that skirted the side of the house, and out onto the lawn in back.

"Follow me, princess," he told her, leading her across the grass and up the stairs of the big gazebo that looked out onto the beach. Red sat in one of the wicker armchairs and pulled Piper into his lap, wrapping his arms around her and holding her close.

They stayed like that for a long time, talking softly. He asked her what she liked best about the area where she lived, and it was a lot to compete with. Red weighed comparable places close to him in New York while he traced patterns on her thigh and toyed with her hair.

Piper's mind wasn't on comparisons between New York and Maryland, however. Before long, she'd shifted sideways on his lap, and rested her head on his arm so he could kiss her. One taste of her tongue, one tug of her hands in his hair, and Red was slipping his already-tenuous leash.

Piper's husky moans carried out across the sand and echoed back on the tide, while Red sucked on that sexy space joining her neck to her shoulder. He used his hands to get her off and thanked his lucky stars that he'd inherited those long, deft MacLellan fingers.

Too soon, she sagged across his lap, boneless and sated. Red whispered, "God, you're so beautiful."

"I just hope no one walked by in the middle of that," she smiled.

"No one will come by. Once the tide came in, it cut off the beach down there." Red pointed at the curve of coastline. "Someone would have to cut across private property and scale a very steep and slippery seawall in the dark if they wanted to get this far up the beach now."

"That is very interesting information," Piper told him. She moved off his lap and knelt between his legs.

Red's body cast a looming shadow over her in the moonlight. He clutched the armrests with his hands and ignored the way the back of his shirt kept snagging on the wicker chair. He couldn't quite make out Piper's face in the darkness, but when she ran her palms up his thighs, his heart hammered at her decisive touch.

"Scoot forward," she instructed.

Red was used to being the one in the driver's seat. Normally, his resistance to being ordered around was both immediate and incontrovertible. And he did hesitate at Piper's commanding tone, a small vestige of defiance rearing up in opposition.

But the woman he wanted was on her knees in front of him. If Red expected to receive the gift she was offering, he needed to override that command center miscue, and fast. He made the conscious decision to relax, then scooted the fuck forward like she'd asked.

Piper pushed up the hem of his button-down shirt, already a soft and rumpled phantom of its former perfectly-starched state. Then she reached for the button of his pants, and his internal conflict threw up another last-gasp effort. He clamped his hand over hers.

"What are you—" Red cleared his throat. He knew damn well what Piper was doing, and so did she. "Wait," he tried.

Under his restraining hand, Piper had managed to work his button free. She was clearly heading for zipper territory but at the discomfort in his voice, she stopped cold.

"You don't want me to?"

"Yes, of course I do." He did. God, he really did. "But…" *What?* What, exactly? Did Red have to be able to tell her what to do, or did he have to take a strong and immediate chill pill?

Piper pulled her hands away and sank back on her heels, giving him space. "I'm making you uncomfortable," she said. "Why?"

"It's not that," Red tried. He attempted to force his scrambled thoughts into some kind of logical order. Hadn't he already determined that all the control bullshit didn't apply with this woman? That he was completely cool without it? "I just don't want you to feel like you have to," he said. His voice came out weird and guttural, and Red was sure Piper would call him on it.

But she took his words at face value. "I do feel like I have to. But not because of anything you're doing. It's because I want this. I want you, like this." She took a deep breath. "But only if you're okay with it."

Red's reservations melted in the face of her calm, reasonable assurance. He gave her a jerky nod and relaxed back into the seat.

Piper moved slowly, carefully lowering his zipper the rest of the way, then brushing aside the edges of his khaki pants. She shuffled closer to inspect his boxers, then smiled suddenly when she realized they had red anchors all over them.

"Ahoy," Piper murmured appreciatively.

Red huffed out a short laugh, trying to retain the semblance of a casual sprawl despite the fact that every muscle in his body felt tense. When he'd leaned back, his shadow had moved off her face, and Piper's lovely, willing lips were quite easy to discern.

"Do you want me to stop?" She studied him, trying to gauge his mood. She probably thought he was acting bizarrely. Red would bet his mother's entire collection of jewelry that Piper had never encountered resistance to a blow job in her entire adult life.

"God," he laughed again, feeling unhinged. "No, I don't want you to stop. I want you to do this like I want my next breath."

When Piper dragged one fingernail up his boxers, tracing the outline of his cock, Red's swallow sounded too loud in the soft autumn night. His erection was all-in on the plan, clearly not having gotten the message that there was a previously-determined protocol to be followed.

"I see that," she grinned, the little imp.

The combination of her sass and her touch made it difficult to put two words—two thoughts—together. Red forced out something of a non-sequitur: "I don't want to make you feel uncomfortable," he murmured, then had to stop when she kissed the small button on the placket of his boxers. Eventually, he was able to press on, "Because…because of what happened last time. When you didn't like the spanking."

"You won't. I want to do this," Piper assured him. She eased down his boxers and pants, then looked very proud of herself when Red lifted his hips to aid her efforts. "Last chance to back out," she added.

Red shook his head quickly, his eyes boring into her in the starlit night. He could do this with his hands tied behind his back. He merely had to keep his eyes on the prize as it were.

"Then let's proceed, Captain."

Red hissed out another tortured laugh when Piper put her lips on the head of his cock, and wished he hadn't given himself quite the pep talk he had. Now all he could think about was *her* hands tied behind her back. And no one would have to close their eyes if he blindfolded her, too.

Any amusement Red might have felt was cut off quickly, though, when Piper cupped his balls in one hand and tightly gripped the base of his shaft with the other. She slid her mouth down his length as far as she could manage, and when Red groaned softly—she sucked. She sucked him so fucking hard it made him see stars. *More* stars.

Piper took her time, using her lips and her tongue to wind him up and up, before backing off again. She was so incredibly gorgeous kneeling there, not trying to be gentle, not letting up. Red held off his climax as long as he could because he never wanted this to end.

It came barreling down his spine without warning, though, sizzling through his nervous system like an electrical current.

"Coming *now*, baby," he warned.

Red sank his fingers into Piper's silky hair to hold her still and took in a huge gulp of air. It stuck in his lungs for an interminable moment while the world stopped turning and he hovered on the edge, but seconds later, Red was growling and shuddering in release.

He cupped Piper's head in trembling hands. She pressed a shaky kiss to the inside of his thigh.

"So unbelievably beautiful," he told her again.

Piper laid her head on his leg and smiled up at him, ignoring the rough wood and grains of sand that had to be digging into her knees and shins. Red could barely believe he'd been the one to put that expression on her face.

When he could stand up without embarrassing himself, Red helped Piper to her feet, too, and led her back across the boardwalk. He brought her over to the outdoor shower outside the pool house and crouched to wash off her legs and feet.

He left the lights off inside the main house, and walked quietly beside her, straight up to his bedroom. Piper crawled into bed beside him and sounded happy when he mentioned visiting her sometime in the coming week. She reminded Red what time her train left from Penn Station the next day, and then she fell sound asleep.

They didn't talk about ex-fiancés or penchants for bondage or financial headaches at the office. In the morning, they would fly back to the city, and Red would deliver Piper to her train in plenty of time.

And all that was okay, because Red deserved this happiness, just like Piper deserved him. He could trust this astonishing thing that had dropped smack into the middle of his life, and so could Piper.

He didn't need to worry. He wouldn't worry. Red was in charge, and he was capable. Everything would happen exactly the way it was supposed to.

Nineteen

PIPER HADN'T REALIZED before now that she was quite so terrible at going down on a man. Though to be fair, she hadn't had a ton of practice—and the last time she'd tried had been three effing years ago. Come to think of it, though, Kyle wasn't exactly bowled over by her efforts, was he?

Still, Piper thought that her enthusiasm on her most recent attempt would have smoothed over any deficiencies in technique. Red had certainly seemed happy with how things went, but that was before he'd flown the coop.

Maybe that was overstating things. But he *had* said he would visit Piper that week and it was already Thursday with no sign of him. Red had texted and called her every day as he always did, but he'd made no reference whatsoever to his potential travel plans.

She'd been normal enough at first, talking herself through the most obvious explanation—that Red was simply a very busy man, working through whatever he'd missed by whisking her off to the Hamptons on Monday.

But then she'd begun to dissect whether he might be avoiding a visit because of her sudden U-turn on the spanking issue. She had enjoyed it the first time they tried. It was just that Red's mood had been so different the second time around. It had felt—still felt—like he'd been taking out his annoyance at Jim Denton on her tender derriere.

Which meant that over the last three days, Piper's brain had hashed out every possible thing she might have done to dissuade him. Clearly, she had to add social anxiety to the list of things she hadn't known about herself.

She hadn't considered that she might suck at sucking, as it were, until she'd hit the dairy aisle at the grocery store this morning. Once she did, however, it seemed to make an odd kind of sense. There'd been Red's initial reluctance to the idea, and his pensive mood after the fact.

She wished he would call her, anyhow. Then maybe Piper could ask for some tips, so she wouldn't blow it again. And, *great*, now every thought she had was apparently going to sound like a fellatio euphemism. She had to get a grip. She had to…oh. *God*.

Piper felt her face get hot and looked quickly around. Somehow, she'd ended up in the freezer section on the other side of the store, which was probably as close to a cold shower as the market was likely to provide her. She snatched a container of mango sorbet, tossed it in with the rest of her food, and powered over to the checkout lanes.

Her humiliation at being the world's only erotic romance author who could botch real-life oral sex flamed disconcertingly bright for nearly the entire drive home. She was two blocks from her driveway before her brain changed channels again, and she thought of yet another possibility for Red's evident disinterest.

Might it be because Piper hadn't wanted to tell him more about Kyle? At the time, she'd only been thinking that she didn't want her ex to intrude on such a wonderful day. Well, that and not wanting to look dumb in front of Red. Now, it occurred to her that not explaining probably made it seem like she had something to hide.

She didn't, of course. The only thing Piper had done wrong was to entrust a horse's ass with her heart. But how was Red supposed to know, if she didn't have the guts to tell him?

He'd said he'd come to see her. He hadn't. But oh, how she still wanted him to. Piper wanted to see Red's face and touch his skin, and banter back and forth with him over desserts that started life in boxes.

She sighed and slowed to make her turn. It was impossible to maintain a sense of anticipation for long—the high-alert pounding of her heart when she knew she was going to see him again had faded within forty-eight hours. Little by little, Piper had dropped her guard and let her normal life—and abnormal fears—distract her.

That was probably why it took several moments for it to dawn on her that there was another car parked in her driveway when she pulled in. A very shiny, very black…*something*. Piper was terrible with car names, but even she could tell it was fancy, and exactly the sort of thing that Red MacLellan might drive.

Her heart stuttered in her chest, and Piper gave herself a mental shake. Just because he made her feel giddy as a child sometimes, did not mean she had to act like one, too. Anxious thoughts notwithstanding, she ought to play this cool. Lord knew nothing seemed to fluster Red.

If it even was him. Which it might not be. If it wasn't, she'd be totally cool with that, too.

Piper snorted. If she felt the need to pretend like this when she was sitting alone in the silence and solitude of her own damn car, then maybe she really was off her rocker.

She meted out one small, undignified squeak of excitement. She gathered her bags, locked her car, and marched staunchly onto her porch. Once there, she stopped and eyed her front door suspiciously. Piper hitched her purse higher onto her shoulder and switched the grocery bags to her other hand.

Was Red in there right now? She'd gone out on a limb and made a copy of her key for him, something she'd never done before. Red had promptly turned around and sort-of ghosted her, acting like it was no big whoop.

Maybe Piper was remembering wrong, and he hadn't said he'd visit this week. In person, it was impossible to doubt the things he told her but after a few days away Piper began to question all kinds of things—such as her ability to recall basic information or whether she held any appeal for a man who assured her repeatedly that he was crazy about her.

God. She had to stop acting like such a nitwit.

Piper steeled herself, unlocked her own damn door, and swung it wide.

Keys. On the table in the foyer, placed neatly in the wooden bowl that usually held hers. A trim black travel bag perched stolidly at the foot of her stairs. A dark suit jacket was folded lengthwise and slung over the banister. And total silence reigned.

Piper waited on the threshold, listening for some sign of Red's presence, her heart tripping along in double-time. There wasn't a single creak or rustle or sigh to indicate he was here—nothing at all except his things.

Maybe…maybe he'd seen that she was out, dropped off his stuff, and gone out again. But, no—his keys and car were still here. Piper stepped the rest of the way inside and closed the door behind her. She was assuming it was Red. Who else could it be? Even Kyle hadn't had a key to this place.

She dropped her keys and her phone into her pocket and set her purse and groceries on the floor. She slipped off her shoes and padded across the entryway with silent steps. Piper peeked into the living room, knowing she was being ridiculous, but unnerved by the pervasive quiet anyway.

She didn't see Red at first. It was only when she inched further into the room that she had a view of the front of her couch, and him.

Her tension released her with a snap. Red was out cold, poor guy. Piper smiled and studied him unabashedly.

His tall frame stretched from end to end on the couch, his arms folded on his chest, and his long legs crossed at the ankles. His polished wingtips were angled carefully to the side, where they wouldn't get the upholstery dirty. The top button of his dress shirt was undone, his tie a little loose and his sleeves rolled to his elbows.

Even like that, Red still looked perfectly put together, freshly showered and shaved, without a single errant piece of lint anywhere to be seen. Of course, he did. No wrinkle or speck of dust would dare defile His Majesty.

Piper crept closer. Those forearms. Those wrists. Red's big, beautiful hands—what *was* it about those elegant hands? She found them totally irresistible. She loved that she knew how sensitive the skin on his arms was—from wrist to elbow to shoulder, Piper could touch Red there and make this big, strong man tremble.

She watched his face and chest, but he was so still, dead asleep while he waited for her. He must have been exhausted—she hadn't been gone long enough for him to have waited more than a half hour or so.

Piper tried to stay quiet—she'd always hated to wake someone that was sleeping so soundly. But she couldn't quite keep her hands off Red, either. Where he was concerned, Piper was weak.

She stood right next to the couch—right next to him. Reaching out, she touched her fingertips lightly to his hand, then ran them up his forearm. Red, who spoiled her lavishly and routinely said things too good to be true, was warm and soft and didn't budge. She hadn't felt attraction like this in so many years. Maybe ever.

Piper turned aside, however. She had groceries to put away, and Red obviously needed to rest. But just like that, she was dragged back and landing on top of him. There was no time to gasp, much less scream—but Piper felt both those things stuck in her throat when she blinked down at him.

Red gripped her waist and held her tightly against his belly. Grinning up at her, he winked and asked, "Miss me?"

Cheeky bastard. Piper managed a nod, and he lifted her hand from his shoulder, kissed it, then pulled her head down so he could kiss her mouth. He held his lips still against hers and lingered a long moment, savoring her.

And then Red kissed her for real. Hot, hard, hungry—his mouth opened under hers as if she'd missed the beginning and had been dropped smack into the middle of some very salty proceedings.

She'd have to remember the way this felt. Piper could definitely use this in a book. In every book. If she could recreate this sensation somehow, her fans would go wild for it.

"I really like having the key to your place," Red said eventually. He murmured against her mouth, "Why does it feel so illicit?"

"I have no idea. Maybe because you didn't *warn me* you were coming?"

"I thought it would be fun to surprise you. But I took the 5 a.m. shuttle to get to an eight o'clock meeting in D.C. and it must have caught up with me. Sorry." Red yawned and stretched beneath her. "I almost waited for you upstairs, but I didn't want to scare you."

Piper felt her cheeks flush.

He touched one with his fingertips. "Damn. I scared you anyway, didn't I?"

"Only a little. I saw your stuff, but it was creepy-quiet in here, and I didn't spot you right away."

Piper rolled against the cushions, cuddling up along Red's side. His arms wrapped around her, and he let out a contented groan.

Her feet encountered a large purring blob of fur near Red's ankles, and it growled when she nudged it. Piper should have known—Fredo had already staked his claim and wasn't about to be ejected by the likes of her.

At Red's chuckle, she rolled her eyes. "I see you've met Fredo," she said.

Red raised his head and smiled down at the sneaky gray beast. "I knew it was you, didn't I, buddy?"

Fredo squinted, then flopped over to look at them upside-down.

"He actually let you pet him?"

"No, I just wanted to say the line. He must have gotten comfortable once I was asleep." Red kissed her on the temple. "But there are two, right? I haven't seen the other one."

Piper glanced around the room, then smirked and pointed toward the stairs. She could just make out a black ear and some whiskers, where the other cat peeked between the stair rails at them.

"There," she pointed.

Red called, "Here, kitty kitty," and burst out laughing when they heard Sonny take off up the stairs. The sudden sound scared Fredo, who instantly leaped up and over the arm of the couch before disappearing, too.

"At last, I have you alone," Red drawled in a campy Dracula voice. He bent his head to nuzzle her neck.

"I didn't think you were coming," Piper admitted softly.

He reared back to look into her face. "I said I would."

"I know, but when I tried to pin you down, you either avoided the question or said you didn't know. It seemed like maybe you'd changed your mind."

"I'm sorry," Red said. "It was a crazy week and I wanted to surprise you. I didn't think about how it might look from your end."

"Oh."

"You didn't believe me, did you?"

Piper objected, "Sure I did."

Red studied her face, then shook his head. "I don't think that's actually true."

Piper shrugged and moved to get off the couch, but he held her in place along his side.

"I told you that you could trust me, Piper. I wasn't just saying that to fill the time, you know."

"Just because people tell you something," she said, swinging her legs over his lap so she could get to her feet, "Doesn't make it true. If you want me to trust you so badly, then earn it."

"Man, that ex-fiancé did a number on you, didn't he?" But then Red grinned, not intimidated in the least. "No biggie. Challenge accepted," he said. And then he yawned so widely she could hear his jaw crack.

"God, what time did you have to get up this morning?"

"I don't know. Three-something? I think. Everything is sort of hazy before about 7:45."

Piper laughed. "Why don't you go up and crawl into bed for another couple of hours? I have to put away my groceries, but I'll still be here when you wake up. I promise."

Red shook his head and sat up. "No way." He shoved himself off the cushion, then clapped his hands briskly once he was upright. "I must've sacked out for thirty or forty minutes. I'm totally good to go now."

He tried to stifle his next yawn. When that didn't work, Red reached up to scratch his neck and attempted to hide his gaping mouth against his sleeve. Piper raised her eyebrows at him.

He said, "You know what? I will definitely be good as new once I shower and change into casual clothes."

"While you do that, I'll brew some coffee," she told him. "And maybe I'll even make the box of tapioca I just bought at the store."

Red caught her in his arms and squeezed her tight. "See? You *did* think I was coming."

"I like to be prepared," Piper said. "You never know."

There was a sudden commotion in her front hall that sounded an awful lot like the cats had found the grocery bags. Piper shooed Red away and went to save her food.

Cats vs. Bags, however, turned out to have nothing on the destruction she found in her kitchen. It seemed that her surprise visitor had not come empty-handed—there was a big bouquet of hot-pink roses in a vase on her counter.

Red could not have known about the long-standing blood-feud between Sonny and Fredo and anything botanical, however. The evidence was everywhere. There were shreds of leaves strewn across the counter and floor, edges nibbled off several blooms, and at least three puddles of shockingly pink vomit on the tile.

Piper sighed, grabbed the paper towels, and rushed to clean up as much of the mess as possible before Red returned.

HE WAS A shockingly fast bather, sauntering into her kitchen with damp hair and flushed cheeks before the pot of coffee had even finished brewing. The scent of his soap mixed quite nicely with the sugary smell of the pudding Piper was stirring on the stove, and her brain tumbled headlong into a dirty cavalcade of images involving Red, a bath, and tapioca.

She cleared her throat. Red looked up from the ragged rose he was touching.

"Feeling better?" she asked.

"Much. And I also didn't spot any water on the floor up there. Did you get that plumber out already?"

"Yup, he came out yesterday. He said the valve under the sink was cracked, so he replaced it."

Red nodded. "Good. Good," he said. "What about the pipes?"

"Status unchanged," Piper responded. "How about some coffee?"

He accepted both the mug and the change in topic with good grace, then sank into a chair and looked around cheerfully. Red fit so perfectly there, which was strange considering what a recent addition to her life he was.

"How long can you stay?" Piper wondered.

"Until Sunday—I have a few things early Monday that I have to get back for."

"Damn, I was going to call you in sick and fly you to Florida on my private jet that day," she sulked, snapping her fingers. "Oh well. Maybe next time."

Twenty

M ONDAY MORNING, RED was back at his desk and fresh off a conference call with some of the biotech managers when Rob stuck his head in and begged for another meeting.

Trident's point man looked positively gray when he intoned, "We…have a bit of a problem."

Red sighed. His post-Piper high had lasted less than twenty-four hours, and he had no idea how soon he would be able to see her again. "Rob, why do you always say that?"

"Because that's what you pay me the big bucks for?"

"Right. And we've had some version of this conversation, what—ten or twenty times now?"

"Give or take."

"Okay, so why does the look on your face make me happy I'm sitting down right now?" Red wondered.

"This is an emergency. You remember that conversation we had a while ago?" After a loaded pause, he added, "About those diverted Trident funds?"

"How could I forget?" The problem had been simmering at the back of Red's brain, making him antsy while he waited for the other shoe to drop. He hadn't followed up with Rob yet because he'd wanted to give the man and his team time to do their damn jobs.

But Red had also been distracted, chasing like a rutting deer after the first intriguing woman he'd met in an eternity. If he'd been in his right mind, he would've comprehended that this little headache wouldn't stay quiet for long.

"Well, I have some more information for you." Rob slid a chart across Red's desk and pointed. "See here?"

Red's stomach dropped. "They were stealing royalties?"

"Yeah. That's putting it mildly." He shuffled some papers and place a second paper on top of the first.

Red stared down at the numbers in front of him. Too many numbers. Attached to one very inconvenient name.

"From Miss Corelli," he stated, though the words tasted like gravel on his tongue.

Rob nodded. "I mean, who else were the Dentons going to steal from? She's the only one who was making them any real money."

"*Fuck.*" Red massaged his forehead. This could not be happening. This. Could not. Be. Happening.

Rob started babbling, "Right? We have to tell her. How are we going to tell her? Maybe we shouldn't. *Shit*, no. What am I saying? That's crazy pants. Of course, we have to."

"Get a grip," Red said, needing to shut the man up so he could goddamn *think*. "Obviously we are going to tell her. But…"

He flexed his fingers, then drummed them on those disastrous charts. He shifted in his chair and blinked. Red tried out every nervous tic known to man, attempting to puzzle out how the hell he could fix this clusterfuck without ruining his chances with the one woman he was over the moon for.

Rob waited, looking peaked.

"Okay. We do have to tell her," Red said, feeling his way forward. "But have your people keep this under wraps for just a little bit, until I can figure out if I can line up a few new investors to get us past the worst of it. When we do go to Corelli, I want to make sure we have a game plan in place for how she's going to get her money back."

"Red, this goes back years," Rob said darkly. "It's a lot of freaking cash."

"I fucking know that, Robert."

"Keeping it from her is a bad idea. We could be opening ourselves up to litigation."

"Also aware of that."

"And you still think this is a good idea?"

He wasn't sure at all. But what other choice did Red have? He could not bring this to Piper without having a no-fail strategy to offer her as well. God *damn* it.

"*No one* finds out about this. You hear me?" Red said. "This whole thing is on fucking lockdown as of right the fuck now."

"I'll do my best."

Red had never threatened an employee in all his years at PKM, but he was sorely tempted to do it now. Instead, he muttered, "I know you will. Don't let me down."

Red's Abysmally Long day finally dragged into night, but it wasn't the early autumn darkness blanketing the city outside his office windows that eventually drove him toward home. It was his bone-deep exhaustion.

On his way down to the lobby, he stopped the elevator at Rob's floor and wasn't the least bit surprised to find all the lights on and most of the team still hunched over their desks.

He sent them all home, too.

Downstairs, he pushed his way out of the revolving door fronting PKM's main lobby but stalled once he hit the sidewalk. Rush hour was over, the pretzel vendor who usually worked that part of the block was long gone, and the usual throng of weekday commuters had dispersed.

Red stood there, warming his hands in his pockets and trying to decide what to do. He'd forgotten to send for his car and didn't want to mess with hailing a cab. Instead, Red turned north and hoofed it up Broadway, his steps decimating block after block while his brain circled through the same excruciating loop it'd been in all day.

Eventually, he came to the Canal Street station, so he trotted down the steps and climbed aboard the next train heading toward home. For once, Red was happy Piper didn't live here in the city. If she had, he'd almost certainly end up on her doorstep, and that would be a *bad* plan.

He had no idea how he was going to keep this secret from her, but the idea of telling her without having a ready solution to ease her mind seemed like an even worse proposition. Piper had enough to worry about with the leaking pipes at her house and the new series being drafted. This was one thing Red could take off her plate. A nuisance he could spare her.

It was a totally logical assessment of the situation, so it begged the question—why did it still feel so fucking horrible? Red marinated in that uncomfortable feeling for what felt like an infinity, one more New Yorker in a sea of them, slouched on the subway while it screeched through the tunnels at the end of the day.

Once he hit Chelsea, Red got off the train and walked the last three blocks to his building. His loft was too quiet and too full of ugly things that he could no longer ignore. Now, Red despised every garish thing in the place—and there was a whole hell of a lot of them.

He grabbed a beer from the fridge, dropped onto the stupid couch, and groaned. He had Piper to thank for his sudden disaffection with his own home.

Inside his jacket, his cell started ringing, and he groaned again. He wanted it to be Piper, wanted to hear her sweet voice, wanted to tease her and be comforted by her. Red wasn't sure he could do it, though, not right now.

Right before the call shuttled over into voicemail, he regretted his cowardice and fumbled the phone out—but it wasn't her. Instead, it was Luca, and he hung up before Red could answer.

Between the New York/Rome time difference and Luca's crazy hours at the hospital where he worked, Red didn't get to talk to his old friend as much as he'd like to. However, if there was ever a time when he could use the man's sage advice, it was now. Red dialed him back and breathed a sigh of relief when Luca answered on the first ring.

"Screening my calls now, *bastardo?*"

Red said, "Find a quiet corner. I'm in a shitload of trouble and I need help."

His friend griped, "What else is new? This is why I call. Someone has to save you from yourself, and we both know it won't be Tate."

AN HOUR LATER, Red sighed and checked his watch again. The six-hour time difference between his home and Luca's was an annoyance, but occasionally it came in handy—as it had tonight, when Red was up too late, and his buddy was clearly up too early.

"Maybe I should just tell Piper now and get it over with," he said again. "Like ripping off a bandage." He eyed the two empty beer bottles lined up on the coffee table in front of him, twins to the one in his hand, and wondered how they had multiplied so fast.

Luca made a considering sound, as if Red had spoken those words for the first time and had not been crying on his figurative shoulder for the last sixty minutes. "What would be the harm?"

"I suppose…" Red scrubbed a hand over his face, indescribably exhausted. "Because we've got something good going right now. Something I didn't think I'd ever find. I don't want to ruin it with some stupid knee-jerk reaction."

"Honesty is usually not what ruins love. Lack of honesty, however…" Red could almost hear his friend's casual Italian shrug through the phone line.

"That may be true, but Piper is pretty gun-shy. I'm trying to prove to her that she can count on me—that she can trust me. If I tell her what's happening and then have to admit that I don't know what to do about it, it's going to make me look really bad."

Luca was silent for several beats. Red could hear car horns and the occasional burst of rapid-fire Italian, and then a rush of quiet.

"Hello?"

"You're worried about how you'll look? That seems like the least of your problems."

"Besides," Red reasoned, shifting gears, "Who said anything about love, anyway?"

Luca's deep chuckle rumbled over the line. "My father often says something about exactly this problem."

"About owing your new girlfriend money? Something you need to tell me, bro?"

"No, *idiota*. About delivering bad news to your woman."

"This from the man who was raised in a miniscule one-horse village?"

"I beg your pardon, Your Highness. You seemed to enjoy my hometown just fine when I took you there."

"The entire tour you gave me took five fucking minutes."

"Besides, I'll have you know that they've acquired two more horses and at least five mules since your last visit."

"A virtual metropolis. How old was your dad when he finally left it?"

"He worked in *Roma* as a young man, before he and my mother opened the Tivoli office. But that is not what is important."

"Okay, so tell me. What's important?"

"The fact that my parents have been married to each other for forty years. *Non essere stupido*—don't be stupid. Have you been getting enough rest?"

Red decided to ignore most of that and focused only on the relevant part. "You make an excellent point. Carry on."

"*Sì*, so Papa always told me that, most of the time, the bitter pill goes down better with a little sweetness on top. A man shields his wife from life's ugliness when it is possible, and when it is not possible, he delivers the dose of medicine with a better-tasting flavor after. Papa says this saves much *agitazione* for everyone."

"That sounds very practical, and also suspiciously prescriptive. Are you sure that isn't your own advice, Doc?"

"My father was always very clever about tailoring his wisdom to the mind of each of his children. How do you think I ended up becoming a doctor? You should have heard the things he told poor Paolo."

Red paused, considering that. "Isn't your brother a chef?"

"Indeed. Suffice it to say, none of us were able to look at eggplants—or even knives—in quite the same way, once Paolo hit puberty."

"*Jesus.*" Red winced and tried to expunge that from his brain. "Anyway, is your dad aware that you don't currently *have* a wife?"

"He likes to plan ahead, and I cannot argue with his results. His body of research is very persuasive. As for you, I am wondering if your current mood can be explained by dehydration. You should be drinking more water than whiskey, *amico.* You'll feel better and think much more clearly."

Red sighed. "Can you please stop trying to mother me, Luc?"

"Someone has to. Lord knows your own mother doesn't get it right."

"You keep saying that. But, listen—do we agree that I should definitely hold off on telling Piper about the money right away? Once I have an actual plan in place, then I can spill the beans. Sound about right?"

"Beans?" Luca asked distractedly.

In the background, Red could hear the sounds of the bustling hospital where his friend worked and knew at once he'd used up his brief allotment of the good doctor's time. As usual, he'd wasted most of it busting the man's balls, instead of being polite and asking after his family or some shit. It figured.

"Spill the beans," he explained irritably. "Tell the secret. You remember."

"Ah. Yes."

"Seriously, Luc. It's been too long. When can I get you here for a visit?"

"It's funny that you say that. I met an American woman here last summer. We…"

Luca's words cut off, and he erupted in a flurry of Italian too fast for Red to follow. Red listened to the man's commanding tone and knew some crisis or other required the capable skills of the unflappable Dr. Delledonna.

Luca's voice switched back into English abruptly. "I have to go. Remember what we always said, *mio fratello*. *L'amore domina senza regole*. I'll call in a few days." The line went dead.

All's fair in love and war. Red ought to have known Luca would throw that one back in his face. How many times had Red cheerfully tossed that phrase at Luca or Tate when they'd been lamenting some girl or another? Red hadn't lamented a single soul—back then or more recently—but he supposed there was a first goddamn time for everything.

He texted Piper a quick goodnight, left the empty soldiers where they stood—in a soggy, ragged line on the coffee table—and trudged upstairs. He dropped his clothes in a heap on the floor and went into the bathroom to brush his teeth and guzzle a few cups of water. Then Red crawled into bed. Hydrate and rest—doctor's orders.

Tomorrow, things would look better. Tomorrow, he'd figure out what to do.

Twenty-One

G OD, I WANT you right now." Red's gravelly voice filtered through the phone. Piper pressed it tighter to her ear, so she wouldn't miss a single syllable.

Happily, she was already in bed. Now she leaned over to switch off her bedside lamp, so she could focus completely on the seductive spell Red was weaving around her.

"I wake up hard for you, too," he continued. "Every morning, I've got a telephone pole under my sheets."

Piper laughed at his hyperbole. "Really. Well, that sounds like quite a problem. How's a guy supposed to handle that?" Given how her heart was hammering, it was a wonder her voice came out sounding so even. Red had to know how he affected her, though. He always knew.

"Today, I tried ignoring it. Wishful thinking, hoping it would go away by itself," he mused darkly.

"Didn't work out for you, huh."

"Nope. Not at all. I was tragically unproductive all day."

"I see. And now?"

"I took steps." Red cleared his throat meaningfully, but he didn't need to elaborate. Piper could picture his solution just fine, thank you. He waited for her to answer, but it was a comfortable quiet—expectant maybe, but not impatient.

"It's the same for me, too, you know," she whispered tentatively. "The wanting, I mean. In the morning, but especially at night."

"Oh really?" he inquired. "And do you touch yourself, Piper? Do you get yourself off while you think about me?"

She should've known he wouldn't let her off the hook. Piper paused, then confessed quietly, "It does seem to be the most efficient solution."

"Tell me" he commanded, sinking into bossiness as easily as he breathed.

"Uh," she hedged. Piper stalled, not sure what to say next.

Red had a distinct knack for luring her out on the ledge, right out to the threshold of her comfort zone, where she had to decide in an instant whether to cower or fly. Piper knew too well how it felt to cower, though. With Red, she wanted to fly—to soar—in real life, and not just on paper.

"Do you touch your beautiful breasts like I would? Or are you already hot and slick just from thinking about us?" Red's voice was deep and husky, and so unbelievably sexy. It was like he was really there with her, whispering filthy things in her ear and winding her up. "Do you imagine it's me when you come apart, Piper?"

There was only one thing to say to that. "Yes."

The line went silent again, but she knew Red was still with her. She could *feel* him breathing, feel the heat brushing over her skin.

Suddenly, he blurted out, "Come see me. Tomorrow. I'll arrange a flight for you. You can stay here for a couple of nights, and then I'll take you back home on Saturday. I'll stay the weekend there with you again."

Piper processed that for a beat. She asked, "Seriously?" But a lightning-quick review of the rest of her week told her what she already knew—she had absolutely nothing going on but the writing, and lately she could do that anywhere.

As long as it was quiet enough, the words flowed, and Piper's work got done. There was a lot to be said for feeling inspired.

Writer's block was a vague and distant memory with Red MacLellan in her life.

He demanded, "When am I ever *not* serious?"

"Never?"

"Right. I would come there first, but I have a few meetings here tomorrow and Friday that I can't blow off. If you can make it, we'll still have the afternoons and the evenings, together though. And the mornings, of course," he emphasized mildly.

He was hard to refuse. So hard. Piper caved like a house of cards. "All right," she said. "You win. What do I have to do?"

Red exhaled loudly, and it sounded an awful lot like relief. "I'll text you the particulars, but...let's have a car pick you up tomorrow morning to bring you to the airport. Felix can pick you up on my end and bring you back to the loft. Just make yourself at home, and I'll meet you as soon as I can swing it."

"Sounds like you have it all figured out," Piper laughed.

"I always do," Red assured her. "Now go to sleep. You have a big day tomorrow."

Piper grinned from ear to ear in the darkness. "Can't wait," she told him.

THE TEXTS BEGAN rolling in about half an hour later. Piper, too excited to sleep, was still clutching her phone, planning what to bring. But once the travel particulars were dispensed with, Red ended on a weirdly formal note.

Please be prepared to dine out Friday night. Attire is dressy casual.

She couldn't resist teasing him. *What the heck does that mean? Is it dressy or is it casual?*

As expected, Red was quick on the uptake. He sent her a scowling emoji and a huffy retort that made her grin. *It's BOTH you hayseed. Pretend it's date nite!!*

Piper gave up on sleep and turned her light back on. She typed out, **Why pretend?** then went to her closet to pull out her travel bag. The thing was getting more action than it had in years.

Christ, woman. For once, just do as I ask.

Piper raised an eyebrow at the glowing screen, even though Red couldn't see her. **NEVER,** she wrote, then tossed the phone aside and started packing.

TRUE TO HIS word, Red didn't meet Piper at the airport the next day. His driver was right on time, though, waiting in baggage claim with a printed-out sign, an armful of fragrant yellow and orange roses, and a scrawled card from Red that said simply, "Welcome Back."

Felix offered to drive Piper wherever she wanted, but she figured she'd save the sightseeing for another time. They went straight back to Red's loft instead, where Felix parallel-parked at the curb so he could walk Piper inside with her bags.

This visit was one hundred percent personal, so Red hadn't bothered with a hotel room this time. She was unlikely to ever see the inside of one—what was the point?

Piper texted Red to let him know that she'd arrived, and he quickly replied that someone was waiting for her. She hoped to hell it wasn't going to be his mother.

Instead, a brisk older woman ushered her inside the second Piper stepped off the elevator.

"Oh, good. Mr. MacLellan let me know you were here. I'm Mrs. Markham, the housekeeper. You must be Piper."

"I am," she agreed. The woman wrested Piper's bags from her and hauled them toward the stairs.

"Was your trip all right?"

"Yes, thank you." Piper glanced around, hoping to see Red emerge from around some corner of the vast space.

"Mr. MacLellan asked me to extend his apologies for not meeting you himself. He was detained at the office but promises to be home in time for dinner. He asked me to tell you to make yourself at home."

"Oh. Okay." Piper felt like a homecoming queen, standing there holding her flowers while Mrs. Markham looked her over.

"I'll bring your things upstairs and then I'll be out of your hair," the woman said. "Also, I left some snacks and lunch things in the kitchen for you, if you're hungry."

"I'm okay for right now but thank you."

While the other woman disappeared up the winding staircase, Piper wandered around. It felt less intrusive to study Red's home without him there to gauge her reactions.

The open kitchen was exceptionally modern, all blocky angles of chrome and matte black. She set her flowers on the counter and kept moving. The main room still contained the same pretentious assortment of modern art and space-age furniture, but the small hallway opposite the stairs was somewhere Piper had never ventured before.

She followed it, discovering a home office first. Piper stepped in, her curiosity pricked by the dramatic change in decorating style. She was surrounded by dark paneling and built-in bookshelves, a large leather couch and chairs, and a heavy mahogany desk near the soaring factory window. The entire effect was masculine in the extreme, like a hundred-year-old men's club filled with cigars and scotch.

There wasn't a single piece of frippery to be seen, and it was so sophisticated it was almost exotic compared to the common rooms of the loft. It was a place where anything feminine would stick out like a sore thumb, Piper reflected.

She tiptoed lightly across the rug and peered out the window at the city beyond. Through the buildings, Piper could just catch the reflection of the midday sun hitting the surface of the Hudson River.

"It suits him, doesn't it?" Mrs. Markham said. "More than out there, anyway."

Piper spun around to find the housekeeper smiling at her from the doorway. "It really does," she agreed.

"Did you need anything else before I leave?"

"No, I'm fine. Thank you so much for letting me in."

"My pleasure. Enjoy your visit." And, with another friendly smile, the woman departed.

Piper sat in the leather desk chair and pictured Red working at his laptop. Then she imagined, in vivid, throbbing detail, climbing into his lap and distracting him.

She shot up, feeling a little guilty, and glanced at the clock on his desk. Red might not be home for hours. She needed to find something productive to take her mind off him before she embarrassed herself.

Mrs. Markham had already laid out Piper's things in Red's bedroom. She'd also put the flowers in an odd ceramic vase on the kitchen counter.

Piper munched on some carrot sticks she found in the fridge, smiled at the towering stack of dessert mixes she saw in the pantry and wondered a bit at the pile of beer bottles in Red's recycling bin. She took another lap around the living room.

Eventually, she split the difference. Piper grabbed her notebook and her computer from her luggage upstairs and set up camp on the big leather couch in the study. If certain scorching-hot traits of one tall, auburn-haired stud muffin made it into her new book, well…who would be the wiser? Inspiration came in many forms, and some of them happened to be very good in the sack.

IT WAS WELL after dark when Red finally came home. Piper had relocated to the kitchen by then, where she was nursing a cup of tea and trying to decide if she should make one of the boxes of pudding for dessert. He set a big paper bag full of Indian take-out on the counter, then bent Piper over his arm in a kiss straight out of the movies.

Once he let her up for air, Red told her, "Man, am I happy to see you."

"I thought you'd never get here," Piper smiled. "Long day?"

"Very. But let's not talk about that. What'd you do?"

"I worked for a while. Watched a movie. Oh, and I found the game room! I wish you'd shown it to me sooner. I love pool—do you want to play while we eat?"

"I absolutely do," he said. "Let me run upstairs and get out of this suit, and then you're on."

In the game room, black-and-white portraits marched in a straight line across the walls, an eye-catching gallery of interesting faces. While she waited for Red, Piper examined them more closely, until it dawned on her what she was seeing.

"These are all authors," she exclaimed when he returned. "Aren't they? That's the requisite Ernest Hemingway and Dorothy Parker, I know. Is that Orwell?"

"Yes. And Kerouac there. Then Maya Angelou, Harper Lee, and Flannery O'Connor. And Tolkien over in the corner."

"This is quite a collection. All people you like to read?"

"Of course." Red set the two laden plates he was holding on a bar table against the wall. "You're surprised?"

Piper nodded.

He grinned back. "I'm a publisher, Piper. What did you expect?" He ducked out for a minute, then returned with two beers and a few napkins.

"No, you're a businessman who recently added a publishing house to his portfolio. That's a little different." Piper accepted the beer he offered her, clinked her bottle against his, and took a long sip.

"And why would I do that, if I didn't love reading?"

"Because it was a savvy financial decision?"

"I hate to break it you, but—your career aside—there isn't a ton of money to be made in traditional publishing anymore." Suddenly, Red's smile seemed a little forced. He looked away and busied himself with gathering the billiard balls and racking them.

"Don't tell me you have buyer's remorse already?" Piper asked. She tried to keep the quaver from her voice, she really did—but his expression was scaring her.

Red must have heard, though. He dropped what he was doing and came toward her immediately, taking Piper's face in his large, gentle hands and staring right into her eyes.

"If I'd never bought Trident, I would never have met you," he said softly. "I'll never regret that. Not for one minute."

LATER, THEY SAT propped in his bed, watching TV in the dark. Neither was quite ready for sleep. With his right hand, Red wielded the television remote, idly flipping through channels. His left hand rested possessively on Piper's thigh but didn't wander. He seemed content, for the moment, just to be together.

She leaned against Red's shoulder, thinking about how even a few days away already seemed like a long time. Piper thought it was strange that she hadn't considered herself particularly deprived or lonely before she met Red. Now, Piper missed little moments like this when she was home.

She wondered, painfully, if Red did, too. Even though she knew she ought to, she couldn't quite keep that thought to herself.

"Red?"

"Hm?" he murmured.

"Do you ever think about me when we're apart?"

He snorted and tossed the remote aside. "Uh, yeah," he laughed. "I think that's fair to say."

"Was that a funny thing to ask?"

An old movie flickered on the television, the dashing couple twirling and dancing their way around an opulent living room, smiling placidly as they leaped over ottomans and skirted end tables.

"Oh, I don't know. Could be. I wake up horny and wishing for you, when I fall asleep I dream about doing filthy things with you, and I probably spend fifty percent of my lunch hours jacking off in my office bathroom, because I can't stop picturing you there with me."

"Ah," Piper smiled. Red was taking her dumb question in stride, instead of getting weirded-out by her sudden bout of clingy insecurity. "I get it. This is purely a physical deprivation problem for you."

"Hardly," he scoffed. "I also spend the intervening hours obsessing about where you are, what you're doing, who you're seeing, what you're wearing, what you're eating, what you're thinking, and what you're feeling."

"I…see." He appeared to be completely serious.

"Oh, I doubt that you do. I've got it bad for you, Piper Mae." And then Red rolled to the side, flattened her beneath him, and began licking her neck.

"Me, too. For you." She giggled when he tickled the sensitive underside of her chin with his tongue. It was probably better not to think about how or when she'd become a chronic giggler.

"For this?" Red asked, sliding his hand up to cover her breast, grazing her nipple lightly through her t-shirt with his palm.

Piper dug the remote out from under her hip and tossed it toward the nightstand. Red's nimble fingers found their way up the inside of her thigh, and then between her legs.

"Or maybe you've got it bad for this," he growled in her ear. His lips were hot and soft against her skin and made her tremble with each teasing breath that escaped them.

"All of that," Piper admitted, turning his head so she could kiss him full on the mouth. Against his lips, she confessed, "But really all of you."

Twenty-Two

R ED HUNG UP the phone and propped his elbows on his desk. He tried to massage away the tension taking root at the base of his skull.

Fuck 'taking root.' The stress was branching out like one of the great goddamn elms in Central Park, twisting and spreading and casting its damning shadow across his day. Even so, Red rolled his shoulders and steeled himself for one more phone call.

He'd been at it for hours, but lining up new investors to paper over the royalty issue they'd uncovered at Trident was turning out to be unexpectedly difficult.

It wasn't like he kept a whole fleet full of destroyers in the water, ready and willing to vanquish any cash-flow problems that came his way—not book-related problems, anyway.

No, the investors Red usually worked with saved their bachelorette-at-a-strip-club routines for the boats and the biotech projects. He couldn't fathom why the booze and the books should be any different, but they were.

Any smile that might have threatened at the memory of Piper's apt assonance regarding PKM's main business lines—Christ, now Red was beginning to sound like her—was squelched by the thought that came on its heels.

His usual roster of donors was proving to be a dead end. They'd spent the last few hours telling him in great detail about his foolishness, recklessness, and vanity.

The thing was, Red's wrists were cuffed on this one, and not in a good way. The feelers he'd put out across the industry months ago were now bearing fruit at the most inconvenient time. No way was Red going to let the opportunity pass him—or Trident—by, though.

When the biggest, most well-known chain of bookstores in the country finally came calling, you answered the hell out of that phone. But, if Red was going to successfully woo Millhouse & Rock into bed with PKM, then…well, suffice it say, the crap currently brewing at Trident needed to stay under wraps.

Which meant Red had been knocking on doors all morning, hamstrung. He couldn't explain why he needed more money, or the gossip would start making the rounds and Trident's woes would become common knowledge.

And he couldn't sweeten the pot by dangling the bookstore deal in front of people, in case the assholes at M&R decided to pull the plug at the last minute. They were like tentative, crotchety old ladies, and they'd developed a real fondness for playing him like a marionette.

Even more unpleasant than any of that was something Red ought to have anticipated beforehand—books and reading simply weren't cool enough for the popular kids.

Patrons of the symphony or the ballet could expect to have their names plastered on signs and printed in programs where many people see it. They could swan around on opening night, receiving the accolades of their friends, secure in the social glory that came with supporting the performing arts.

Books, though, were essentially a solitary endeavor. You read them alone and expounding on them too much at parties tended to make you sound like a pretentious bore. And, there were no goddamn opening nights at which to see and be seen, and to get your photo in the paper the next day.

Red groaned and swiveled his chair around to stare out the window at the buildings marching down Pearl Street. He was obviously going about this all wrong. He needed a new plan of attack.

He could try to make Trident more appealing to the usual artsy crowd. Throw galas for book launches and set up exclusive per-plate dinners to meet authors and hear readings. Except Red hated to embark on things he wasn't confident he could succeed at, and it would take time to change perceptions—time he did not have.

And forget about what the business and investing worlds were going to say if they discovered the straits that Trident was in. If Piper found out before Red was ready—if she found out from anyone but him—then Red's life was going to suck balls even worse than it had before.

So, if slapping some lipstick on this pig and hoping to market it to the usual buyers wasn't going to work…then maybe Red needed to bring in a fresh set of eyes.

Wayne buzzed in.

"What's up?"

"Your mother is on line three," his assistant said.

Red groaned. It was so not the time. She'd undoubtedly have some luncheon she wanted him to fund, or a tea, or a lecture, or God only knew what.

Wayne asked, "Want me to tell her you're busy?"

Fresh eyes. Red had to find new, different investors to dangle Trident in front of. And as loathe as he was to admit it, Gina MacLellan might just be the person he needed most right now.

He'd never met a more socially-connected person in his life. His mother genuinely knew every single person who had cash to burn in this entire city. If there were any doddering old widows or reclusive matrons left who might get off on being patrons to authors, then Red's mom could find them.

He focused, allowing himself a flare of optimism.

"No," he told Wayne. "Put her through. I'll talk to her."

Line three began ringing. Red took a deep breath and answered.

"Ah, Red darling. How kind of you to take my call." As intended, the sarcasm was hard to miss.

"Mom, it's been a long day. Could you not, please?"

"All right, fine. Then maybe you can shed some light on something."

"What's that?"

"You father and I stopped at that club of yours last night after the opera, hoping for a nightcap. And while we were there, your security man said the strangest thing."

"You mean Terry?"

"Perhaps. We don't go there often since you keep the music so loud. I can never really keep the men straight."

Red rolled his eyes. "Well, what did the mystery man say?"

"He told us you'd been there recently with a woman."

"Could be." Red felt a frisson of concern. He'd taken exactly one woman to his club recently, and Piper was not someone he wanted in his mother's crosshairs, particularly after that impromptu run-in they'd had.

"Must you always be so terse?" she snipped. "Anyway, when he described her to us, it sounded an awful lot like that person I met at your house a few weeks ago. The timing is right, too."

No use denying it now, he supposed. "What's your point?"

"Padraig, you're not pursuing a relationship with that woman, are you? She's incredibly inappropriate."

"How would you know? Besides, I don't think my personal life is any of your business." Red *liked* Piper when she was inappropriate. The more inappropriate the better, as a matter of fact.

"Which is it, darling? Personal or business?"

Painfully, it was both. But his mother was the very last person with whom he wanted to delve into the complexities of his new relationship. The longer Red could keep the two women apart, the better his life would be.

"Forget about that," he said. Time for some deflection. "I have a project for you."

There was a loaded pause, while his mother decided whether she would let him divert her or not. Finally, she took the bait, as he'd known she would. The woman absolutely thrived on being useful to him, even if her results were hit-or-miss.

"Oh really? Do tell." she purred.

AND GINA MACLELLAN had come through for him in a big way. Red had expected her to toss off a potential name or two. From there, he'd have followed the cobweb of connections, in an effort to find others.

Instead, his mother had produced five individuals with deep pockets and a decided interest in the less-flashy arts. Fuck if Red knew where she'd unearthed them.

She'd even engineered five low-key introductions, and though Red had drunk more tea and perched on more uncomfortable divans in the last two days than any grown man should have to do—it had mostly accomplished the job.

Now, if he was very careful and very fucking lucky, they might have a chance.

Trident had a chance.

And that meant, if the gods of love and war were kind, Red might actually get to keep Piper Mae Fulham.

HE HADN'T BEEN able to hold out long without her. Within a day of his unsatisfying conversation with Luca, Red found his balls and could act reasonably normally with Piper on the phone. And the day after his talk with his mom, he'd practically been begging Piper to visit him again.

Thank fuck for his own deep pockets. Red had no idea how most people conducted long distance relationships successfully, given how many planes and trains were involved. And while the phone sex thing certainly had its appeal, it was utter shit as a replacement for the real thing.

Red was hooked on Piper, through and through, and that meant he wanted eyes and hands on her as much as humanly possible.

However, when he'd had the impulsive idea to drag Piper back up to New York so soon, he'd hadn't realized quite how efficiently his mother would be working her connections. On that score, Friday had dawned with both good news and bad.

In the pro column was the fact that he'd convinced Piper to stay on through the weekend, as well as the news that his mom had uncovered yet another promising name for him.

In the cons? That would be the part where his mother, completely oblivious to Piper's presence in town, had finagled Red an invite to a private dinner she was attending that evening— a dinner his potential investor was also attending.

A dinner that was occurring at the exact time Red was supposed to be going out with Piper. Hell, she hadn't even been ensconced in his loft for a full day before Red had to cancel their date, and he couldn't even tell her why it was so goddamn important that he do it.

He also couldn't bring Piper along, not when his own attendance was so spur-of-the-moment. Trying to arrange for a plus-one would've been like broadcasting his connection to Piper with a virtual bullhorn. In no time, inquiring minds would've then made the connection to Antoinette Corelli and Trident, and that was an outcome Red could not risk yet.

Only something as critical as scrounging up more cash for Trident could have dragged him away from his precious few days with Piper. Red had hated to leave, and found himself thinking about Piper, sweet and warm in his home—and in his bed— throughout the evening.

Could he have brought Piper with him that night, instead of having her wait for him at home? Despite his excuses, he probably could have. Red had spent the entire evening picturing her there, anyway, trying to envision how or if Piper might fit in with his mother's friends.

He'd been paired with the host's daughter at dinner, of course, a quiet divorcee with at least ten years on him—and felt a little sullen about the fact that she wasn't Piper. The evening might have been a complete loss if his mother hadn't managed to subtly convey that the daughter was, in fact, his mark. She'd saved him from making a total fool of himself.

When he finally left the party and went home, he didn't head straight for her, as he'd wanted to all night. Instead, Red stood in his suit in the dark living room, staring gloomily out at the city lights and brooding about his real motives.

God. Was it *really* so vital to keep Piper in the dark about what was happening at Trident?

All night, Red had been wishing she was on his arm, giving him her opinion on the potential investor and weighing in on how he should proceed. So, when the time came that he could have made an early escape, Red had surprised himself by lingering— procrastinating coming home until he knew Piper would have fallen asleep. Why?

She would definitely have noticed his moodiness, there was that. And Red didn't want to talk about the thundercloud hovering over him—it was difficult enough to withhold the details of what he'd been doing all week, but it would be so much worse if Piper decided to question him directly.

Red was irritated with himself, though, and he wasn't entirely sure why. He kept thinking about how his mother had proclaimed Piper 'inappropriate' after one five-minute meeting.

Was his decision to leave her behind tonight easier because Red was subconsciously ashamed of her? He chafed at his mother's insults, but she was correct that Piper didn't inhabit the same world he did. The society mavens flouncing around tonight's dinner would have picked up on that instantly.

He didn't want to consider the caustic jibes that might've been slipped his way—or hers. Piper wouldn't have complained, of course, but that didn't mean she wouldn't have been hurt by it. She wasn't used to the gossip like Red was.

As if she'd been summoned by his heavy thoughts, Piper appeared behind him, more angel than human in her pale, silky robe. Piper didn't say a word—just slipped her arm around his waist and leaned her head against his shoulder. She searched out the window, looking for what had claimed his attention.

No, Red decided. It hadn't been shame. He'd wanted to protect her from them a little longer—the sharks that looked like swans—but it was such a foreign feeling to him, it was no wonder he hadn't recognized it.

When had he last cared like this? Before Piper, he'd been entirely comfortable letting people sink or swim, to receive what they had coming to them. Before Piper, he hadn't worried over whether he was even capable of shielding someone from the pettiness of others.

But Piper was sweet. Unsullied, despite the raunchy tilt of her brain. She didn't deserve what the people at a lot of those gatherings could dish out if they had a mind to.

What was more—Red wanted to keep Piper to himself just a little longer. His own private haven, untainted by the glare of attention from his acquaintances, from the media, from his mother. Piper was something good, just for him.

Beside him, her breathing was slow and even, like it sounded when she was asleep. The way she stood there—asking nothing, offering her companionship without comment—twisted something dead and gray inside Red and made it pulse with life.

Piper was everything warm and kind in the world. A ripe summer peach in a city of cold, hard stone. A passionate kiss in a parade of obligations.

Red dropped his hand from the window sill, hoping to catch hold of hers—but his fingertips encountered a drifting whisper of silk, instead. He only had to move them back a scant couple inches to find the opening of her robe, and beneath that, the juncture of her thighs.

Piper was bare for him. Wet and ready already, leaving Red to wonder how long she'd been that way. All night while he'd been gone, or only while he'd been wasting time here, deliberating?

The promise of her body, the melting heat and dark pleasure, called to him. All that was Piper burned off Red's lingering fugue, like it always did, and had him hard and hungry inside his trousers in seconds.

Red slid his fingers through her folds and listened for Piper's quiet intake of breath. In the window's reflection, he watched her bury her face against his sleeve and felt her hand flex against his waist.

Yes. *That.* Nothing mattered but that—the soul-shaking, magnetic thing that was growing and blooming between them— Red would move heaven and earth to shelter that.

Twenty-Three

"R ISE AND SHINE, pretty little dove," Red crooned, his breath already fresh and minty.

Piper burrowed deeper under the covers, but he had hold of her hand and was placing precise kisses on each of her fingertips in turn.

The morning cheerfulness was a switch. Generally, Red was as irritated by the arrival of dawn as Piper was—which made sense, given that he was the one keeping her up half the night, and usually hadn't gotten much sleep either.

From inside her nest of down, Piper demanded, "Why are you so happy?"

"Besides the fact that you're here to wake up with, you mean?"

"Yes, Red. Besides that."

"If you must know, I got some very good news a little while ago. And that means I have a surprise to give you later."

He sounded smug now, on top of happy. Piper cracked open one eye and peered at him from under the covers. "Color me intrigued," she said.

Red smirked, tucked her hand against his chest and moved closer. He switched from kissing her fingers to nibbling on her earlobe, and, while Piper might have been inclined to go back to sleep, her body clearly had other ideas. With each press of Red's teeth and flick of his tongue, traitorous shocks of desire flared through her, waking up nerve endings and speeding up her groggy heart.

And then it occurred to her—Red was showered, shaved, and dressed already.

"Come on, Cupcake, up and at 'em," he urged. "If I know you and your packing skills, we have some shopping to do."

Piper snapped back the covers and frowned. "What's that supposed to mean?"

"That I am completely certain you did not cram a cocktail dress into your little carry-on?"

"I do not like to wait for checked baggage, and neither do you," Piper huffed. "And in my defense, you distinctly said *dressy casual.*"

"That was before the surprise came through."

"Furthermore," she growled, "Did you just call me *Cupcake?*" No one but Perry had ever dared to call her that.

Red got to his feet and gazed down at her from the foot of the bed. He looked good enough to eat, in his low-slung jeans and soft gray henley. Which was ironic, because then he grinned wolfishly and said, "I did. I'd like to lick you all over and then eat what I find underneath."

"Oh my God," Piper dove back under the covers to hide what was surely a vibrant red flush invading her face. "You're worse than my cats!"

Dead silence. Upon reflection, Piper could understand why. She checked to see if Red was still there and found him stuck in place, head tilted while he squinted down at her.

"Not like that, you pervert! Only because you're so freaking awake right now! When you're not there, Sonny and Fredo always pounce on my toes and wrestle with each other next to my head, so I'll get up and feed them."

He considered that, then said, "I'd be up for the wrestling bit, but I'm already dressed. And I can feed myself, so…"

Piper sagged back, hoping he'd go away and leave her in peace.

Red lunged forward suddenly, grabbing her feet exactly like a pouncing animal and scaring a high-pitched shriek right out of her. Piper didn't think she'd ever made such a loud sound before noon in her entire life. She glared at him indignantly.

He obviously considered his job done, however, because he turned and strolled toward the stairs with nothing more than a victorious grin and a wink. Tuneless whistling drifted after him as he descended from view.

"The least you could do is bring me coffee!" Piper belted after him.

"On your right," Red called back, laughing.

Piper spun to the side and groaned—a tall, steaming mug sat on a coaster on the nightstand, the coffee inside the perfect, milky shade of light brown. That man could scale the defenses of even the hardest heart, damn him.

Little by little, he was demolishing all of Piper's armor, and she'd hardly noticed him doing it. *Stay aloof*, her ass. She might as well be the president of the Red MacLellan fan club, at this point.

SHE TOOK HER time showering and getting dressed, partly to stick it to Red, and partly because a number of workmen seemed to have arrived at the loft. There was a good bit of cursing and struggling from under the stairs, while Red banged around in the kitchen.

Piper peeked down and saw some of the men carry an enormous crate out the front door. The rest of the guys had set up an unholy racket below her, complete with alarming metallic clangs and the whine of more than one drill.

Strangely, Red hadn't mentioned anything about it when he'd woken her up. Piper couldn't figure out what was going on. Something to do with her surprise maybe?

The instant the men left and all was quiet again, she crept down the stairs. Red was standing in the middle of the main room, hands on his hips and pleased as could be.

"What's going on?" she asked.

"See for yourself," he said, pointing behind her. "Incidentally, this isn't your surprise. That happens later."

The crime scene painting was gone, replaced by a framework of plumbing pipes bolted in rows to the brick wall. Industrial clamps held black wooden frames filled with photographs, at intervals along each pipe.

"What is this?" Piper breathed, taking in the scale and cleverness of the design. It was industrial and rustic, masculine and homey, all at once. It suited Red's loft much better than anything his mom's decorator had picked out.

"Once we talked about it, I couldn't stop thinking about how much I hated that painting, too. It was getting on my nerves."

Piper pivoted around but didn't spot the offending canvas anywhere else. "What did you do with it?"

"Sold it at an art auction."

"Someone else *bought* that thing?"

Red was sanguine. "Turns out the painter died," he shrugged. "Honestly, I got more for it than I expected to."

"I'm not sure whether to be even more appalled," Piper said, "Or to congratulate you on your business acumen."

Red chuckled and gestured to the new structure. "This is better, though, right?"

"Much. Where did you find it?"

"I made it. I just needed the guys to install it once they got that atrocity packed up and out of here."

"Seriously?"

"I had to do *something* to fill the evenings when you weren't here," Red smirked. "I'm not just a pretty face, Piper Mae."

She grinned back, surprised and pleased by this new side of him. "I never doubted it for a second." Her heart melted into a warm, gooey mess at how proud he looked.

Piper went closer, spotting among the pictures a few favorite places that Red had taken her to around town. There was an action shot of a teenaged Red in hockey gear, gearing up to score a goal. Red as a toddler, crouched beside a pond with an older man and a toy boat. Him as a red-haired baby in an old woman's lap, poring over a storybook.

And several photos of Red as he looked now, with two other men who appeared again and again—smoking cigars, raising drinks, playing cards.

"Who are those guys?" Piper wondered, fascinated.

"My best friends," he murmured, a little shyly. "We were college roommates. The dark one is Luca. And the other one is Tate."

"Where are they now?"

"Luca went home to Italy. He's a doctor there. And Tate is in the Army, stationed in the Middle East."

"Oh, wow."

Red came up behind Piper and wrapped his arms around her. "I hope you can meet them someday."

Piper thought she must be glowing with the affection she felt for him at that moment. When Red had chosen for himself what he wanted to see in his home every day, he'd gone with family, friends, and childhood memories. He'd picked images of the simple beauty secreted all over his city. And Red had gone one step further, designing and constructing the display himself, when he could easily have commissioned someone else to do it for him.

Piper didn't know what his surprise was going to be later, and she didn't care. Coming to New York for the weekend was worth it just for this.

THAT EVENING, PIPER finished showering and toweling off in Red's bathroom, then donned her new strapless bra and lace panties before cracking the door to let out some of the heat and steam. While she combed out her hair in the big mirror over the sink, Red appeared and nudged the door wider.

Shopping for an evening dress with Red had been an experience. He seemed to have a predilection for zippers, buckles, and laces, for one thing—and an aversion to actual material, for another. Piper had determined *that* almost immediately.

What was more, he'd flatly refused to bring her to a simple department store. Instead, they'd gone to several boutiques on a list he had on his phone—culled, apparently, from the suggestions of women he worked with at PKM. Based on the styles displayed in each, Piper had almost been able to pick which employee had steered Red to which store. That confounded him.

He'd lobbied hard for a knee-length navy-blue confection, with one shoulder and an eye-popping price tag, but hadn't been able to convince her. She'd dragged him to two more places before she'd finally settled on a simple, olive velvet slip dress. Red had proclaimed it boring until Piper put it on.

Once he saw the way the material slipped sinuously over her breasts and hips, he'd changed his tune. She bit her lip, remembering how he'd backed her into the dressing room and shut the door, working the narrow satin ribbons off her shoulders and fervently kissing her collar bones. Red's talented hand had found the high slit on one thigh and slipped inside.

Piper took a deep breath and met his eyes in the mirror. He looked impeccable, leaning against the doorjamb in his suit. He still hadn't told her where they were going. Her nerves about the evening ahead were getting the best of her.

His eyes skated over her body, his expression unreadable. She'd quickly purchased this set of lingerie in one of the boutiques earlier, when he wasn't looking. Unfortunately, it wasn't having the effect she'd been hoping for—on her or him.

Maybe she should have skipped that hot dog from the cart in the park. And also the muffin in the coffee shop right afterward.

Besides, it wasn't like Red hadn't seen her body already, right? Although…as Piper's mind cast back over their relationship, she began to wonder. She did have a habit of turning off lamps and changing in the bathroom. Maybe Red *hadn't* ever gotten a good look at her.

"Look, I realize I don't have the body of a twenty-year-old model," she muttered defensively. "But I've been living a full life and I clearly have the marks to prove it."

Red's eyes twinkled in the reflection, the first sign of life he'd shown since he'd barged in. Did he think that was funny?

Piper squared her shoulders and raised her chin, defying him to say one word about her imperfections. If he wanted to go back to dating rail-thin models barely out of their teens again, then she wasn't going to stop him.

"*What?* I like carbs, all right?" Piper spat. "Preferably with cheese. Do we have anything else to discuss, or can I finish getting ready?"

Red laughed outright then, a dark rolling chuckle from deep inside him. He gave Piper a patently obvious once-over, from her heels to the crown of her head, then grinned at her image in the glass.

"Settle down, little dove. You look amazing, as always. I was just wondering how you managed to slip that little scrap of naughtiness past me," Red snorted, coming closer. He cupped her ass, then bent to murmur hotly in Piper's ear. "But after that outburst, I think we have plenty more to talk about. Why don't you finish up in here, so we can figure out why you're so worried about one little surprise?"

He sauntered away with another amused laugh, leaving Piper to stare in shock at his retreating back in the mirror. What the hell was she doing with a guy like him? She had to be insane.

THE CAR TOOK them straight to the garage under PKM's headquarters, and Piper's initial trepidation grew. When Red turned to her and displayed the smallest hint of uncertainty, that feeling turned right into worry.

"Okay, here's the deal," Red said. "We don't have to stay all night, but we should probably stick around for a couple of hours, at least."

"All right."

"I think you're really going to be excited about what happens, but…" He paused and took a deep breath. "We probably shouldn't go in together." Piper began to reply, but Red cut her off. "Or act like we're a couple. I'm sorry. I don't like it, but it's for the best. I'd hate for my employees or your coworkers to get the wrong idea about us."

"Red—I get it, but this is weird. What is going on?"

"Trust me, honey. It'll be good. I promise. Just head up to the fifth floor and I'll come find you soon."

UPSTAIRS, THERE WAS a large party already in full swing. Apparently, Red's employees had put together the entire thing in one day. From Anika, Piper learned that they'd ordered take-out appetizers from five different restaurants in order to have enough on such short notice. A guy named Rob admitted that he and the other members of Trident's transition team had to visit three liquor stores to get enough beer and wine for the crowd.

And Red's assistant Wayne explained how he and his mother had driven all the way to a warehouse store in Jersey for the napkins and paper plates, and the water and sodas. In addition, he told Piper that the small band playing credible Sinatra covers in the corner was comprised of his law school classmates.

None of the other guests she spoke to wanted to enlighten her on *why* they had gone to so much trouble, though. Piper sipped her wine and circulated and tried to uncover what the big mystery was. Red, head-and-shoulders taller than everyone else, mingled on the other side of the room, but caught her eye occasionally and sent her flirty looks.

It was exasperating. Piper had been promised a surprise and was dressed to kill—but the man responsible for all that was keeping his distance, having a grand old time with pretty much everyone else but her.

Piper had just parked herself next to a mystery writer named Lyla when Wayne whistled, loud and shrill, with his fingers. Behind him, Rob was helping PKM's legal director up onto a chair.

Anika's grin was wide as she addressed the room. "I'm sure most of you have heard the good news already, but I'd like to officially confirm that, as of six-thirty this morning, PKM is now party to an exclusive deal with the Millhouse & Rock bookstore chain! The deal is signed, sealed, and delivered, people."

Piper froze, searching the room until she found Red—leaning against a wall off to the side and watching her expectantly.

There was a round of cheering and applause. Anika laughed, then shushed everyone.

"Listen guys, a lot of you have worked really hard to make this happen, and that's why we wanted to celebrate. This is going to be a terrific thing for PKM, for Trident, and for all of Trident's amazing authors." She tipped her head at Piper and Lyla, at Rachel Wilbon, and at a few others scattered around.

Unsurprisingly, Jim Denton and his friends did not seem to be in attendance. Piper wondered if they had already gotten the ax, or just weren't invited. She couldn't imagine them choosing not to attend.

Red kept his eyes on Piper's face as Anika explained how Millhouse & Rock would carry all of Trident's current titles in a dedicated, preferential section of its stores and website. Piper didn't dare look back at him, sure that he'd see how flustered she was.

"Incidentally," Anika was saying, "We threw this shindig together on the fly, so if you have any criticisms you can keep them to yourself. Also, if you were one of the stupendous people who picked up food or supplies for us, don't leave without giving me your receipts. Our dear leader has promised me we'll be reimbursed."

More whistles and applause rang out, Rob helped Anika down from her chair and high-fived Red, and the music started again, louder than before.

Lyla turned to Piper and said, "Well, I have to say, I did not know what to expect when I heard PKM had bought out Trident, but this is really great news."

"Yeah, maybe," Piper said.

"You don't think so?"

"I really don't know. But I guess we'll see."

Piper definitely had to talk to Red, though. She broke away from Lyla with a vague excuse and wound her way through the excited crowd, toward the place she'd seen him last. He met her near the center of the room, and once she was next to him, it took real effort not to be too obvious or demonstrative.

"Well, what do you think of your surprise?" he murmured.

Piper didn't have a chance to answer. They were immediately waylaid by Rachel Wilbon, blowsy and overdone in black sequined chiffon. The other woman leaned heavily on Red so she could adjust her platform heel, then craned up to plant a too-long kiss on his cheek.

Red winced, pulled a handkerchief from his jacket, and rubbed at the lipstick she left behind. Rachel's perfume was strong enough that Piper had to breathe through her mouth. Red would probably need to dry-clean his suit three times to get rid of the smell.

Piper couldn't believe the other woman's lack of restraint, but who was she to talk? She'd been hot and heavy with the "dear leader" within a day of meeting him—the man whose company had bought out her publisher. The top banana, the boss of bosses.

Maybe Rachel was no worse than Piper was. Office romances were a favorite novel trope for a reason, after all. Bosses like Red, powerful and confident, were *hot*.

In a breathy, boozy purr, Rachel griped about having to come all the way in from Brooklyn unexpectedly. "You could at least make it worth a girl's while," she said to Red, waving her empty plastic wineglass around.

She was clearly three sheets to the wind and Red sent Piper a desperate look. She shrugged—it wasn't like she could stake a claim in front of everyone. He was on his own.

And that meant she had to watch the woman continue to hit on Red. All the while, Piper was noticing Rachel's curiously-dated hairstyle, her chipped nail polish, and the lipstick on her teeth.

The other author had always been a bit over the top, but she was a mess tonight, even for her. Her manner was coy and her banter heavy on the innuendo, but Rachel was giving off a disturbingly brittle vibe. She looked painfully thin. Piper frowned, trying to figure out what was going on with her.

Red didn't give Rachel much, despite her striving. Eventually it dawned on her, and she broke awkwardly away again, sashaying around the room with a languid, one-foot-in-bed gait. Between knocking back glasses of wine, Rachel draped herself on a panicked-looking guy from the legal department, a burly security guard, and Wayne.

Red's assistant was not amused. Unceremoniously, Wayne pulled the woman to the side of the room and gave her a stern talking to. Seconds later, he handed Rachel her wrap and clutch and pointed her toward the door.

Piper was still loitering beside Red, doing her best to look casual, when Rachel detoured over to say goodbye. Rachel's kiss landed sloppily left of center, thanks to Red jerking his face aside just in the nick of time. He pulled the woman away and steadied her on her heels.

Piper couldn't stand to watch anymore, so she turned and wandered resolutely away from them. She had never liked Rachel much, but now that dislike had grown into outright loathing. It wasn't fair that Rachel got to hug and kiss Red, and Piper couldn't. How long would it be, anyway, before she and Red could go public? Would they ever be able to?

Speaking of Mr. Tall, Buff, and Bossy…it was hard to ignore the way this whole evening was getting under Piper's skin and setting off warning bells. The parallels to her last date with Kyle were beating her over the head with each moment more she had to be there.

There was the way the PKM employees bantered with Red, like they'd been friends for years. And there was the way that Rachel's advances engendered more amusement than anger in him. Hell, Piper had only learned that morning that he had two best friends—or what their names were—and she'd been dating Red for weeks.

Forced to watch him from the sidelines, Piper had seen a different version of Red tonight, one that was unknown to her. It felt like she knew him so well, but that was just an illusion, wasn't it? When Piper visited, she and Red spent most of their time alone. For all she knew, he could be living out a whole other life when she wasn't in New York.

After all, no one understood better than her that just because someone *said* they were honest, didn't make it true. Did truly trustworthy people walk around telling people to trust them all the time? No, they did not. They didn't have to.

Which gave Piper a lot to think about.

Red found her near the food table about fifteen minutes later. "Shake it off," he said calmly, sensing her unease. "Rachel acts trashy, but I think she's essentially harmless."

Piper had been studying people for a lifetime, though, letting her heart and mind work together to discover what made them tick. And with Rachel, the calculation was always there, lurking just under her innocuous barfly façade.

Piper didn't trust her. Not around her man, and not around her business.

Red disappeared a while later, leaving her alone at the party that he'd meant to be a good surprise. He sent his driver in soon after, though, to fetch Piper with a handwritten note.

For the second time that day, she took her own sweet time obeying his summons. It would do Red good to realize that not everyone was at his beck-and-call all the time. Piper used the facilities, touched up her lipstick, and said goodbye to Lyla and Wayne. *Then* she left.

The underground garage was cold when she came out of the elevator, the autumn bite in the air worse now that the sun had been down for a while. Red stood next to the car, hands in his pockets, waiting for her. When he noticed her shiver, he immediately removed his jacket to drape around her shoulders.

Piper gathered her composure around her like his coat while the car pulled up the ramp and out onto the street, then told Red, "You have a lot of explaining to do, mister."

She was surprised and worried about the Millhouse deal, for sure. Piper couldn't believe Red hadn't warned her, knowing how she felt about the company. But she was also furious about Rachel's skeevy performance, and at herself for letting her guard down so soon.

"Oh, do I?"

"Red, I'm serious. You shouldn't have let Rachel hang all over you like that. But more importantly, we need to talk about this Millhouse thing."

"I don't want to talk right now," he replied. "Pretending to barely know you tonight was murder. Stop scowling and kiss me."

"You're really freaking bossy, you know that?" she fumed.

Red grinned. "Better be careful, Piper Mae. If you keep that up, I'll have you tied to my bed in two minutes flat, so I can boss that sass right out of you. You'll be begging me to tell you what to do, then—begging me to let you scream my name, to let you touch me, to let you climax…"

Piper nearly swallowed her own tongue. "Wh—what?"

Red's voice was full of dusky promise. "Just try me."

She pressed her knees together against the rush of desire that swamped her at his tone. His mouth twitched as he stared at her. He touched his fingers to her chin, and she squirmed on her seat at the contact. All thoughts of walling off her heart and giving him what for flew right out the window.

"Dear Lord," he muttered, sounding stunned. "Don't tell me you actually like that idea, too? You *want* that?"

Twenty-Four

RED STARED AT Piper in shock. She sat next to him in the back of the semi-dark car, looking like a glowing jewel against the charcoal smudge of streets moving past the window behind her.

"I think I do," she whispered.

The thought of her in restraints was almost unbearably seductive, and that went double for tonight, when Red was feeling so untethered. He should've known his surprise would play out differently than he'd planned. There were simply too many moving parts.

His logic-loving brain was scrambling, trying to make sense of it, and lately that was becoming a common refrain.

Red gripped the edge of the leather seat and held on so he wouldn't do something stupid—like truss Piper up with his goddamn necktie. He needed to get the lay of the land first. Make sure she was okay.

After all, the need to act like disinterested business acquaintances tonight—annoying all on its own—had had an unintended consequence. Flying solo at the PKM party, as it turned out, had cleared the way for Rachel Wilbon to try out all her wiles on him. Without her agent to rein her in, Rachel's efforts to seduce him into submission had progressed from mildly bothersome to outright inappropriate.

It might have been laughable if Piper hadn't been forced to watch the whole fucking farce. And, while his secret girlfriend certainly hadn't enjoyed that, Red could safely say that he'd liked it even less. Jesus—he could still smell Rachel's overwhelming perfume, occasionally drifting up from his jacket when he moved.

When charm hadn't worked, Rachel had tried to strong-arm Red into keeping her on at Trident, predicting all sorts of doom and destruction if he tried to get rid of her. Which, honestly, merely confirmed for Red what he already knew—if Rachel had a new project in the works at all (something he doubted) it was not going well.

He'd said as much. The floor show took a right turn into the ludicrous.

Eyes narrowed to black-rimmed slits, Rachel had hissed, "You think you're so high and mighty, Red MacLellan, but you're not. You're on very, very thin ice and you don't even know it."

He'd laughed. Of course, he had. Red had been deflecting pissed-off, spurned women for nearly his entire adult life. Rachel was the exact opposite of terrifying to him.

"Rachel, you've had too much to drink," he'd fired back. "You know what our deal is, and you know what you have to do to stay on at Trident. Now knock off the vaudeville act before you say something you can't take back."

Red had tried to walk away then, tried to head casually in Piper's direction so he could find some way to flirt inconspicuously with her, or to touch her silky skin without anyone noticing.

Rachel had sunk her nails into his arm, though, keeping him in place for one more salvo. "You'll regret this. You'll be sorry you ever belittled me."

Red had been riding the buzz of success, however. He'd smiled his coldest, fakest smile, and assured her, "That is never going to happen."

That buzz had faded now. Next to him was the woman he wanted, and Piper could try to seduce him all night long if she so chose. Sadly, Red suspected they had a couple of things to get out of the way first.

He'd watched her all through Anika's speech, and his big surprise hadn't, in fact, put a happy expression on Piper's face. Red had thought, given the way she'd talked about Millhouse & Rock, that handing them to her on a silver platter would be a pretty spectacular offering. The Dentons might not have been able to give Piper a huge distribution deal with the bookstore chain, but PKM could—and had.

So why hadn't she looked excited? Once Red had a chance to explain all the details, Piper would understand precisely how the deal benefited her. She had undoubtedly figured that part out already.

Therefore, maybe this wasn't about Millhouse—maybe her somber mood had more to do with having to play it cool in front of all their colleagues tonight. Maybe this was about Rachel glomming onto him like a cheap suit for half the party.

If Red had to bet, he'd guess that Piper had not only been uncomfortable with the cloak and dagger routine, she was perhaps a bit jealous of her fellow author.

Now that they were alone, Red was free to put her mind at ease on both those scores. And, once he had her tied to his bed, she'd be singing a happier tune in no time.

Red hadn't attempted much kink with her yet because Piper just hadn't seemed the type, despite the steaminess of her backlist. The few half-assed attempts he had made hadn't exactly gone according to plan.

It was something of a surprise that Piper was suddenly into the idea of a little bondage now. Red was quick on his feet, though. He recovered as quickly as he could.

"If you really want this, little dove," he told her now, "I am willing and able to make it happen. Tonight, even."

The way Piper had done her makeup earlier made her pretty amber eyes look smoky and exotic in the irregular illumination from the streetlights. Her gaze went wide at Red's offer, and her nervous swallow seemed loud in the quiet confines of the car.

She nodded in agreement. "Okay. Yes," she said. "Let's do that."

Red's dick stood at attention, and he willed it to calm the fuck down. Its services weren't needed quite yet, but if he did his job well, tonight could be the start of many such evenings. Maybe, if Piper liked—no, loved—how this went, it could be a regular thing for them.

Dream come true.

TRUST, OR LACK thereof, was obviously a big deal for Piper. As it turned out, that was kind of convenient—if Piper was questioning his commitment after that crap with Rachel, it wouldn't last much longer. Red had been telling Piper all along that she was the only one for him, and now he'd make that message stick.

He knew clear as day that Piper was no submissive, but he thought a lesson or two from his bag of tricks could be the thing that finally turned the tide between them. Perhaps this would help prove to her that she could depend on him—that she could trust the things he told her.

Piper was balanced on the edge of Red's mattress, watching him warily while he retrieved the gear they'd need from a shelf in his closet. Red set it beside her and helped her to her feet. While he busied himself slipping that insidiously sexy gown off her shoulders, she started in with the questions.

"Wait, you actually have a box of stuff? Just hanging around the house?"

Red grinned at her and ran his fingers over the thin cords lacing up the front of her black strapless bra and the sides of her matching panties. The design was devilishly appropriate. "Yup."

"So, you've done this before. Obviously."

"You could say that." He leaned down and leisurely tasted her mouth, getting a hint of the red wine she'd had at the party, and maybe something sweeter.

"But like, often enough to have your own equipment, though?"

"Clearly," Red pointed out. "Now sit here." His heart was thumping out a relentless drum solo, and he marveled that Piper couldn't hear it. She would probably have questions about that, too.

Red had never used the restraints on his own bed before, but luck was on his side and he got them set up relatively efficiently. After that, he spread Piper out and worked slowly and gently on each of her wrists, and then her ankles. Red explained carefully how she could release the restraints herself, until he was certain that she understood.

"How are we doing?" he murmured, stepping back to take in the picture she presented. She looked…heart-stoppingly perfect.

Piper's expression was a little uncertain. Her breath hitched a bit when she said, "All right," even though she smiled tentatively at him.

That was to be expected. She was nervous and so was he, but Red would prove to her that she could count on him implicitly. He'd never let her down.

He tested everything, making sure it was firm, but not too tight, then reached for the blindfold he'd pulled out. The look in Piper's eyes turned a little wild when she saw it, though, so Red jammed the length of fabric in his pocket, sat beside her and kissed her neck—right where he knew she was the most sensitive.

She trembled a bit when his lips made contact. Red reconsidered, scrapping the idea of the blindfold altogether. He didn't want to overload Piper with too much, too soon. If this went well, there'd be plenty of time later to try other things.

"Got any other dark secrets up your sleeve?" she tried to joke.

Red paused, thinking of the storm brewing at Trident. This was not the time, however. He murmured, "All in due time, little dove. All in due time."

He dropped another light kiss on Piper's luscious mouth, then moved over to his dresser. He stalled at the open top drawer for a few minutes, looking over the few items he had stashed there—things that had never made it into the rotation with anyone else. He wanted this to be perfect.

Red already had a pretty good idea which toys might intensify Piper's pleasure without scandalizing her. He reviewed them now, making extra sure he chose well.

Anticipation lay heavy along his spine. His nerves sparked and jumped. Red was determined to do right by her, to win Piper over to the bondage game come hell or high water.

His reverie was broken suddenly, though, when his ears picked up the change in Piper's breathing, jarring against the soft music he had playing on the sound system. Red spun around.

One look at her Piper's face told him everything he needed to know. She was freaking out—sucking in gasping breaths like she might start hyperventilating, eyes feral, face suddenly damp with tears. Red was horrified. How the fuck had that happened so fast?

In two strides, he was back at the bed. He released Piper's ankles since he'd gotten there first, but she was already twisting at her wrists, pulling with panicky jerks of her arms that basically ensured she'd never get free.

"Whoa. It's okay, baby. You're okay," Red told her. He moved to her wrists as fast as he could. "Shh, I got you. It's okay." It was a dumb comment, though. She was obviously not okay. "Piper honey, what happened?"

Defensively, she drew up her knees while his shaking fingers worked on the buckles. She couldn't seem to force actual words out, and she wouldn't maintain any eye contact with him.

"Please," she gasped. "I can't get out." There was more, but the rest was mostly incomprehensible. For fuck's sake, her teeth were chattering.

Red finally got her free, regardless. He hated how he had to hold each arm still with a pretty solid grip just to do it, though. He hated the way Piper curled in on herself like a bug, quivering in a tight, terrified ball in the middle of his mattress. God *damn* it.

Red yanked at the hem of the heavy down duvet, tucking it snugly around her even though it was plenty warm in the room.

"Piper, honey," he tried again. "What happened? Did you forget how to free yourself?"

Slowly, he slid onto the side of the bed, sitting carefully beside her. He didn't try to touch her yet. She was still eyeing him like a cornered animal.

"I couldn't get out," she whimpered, burrowing deeper into her cocoon. "It wouldn't work."

Red stroked a gentle hand down her shaking back and studied her. Something inside his chest was squeezed so tight, he wondered if he was heading for a total meltdown himself. What had he done? Where had he gone wrong?

"You got scared?" he asked. But that was moronic—it was plenty apparent she had. "By what?" he tried.

No answer. Nothing but a shiver.

"By me?"

Red wasn't sure but he thought maybe Piper shrugged.

"Honey, please believe me. I would never hurt a single hair on your head—not in a million years. I adore you, you must know that." It sounded lame, given the circumstances.

"I'm sorry," she hiccupped, not quite sobbing, but not quite breathing right, either. Piper's eyes were enormous muddied pools, filling up and spilling over every couple of seconds. Red felt like an ogre, and he hadn't even done anything but turn his back.

"No, don't be sorry." he petted her hair, smoothing the thick silken fall of it across her shoulder. "I'm the one who's sorry."

"It's okay," she murmured soggily, gripping the covers tights around her like a shield.

"Piper…" Red shook his head, utterly poleaxed by this turn of events. She was a damn erotic romance author—hell, she'd probably written five books or more about BDSM relationships. How could this even be happening right now? Then something awful occurred to him.

"Have you done this before?" he forced himself to ask. "And had a bad experience, maybe?" If some bastard—that Kyle character, perhaps—had roughed her up while she couldn't fight back, Red swore on all that he held holy he would find the fucker and *end* him.

"No, never." Piper peeked at him with watery, blinking eyes. Her breathing was settling down, at least.

"If this was your first time," Red floundered, casting around for what to say, "then you didn't know this would happen, huh?"

Piper shook her head emphatically.

Naturally, she hadn't known—she wouldn't have agreed to it, otherwise. Mentally, Red berated himself. He was, undeniably, a venal motherfucker to have ever thought this would work. Piper was simply too damn sweet, even if she did know all the filthy words.

Slowly, carefully, Red pulled and lifted her, nestling Piper securely in his lap. He cradled her in his arms, surrounding her gently with his warmth and strength, trying to protect her from all her fears—even the one of him.

It hurt like hell to do it, but Red stayed alert for any sign at all that she didn't want to be there, that Piper needed her space from him. She rested her head on his shoulder, though, and relaxed into his hold.

"I am so, so sorry you got scared, little dove. I shouldn't have left you alone for even a minute on your first time. I should've stayed with you and explained what I was doing. I don't know," he fumbled, "I just…I really didn't intend for it to go this way."

"Not as hot as I thought it would be," Piper agreed dryly.

"No," Red laughed, relieved to see the color coming back to her cheeks. "It wasn't. I feel awful. What can I do for you?"

Piper simply said, "This."

Yes, *this*, this connection between them. This was good. This was right. It had to be, because it was all Red could offer until Piper decided to forgive him for his lapse. *If* she decided to forgive him.

After a long quiet while, Red asked her, "Can we talk about what just happened a little more?"

Piper's gaze skated away from his. Her jaw was set but as he studied her, Red saw her lip quivering the tiniest bit.

He stated the obvious. "You were afraid?"

Her beautiful eyes flicked to his. Her lovely throat moved as she swallowed. Yes. She was.

"Of me?" Red cupped her cheek and turned her face to his.

She nodded and turned away.

After that spanking thing, he'd been careful to reassure Piper that pain was not a part of this package. Either she didn't believe him, or there was more at play here.

Red couldn't let her withdraw, though, not if they were going to work out what had gone wrong. They needed to clear the air so this wouldn't dog them going forward.

"I'll say it, okay?" He nudged her chin, so Piper would look at him again. "So you won't have to. You're afraid I'm lying. That I'll really hurt you, or worse. And you're scared you won't be able to do anything about it."

Piper's tawny eyes were watery, glittering like topaz in her precious face.

"Maybe you were afraid I'd leave—walk out and strand you, alone and powerless. And then maybe someone else would find you and make *you* feel ashamed for what *I* did. Add in humiliation on top of everything else."

She watched Red quietly but didn't say anything.

"Am I close?" Nothing. "Piper? Am I close?" Red caressed her cheek, suspecting that he was not only close, but spot on.

Finally, she admitted softly, "It's not just you. I barely trust anyone."

Red nodded. *Finally.* "I know, honey. But I want you to trust me."

"I can't."

"You can. That's what all this was supposed to prove. The control thing—it's arousing, sure. I love being the one who gets you off. And I would love being in control of how much, how soon…just how. I want to play your body like a fucking instrument and make it sing."

Red trailed a fingertip down the center of her chest and watched Piper shiver.

"But I only want that if it means you truly trust me—not to leave, not to hurt, not to lie. If it means you actually let yourself be vulnerable with me." He picked up her hand and kissed her palm. "If you believed that I wasn't going to disappear if you were in a bad mood, or you gained a few pounds, or you got wrinkles or gray hair, then you might open yourself up to what's possible between us…what I know in my bones we could be together."

"So, it's all about me," Piper said dubiously.

"Not just you," Red explained. "*I* need you to trust me, too. I need to be the man that won't leave you, won't hurt you, and won't lie. I need to be the person you can depend on. It would feel incredible, knowing that I earned that privilege. That I can be that for you if you let me."

"Why?"

"Why do I like to do things this way? Or why with you?"

"Probably both."

Red was petting her skin the way he'd soothe a panicked animal, but it seemed to be helping.

"Maybe you were right. Maybe all this domineering crap stems from not having control of some of the important stuff. I've been thinking about it, and I guess it makes as much sense as anything. Or maybe…I don't know, Piper, maybe this is just the way I'm built."

"Bossy," Piper sighed. "Then what about me? Why choose me?"

"Because, Piper, I suspected you were the one for me the second I laid eyes on you. After feeling nothing but irritation or indifference for women for years—*years*—my mind and my body and my heart all stood at attention when you walked in my office that day. They woke up, came alive, and said, *yes*."

"Oh, Red." She snuggled closer.

"Piper—" God, this part was trickier, because it was too damn soon, but Red had to rid her of her anxiety like he needed air. "—my soul knew you, too. Reached right out and declared, *Mine*. Don't you feel it?"

"Maybe. Honestly, I'm not sure what I'm feeling, at the moment."

Red nodded. *Understandable*. "Why do I suspect there's something else, too?"

Once again, Piper kept quiet, like that would stop him. Like it could keep him out as it'd probably kept out all the other men she'd known.

"Say it, honey."

"I just don't understand," she relented in a rush, "what's wrong with me. Why can't I just…"

Red was too impatient to let her finish. He was so furious with her goddamn father, or Kyle, or whoever, for saddling Piper with this insecurity, he'd like to obliterate them with his bare hands.

"Why can't you catch a nice man—one who won't want difficult things from you?" he demanded gently. "How about a guy who won't push you? Maybe he'll let you hide somewhere safe where you won't have to worry about getting hurt. I doubt you'd see much of each other, though."

Piper winced.

"That guy's not me, Piper Mae. If I'm going to have you, I want all of you. Not some cardboard cutout that only looks like you. Where's the fun in that? We'd be no better than a couple of wax figures in a museum that way."

"You seemed like a stranger tonight," she whispered quietly. "Someone I didn't know. And not just because we had to pretend at the party. It was…realizing you had all these friends that know you better than I do. This life that I'm not a part of most of the time. Not to mention, boxes of secret toys stashed around."

Red arched a brow at her.

"When you turned away before, all I could think was, *Who is this guy? I don't even know him.* It freaked me out."

"Oh, Piper," Red said sadly, "What the hell did that asshole Kyle do to you?"

"Enough," she said.

"How long am I going to have to pay for it?"

"You don't."

"Are you sure?"

Piper's eyes were wide. She looked so gorgeous, so sweetly vulnerable in the center of his big bed, that Red had to turn away for a moment to compose himself.

"Hell, Piper. Look at me. You've already got me wrapped around your little finger. I'll pay whatever I have to if it means I get to keep you."

She didn't quite look like he'd convinced her, but at least she looked stable and whole again.

Red nudged away the closest restraint, lying black and damning against the pale covers. "We obviously need to table this idea, anyway."

"No, I…I don't want to," Piper said. "Now that we've talked more about it, I'll be fine next time. I swear. Maybe not tonight, but soon."

"I'd rather you be something a bit less neutral than fine."

Piper huffed in annoyance. "Okay. How about this? You're a total sex god and I definitely want you to have your wicked way with me. *Next* time."

Red gave her his wickedest grin, since she'd asked so nicely. "Okay, sweetheart. You have a deal. And you are definitely going to be invoking God by the time I'm through with you."

Twenty-Five

THEY STAYED IN on Sunday morning because Red was expecting yet another delivery—and it turned out to be two comfortable couches of soft caramel-colored leather for his living room, as well as a couple of other nondescript boxes that the movers set in the corner.

The guys carted away the hard, white couches on their way out. Piper wondered where they would take them—some modern, high-end bridal boutique, perhaps? Or would it be Gina MacLellan's garage? Not that it mattered. Piper was just happy to see them gone.

After they ate a late, lazy breakfast, Red produced several large and sturdy boxes from his study. Then he commandeered Piper's help in gathering up all the assorted lamps and strange, misshapen pieces of sculpture from the main rooms. They packed them all up for the movers to fetch later that week.

The new cartons were next on Red's to-do list. When he cut them open, Piper saw that they contained new lamps for the apartment, in understated mercury glass and simple bronze. Before her eyes, Red's loft was undergoing a transformation, and Piper admired the way it was finally becoming a space that truly reflected its owner. She already felt more comfortable in the living room and hoped he would, too.

By late afternoon, they were tired and ready to call it quits. The autumn sun was sinking low behind the buildings outside, throwing the living room into darkness. Red left the new lamps unlit—commenting wryly that there was still plenty of ugliness left to banish, despite the hill of boxes stacked near the front door.

Lights were beginning to wink on in the buildings outside his windows. Piper turned on the bulb over the stove, then grabbed a bottle of wine and two glasses from the kitchen counter. When she turned back, Red had turned on the television, and its pale ghostly glow illuminated the rest of the cavernous space.

Red sank onto one of the new couches and used the remote to cue up the spy thriller they'd decided to watch. Then, he sprawled back and watched Piper walk over.

She set the bottle and wine glasses on the plexiglass coffee table and wondered how long it would be before Red replaced that, too. Not long, she'd guess. It stuck out like a sore thumb, now that the items around it had been changed.

She went to sit next to him.

"Wait," Red burst out. This close, Piper could see how determined he looked. He stood and moved behind her, wrapping an arm around her waist and leaning down to murmur in her ear. His mouth was hot against her skin.

"Close your eyes," Red told her.

Piper did as he asked but wished she could hide the way she was suddenly shaking. It made no sense. She *loved* when Red touched her. Still, she couldn't help wondering what he intended to do. After last night's failed escapade, everything felt…ambiguous.

He'd absolutely noticed, of course. Red made a reassuring sound against her cheek, then kissed her softly.

"It's okay, little dove," he whispered. "I promise. Nothing scary, okay?"

Piper swallowed hard, hating that her confidence had failed her, that she needed a minute to decide. Why couldn't she be different? More like the Antoinette Corelli people expected?

With feather-light fingertips, Red caressed her shoulders and arms.

"Piper?" he asked again. "Will you trust me?" His voice cracked just the smallest amount, and that was what finally did it. The infinitesimal flash of vulnerability in a man so in charge of everything else—it demolished her reservations.

Piper nodded, squeezing her eyes shut again. Red's fingers moved deftly down the buttons of her shirt, undoing them so he could slip it from her shoulders and set it aside.

"Oh, honey," he murmured, unbuttoning her jeans, too. When he pushed them down her legs, he took her panties along with them. Piper stood there with her knees quivering, like she was a skittish cat about to bolt.

She waited for Red to unclasp her bra next but instead, he set his hands on her hips and sat back down, pulling her into his lap. Red arranged her legs so that her thighs were draped wide across his. When he moved his knees further apart, it spread her open even more. She shivered at the sensation of the cool air hitting her, and Red growled low in his throat in appreciation.

"Now, then. Where were we?" he wondered. "Watching a movie, wasn't it?" He brushed her hair back and delicately kissed the rim of her ear. "Open your eyes, dove. Watch the show."

The TV screen flared too brightly in the dark room. For the first several minutes of the movie, cars chased each other through narrow streets, explosions detonated, good guys charged after bad ones—and Red's careful fingers trailed over her thighs and stomach and the inside of her forearms.

He stroked and teased and caressed, and Piper tried to ignore how exposed she felt, so she could focus on the movie, or on her mounting desire. Anything but the worry that she wasn't enough for this burning hot man—and wouldn't ever be.

Soon Red was scooping her breasts out of the lacy cups of her bra to toy with them. He kneaded and massaged her, rubbing her nipples between his fingers while she tried not to squirm.

Sometimes she felt his breath tickle across her temple. Sometimes his hot tongue flicked out for a second to taste her earlobe or her neck. Piper was hyperaware of the material of his jeans, soft against the back of her thighs and rear. She was lulled by his touch and the rise and fall of his chest, his cotton shirt sliding silkily across her back.

Piper shifted, trying to ease the tension building inside her. Red still held her legs wide with his, but he hadn't ventured very far south yet. When she whimpered in frustration, she felt him smile against her hair.

"Shh," he soothed. "Keep watching. This is the best part."

At last, his maddeningly-light touch dipper lower, to trail through the slick folds between her legs. He drew out her pleasure as long as she could stand it, until her moans were louder than anything happening onscreen.

By the time Red guided her skillfully over the cliff, a sniper on the big TV was taking out the unsuspecting players in a high-stakes poker game, and Piper was a vibrating, boneless heap of flesh, splayed across his lap and panting like some kind of erogenous blanket.

Red was definitely grinning now, planting kiss after kiss on the top of her head, her temple and ear and cheek and jaw, his palms stroking her in soft, soothing caresses, easing her back down to earth.

Before Piper knew it, he'd cast aside her bra and pulled a throw from the back of the couch to tuck around her, nestling her sideways in his arms to curl close against his chest. His heart thumped loud and steady beneath her cheek, anchoring her.

Once again, the blazing chemistry between them had managed to leap right over her hesitation. Piper probably ought to be more worried about that, but damn, it was fun. She'd taken a chance, trusted him, and it had worked out fine.

Piper peered at Red's face in the flickering light, then back at the screen. The movie had ended. She couldn't imagine he was overly interested in the credits rolling up the screen. She ought to say something. She should say…anything that was less lame than "thank you."

She managed a breathy, "Whoa," and immediately winced at how juvenile it sounded.

"Indeed," Red agreed cheerfully. "I'd like to bring you upstairs now," he added more carefully, "Unless you'd rather watch another movie?"

The cheeky bastard. Piper glared at him. "Not just yet," she said. She rearranged herself until she was straddling his lap, whipping off his shirt, and wiping that smug look off his face.

Red's eyes glinted in the TV's weak light, then widened when she ground down against the admirable bulge behind his zipper. At least one part of him couldn't play dumb—his erection, as always, was *quite* happy to make Piper's acquaintance.

"No?" he inquired mildly.

"Uh-uh," she confirmed. "I've got things to do right here, as it turns out."

"Please let me be one of them," he muttered fervently.

"You are. And after that, I'll even let you take me to dinner."

"You are everything kind in this world," Red told her.

THEY ARRIVED A bit early for their dinner reservation in SoHo. Felix dropped them off at the corner, so they could stroll up the block and enjoy the mild fall night before they ate. The street was lined with boutiques, and since he'd kept Piper inside all day, Red thought she might like to do a little window shopping.

Besides, it could be eye-opening to wander stores with a woman. The things they pointed out, even the way they did it, always gave Red interesting insight into who he was dealing with. It was an old gambit better suited to a different kind of person, but maybe he'd find out a little bit more about what made Piper tick.

There was a steady stream of people who were also out enjoying the weather but, of course, Piper was unique. She didn't seem overly aware that they were walking past open shop doors at all, and that included two different luxury shoe boutiques.

That was remarkable for a woman who loved shoes as much as Piper. He hadn't forgotten those fiendish leopard-printed numbers she'd worn to their first meeting. They hadn't made another appearance yet, a fact which saddened him deeply. He'd like to see her in them again. Only them.

Piper did a quick double-take when they passed a display of handbags in a large window, noting the sign over the door, and passing a keen eye over the brightly-colored leathers. And then she kept walking, with barely a pause in her step.

Purses, Red thought, possibly she liked purses, just—not these particular ones. He glanced back at the store over her shoulder. They might be haute couture, but he wasn't surprised that she'd passed them by. They would have fit right in with his former home décor.

Red ran an admiring eye over Piper, taking in her ivory cashmere turtleneck and tall suede boots. She mostly wore classic, streamlined pieces, nothing fussy or frilly. Occasionally she threw in a flourish like those animal-print heels, but she managed to be judicious about it. She wasn't flashy or terribly trendy. She was…as elegant as a goddamn duchess.

Shitty home repairs notwithstanding, Piper didn't appear to be hurting for money too badly, but Red couldn't help wondering what she might do with a bank account like his to play with. Somehow Red suspected there still wouldn't be any great influx of spangles and flounces. Piper was an understated woman. A practical one.

Honestly, it drove him crazy. Red couldn't remember ever wanting to rile up a woman more. Which was a switch—normally, he preferred women to stay reserved, unless he told them when and how to let go. But Piper had him nearly slavering with the desire to make her lose her undentable composure. Oh, how the tables had turned—how the mighty had fallen.

Red grinned, peeking down at the siren who'd felled him.

Piper's attention had finally been snagged by no less than the venerable jewelry store known for its turquoise blue boxes. Her attempts to peruse the window displays without obviously craning her neck or losing a step were clearly requiring some effort. Piper had totally forgotten to keep making conversation or to walk in a straight line.

Red chuckled—oh well, she was only human. Something on this street of temptations had been bound to entice her. He checked the time, then tugged her to a full stop.

"Hey, Piper?"

He'd been taking a strange amount of pleasure in the way her hand felt tucked in his elbow. Now it fell away, and she looked up at him in query.

"Wanna go in?" he asked, smiling at her.

"Oh!" Piper was startled.

Busted. Red laughed harder.

"Well…" she hemmed. "Do we have time?" She tried and failed to keep the note of hope out of her voice.

"Plenty. Come on, it'll be fun," he urged, holding the door open and grabbing her hand.

She looked cautious, but she came along anyway. That was good. Maybe he was making some headway with her.

The second they entered, however, Red was hit with an icy blast of wrath. *Damn it.* His ex, Monika, sailed toward them, an infuriated expression on her face. He'd forgotten that she lived nearby and loved to linger here, trolling for her next conquest, drafting a wish list…whatever it was that she did.

How long had it been? Two years? Three? Monika had lasted longer than many, but Red struggled, just then, to remember *why.* She certainly didn't have an ounce of submission in her. She'd only been an ornament for his arm when an event had called for it—nothing more.

Now that he had Piper, he couldn't believe he'd lived like that for so long.

By way of greeting, Monika barked, "Red." He hadn't missed that tone of hers, that was for damn sure.

She looked pointedly from his face to Piper's, then down at their still-linked hands. Monika snorted in amusement, or possibly derision. Was it really so hard to believe that he'd found something real, or was this just disbelief that it hadn't been with her? Hardly mattered, at this point.

"Seriously?" she demanded. "This is who you're with now? And when have you ever brought someone *here?*"

In the past, Red's pride might have been pricked. He might've dropped his date's hand so he could face off with Monika and deliver her the set-down she so clearly deserved. He would have been disgusted with the situation for any number of reasons, but he would've been most unhappy with himself for giving Monika the opening to take a shot at him.

But Red couldn't ever recall caring quite so much about the feelings of the woman he was *with* before. He looked at Piper, checking her reaction, and decided she could use some bolstering. For the hell of it, he lifted their joined hands and kissed her knuckles, putting as much apology and reassurance into his gaze as he could muster.

Monika emitted a harsh sound, but when Red turned back to her the sneer had slipped a bit. A flicker of uncertainty crossed her face. It seemed he wasn't the only one parading around vulnerable today.

And she'd asked him a question. Red supposed he ought to reply.

"I could not be more serious if I tried," he told her. Monika edged back at that, so he moved past her with Piper in tow. Red registered his ex's silent departure somewhat absently, though, because now Piper was frozen in place, refusing to venture further into the store.

She studied him a moment, then looked away. "So, how long did you date *her*?"

No point in denying it, he supposed. "Long enough," he admitted.

Piper watched Red's face. "You really weren't exaggerating about the kind of women you know, were you?"

"Not at all."

"I see. And, just estimating, how many people like that did you go out with, would you say?"

He smiled. He couldn't even venture to guess, but, "Even the one was too many, don't you think?"

"Yup. Sure do." With that out of the way, though, Piper still didn't seem inclined to move her feet. Other patrons were starting to circumvent them with curious stares.

Red wasn't in a huge hurry, but he did hope to eventually eat dinner tonight. "So, what happens here," he said, "Is that we browse around and look in the cases. When you see something you like, you point it out to me. You say, 'Isn't that pretty?' and then I nod and try to commit it to memory. The next time I want to buy you something, I'll come back here and look for it."

Piper's eyes rounded at that, so Red took her arm and guided her to the first case, an innocuous collection of delicate silver necklaces meant for kids. Her eyes passed dispassionately over the display, so he nudged her along the row. Next came charms for bracelets, then men's watches. The real fun was in the center of the store, with its glittering banks of diamonds.

Red slid his arm around Piper's waist and spun her in that direction.

"When you want to try something on, just let me know and I'll make it happen," he murmured into her ear.

"But," Piper argued, "How am I supposed to…" Her mouth snapped shut at the sight of the rows and rows of sparkling earrings, and she squeaked a little. "Oh. *Wow*."

"Just like that," Red smiled, and gestured over the keen-eyed employee watching them.

"I have stuff like this saved on my online pinboard," she whispered furtively, "But I've never actually been brave enough to come in here and try it on."

"Why not?"

"Because then they expect you to buy stuff!"

"Not necessarily," he replied.

The salesman approached and rested his hands on the glass. "How can I help you today?" he inquired, looking between them and sizing them up.

Red chuckled—Piper stood ramrod straight beside him, a serious expression plastered on her face. She shot him a panicked look, and he knew he'd have to do the talking.

"We'd like to take a look at this pair," he announced, hazarding a guess and stabbing a finger toward the middle of the pack. The employee nodded and reached for his keyring.

"Actually," Piper cleared her throat. "It was these."

Game on.

Twenty-Six

OVER DINNER, PIPER had worried that she might have gone a little overboard at the jewelry store. Once her intimidation had worn off and it became clear that the sales guy was happily on board, she'd gone All. In. How often did a girl get to try on diamonds with five- and six-digit price tags, after all? Not often enough, if you asked her.

Still, in case Red started drawing unfortunate parallels between her and that horrid ex of his, Piper had reached for the quickest change of subject she could think of.

She'd mentioned a Broadway billboard she'd seen on the way there, then told Red that they ought to catch a show sometime. Red, master of making things happen, had immediately whipped out his phone.

"If you can hang around for another couple days," he'd said, "I could probably get us tickets for tomorrow night." That, at least, had to be a perk of being who he was.

Piper's eyes must've lit up—how could they not? "I'd love that! Let me see if the cat sitter can do the extra days." She'd smiled, "Again."

"That woman is going to be buying her own island at this rate."

"That's the truth. But this time, my sitter is a teenaged boy," she'd laughed. "He lives down the street and he's saving up for a new video game. Though I'm positive he's going to be a vet someday. He loves animals. He'd probably bring home strays all the time if his dad wasn't allergic."

AS SHE'D EXPECTED, Piper's cat sitter was not only available, he was thrilled. Piper had told him that if he also got her mail and watered her plants, she'd throw in a good bonus, too.

Overhearing that, Red had pulled out his phone, ordered the new game her neighbor wanted so badly and said he'd pick it up at the store the next day for her.

All of which explained why Piper found herself sitting pretty at the theater with Red on Monday night, instead of moping around Maryland all by herself, missing him. Out on the town with her tall, handsome date, worries about work and her house seemed very far away.

After the show, however, she and Red ran into Trident's former owners in the lobby. Lisa Denton made a beeline right for them, towing her husband along in her wake.

She had transformed, somewhat, since Piper had seen her last. The bookish grandmother persona had been scrapped, disconcertingly replaced with a society maven that was all hard angles.

Mrs. Denton looked Piper and Red over, then said coyly, "How peculiar to see the two of you here together. And, also oddly fitting."

"Don't be mysterious, Lisa," John said, giving her a repressive look. "Why shouldn't they spend time with each other? They work together now."

"You're absolutely correct, though of course she never had much time for Jim." Mrs. Denton pursed her lips, hiding an unkind smirk. "Anyway—what did you think, Piper? Did you enjoy the show?"

"I did. The cast did a terrific job," Piper said, as neutrally as possible. Red stood tense and bristling at her side, making her wonder if the Trident negotiations had been testier than she realized.

"As they do," Lisa agreed, her eyes skipping back and forth between them, measuring. Calculating.

John Denton leaned on his cane with one hand and reached for his wife with the other. "I think that should do it," he told her. "We're done here."

"Not quite," Red gritted out between clenched teeth. He gestured to Felix, waiting at the curb, then asked the Dentons, "Might I have a private word?"

Mrs. Denton turned to her husband with a wide, triumphant smile. "I told you, John. Didn't I tell you?"

Denton, gray and rigid, assented with a short, cursory nod.

Red pulled Piper a few steps away. "Listen, I need to talk to these two, but I don't know how long it might take. It's freezing, though, and you don't have a coat. Why don't you head home in the car so you can get warmed up, and I'll grab a cab as soon as I'm done?"

Something odd was going on. Piper asked, "Is everything okay?"

"Totally fine."

"You sure about that?"

"I promise," Red told her, though he didn't look fine at all. He was absolutely seething. "Go on and have a nice long bath. I'll be there before you know it."

He was packing her off, but what choice did she have? These people could have all kinds of unfinished business with each other. If they were going to have words, she'd really rather not be a bystander in the paparazzi photos that were bound to surface.

Red had managed to keep that from happening once, but odds were that he wouldn't be able to do it again.

Piper let him kiss her on the cheek, then she waved at the Dentons and left.

AS MONDAY MORNINGS went, Red's had been spectacularly unproductive. Wayne had called in sick but still managed to email him his schedule for the day. Red had tooled around on the internet for a while, then sat through a short debriefing with Rob and some of his team members—but walked away having learned nothing new about the Denton's skullduggery.

Around lunchtime, he'd broken out of his office to pick up the video game for Piper's cat-sitting neighbor, then grabbed a second one for the kid that the store manager insisted was the newest, hottest thing. After all, if it wasn't for Dr. Teen, DVM, Piper would've been on a plane home instead of spending more time with Red.

He'd taken a walk and run smack into the Wall Street location of that jewelry store they'd visited. And then Red had gone inside. He'd excused that bit of absurdity by reminding himself that he needed to buy a gift for Anika's upcoming wedding. That had worked reasonably well, too, since Red managed to purchase her a very nice set of candlesticks from her registry.

But he also bought Piper a ring. Not the life-changing kind, God help him, though he had strolled pretty slowly by that case. No, Red only lost his mind once he spotted the very ring he'd seen on Piper's online pinboard account that morning. Like magic, he remembered the salesman from the day before announcing Piper's ring size, and the rest was wallet-shrinking history.

Red had spent the rest of the day getting used to the shape and feel of a ring box in his pocket and found that it didn't bother him as much as he would've expected. Still, Piper was going to blow a gasket when he gave it to her. Therefore, he had spent the better part of his afternoon concocting the perfect plan.

HE'D INTENDED TO give Piper the ring before they went to the theater. By the time Red headed home that evening, he'd had it all planned out. What he'd say—how he'd kiss her.

Instead, she'd walked down the stairs from his bedroom wearing a sinful pair of shoes he'd bought her many weeks ago, taunting him with crisscrossing black laces that marched up the tops of her pale feet and ankles.

They'd turned Piper's simple little sheath dress into something painfully erotic.

So Red had sat next to her at his dinner table and made normal small talk for a while. They ate the take-out he'd picked up on his way home, and Piper got excited about seeing her first Broadway show.

When Piper finished, he dumped their plates in the kitchen sink, grabbed dessert from the bag on the counter, and set hers in front of her. Chocolate mousse. Piper liked chocolate. Red had taken her fork and fed her a bite and enjoyed the way her lashes fluttered in pleasure.

He did not say, *I got you something,* as he'd planned.

Piper didn't have the chance to be perplexed, to wonder why, though. He knew she would've, and he loved that she didn't appear to have an avaricious bone in her body.

In the face of all her mousse-induced groans of pleasure, all his pre-arranged words had evaporated like they'd never existed. Red hadn't felt like explaining why he'd been stalking the aisles of that store that day. He honestly wasn't sure he knew for himself.

Red had simply needed her. So, he'd urged Piper up onto the edge of the table, smoothed his hands over her ankles, then undid the thin leather cords tied in bows there—those fiendish little tassels dangling seductively from each end.

He'd dropped Piper's shoes on the chair next to him, slipped a hand inside his suit jacket, and touched the small box hidden there. Her eyes would've gotten big as moons if she'd spotted it, Red knew. She might not have managed to stay quiet long enough for him to even explain.

It's not what it looks like, he'd meant to say. *I imagine we'll get there soon enough, but I wanted you to have something to wear until then. So, this ring is for your right hand—they called it an eternity band.* Aptly put, since he didn't think eternity would be long enough for him to get his fill of Piper Mae Fulham.

Red was supposed to have taken out the ring and said, *I liked the sound of that, and I thought it was perfect for you.* Then he should have taken Piper's hand and placed the damn thing on her finger.

He did *none* of that. As always, the plans Red made for Piper took on water faster than a torpedoed cargo ship.

Instead of declaring himself, he'd simply leaned in and kissed her. Piper had tasted like chocolate, and melted like it, too. Red had left the ring in his pocket and reached around to unzip her dress. He'd smoothed the straps off her shoulders, hiked the hem up to her hips, and taken Piper hard on his dining room table.

And then Red brought her to the theater, sated and starry-eyed because of him and what they had done together. Later, in the dark of the private theater box, it might've occurred to Piper what he'd meant by, *We'll get there soon enough.*

Only Red hadn't said it. Any of it.

He still might have salvaged his romantic plan if they hadn't run into the Dentons after the show—John Senior looking grim as death and Lisa acting so sly and self-satisfied. Red hadn't wanted to tip them off before he'd had a chance to make the net around them nice and snug, but damn, that woman had goaded him.

He'd had to hustle Piper into the car and away, just so he could make it clear to those greedy fools that he knew all their ducks were not in a tidy row.

Except then their son had strolled up, breathing fire and cheap bourbon fumes.

"It's bad enough you took our family legacy away," Jim had complained, "Right out from under us."

Red had frowned and so did John, both remembering the Trident transaction quite a bit differently.

But Jim had gone on. "You don't have to stand here on the street and threaten my parents. They're only a couple of retirees now. You can't take any more from them. From us."

Lisa had castigated Red for firing her son, the 'best damn crime writer in the country.'

John had attempted, once more, to get his family to leave.

And the theater workers had very politely invited them to retire to the cigar lounge next door, where they would be more comfortable. Red had set aside a flash of guilt when he thought of Piper, ringless and waiting for him at home. He'd ridden off into an odd, weaponless sort of battle, where he attempted to say what he needed to without giving any of his strategy—such as it was—away.

Twenty-Seven

J UST AS PIPER was exiting the hot bath Red had prescribed, he'd texted to let her know he was going to be a while more yet. By then, Piper hadn't been able to keep her eyes open any longer, even with her rampant curiosity about what was happening with the Dentons. She'd climbed into his bed to wait for him and figured Red was bound to show up there eventually.

At some point, he had. As Piper came slowly awake, she registered that Red had already shucked his suit and crawled into bed in his t-shirt and boxers. He lay face-to-face with her and was nudging her gradually into consciousness with light caresses along her arm and kisses to her forehead.

When Piper opened her eyes, Red was smiling sheepishly back at her. His head was nestled on the pillow next to hers, his long body mirroring her own posture. He smelled wonderfully clean and masculine, crisp and fresh—he obviously hadn't slept at all yet.

"You made it," Piper croaked out, her voice scratchy with sleep.

He nodded. "Seems like I keep making you wait for me. I'm sorry."

"You're a very bad boy."

"True," Red's eyes crinkled at the edges when he laughed, then he shifted forward, easing her onto her back. "Can you find it in your heart to forgive me?" He propped himself on his elbow and trailed his fingers through Piper's hair, spreading it across the pillow.

"Probably."

"I wonder how I can convince you to?"

"I'm sure you'll think of something." Piper was happy to see him, but underneath it burrowed a small, niggling tendril of doubt. How many nights would she have to spend, exactly, waiting for this man to show up? That assumed, of course, that this whole thing with him went anywhere—that he didn't tire of her too fast for it to even matter.

Red lowered his face to her neck, and his lips grazed her skin before moving on to her ear and down the sensitive side of her throat again. Piper's eyes drifted closed as she absorbed his presence above her—warm and large, strong and careful. It was hard to be skeptical of someone so solid, but she'd be foolish not to.

"My job is demanding," he murmured against her skin. "But most of the time, I love it. I get off on it. Overcoming the challenges."

Piper nodded. He would.

"Except now, there's somewhere else I want to be. When I can't get away, it chafes." Red raised his head and gazed down at her, and she felt the intensity of it before she even opened her eyes. When she did, though, it was too hard to look back. She felt too exposed.

Piper looked away.

"It's like everyone's expectations of me got all out of proportion," he continued, returning to brush his lips over her neck and collarbone. "I never cared before. But now, knowing you're out there somewhere, being enticing without even meaning to…"

His voice faded away and Piper could feel his breath against her sternum. Suddenly, he rubbed his face against her pajama top like a puppy.

"I don't want to sit in an office all day," Red told her.

"I don't know," Piper teased. "It seemed pretty nice when I was there."

He raised up on his arms and looked down at her. "It's different with you," he said. "Everything's different with you."

Before she could respond to that, Red scooted down and inched up the hem of her top, placing blazing hot kisses along the sliver of skin he exposed. He ran his lips back and forth, tickling the fine hairs there and sending a shiver through her.

"I have something for you. A couple little gifts," he said quietly.

"I'll bet," Piper laughed before her sleepy brain caught up with the uncertainty in his tone.

"No, really," Red chastised. "I just wrapped them, and I want to give them to you. But I don't want you to think that I'm trying to buy your forgiveness, or your complacency—or whatever— for being late all the time. It's not like that."

"Okay. So, what's it like, then?"

"I spotted one of them in a store today, when I was picking up a wedding gift for Anika. It made me think of you so much that I just couldn't leave it there. I wanted you to have it. I wanted to see it on you."

Piper squinted up at him, trying to parse Red's explanation. He was making a big deal out of what was bound to be some little trinkets. So *why* was she catching the faintest whiff of vulnerability coming off him?

Suddenly wary, she wriggled out from under him, needing a little more space for herself. Red sat up and studied her face. What he saw there must have resolved something for him because he nodded briefly—like he'd come to a decision.

Red leaned forward and reached under the pillow he'd been laying on, extracting a long, slim box covered in black paper. Piper untied the satin ribbon and opened it, and saw a beautiful, glossy-blue fountain pen laying inside. Around it was a ring.

"I know no pen could possibly compete with your favorite one," he began, "But maybe…"

Piper lifted a shaking finger to touch the diamonds winking up at her. Red slid the ring free, lifted her right hand, and put the ring onto her finger.

"What do you think?" he asked softly.

Piper squinted at it, trying to unravel what she was seeing. A wide band of stylized vines and leaves, liberally sprinkled with diamonds, was sparkling up at her. The metal looked different than silver or white gold—platinum, she guessed, by the color of it.

No. Not a guess.

"I *know* this ring," she said in shock.

"Do you?"

"I've been—I've been admiring it for years," she stuttered.

It was amazing that she'd managed to be even that casual when *stalking* or *lusting* were probably better words. But Piper had never gotten it for herself, because—

"I can't accept this!" she gasped, wrenching it off in dismay. She tried to press it into Red's hand. "You're out of your mind. This is way too expensive!"

He refused to take it.

"Stop! What are you doing?" she wailed. "Take it back!"

"No." He sat on his hands like a stubborn child.

"No? What do you mean, *no*?" Her voice had turned shrill. Piper was aware of it—accepted it, even. Why the hell not?

"I mean, no. I refuse to take it back. It made me think of you. A lot. So, I got it and I gave it to you, and it looks beautiful on you. You can't pretend like you don't love it." Piper's chagrin must have been written all over her face, because then he added, "You *do* love it. Admit it."

She bit back the automatic denial that bubbled up to her lips and nodded instead. It was totally appalling because she *did* love the ring—insanely, irrationally so.

She might've tried to pretend to herself, but Red was far too perceptive to fall for it. She couldn't lie to him.

He pried it out of her palm and slipped it back onto her finger.

"It belongs here. I didn't want to make a fuss, and I didn't mean to freak you out. I just wanted you to have something special from me. Now, let's just lay here for a little while, okay? It's been a long fucking day and I missed you."

Red held Piper against his chest. His breathing was deep and regular—peaceful. Piper willed her stiff limbs to relax, but it was hard. The ring pressed into her skin where her fingers were entwined with his.

He murmured, "The pen is for you, too. It's a fountain pen that writes like a…fountain pen. I hope you like it."

"I love it," Piper smiled. "Thank you."

For the last couple of years, she'd sworn to herself that she wouldn't be duped by smooth words and a pretty face again. For the most part, she'd been successful, too. But nothing could have prepared her for Red's will—it was both excruciatingly simple and dreadfully complicated, and Piper was weak in the face of it.

To her everlasting mortification, it seemed she had no fortitude to withstand his blunt words, his direct manner, or his horribly perfect gifts. She couldn't possibly hope to contain Red or to keep him.

Since she was beginning to suspect she'd stupidly lost her heart already, that meant Piper was doomed.

LYING NEXT TO Piper, Red still hadn't been able to summon most of the words he'd crafted so carefully earlier that day. Not after he'd had to send her back to his loft alone while he tried to handle the Dentons.

Because—while he might believe they had a future together—Piper might find that hard to envision. What kind of life would it be, constantly playing second fiddle to his job? To his responsibilities?

At least he'd won this tiny victory. The eternity band took up almost all the space below her knuckle, starbursts of diamonds flowing around the circlet with white fire at their hearts. Red had remembered her size correctly, at least—the ring fit Piper precisely and she wasn't trying to give it back anymore.

Piper's patent stupefaction had been excruciatingly clear when she'd first stared down at his gift. Once she recognized the ring, she was predictably horrified. Not only had she known where Red purchased it, she knew how much he'd paid for it—because she'd picked it out herself. Red wondered if she regretted saving it to her wish list now.

Had she forgotten mentioning the website to him over dinner? Or that Red was a quick study? It hadn't taken him long to investigate what she'd been chatting about, and he'd been intrigued to discover, tucked among the photos of home décor and snarky cat memes, all sorts of helpful gift ideas for her.

Shoes and more shoes, but also handbags and lingerie. Sparkling jewels. Mountain cabins. The possibilities were intoxicating.

Yeah, Piper would wear his ring. She'd wear the clothes Red bought her, and the kisses he laid on her, too. She'd wear every single one of his marks of possession, and any other man who spotted them would know to keep on walking.

Piper was *his*. Once she figured that out, once she began believing it—maybe she wouldn't question what was growing between them anymore.

Red realized, of course, that he was reverting into caveman territory—he knew he didn't *own* her.

Red wanted to be hers as much as she was his. Red wanted Piper to claim him once and for all, and he wanted to be worthy of it. When the time came that they could finally take their relationship public, there'd be no stopping them.

Red knew it like he knew his own name.

IN THE MORNING, Piper's flight home was delayed while a treacherous front of thunderstorms skated across the Baltimore area. The sudden change in plan seemed to throw her for a bit of a loop.

After watching her pace around the loft for a while, Red finally dragged her into his game room to pass the time, and to take her mind off worrying about the weather.

There was something different about Piper's expression when she gazed at his pool table this time, some flicker that he'd never spotted on her face before. He wanted to know what it was.

Red leaned over to rack the balls. "Let's play," he said, handing her a cue stick before she could whip out her phone to check the Maryland weather for the umpteenth time.

Piper went along with it, smiling a little but not saying much through their first few shots. Red watched the way she moved around the table and contemplated the angles her balls took.

"You're a good player, aren't you?" he commented. "Maybe more than good." She improved more and more with each shot she took.

"I used to play every chance I got," Piper told him wistfully. "Once upon a time."

"I can tell."

"That was a long time ago, though. I don't find myself in many pool halls anymore. Not too many bars, either." She frowned at the wall. "None, as a matter of fact."

Red studied her. "You loved it." No question. She missed it, too.

Piper sniffed a little, deriding her long-ago self. "I had a bad-ass conception of myself back then. You know—that girl who drinks whiskey, shoots pool, and swears like a sailor. All the guys are supposed to love her. And if I got a couple tattoos and a lot of ear piercings, then maybe I'd be edgier than all the other kids in middle-class suburbia. What did I know?"

"Sounds like fun." Red's younger self would've killed to meet a girl like her then.

Piper clearly didn't agree. "No, it didn't take me long to figure out how naïve I was. I wasn't actually tough. It was all just foolish posturing."

Whatever had nudged her out of that life stage still stung, it seemed. "Isn't that par for the course when you're twenty?" It wasn't often that she dropped tidbits from her past into conversation. Red kept his tone mild, hoping to keep Piper talking.

She shrugged, her eyes drifting over the table, studying her options. "When I was twenty, I was still under the impression that I had some fierce spark within me that other people didn't have. It was going to turn my life into something extraordinary, I knew it. I just…" Piper peeked at him, then quickly looked away. "It took some time to come to terms with the fact that I'm actually pretty ordinary."

Red tried to school his expression into impassivity. Normally, he'd have thought that this was all an affectation, the kind that so many women of his acquaintance used to fish for compliments he didn't dole out easily. Only, Piper's entire demeanor was so woebegone that he knew it was no act.

The question became, why would a woman as lovely and accomplished as her be so intent on minimizing herself? Piper had that spark all right, and had probably possessed it all along. Any person with half a brain could see it—in fact, it was probably why she'd done so well in her career.

The conundrum intrigued him. Instead of singing her own praises so Red would understand why he should spoil her rotten, Piper was awfully keen on making the point that she was really nothing special—despite all appearances to the contrary.

And she did that because…Red watched her and considered the way her mind worked. If Piper could convince him that she wasn't exceptional enough to want, then he would probably ditch her before this thing between them even had a chance to get off the ground.

Maybe even before anyone's hearts were on the table. Which made Red wonder—did Piper already like him enough that she thought he had the ability to hurt her? By submarining her chances before he got too interested, she could be trying to protect herself.

Red shook his head. That was a lot of logical leaps to make, without any of the pertinent background data. But if that *was* what Piper felt, he probably ought to warn her—telling Red MacLellan not to want something, telling him that he couldn't have it and shouldn't try—well, that was throwing down the gauntlet for a man like him.

Red wouldn't quit until Piper gave him her heart and soul.

"You're a lot of things, sweetheart," he told her. "Ordinary isn't one of them."

Twenty-Eight

THE THUNDERSTORMS IN the Mid-Atlantic had turned into torrential rains, and over the course of the day, half of the eastern seaboard had ended up grounded. Piper's flight, which had been delayed over and over, was finally canceled altogether.

Red went looking for her, so he could give her the good news. Or was it bad? Hard to say. She wasn't in his study working, as he expected. Instead, Red found her, silent as a tomb, in his kitchen.

Piper's spine was stiff, and she was knocking back a measure of alcohol with a quick and unmistakable tilt of her head.

Red cleared his throat to let her know he was there, but only managed to startle her—Piper nearly jumped out of her skin and began sputtering. Whether that was from his sudden appearance or from the burn of the scotch was unclear.

"Did you just shoot 50-year-old Macallan?" he wondered.

She stared down at the bottle's label a moment before defiantly meeting his eye.

"Might've," she muttered.

When he smiled, Piper's chin tilted up, but her eyes slid guiltily away. Red stepped carefully closer.

"Why?"

"You don't seem to stock anything cheaper," she declared.

He snorted, "Nice try."

Piper huffed in irritation, but finally admitted, "I'm a little on edge."

"Again," Red asked, "Why? Dying to be rid of me already?"

"No, nothing like that." She blew out a long, discouraged breath, then went over to slump onto the couch.

Red grabbed the Macallan and followed. "What's the matter, little dove?"

"It's just—this long-distance thing is tough, you know? I love being together, but it's hard not to worry about how much time I'm spending away from home. My cats and my parents miss me. I'm completely burying my head about the work I need to do on my house. And…I'm writing, but not as much as I would be if I were home alone. I can't start blowing deadlines, now. How awkward would that be, if PKM had to fire my ass?"

Red sighed, feeling guilty. "I'm sorry. It's selfish of me, dragging you up here and then convincing you to stay longer every time."

"I wouldn't say that. You've come to see me, too. But your life is here, and mine is there, and there isn't a good solution to that. We're grownups, Red. We can't just ignore our responsibilities because they're inconvenient."

"That's true. We can only do the best we can."

She turned her pretty caramel-colored eyes on him, and Red hated to see them brimming over.

"What if our best isn't enough?"

"It will be." He took her hands in his and ran his thumb over the ring he'd given her. It looked like it had been made for her. "What brought this on, anyway? Just worried about the flight, or something else?"

Piper stared at the floor for a long time. "The neighbor kid found more water downstairs," she admitted softly. "He couldn't tell where it was coming from. With all the rain we've had, I'm worried it might not be the pipes this time. Maybe a window is leaking, or the roof. I need to get home and find out, though. I should've been there already."

"Oh God, I'm sorry to hear that. But I promise you—we'll figure this out. Just trust me, okay? Trust us."

"I'm trying."

Red wasn't sure he believed that, but now wasn't the time to press the point. "I hope so," he said. He hesitated a long time, but there really wasn't any getting around it. "Your flight was canceled."

Piper dropped her head. "Yeah, I figured. I guess you're stuck with me another night."

"You can stay as long as you like," he told her. "But don't worry. I'm sure everything will be fine in the morning. We'll get you home one way or another."

"I know. Thanks." Piper tried to shake off her gloomy mood and turned a brighter face on him. "We may as well make the best of it. Want to watch another movie? We can try that rice pudding mix you got."

"Not…not yet. I want to ask you something first."

"What is it?"

"Have you thought any more about my offer? About me helping with the house?" Red desperately wanted to erase the heavy cloud of discouragement blanketing her, to restore the intimacy and comfort they usually shared.

"Why do you care so much about this?" Piper sighed. "It's my house and I'll deal with it. Now, come on. We have some bonus time together, and after this, we might not get to see each other again for weeks."

Red scowled. No way would he let that happen. "I care because you care. Because it's weighing on you, and I can help."

"Red, sometimes you're too much, you know that?"

"I know. I'm sorry."

Piper turned away and fussed with a piece of her hair. "And I'm not…" She trailed off. Dropped the hair and waved her hand vaguely around.

"What? You're not what?"

"Not as much. We're not the same. I don't understand why I can see it, and you can't."

Red exhaled. He did not like where Piper's head was tonight, and he couldn't shake the sense that maybe he was missing something—some vital detail that would make sense of all this. "Hey," he murmured, "Come here."

He repositioned Piper until she was facing him on the couch, then slipped her sweater off her shoulders. Piper looked away while he ran his fingers over her, tracing her outline, etching her shape and feel deeper into his memory.

After a while, he spoke again. "The thing is, you're beautiful. That's the first thought that hits a man over the head when you walk into a room," he told her. "Punches him in the chest. Grabs hold of his dick and pulls."

He'd hoped to get her attention, and thankfully, it worked. Piper met his eyes and looked surprised.

"But it's all your other small sweetnesses that pile up and make it impossible not to worship you," Red said.

Piper opened her mouth to refute what she clearly viewed as insanity, so he laid his fingers lightly against her lips and shook his head.

"Let me," he whispered, then continued his recitation. "It's your impossibly soft and fragrant hair. And your skin, too—stunning velvet against mine. It's the curve of your throat and your delicate ankles, and it's the veins that I can trace up the inside of your wrists, all the way to your elbows. It's the tender, vulnerable heat behind your knees," he explained.

"Red, stop."

"No. Have I told you how much I adore your expressions? So many expressions. Your face is always changing, with a million different ways to smile and frown and weep. And your fingers—I'm crazy about how your fingers are always looking for my skin, and always finding it."

Piper went for a half-assed joke, but there was nothing that could dilute what he wanted her to hear. "Well, you're one to talk," she said. "Your fingers are pretty magical, too."

Red snorted, acknowledging that, but she ought to have known he wouldn't be deterred. "All the little things," he murmured, "Layer after layer after layer in an inescapable onslaught—a heady, bewitching net—that's you, Piper."

She rested her hands on his shoulders, and he was surprised by how chilly they felt through his shirt. He pulled her sweater back around her before she could start shivering and wondered if he ought to turn up the heat.

Piper tried deflection next. "You're crazy."

"Maybe. I can't for the life of me figure out how you haven't been snapped up by someone else. But if you think for one moment, now that you're mine, that I'm not going to do my damnedest to make sure you're taken care of, then you're the crazy one."

"Red, come on," she sighed. "If I let you do this, then I'll be no different than all those other women you so fondly labeled *vultures*."

"You are nothing like them, something I keep telling you. And you aren't asking—I'm offering. Let me help with the house, Piper."

"Honestly? There's so much to do, I wouldn't even know where to begin."

PIPER MIGHT NOT know where to start, but Red had a pretty good idea. Once she had fallen asleep with her head in his lap, while the cooking channel flickered silently on the television, Red dialed Tate's number and left him a message.

His buddy finally got back to him early the next morning, before Piper woke up. Red crept downstairs and answered before the call could go to voicemail.

"Tate?"

"What's good, Holmes?" his old friend drawled. He sounded drunk—or exhausted. With Tate, they amounted to about the same thing.

"Who dis?" Red retorted. "Do I know you?"

"Better than your right hand, asshole. What's up? I don't have a ton of time."

"Okay. Didn't you tell me you knew a dude working construction in the D.C. area one time?"

"Yeah. Eric Whittier. He got out of the service last year and started his own remodeling business."

"He any good?"

"From what I hear. But I can look into that more, see what I can find out. Can I get back to you in a couple weeks?"

"Nope. I need a name as soon as possible. Someone really good, and..." Red paused, then bit the bullet. Tate would find out soon enough, anyway. "No 'fraternity members.' You hear me?" It was their old code for ladies' men, and Tate understood immediately.

The fucker chuckled, though. "Could this be, perchance, for a lady friend? In the D.C. area?"

"Maryland suburbs," Red gritted out. "To be specific."

"You have a woman in Maryland, now? How the fuck did you manage that?"

Red waited silently, wishing he could reach through the phone and throttle him.

Tate laughed harder, not conceding. "You're refusing to answer? That's your strategy? You're regressing, brother. Big time."

Red chuckled, but figured the silent treatment was still working fine. He kept at it.

"For the love of God, I can picture your expression perfectly right now. Hang on, motherfucker. Lemme ask around for a minute."

Red tried to be patient, listening to the echoes of his old roommate joking and laughing with the guys in his unit. At least if they were happy, if they had time for everyday nonsense like this phone call, then it meant no one was shooting at them. One thing to be grateful for, at least.

Finally, Tate came back on the line. "All right, Romeo, here you go. Word is, Whittier knows his shit. He's based in Potomac. I'll text you his number once we hang up."

"Thanks, man. I appreciate it."

"Roger that. And, for the record, Eric is reportedly a *man's* man, not a ladies' man. Happy now?"

"Very. You staying safe?"

"Not even a little bit," Tate told him cheerfully.

"You're so predictable." Red missed him, missed having friends nearby that wouldn't stand for his shit, and who always had his back. It reverberated, deep in his chest. "When are you coming home?"

"That, my friend, is classified."

Red wandered over to the new photos on his wall and found the one of him, Tate, and Luca at the party they'd thrown after Red took over from his dad at PKM. "Shocker. Okay, well, try not to get your junk shot off before I see you again." Tate grinned back at him from the old black-and-white, hair as messy as always.

"Trust me, bro, that's priority number one. Gotta go." And the line went dead.

For the next hour, Red kept watching his phone and worrying, until Tate's name finally popped up in his text messages. He thumbed it open to find a gif of a soldier, winking and blowing the smoke off the muzzle of his gun. For now, the 'handsome' member of their little trio was still alive and well, and Red fervently hoped he'd stay that way.

Seconds later, a text arrived with a link to Eric Whittier's webpage. Tate had managed to make himself useful, even from six thousand miles away. *That stud.*

His determination solidified, Red went to wake up Piper so she wouldn't be late for her new flight.

Twenty-Nine

TWO WEEKS LATER, they were right back at it again. Red had found a couple of free days in his schedule and blown into town with a vengeance. Unfortunately for Piper, he'd noticed the two bum windows in her family room within moments of arriving.

"What's that all about?" he demanded, a tremendous scowl on his face.

Piper sighed. This was not going to help her *I've got it covered* defense. "That is where the water was coming in when my flight got canceled. I tried to caulk them once everything dried out, but it didn't really work. I think the wood is too old and warped."

Red strode over to examine what he could through the heavy plastic Piper had taped over the frames. It wasn't pretty, but at least it let light through, and it kept out the rain.

"My dad took a look a couple days ago," she added. "He said he might be able to order some replacement parts or something."

Red glanced over his shoulder at her. "Are these the original windows?"

"Oh no, of course not. My mom and dad had those replaced years ago."

"How many years ago?" He poked around the edges, and the crinkling plastic spooked Sonny, dozing in a patch of sun in the corner. The cat jumped up, shook his head, and stalked off into the kitchen.

"Umm, let me see. I remember getting ready to go to school when the guys came out. That must have been kindergarten, maybe? Or was it first grade?"

"Piper! That was nearly thirty years ago!" he blurted, giving her the universal, palms-out WTF gesture.

Like she didn't realize this was a problem. "So?" she said, knowing it would only rile him up further.

"So, your dad isn't going to be able to find parts for these. They probably need to be replaced altogether."

Piper bit her lip, thinking back to her dad's supreme annoyance. He'd stomped around grumbling, muttering under his breath about still having to fix the impossible, despite having finally unloaded the damn place.

"Yeah, we're not going to tell him that. Dad is definitely going to sit out that discussion."

Red crossed his arms over his broad chest and leaned against the wall. "First the pipes, and now the windows. Jesus, Piper, you don't mess around, do you?"

Piper shuffled over to her favorite armchair and dropped into it. "I know. And they're both so bad. Are the pipes worse than the windows? I don't know. I don't know what to do, and I just wish it was someone else's problem. You know? Just…someone tell me what to do."

Red's expression changed subtly, but it transformed his face. One minute he was a brooding, grumpy bear, and the next—the next that sexy glint had come into his eyes. His lips had quirked up in a sardonic smirk that told Piper she'd said something dirty without meaning to. He straightened and headed right for her.

"Tell you what to do, huh?" he growled, low and dangerous.

Piper's breath caught in her throat. She couldn't speak and she couldn't take her eyes off him, so she nodded, quick and fast.

"Then get down on your knees, sweetheart," he barked. "I've missed you." Red advanced on her, his hands dropping to unfasten his belt buckle.

A small sound escaped Piper's mouth—a half-snort, half-giggle kind of sound. It wasn't very accommodating of her. She stifled it as quickly as she could and slid down onto the carpet.

But Red was staring at her, and he quickly noted the mirth that must be dancing in her eyes. He froze.

"What?" he demanded.

Her neck was starting to ache from having to look up that far. Another betraying squeak snuck out. "You know, I don't think I've ever asked how tall you are before. You've got to be, what? 6'3? 6'4?" Piper was undershooting, and she didn't care.

"6'6, actually," he responded.

"Holy smokes. It's kind of hilarious, to be honest, because I'm not sure this position is going to work the way you're intending. I mean, I'm way down here, and unless things have changed substantially since last I saw you, even your very generous endowments wouldn't be able to span the—"

"I'm begging you to stop talking," Red stated calmly and clearly.

Piper didn't. She was getting a kick out of his discomfiture, all of a sudden. She said, "Why are you so freaking serious?"

Red took a step back and sank onto the couch, looking like *serious* was kind of the point. Was it?

"Freaking?" he asked her. "How old are we right now?"

Piper settled back onto her heels, feeling far more chipper than she had moments before. "I'm 33. You?"

Red looked like he was trying to get a handle on how his badass sex plan was sliding so far sideways. "36."

He eyed her, perched on the floor in front of him. Not tractable, not in the least. And miraculously not depressed anymore, either. Piper had missed him, too.

"You're very cute, you know that?" he grumbled.

She struggled to mask the reflexive flinch that always accompanied that dumb word, but Red never missed a trick.

Immediately, a deep divot formed between his eyebrows, and he said, "Come here."

When Piper rose and stepped close, he spread his knees and pulled her between them. Red looped his arms loosely around her waist and looked gratified when she rested hers on his shoulders.

Touch was good. Touch would anchor her through whatever he was about to make her say. Piper lightly brushed the short hairs on his nape with her fingers and watched with interest as a shiver snaked through him.

She should concentrate, though.

"Tell me," he instructed her, "What's wrong with being cute?"

"Nothing. On the face of it." Piper focused on a spot on the wall, avoiding his too-keen eyes.

Red tried again. "Care to elaborate?"

Blandly, she intoned, "*Cute* is exactly the same sort of compliment as *nice*." Like that cleared things up—both were insidious curses.

"Last time I checked, most people like cute and nice things."

Piper winced again, just a little. With all her emotional repression going on, Red would be lucky if he got one straight word out of her—but at least she knew he enjoyed challenges.

"People like white bread, too," she retorted. "But white bread isn't exactly out there tilting the world on its axis, is it?" She stood stiff and inflexible in his arms.

Red's expression cleared, but in the wake of it came the realization that he was going to make Piper admit what she wasn't saying out loud. Now that he had uncovered a problem, he'd clearly decided to goad her until she coughed up the goods.

"I'm not sure I see the problem," he said silkily.

"Let me put it this way," Piper explained. "I doubt very much that someone like…like…Salma Hayek gets called *cute* regularly. Or, uh…" she gestured loosely, nearly cuffing him on the ear, "Eva Mendes."

"Okay, so those actresses play roles. Tempestuous, volatile *roles*," Red countered.

They also had a completely different look than Piper—but she'd leave that alone for the moment. "Yeah but see—you say that with the teensiest bit of admiration in your voice."

"I think you're confusing admiration with trepidation. That's fear you're hearing."

Piper scoffed.

"Piper, those actresses play characters that would torch a guy's car if he forgot their pet's birthday. They'd kill him if he forgot theirs."

"But no one would dare underestimate them, would they?" And there it was. *Oops.*

"I don't imagine people would let their guard down around them, either," Red pointed out.

"Which means, by extrapolation," Piper replied, "That they *can* let their guard down around cute and nice women. Because those women are *safe.* Guaranteed not to make a scene, guaranteed to be passive. Sort of like doormats."

"So, you think stormy women aren't to be taken lightly?" Red bit out.

"Correct."

"I see." Red's eyes were turbulent, boring into hers with an intensity that made Piper swallow hard. "While we're here, why don't you tell me about the sex appeal part of this equation of yours."

She wanted to stand firm, but her eyes darted cagily away. *Damn it.* "What do you mean?"

"Piper, you just cited two women that represent a passionate, over-the-top stereotype. That may appeal to some men, but it isn't the gold standard. There are other tastes out there. Other appetites." Red's fingers flexed into the meat of her hips.

Her voice came out shaky when she joked, "I know. Like those trophy wives who look like Barbies."

Red shuddered. "Ew. No."

"Tall, hot-tempered redheads?"

"For crying out loud," he complained, getting vexed. "Are you going to enumerate every kind of woman but yourself? Putting aside the fact that those are all stereotypical tropes that may or may not resemble real human beings."

WHEN WAS THE last time Red had engaged in pillow talk that included words like *extrapolation* and *tropes*? Never, that was when.

He tightened his arms around Piper. She gave him a charge, that was for damn sure. She was the most unexpected person he'd ever met, and maybe that was why he found her flare of insecurity so damn amusing.

This was the exact opposite of the dirty scene of acquiescence he'd been envisioning all day. It was, however, a lot more engaging.

"White bread and doormats have no sex appeal whatsoever," she muttered. Luckily, she stopped short of adding, *and neither do I.*

Red dropped backward on the couch, bringing Piper with him. She didn't bat an eye when he propped himself on the pillows, keeping her warm, wonderful body draped over his.

"Good thing you are neither of those things."

Piper laid her head on his shoulder with a disbelieving, "Hmph."

He lifted her chin, so she'd look at him again. "Do you think I underestimate you?"

"No, of course not."

"Then, do you think I only want you because I believe you're meek and docile?"

Piper remained mute. Her lovely brandy eyes shimmered. *Fuck.*

"What's really going on here, Piper?" he asked.

"I can't tell you."

"You can tell me anything, little dove. Always. I want you to. I want to know it all."

"I don't…" she hesitated, then shook her head. "You won't look at me the same."

"Piper, in case you haven't noticed, I look at you like I want to take a bite of you. I look at you like I want to tear your clothes off and fuck you senseless."

At least that got a small, lopsided smile out of her. "No one else has ever done that," she told him. "I don't want to give it up yet."

Yet? "You don't have to. But I wish you'd tell me what this is really about."

She groaned. "Fine. You know what? Fine. You think I haven't dated men before who found out I was an erotic romance author, and then expected me to be some kind of porn star in the sack? I'm not, though. I'm just a regular person. And…not a very experienced one, at that. I haven't done most of the things I've written about. I just…have a good imagination, that's all."

"That is true," Red agreed. Piper's imagination was epic.

"It's exhausting trying to date with the weight of all those expectations on me. When you started trying to do all this dominant/submissive stuff with me, I…"

Red held his breath and waited for her to go on, feeling like an anvil was about to drop on his head.

"…I figured it was the same old song and dance. Kyle was always telling me what a dud I was—what a disappointment. I can't do that again."

"Piper," he said, dismayed, "The way I feel about you has nothing whatsoever to do with your profession. I'm attracted to you because you are a beautiful woman, inside and out, not because you can write a sex scene like it's your superpower."

"But…"

"Listen. In the past, I have done some of that BDSM stuff, it's true. I thought it would be fun to try it with you, but I don't need it to be happy. I only want you to be…you. That's plenty for me. That's all I want."

And, with a shock, Red realized it was true. That elusive extra zing that he'd always hunted for in relationships wasn't, in fact, some trendy bit of kink like he'd thought. It was an even rarer prize, that once-in-a-lifetime, needle in the haystack. It was simply…Piper.

This woman, in all her maddening, adorable, impossible glory, was the one he'd spent a lifetime searching for. She was everything he needed and everything he wanted.

Red was in love with Piper Mae Fulham. She'd never believe it. Hell, he barely could. But suddenly, anything and everything that had come before her was meaningless, and Red was wrecked. Completely.

He grinned up at her. "*Now*, will you get on your knees? It's been fourteen days and six hours since I felt your mouth on my cock. I'm almost positive I'm dying."

A startled laugh burst out of her. "After that pep talk? You bet your sweet ass I will."

RED WOKE UP at dawn to an overarching feeling of Otherness. He blinked slowly, letting awareness descend by degrees until he realized what was different, what was new. *Piper.* Piper was there, curled next to him, asleep in her bed.

The sheet was tucked between her knees—she must've gotten hot sometime during the night. Weak bars of sunlight fell across the lower half of her. She was so beautiful it hurt.

Red rose carefully and used the bathroom, then stood and watched her some more. Piper stretched across her side of the bed like one of her cats in a warm square of sunshine. Her faded, old t-shirt was riding up her hip, revealing the waistband of her loose pajama bottoms. Soft cotton, pastel…paisley. Simple and feminine, just like Piper. Soft like her, too.

Despite how overtly unsexy she ought to look in that get-up, there was something so unguarded and intimate about her like this. Something private, only for him. That, coupled with his feelings for her, made it erotic in the extreme.

She had one knee pulled up toward her stomach. Her arms were tucked close, her two fists nestled under her chin. Piper's face was relaxed and serene. Red took it as a compliment.

He'd noticed she didn't sleep nearly as well here at her house as she did at his. Here, she tossed and turned, waking often, and dreaming often, her expressions changing even in sleep. Piper talked in her sleep here, too—urgent, unintelligible syllables that hinted at distress.

Red had no idea what could be bothering her enough to invade her sleep like that. Well…maybe he did. Water from pipes. Water from windows. Big, domineering men with crass desires and tyrannical attitudes.

Gingerly, he slipped into the bed behind her. Piper's body fit into the cradle of his like she'd been made for exactly that purpose. Red stroked his hand down her leg and spread his palm across the top of her thigh, feeling the strong muscle under the soft cotton. The back of her thigh curved delectably upward toward her heart-stopping ass.

To his eternal joy, Piper was like that all over—taut and firm and overlaid with a sweet softness that thoroughly destroyed him. She wasn't wiry and hard like she lived in a gym. Piper looked like she would feel spectacular against a man's body, wonderful under his hands—an exquisite counterpoint to all those hard, male contours and angles.

And Red was the lucky son-of-a-bitch who could attest that the visual impression was one hundred percent accurate.

Piper's hair tickled his face, and his throat got tight when he caught the delicate scent of it. The odd combination of tenderness and lust that kept swamping him in unexpected moments like these was beginning to feel familiar. Comforting.

He wanted to whisper things to her in a secret language only they shared, imparting confidences that weren't for the consumption of others. Impossible things like *trust me* and *I love you*. But if Piper knew what Red knew, she wouldn't do either.

He laid there feeling her breathing, watching the room get brighter and warmer with each passing minute. He wanted to freeze time. Too soon, Piper would wake up. Red would probably act overbearing and try to fix things he had no business interfering with. Piper would misunderstand, be offended, and speculate about his motives.

If she only knew.

Had she ever been able to rely on the people in her life? Red wondered how often she'd been let down. It seemed like the only viable explanation for Piper's occasional flashes of self-deprecation.

He wasn't surprised to learn that Piper had once been engaged. It made perfect sense that some man—probably several men—had wanted her that much. What Red couldn't fathom was why the asshole who'd won her hadn't been clear on the gift he'd been given. And whatever that knucklehead Kyle had done to Piper, she still carried a shadow in her eyes from it.

And much as Red wished he was different, he was likely no better.

He wanted to erase her hurts. He wanted to be the one Piper counted on, wanted to prove to her that his words were true. Red wanted her to entrust him with her whole heart, her deepest thoughts, her gorgeous soul and her beautiful body. He wanted her to want him back.

But as long as he kept his gnawing, impossible secret about Trident, Red would have to be a bigger joker than Kyle to expect any of those things. As it was, it was going to be a close call whether Red could fix it all and sell the result to Piper in a way she'd accept.

He must have been clutching her a little tighter than he'd thought. Piper stirred in his arms, battling into consciousness. She went rigid for half a second, then melted gratifyingly back into him with a languid, happy sigh.

Last night, Red had explained to her about Eric Whittier. The dude was as jazzed to tackle Piper's project as Red had ever seen someone. An old farmhouse like hers, with great bones and an owner with impeccable taste? Eric had sounded like he was in heaven.

With Red footing the bill, Eric probably knew he'd have carte blanche to do things right. And Piper wouldn't have to count on a single royalty—embezzled or otherwise—to fix up her grandparents' home.

The problem was, Piper hadn't exactly been thrilled.

Red had intended to unleash Eric on Piper this week, before he returned home. Now, he wondered if she'd even let him.

It wasn't like he was trying to buy Piper a new car, not yet. Red hadn't even asked her if she had any bills that he could pay off for her. All he was trying to do was take care of this one thing— this thing that he knew meant so much to her. But Piper Mae Fulham wanted no part of Red's largesse, and she was being nearly as stubborn as himself about it.

How many times in the past had it rankled, when a woman he'd just met was intent on spending his money for him? Piper never seemed to want a dime from him. It ought to be depressing that she was in such a minority. Instead, Red was too busy feeling irritated that she had once again managed to sidestep what he wanted.

It figured. The one time Red tried to throw around his money with a woman, it was the exact wrong thing to do. Somewhere, the deity in charge of balancing karmic scales had to be laughing their ass off right now.

If Red took a gamble and forced the issue, he risked ruining everything between them. Sadly, that was becoming a recurrent theme.

Piper mumbled a muffled, "Good morning," and stretched against him.

Predictably, Red's body roared to life. He kissed the side of her neck. "How'd you sleep?"

"Like a rock." She sounded so content. He hated to rock the boat. "I have a question," Piper said.

Red smiled, loving the way her brain worked. It often picked up right where it'd left off, hours—or even days—earlier. "Proceed."

"Why are you trying to do all this? With the house, I mean?"

The secret hanging between them made Red feel abruptly, achingly, ill. He reviewed all the possible answers to Piper's question that did not include the words *guilty* or *conscience* and eventually settled on the simplest version of the truth.

"It makes me feel useful. I like it. I want to be useful to you."

Piper rolled over to face him. She was less annoyed than she'd been last night, which was good. She also looked more curious, though, and that was decidedly *not* good.

"You don't think you're useful to me without the money?" Real amusement crinkled the bridge of her nose and the corners of her eyes.

Was he? What else did Red have to offer, anyway? He was kind of a pain in the ass.

Piper picked right up on his uncertainty. Before he could blink, she was grinning with mischief and dragging her fingers straight down his stomach, stopping only when she hit the waistband of his pajama bottoms. She curled her fingers just under the edge but didn't dip lower.

"Are you seriously implying that your entire utility to me is in your bank account? That would make me awfully craven, wouldn't it?"

Red laughed. He couldn't help it. It was such a Piper thing to say. When she uttered things like that, as if they were the most normal thing to say in the world, it gave him the weirdest, warmest joy.

"If it's not the money," he growled, "Then you must be using me for my body."

He spread her arms wide and pinned them over her head in an instant, his body pressing hers into the mattress. Piper shrieked and giggled a little, in that cute way she had.

"How do I know you aren't using me for *my* body?" she demanded, breathless.

Red took her tender earlobe between his teeth, then nipped at her neck—eliciting another, louder yelp.

"Oh, I'll use the hell out of you, sweetheart. Whenever I want. What do you have to say about that?" He flexed his hips, enjoying Piper's sudden inhale when he made sweet, sweet contact.

His body was beginning to take over the proceedings, and Red still hadn't told her the rest of his plan like he needed to.

"I'm down with that." Piper wrapped her legs around his hips and tugged on her hands. "You aren't going to try tying me up again, are you?"

Cheeky little woman. "No. I love to feel your hands on me." Red released her, and she stroked his back.

"And I love to touch you," she murmured.

His control was slipping. Quickly.

"There's something else," he managed.

"What?" Piper was hot and soft beneath him, her voice sweetly concerned.

"Eric—I talked to Eric," he gritted out, attention almost totally diverted by the t-shirt he was working up her ribcage. "He thought it would be better if you moved out for a couple months."

Thirty

M OVED OUT? OF my *house?*" Piper yelped, abruptly flipping from amorous to alarmed.

"Just for a little while. Eric's crew will operate faster if they don't have to work around you. And you and your little furry friends will be a lot more comfortable not having to deal with all that noise and mess."

"But where—"

"I looked around and found a nice condo about ten minutes from you. If you want, we could go see it." Red had agonized over the various options, determined to find the perfect place. Eric had already looked at it, too, and said he could have it ready for Piper by the end of the month.

Maybe she'd hate it, though. Maybe Red didn't know what the fuck he was doing.

"You found…already?" she stuttered out. Her sleepy brain was clearly struggling to catch up and process this new information. "What's the rent like?"

Piper's eyes were wide and dancing around his features, taking in every available cue of expression and body language while she tried to unravel this development.

Red set a gentle kiss on her forehead. "No rent," he admitted. "If you like it, I'll buy it as an investment, and probably flip it next year."

"I—oh."

"It's okay if you don't, though. We'll find you something else that you like better. If that's what you want to do."

Last night, Piper had made her position quite clear. Now she just looked bewildered.

"Tell you what," Red said, pressing ahead. "Why don't we have some breakfast, and I'll show you the photos Eric and I took. Then you'll have more information while you think about it. How's that sound?"

Red forced himself to back off, rolling away from her and propping himself up against the headboard. He tried to look as non-threatening as possible, a task made infinitely more difficult by how much goddamn space he seemed to take up in her bed.

Piper sprang upright immediately. Red watched her t-shirt fall back down with real regret and wondered if he'd ever get his fill of this woman.

THEY RECONVENED OVER coffee and bacon and eggs at the wood table in the kitchen. Piper tried to look aloof when Red showed her the photos on his phone, but she was too transparent to disguise the gleam of interest in her eyes.

Nonetheless, it was obvious she still had doubts. Red tried not to push, even though it went against all his instincts. Any coaxing he attempted now would only make him look less trustworthy to her, not more.

He was impatient, however. By the end of breakfast, Red couldn't help asking, "So? What do you think?"

Piper rose to clear her plate. Red grabbed his, too, and followed her to the sink. He kept a little distance, though, like she was some kind of skittish animal, and not a woman bent on maintaining her independence from him.

"Want to have a look in person? We could go today."

"I don't know, Red." She shook her head and frowned. "This is all so..." She drifted away to slump back into her chair. "What if..."

"Listen, I know what you must be thinking," he sighed. "*What if he's not for real? What if I can't trust him? What if it all goes wrong?*"

The guilty look on Piper's face said it all.

"I get it, little dove. I'm asking you to move out of your home. To hand over the keys to a place that's been in your family for a very long time. I recognize that it's a lot to ask."

"What I don't understand," she said, "is how you are so sure of me. Doesn't it occur to you to wonder if *you* can trust *me*? What if I'm not what I seem? What if I'm just trying to take you for a ride?"

Red swallowed, not liking how close to home her words hit. Before he'd met her, that would've been exactly the direction of his thoughts. Piper must have seen her arrow land, too, because she rushed to reassure him.

"Red. That's not at all what I'm doing, I promise. But I'm amazed that you aren't more suspicious of me, given what you've said about the other women you've been with."

The chair next to her creaked slightly when he lowered himself into it. "Piper, from the very beginning, my gut has told me that you are exactly what you seem." He leaned in, holding her gaze with his. "My gut is not often wrong. And here—in my shriveled, dark little heart—this thing between us feels all kinds of right. So, you tell me. Why *shouldn't* I do this for you? When I have the means, and I know it would help? To me, right now, *not* helping feels like the dick move."

WITH THE PROMISE of Eric and his renovation magic dangled in front of her, Piper had been easily enticed into coming back to New York with him for a few days. Red might not have asked if she hadn't looked so forlorn watching him pack to go home.

But finding her a seat next to him had been simple, and he'd promised not to cajole her into staying longer than planned. The weather report even looked good—cool and clear, with no storms and no early snow in the forecast.

Piper still hadn't seemed completely enamored with the new condo idea, even after visiting it and admitting it was nice. So, after mulling it over for most of their flight, Red had eventually burst out with his *other* idea on the car ride home from the airport—a notion that would've seemed inconceivable only a few short months ago.

Now though? The thought of having Piper there in Manhattan with him—all the time—got Red's heart thumping in an entirely new way. Maybe, if she liked it enough, she wouldn't want to leave. Maybe Piper would actually want to stay.

He could make it good for her. Red knew he could.

She was hesitating, however, in that way she had—standing in the middle of his living room and looking around with a gimlet eye.

"What am I supposed to do?" she demanded. "Just move all my stuff in *here*? With —" She waved her hands around, broadly encompassing the contents of the loft. "—all *this*?"

Red shrugged. "Yeah. Why not?"

"Oh, right," Piper sneered. "Like that would work."

"Why wouldn't it?" Red got close and stroked her arm. "Piper, I thought by now you'd get it. All of this stuff is meaningless to me. I couldn't care less if you gutted the place and started from scratch. Shit, you could burn it down while I was at work if you wanted. I just want us to be together."

She wasn't buying it. That much was clear. "I'm seriously supposed to believe that you don't care about one single thing in this entire loft? What about those new pictures on the wall? Or your new couch?"

Red thought hard. Piper was right. "Well…" He debated telling her, but he was in this far—what could be the harm in digging a little deeper? "Okay. Maybe there is one thing."

"*One*?" she squawked.

He nodded.

"Show me."

Red lingered, wondering if he was crazy to play this out. But if he didn't put anything on the line, how could he expect to gain what he wanted? His feet were moving before he'd really made the decision, carrying him to his study while Piper trailed behind.

He led her over to the desk chair, sat her down, and pointed to the top drawer.

"Open it."

She glanced at him, curious, then did as he'd instructed.

Inside, right where it always lay, was the folding frame. Its two photos sat side-by-side in easy reach, where Red could look at them quickly or contemplate them at length, depending on what the day or the moment required. He kept a twin of it in the same place at his office, too.

Piper lifted it out of the drawer and studied the images. In one, she was soft and vulnerable in sleep, her hair making a halo on his pillow. In the other, she was laughing directly at him—eyes shining, dimples so damn cute they made his chest seize up, her incomparable heart etched into every plane of her beautiful face.

"These—where did you get these?" Piper stammered.

Red slipped his phone from his pocket and waggled it at her sheepishly. If she asked him why he'd bothered getting the photos printed and framed when he could just as easily have kept them on his phone, he'd never be able to explain it to her. Red wasn't sure he understood it himself. He only knew, at one point, the impulse had felt necessary.

It was hard to read her expression. Maybe he'd crossed a line, stepped clear into stalker territory. It would probably be smart of her to consider him capable.

"There must be millions of dollars of art and…and stuff in this place, and you're worried about two little crappy pictures of me?" Piper sputtered. "You're insane!"

Red smiled. She was most likely right.

"It would be hard to convince me to part with these," he said, taking the frame from her and cradling it in his hands. "But if I had you here with me instead, maybe I could be persuaded."

She huffed out a disbelieving breath and stared at him. Then she dropped her head to the desk, hiding her face from Red entirely.

From inside the cave of her arms, he heard, "You drive a very hard bargain, mister."

His heart leaped into life, beating double-time while he waited for Piper's answer.

Eventually, she said, "Okay. I'll…I'll do it."

"Really?" Red didn't pump his fist, but *damn*, he wanted to. Then it occurred to him that he wasn't sure what she'd agreed to. "Wait—do you mean the condo? Or here?"

"Only the condo," she glowered, standing. "While we're at it, however…you've badgered me relentlessly about your little pet project, but I haven't pestered you one bit about my thing. Now, though—now you owe me a discussion about that stupid Millhouse & Rock deal."

Red groaned. He'd forgotten that wasn't in the 'done' drawer yet. "All right. Fair enough. What do you want to know?"

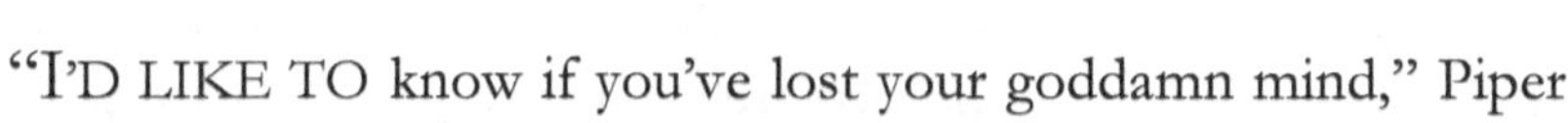

"I'D LIKE TO know if you've lost your goddamn mind," Piper snarled, doing her level best to shoot daggers at him with her eyes.

Red appeared to be immune. Cool as an autumn breeze, he said, "Piper, I know you don't care for Millhouse & Rock, but calm down and listen to me for a minute. This is going to be great for you."

Naturally, she ignored that asinine directive. Any woman worth her salt would.

"In case I wasn't clear before, let me reiterate," she said, her voice emerging from her throat with a deathly chill to it. "Millhouse & Rock wouldn't know a good romance if it whacked them upside the head. We are going to have to battle for every inch of shelf space, every front table placement, and every window display. What's more, the second some ex-president decides to write a memoir, those pretentious assholes are going to kick my 'inane girly books' right into the recycling bin."

Red flinched, and Piper knew the M&R executives had probably used exactly that term with him, too—it certainly was one of their favorites.

He powered on, though. "That's the beauty of this deal, don't you get it? They can't do that, because now they're under contract. They'll have to give you a fair shake, or they won't make any money. It's like the biggest middle finger you could give them. We've got them by the proverbial purse strings now."

"Oh, Red." Piper almost felt sorry for the guy. He really had no idea how wrong he was. "They're only going to resent us more for that. People don't *like* being cornered—it makes them *bitter.*"

"You can't possibly believe they don't want to make any money, here? All their old sales models are failing. They're desperate for it!" he exclaimed.

"And those models are failing because of one thing: Millhouse only likes making money if they can be pompous pricks while doing it."

Red scowled. "Who cares about the why? The important part is that now we have a foot in the door—and the chance to win them over. We'll force them to see what they've been missing."

"Tell me you don't really believe that," Piper groaned.

"If I didn't, I wouldn't have brokered this deal."

"Red, you and I both know they only agreed to this because they want Rachel Wilbon—*and* her stupid Goldstein Award."

He squeezed his eyes shut and massaged his forehead. She knew she'd hit a nerve.

"Have you even *read* her book?" Piper prodded.

"Unfortunately, yes."

"Forget about happy endings," she fumed. "There wasn't even an ending at all! The entire last chapter was *blank!*"

"I'll admit, that was a strange choice."

"I assure you—literary critics may be a rare breed, but actual readers get tired of schticks like that real quick."

He scrubbed his hands over his face and groaned. He'd obviously decided to dig in his heels, the bone-headed man. But he'd learn, just like Piper and all of her love-peddling sisters and brothers had.

Finally, Red sighed, "Piper, Millhouse may have been reluctant to take on romance but, ultimately, we are providing them with a product that is a known, verified seller. If hunger for cash is what got us through the gate, then so be it. They won't be nearly so precious once your books start making them serious dough."

Piper examined him. "Is that what you thought when you first started sniffing around Trident? Is that how you sold the idea to the PKM board?"

To his credit, he looked her dead in the eye and didn't hesitate. "Yes," he admitted. "But you may have noticed that I am a very fast learner."

Red certainly was, but Piper wasn't about to give him the satisfaction of admitting it. He approached her gingerly, probably worried that she was going to stab him with her new fountain pen—and, as ideas went, it had merit.

"Piper, honey, this kind of thing—this is what I'm good at. This is what I *do*. You have to trust me on this. I'm not going to let those bastards screw you over." He reached out and stroked her cheek.

He really, really believed that. Of course, he did.

"The least you could have done is tried for Eva East Books first," she grumbled. "At least they care about the genre."

"Piper, who the hell is that? I've never even heard of them." Red's exasperation was growing, but she wasn't done.

"Your loss, then. Kiki Eastman started out as a romance blogger before she and her cousin founded their own romance-only bookstore. When that went well, they opened a micro-chain of them, all over the Northeast."

Red's voice did not even veer into condescension when he said, "I'm sure they're very nice, but they don't sound like they have the scale we need to help launch Trident into the upper echelons."

"We'll see," Piper hummed. Some lessons were simply better learned the hard way.

"Let me guess," he chuckled darkly. "You've already lined someone up to tattoo 'I told you so' across my forehead if this goes bad."

Piper relented and smirked up at him. "Don't worry, Red. I'm sure it'll look very stylish."

Red must have decided she was nonthreatening again because he took her in his arms and held on. Piper could feel his tension—and no matter how sanguine he pretended to be, she knew he was worried about this deal, too.

She'd always assumed that he was merely dabbling with Trident, that it was only a tossed-off deal he could've finessed in his sleep. But maybe Red had more on the line than she'd thought.

The idea that he had some actual skin in the game was what finally allowed her to relent. Piper rested her head against his chest and sighed.

"Now that we're in this," she murmured, "what can I do to help?"

Red's relief was instantly apparent. "Sweetheart," he said, "All you need to do is keep being you. Beautiful, charming, talented *you.*"

Thirty-One

I T WAS OFFICIAL. As they'd planned, PKM's public relations department had made the announcement about the Millhouse deal the afternoon before. Today, Red was certain it would be the talk of the business world. Despite Piper's concerns, it was going to be a game-changer for all of them. On impulse, Red had hopped on the plane bringing Piper back home himself, making the trip to Maryland for the second time in a week.

He wished she'd chosen to move in with him instead of opting for the condo, but it was probably for the best. All along, baby steps were what had worked best with her. Getting them to the point of living in the same zip code would be no different.

Red wandered downstairs in her cozy, creaking house and found Piper in the kitchen making breakfast. She was wearing his undershirt from the day before, and it hung off her shoulders and draped over her breasts in a far lovelier way than it fit him. His eyes tracked down to the hem, where it grazed her thighs several inches below her ass. He knew she was wearing lacy little panties under his shirt—he'd watched her put them on no more than ten minutes ago.

Red poured himself coffee and edged around the kitchen table, choosing the chair that gave him the most unobstructed view of Piper. She was making him eggs, and he was sure they'd be perfectly cooked. Piper was the only person besides himself who could ever get them the way Red liked them. Yet another point in her favor, to add to all the others.

He watched her delicate ankles and feminine bare feet move around the wood floor. Her toes were painted a pale lavender this time. Red had been trying to decide if he could gauge her mood by the colors she chose—they ranged anywhere from black or navy blue to a rusty deep red, to soft pastels. So far, he hadn't quite decided what each variation signified, but he was developing theories.

His eyes trailed up her strong, slim legs, watching for any suggestion of her delectable ass through the shirt. As if she could feel his look singeing her, she turned and shot him an uncertain smile. Piper's fingers stilled on the English muffin she was prying apart when he returned her smile with a grin of his own. She flushed across her cheeks and neck and turned quickly back to the toaster.

Oh, yes—she knew what he was thinking. Piper always knew what he was thinking.

Sunlight streamed through the large arched window over her kitchen sink, catching the diamonds in her ring and casting a spray of white fireworks across the cabinets behind her. His ring, her finger—Red massaged at the pang that somersaulted in his chest.

He'd never in his life given a woman any kind of jewelry. Superstitious about it, he supposed. It had always felt too momentous, too significant an act, to waste it on a virtual stranger. Before Piper, Red had been meticulous about not getting a woman's hopes up, and it had been all too easy to imagine the sort of conniptions a small velvet box might provoke.

He'd had no such qualms with Piper, however. Last week, in that jewelry store…Red still had no idea why he'd gone in himself. He could have had Wayne place an order from Anika's registry for him. Red could have sent the gift, and never thought about it again.

Instead, he'd elected to leave the office in the middle of the day, purchase the candlesticks himself, then linger while they were gift-wrapped. And while he'd waited, he wandered—directly to the sparkling glass cases in the center of the store.

Looking at Piper now, he couldn't regret it. The ring was perfect for her. *She* was perfect. And that knowledge made Red ponder a different sort of ring—one made only for Piper, that only she would wear. It shouldn't feel right to think about it so soon, but it did.

She placed a loaded plate in front of him, wrenching him from his reverie.

"I was wondering," she said. "Have you always been called 'Red'?"

"I'm sorry?" Had he missed a conversational segue somewhere?

"You know. When you were little, were you ever called Pat, like your dad? Or Paddy, even?"

"God. What do I look like—an eighty-year-old man in an Irish sailor hat?"

Piper snickered. "Hmm. You're right. What about Mac? That's a little cooler."

Red couldn't help it—it was like she'd tossed him a fat softball directly over the middle of home plate. "Nailed it. Everyone I knew called me *Mack Daddy*. Still do, as a matter of fact. You should try it sometime."

An eye roll—he could've predicted that.

"More like a Mack truck," she muttered.

Red snorted. "You want me to deny that I like to drive into you? Repeatedly?"

"Not necessary." Piper flamed crimson, making him laugh. He'd seen that coming, too.

She scampered back to the stove to fuss with her own plate, gathering her composure. As far as he was concerned, breakfast couldn't be over soon enough, perfectly-cooked eggs or not.

Red took the newspaper out of its plastic sleeve and unfolded it, satisfied as only a man could be when his business was tight, his woman was cared for, and he'd gotten laid—repeatedly—the night before.

Plus, Piper had cooked him breakfast wearing nothing but his t-shirt. Checks in all the boxes, today.

But the day's headline stared up at him in grim black boldface, putting the lie to all his smug assumptions: *Questions of Funny Money at New PKM Darling.*

He'd run out of time. *Motherfucker.* How could this be happening right now?

"Piper. Honey," he began. Red had to tell her—right the fuck now—but no matter what he said next, the timing was going to look suspicious, and rightly so. Damn Luca's father and his lunatic village advice. Damn himself for being a coward.

She turned up the sound on the little television she had near the stove. "Hey, look," she chirped. "It's you!"

"Piper, no. Let me—" It was too late. It was way too fucking late.

"Credible allegations of financial misconduct have arisen at Trident Publishing this morning," the business correspondent said, reading off an officious-looking clipboard. *"In a serious blow to Padraig MacLellan's PKM conglomerate, who acquired the struggling New York publisher mere months ago."*

Piper stood frozen while Red frantically tried to remember what he'd done with his blasted phone. His jacket—the front hall. He bolted for it and discovered numerous texts and missed calls from Wayne and Rob, and Anika and his parents.

Back in the kitchen, the broadcaster intoned, *"Coming in the wake of yesterday's big announcement by the company, this is hardly welcome news for MacLellan. Sources tell us that investors are jumping ship en masse, and many of Trident's well-known authors are demanding answers."*

Red skidded to a halt ten feet behind Piper, took one look at her rigid posture, and knew he was screwed.

He hadn't turned his grandfather's company into the juggernaut it was without possessing more than luck and a good-looking face, though. Red was a fighter, and he was willing to do whatever it took to win. He just hadn't ever wanted to fight with Piper.

It occurred to him that someone had executed this revelation perfectly. Someone had *done* this to him—set him up for a hideous fall. That someone would pay dearly for what they'd done.

Red felt a growl of rage bubble up out of his chest. Piper spun slowly to look at him, her face an awful shade of gray.

"Red? What's going on?"

He stepped closer to her and said the worst three words he could possibly utter, "I can explain." He might've laughed if he didn't feel so sick.

The television proclaimed, "*The majority of the malfeasance appears to center around three authors…*"

Red wanted to roar again. No, no, *no*. How had this gotten out? He trusted his staff implicitly. No one was supposed to say a word.

"You knew about this?" Piper asked.

"*…James Denton, only son of Trident's founders and a well-respected crime writer; Rachel Wilbon, the award-winning author of* Come Hither, Moon; *and Antoinette Corelli, a romance writer with nearly thirty titles in her backlist.*"

Piper flinched at the mention of her pen name, and demanded again, "You knew?"

"Yes, but I—"

"*Both Wilbon and Corelli figured prominently in PKM's triumphant announcement yesterday, their new projects the apparent linchpins in a last-ditch deal MacLellan reportedly put together personally in order to save the faltering publisher.*"

God *damn* it. Red spun and threw his phone against the far wall. "Will you turn that fucking thing off?" he bellowed.

Piper went from gray to white and shrank into herself. "I will be in my office," she told him coldly. "And you will be gone from this house within the next ten minutes."

Before she left, she looked down at her hand, methodically removed his ring from her finger, and set it precisely on the counter. "Take that with you," she said.

Her voice was flat. Toneless. Red hated it with every fiber of his being. He gripped his skull to keep from punching something.

"No, Piper. You have to listen. Trust me, I took care of all of this already. I don't know what those assholes are talking about, but—"

She advanced on him and stabbed a finger into his solar plexus. "Trust you? *Trust* you? You've got to be kidding me. All this time, I've been telling you I needed my new series to do well so I could get this place in shape, while you sat there like a *pig*, buying me pretentious shit I don't need. While you hounded me about hiring your contractor and moving out. Holy guilty conscience, Batman!"

Red's heart was thundering. "Piper, it wasn't like that."

"What was it like, then, asshole? Because it sure sounds like that to me."

He took a deep breath, striving for calm. "It's true that I knew the Dentons were cooking the books, but I didn't learn the full details until well after we began dating. I made arrangements to fix it, though. Once the Millhouse deal went through, everything was going to be fine."

"Is that so? Well, as it turns out, big shot, I don't care," Piper snarled. "Take your damn ring, get your shit, and get out of my house." She paused at the door but didn't turn around. "Incidentally, how much was it? How much money did it take for you to feel comfortable snowing me, exactly?"

Red rubbed at his jaw, forcing himself to utter the indefensible. "Roughly 1.8 million dollars, give or take, stretching back approximately five years."

Piper's head dropped for only a moment before she squared her shoulders. Jesus, she was a warrior, even now.

"You'll be hearing from my lawyer," she said, and then she was gone.

In the corner of the room, Red's wrecked phone began ringing once more. Inside his ribcage, his heart fractured into sharp, painful shards like a broken fucking mirror.

Thirty-Two

*L*ITTLE DOVE*. THAT'S what Red had called her. Before, Piper thought it was an endearment. Doves, after all, made people think of soft and kind things. Like peace, and love.

Now, sitting on her back porch wrapped in a blanket, Piper saw Red's real meaning. What were doves, really? Nothing but pigeons, and pigeons, Piper knew, were humble, practical birds. No iridescent plumage, and no special talents.

Pigeons were just common creatures that people liked to throw crumbs at. And long after that token offering was gone, they would keep pecking around near your feet, looking for more.

All the time that Piper had thought Red was falling for her the same way she'd fallen for him, he'd only been mocking her. He'd known he could toss a few shock-and-awe kisses her way and she'd probably never bother to look deeper—to look past the crumbs and see the conniving fox throwing them.

She stared across the barren late-autumn grass, toward the leafless trees crowding along the back edge of her property. They were like gray and silent sentries, ominous in their judgment. Telling her that after Kyle, Piper ought to have known better. She was such a fool.

It was cold, but she barely felt it. Her cheeks were wet, though, and that bothered her. Piper mopped at them with a corner of her blanket and was surprised to find that it was already damp.

She really had to stop this stupid crying. It was getting her nowhere.

Red was good, she'd give him that. He'd listened so attentively when she'd told him about her grandparents and the way they'd built this house. And then, later, he'd jumped all over the idea of renovating it in his usual, ridiculously-outsized way.

If Piper had been thinking clearly, she would've smelled a rat right then. Who the hell even suggested stuff like that, much less actually did it? Who, but someone with a very guilty conscience? Who, but a dastardly villain with a damning secret to hide?

She should have realized that once she allowed the fantasy hero to leave the pages of the book, she'd also set free the bad guy. Unfortunately for Piper, she'd gone and mixed up who was who in this little tale. That might not make her the worst writer in the world, but it sure made her the biggest dolt.

She'd have to give all of it up now, anyway. There wasn't going to be a lucrative new contract or a smoking new series to sell. There was absolutely not going to be a real-life happily-ever-after. Now that Red's betrayal was out in the open, Trident would get rid of Antoinette Corelli as fast as they possibly could.

Knowing about her house repair problem as he did, Red would also be aware that Piper wouldn't have the means to take a big company like PKM to court, either. Perry would almost certainly want to sue Red's lying, cheating ass. It wouldn't come cheap, and so Piper couldn't let him. She choked down another humiliating sob.

God. A broken heart. What a goddamn stereotype she'd become. She'd be absolutely infuriated, just as soon as it stopped hurting so much. Piper had been flayed open and left for the birds, and she'd never even seen it coming.

Furious with herself, she pushed to her feet and went back into the house. It took a long, awful minute for her to understand that the tears on her cheeks and the tears making her blanket soggy could not explain why she was standing ankle deep in water. Her cats were blinking owlishly at her from the top of the table.

"Oh, no," Piper whispered, horrified. The phone rang. Fredo yowled.

ERIC WHITTIER'S CALL had come with almost uncanny timing. When Piper explained the situation, he'd arrived on her doorstep within the hour, then immediately sloshed through her kitchen to the basement stairs, so he could make sure she'd turned off the water correctly.

In rapid order, Eric then set about determining which pipe had burst, and what kind of water damage Piper was looking at. She headed into her relatively-dry office and found the number for her insurance company.

When they reconvened outside on the porch, Eric's face was grim.

"As far as I can tell without ripping into the drywall," he told her, "The rupture happened upstairs in the master bath. All the water in your kitchen must have flowed down through the joists."

When she didn't immediately reply, he added gently, "I'm sorry Piper. It's a real mess, but it's nothing we can't handle."

"Yeah, about that. You need to know that Red MacLellan is no longer involved in this project at all. No exceptions. If you want the job, you're going to have to deal directly with me, and that means we are going to have to scale way back on whatever he might have told you."

"That's not a problem," Eric said.

"My homeowner's insurance does not have a flood clause. So, let's figure out how to prioritize what needs to get done, and how much we're looking at." She sat on the porch swing, while Eric sank onto the bench next to her front door and perused the notes he'd made on his phone.

When he spoke, he was calm and unruffled. "Okay, so obviously all the strictly-aesthetic stuff can wait. You can probably milk another five or eight years out of this roof, and we might even be able to do the windows piecemeal. We'll just figure out which ones need to get done first, then pick off the rest, room by room."

"Great."

"However, getting at the old pipes is going to be a bit of an undertaking," Eric warned her. "And I truly hate to tell you this next part, but…"

Piper motioned him on. "Just say it. Nothing can possibly make this week worse than it already is."

The soft-spoken contractor met her square in the eyes, and she knew she was wrong. "Termites," he said dismally. "I found termite damage in the basement, and it's probably other places, too."

Then he told her how much it would all cost.

ULTIMATELY, THERE WASN'T much Piper could do. Camped out on her parents' couch, she reviewed her finances and confronted the fact that all the possible outcomes would suck.

She had a good chunk of money set aside for her property taxes, due at the end of the year. If she used the bulk of it on repairs, she might not be able to earn enough back in time to pay the government.

Not with her career hitting the skids, anyway. If the news was correct, Trident was in complete disarray, and not even Perry could seem to get answers from his contacts at PKM.

Piper had no idea if her new contract would withstand the fire, or if her existing royalties would dry up altogether. She couldn't dip into her savings with that kind of uncertainty—not if she might end up living off them for a while.

It was the exact wrong time to be taking financial risks, of course. Still, Piper called her mortgage company anyway, hoping to secure a home equity loan to cover the worst of the damages. Regrettably, she was turned down flat—told her grandparent's beloved home wouldn't even appraise for half of what it was worth in its current condition.

Piper couldn't fix it and she couldn't sell, and she hadn't written a single word in weeks.

When Eric Whittier met her for coffee a few days later, she could barely force herself to tell him about the impasse she found herself at. He sat and listened, though, and his tranquil demeanor gave her the courage to speak the words that she hated.

The contractor had said all the soothing things, then assured Piper she could call him if anything changed. He'd wished her luck, finished his coffee and left the shop, and then he'd stopped out on the sidewalk, seemingly stuck in place next to his parking meter.

Eric spun around and met Piper's eyes through the plate-glass window, and then he came back inside. He stood awkwardly next to her table and fiddled with his keys.

"What if," he began, and hit his thigh with the overstuffed ring of metal. *Ching. Ching.*

"What?"

"I'm a hyena to even suggest this."

"You have an idea?" Piper prodded, curious about why he looked so uncomfortable.

"I do, but I'd hate for you to think I'm trying to take advantage. I'm not, I promise."

"Tell me."

Eric sat back down with a thud and launched into his proposition. "My older sister was widowed recently," he explained. "Her husband's unit was protecting some senator or something and got caught up in this insurgent attack. She's staying with our parents right now, while they figure out what's what, but she's got three kids and it's a tight squeeze. I thought…maybe…"

Piper saw instantly where he was going. "You thought they might like my house?"

Eric nodded glumly. "Now that she's on her own, she wants to live closer to family. I could take your house off your hands for a fair price, then fix it up for her to live in. We wouldn't even need to involve any real estate agents."

"That would save money," Piper mused.

"It would. Your lawyer guy could look everything over for you, make sure it's what you want."

"The house has four bedrooms," she said.

Eric nodded again. "One for each kid, plus their mom. Big yard, too."

"And good schools." Piper sat across from him and couldn't understand how her way out had fallen into her lap so neatly. It seemed almost too good to believe.

And then Eric Whittier said the kindest thing imaginable. "Someday soon, this whole mess is going to blow over for you, and my sister will get back on her feet. Then you can buy your grandparents' house back from me and bring it into your family again, where it belongs. Until then, we'll take good care of it. I swear."

Some belated flash of suspicion percolated within her, strong enough for Piper to wonder, "Is Red putting you up to this?"

"No. Of course not. I haven't spoken to him since you told me he was off the project."

She consulted her instincts and made up her mind on the spot. "Then I think we have a home sale to discuss."

Thirty-Three

H E COULDN'T MAKE the puzzle pieces fit. Red had been trying, though—trying for what felt like hours, but had probably only been twenty minutes or less. What had he been thinking, anyway, when he bought this stupid thing?

Stress relief, that's what. The woman in the Duane Reade aisle had seen Red looking at the jigsaw puzzles and said her husband did them for stress relief. Next thing Red knew, he'd snatched the first one that caught his eye, and carried the damn thing home.

And now, in all his newfound spare time without Piper, he was at his dinner table with a thousand tiny blue pieces spread in front of him that were supposed to depict either sky or sea—but were indistinguishable from each other.

It was exactly like him, Red thought sulkily, to go completely overboard and get the big, complicated puzzle instead of the smaller, simpler one.

After all, why simply fail, when you could fail spectacularly? He'd always been too fucking big for the world around him.

Red couldn't even manage to find all the border pieces. And he couldn't seem to stop counting all his miscalculations for himself, either. There'd been the part where he'd underestimated his investors, certainly, along with the Dentons. He'd gotten arrogant, and complacent, and that was infuriating.

But Red had behaved like a complete and total idiot when it came to Piper. He had focused so much on pushing her to trust him—like that was the important thing—that he'd totally missed the fact that if he *earned* her goddamn trust, she'd give it to him naturally.

Trying to push the river, as it were. He'd been such a fool. And now, Red's stupid mistakes were going to make him lose her.

He shoved at the mound of impossible pieces, mocking himself for ever telling Piper he'd like to make this a hobby. He was obviously incapable of it, and it was anything but relaxing.

Over and over, Red had sifted through what he knew, trying to make sense of what had happened that day. No one at PKM had leaked the information about the royalties. He was certain of it. Which could only mean that one of the actual people *involved* had.

So, who was that, exactly? John and Lisa Denton. Probably their son Jim. And one other person. As Red had discovered, the reporters had gotten one detail wrong in the early days of their coverage—Rachel Wilbon was not, in fact, a victim. No, she'd been a beneficiary, just like Jim.

It wasn't until Wayne had come into work one day, breathlessly recounting how he'd seen Jim Denton and Rachel out on the town the night before, canoodling happily in the back booth of a bar, that Red had understood why. Sure enough, once Rob and his team started digging, the evidence was all there in black and white.

Red ought to have seen it before, though. Everything from the way the Dentons had acted at the theater, to the way Rachel had vacillated between trying to handle him and trying to threaten him, should have told Red the truth.

Instead, he'd been too busy chasing Piper back and forth from Maryland to pay much attention to the critical details. And in doing so, Red had jeopardized not only their relationship but possibly her career.

Was Rachel the leak, though? Red got up and went to his study and glared down at the three personnel folders on his desk. Piper's shock at the news had been too visceral for her to have been the leak. Besides, this felt like revenge. And that led him to either Jim or Rachel.

Jim did not stand to gain much from disclosing anything—in fact, he probably would've had a vested interest in protecting himself and his parents from legal fallout.

So, Red picked up the folder on the end. Rachel—Rachel was the only one who might've stood to profit. Rachel's relationship with Jim no longer provided her with easy funds, and it didn't shield her from getting fired for not producing new work.

She'd known she was on the verge of being released from her contract. She'd known her efforts to win Red over were failing. If Rachel could discredit Red or PKM, though, she might have been able to buy time to salvage her tanking celebrity.

Red tapped the folder against his desk. He needed information. A *lot* more information. And he might just know where to get it. He went around his desk, parked his ass in his chair, and picked up the phone.

THE FOLLOWING MORNING, Red was already waiting beside his assistant's desk when the man arrived at work. While Wayne unwound his scarf from around his neck and hung up his peacoat, Red stood semi-patiently nearby. He even managed a pleasant smile when Wayne settled into his chair and turned on his monitor.

"Good morning," Wayne said finally, turning to Red with a sardonic look. "How may I be of assistance?"

Red slapped a copy of Rachel's contract on Wayne's desk. He approved of the way the young man only jumped slightly.

"You had Contracts yet?" Red barked.

"I'm taking it right now."

"Your grades any good?"

"Perfect, if you must know."

"Great. Anika tells me this contract is watertight," Red told him. "Find us a way out of it, and you'll have a job at PKM waiting for you the moment you graduate and pass the bar."

"What if I don't pass?"

"That's not really the kind of can-do attitude I like to see in my henchmen," Red frowned.

Wayne gaped, his blue eyes going wide. "Is that actually how you see me? As a *henchman*?"

"Never mind that. About you passing the bar—I'm not really worried about it. Are you?"

"Nope," his assistant grinned.

Red waited him out.

"Seriously?" It was impossible to miss the hope and glee, but then Wayne never had much of a poker face.

Red scowled at him, as a leader of henchmen would.

"What am I saying? Naturally, you're serious. You are always completely serious."

Red slapped him on the back. "Not always. But business is business. Get cracking, my little minion, and the reward will be yours."

WAYNE CAME TO him only two days later, looking exhausted but victorious.

"The reporter who broke the original story is ridiculous with the midnight Twitter," he said. "He tweeted all these hints the night before his story hit the paper, identifying his source as an author well-known not only for her award-winning fiction but also for her famous head of golden curls. He deleted it later, but my friend got a screenshot."

At Red's questioning look, he added, "She knows I work here. She wanted to ask me about it."

Perhaps unnecessarily, Red said, "Rachel has blond curly hair."

"Only Rachel," Wayne agreed, smiling. "Which means that Ms. Wilbon is in violation of this handy non-disclosure addendum the Dentons had her sign, right around the time they began throwing her some extra bucks."

"Wayne, you are amazing."

"I know, right? But wait, there's more."

"What more do we need?"

"How about proof that the Dentons paid off that award committee to make sure Rachel won?"

"You're shitting me."

"Nope. I checked your messages on the way in this morning. That PI you hired talked to some people on the Goldstein committee. Apparently, they'd heard rumors that Rachel might've plagiarized large chunks of her book from her college roommate's senior project. He tracked down the roommate and left her number, so I gave her a call."

"I'm beginning to think you might be pursuing the wrong line of work, you handsome devil," Red smiled.

"Naw. I'm just a detecting dilettante. Anyway, the roommate said the Dentons paid her to retract her accusations, and then went on to grease the wheels for Rachel to win the Goldstein. The roommate's still pissed about it, as you can imagine. Rachel was one of her beta readers."

"I can imagine. And you, my friend, are a prince among men. Do you think the roommate will talk to me?"

"Are you kidding?" Wayne asked. "I couldn't get her to *stop* talking."

Finally, finally Red had what he needed to right his ship. And while the news of Rachel's wrongs probably wouldn't bring back Trident's original investors, he had some new ideas he could try, and he could already see tomorrow's headlines.

"Send this to Allison in PR," Red said. "Quote, *Former Trident darling Wilbon accused of aiding in the embezzlement of royalties. Her highly-lauded book also discovered to derive large passages from college roommate's senior project, on which she was a beta reader.*"

Wayne rubbed his hands together, relishing his role as a perfect vaudeville scoundrel. "Anything else?"

"Give Allison everything you have. She'll know what to do," Red said. "I'll be in my office, calling that district attorney we spoke to."

Thirty-Four

PIPER HAD BEEN trying to break the habit of thinking about Red MacLellan all the damn time, but it was slow going. Despite her best efforts to expunge him, he seemed to have infected every layer of her heart and mind. The bastard. It was just like him.

As she sat in her car and eyed the collection of work trucks in front of her old house, she supposed she ought to thank him, though, for his crack-brained 'move out while a stranger guts your home' scheme.

If Red hadn't pushed the idea so hard, Piper might not have sifted through everything she owned, preparing to give stuff she no longer needed to charity. She might not have planned how to stockpile boxes and bags for a move or have known where to rent a good storage unit.

However, all that preparation had made moving out for good far easier than she'd ever expected it would be. It had taken Piper only a week to pack everything up, stash the bulk of it in storage, and truck the remaining load over to a new apartment she'd rented.

Eric had insisted on paying her the price they'd decided on, despite the additional issues uncovered in the home inspection. He'd raved about how perfect Piper's house was going to be for his sister and her young family. He'd tried to tell Piper their names—to show her photos.

But Piper remained suspicious that Red had somehow found another way to manipulate her life and play games with her emotions. She'd tried to stay aloof. She'd left the settlement and driven straight back to her former home, taken as many photos and videos of the empty house and yard as she could, and then she'd forced herself to walk away with her head held high.

Things. A house was only a thing, and things came and went. Things were shed all the time. Things broke, became outdated, became useless.

Though, come to think of it, so did people. And while prying herself from her childhood home had been physically simple, it had been emotionally hideous.

Fredo had been lost in the move. One minute he was there, terrified by the commotion but still locked securely in the bathroom with Sonny, while Piper got their carriers ready. The next, Fredo was darting around stacks of boxes and through the legs of the movers, then streaking straight out the open front door.

She'd looked and called and waited as long as she could. Well after the moving truck was gone, Piper was still scouring the yard and the trees. In the days after, she posted signs in the neighborhood and drove all over looking for him. She couldn't sleep at night, worrying about how cold it was getting, and how scared her pet must be.

Piper sniffed and scanned the area one last time, then put her car in gear. She hated thinking about what had come next. That first week, she'd hunkered down with a bottle of expensive sherry and her laptop and *forced* herself to write.

Picturing total strangers wandering her home, changing everything, was excruciating. Imagining Fredo frightened, hungry and lost without her, was worse.

Admitting how much she missed dirty, rotten Red was something she refused to do, though. Piper had crafted many, many chapters of breakups and revenge to pass the time.

While she drove down the streets that would bring her to the new apartment, Piper acknowledged to herself that most of what she'd written would never find its way into any of her books—not unless her new series took a boozy, bloodthirsty spin she wasn't expecting.

As it was, she'd taken the step of running her finally-complete manuscript past a developmental editor before handing it over to Trident. Piper trusted herself so little at this point—she'd had to be sure.

The verdict was a mixed bag. Apparently, the first two-thirds were her best work yet, but the last section was so dark and pessimistic that the editor had inquired if Piper had used a ghostwriter. Who could say what would happen to the story now—to the whole project? The happy words she needed just wouldn't come.

Life itself had proven to be very unpredictable lately. Why should her ability to write a book be any different?

Piper pulled into her new garage and forced herself to remember how much she'd cried. She'd felt like an arid wasteland after she'd kicked Red to the curb, but that had been nothing compared to the tears she shed over her grandparents' old house and Fredo—those had been like some kind of biblical flood, annihilating everything in their path. Maybe that was how misfortunes worked—one piggybacked on the next, and the stack grew taller and more devastating.

As Piper trudged up the stairs and unlocked her front door, she tried to see the positives. She'd stayed afloat somehow. Her parents had driven out to help paint and unpack the few things she'd brought to the apartment, and by the time they left again, it had felt almost normal. *She* had felt almost normal.

It helped that they'd been so serene about everything. But then, they'd already gone through their own version of mourning when they'd sold the house to Piper. They'd undoubtedly been able to assuage her feelings of guilt and failure so easily because they'd already had to process those exact emotions themselves.

And, while Piper's father had probably never really believed she was up to the task of caring for that house, he had stoically refrained from saying *"I told you so."*

So…yeah. On the home front, so to speak, Piper was mostly fine. She was at peace. Her apartment was new, easy to clean, and beginning to feel sort of homey. It did not creak or leak, or otherwise behave in ways it shouldn't. It would be fine.

It would give Piper shelter while she decided what she was going to do now that she wasn't saddled with the twin albatrosses of history and nostalgia, or by the promise of a future with a man who only wanted to use her.

Piper wandered into her kitchen and decided to brew herself some tea, to ward off the depressing effects of the cold, gray day. While the water heated, she turned on lights to brighten things up, then wadded a blanket around Sonny, tucked tightly into a corner of the couch while he snoozed.

The only thing left to do, really, was for Piper to exorcise the last, lingering vestiges of Red. However, that job would be a heck of a lot easier if he would stop calling, or texting, or sending cards and letters that she would not read.

Each time Red's handwriting appeared amongst her bills and junk mail, Piper wondered again why she'd bothered having her mail forwarded. What was the point? Nothing Red could say would fix what he'd done. Nothing.

Trust him, her ass. Red could go take a long walk off a short pier for all she cared.

Piper just hoped that the fates would eventually grow tired of being vengeful with her. With luck, they would try out some mercy soon—because once she wrangled her new book into shape, Piper was going to need Red MacLellan to stay as far away from Trident as humanly possible.

Red needed to go out and find some new project to manage the hell out of. If he was distracted, maybe he'd finally give up and leave her alone. Maybe he'd forget all about her.

So Piper could forget about him.

She'd known from the very beginning that they made about as much sense together as…well, two people who made no sense together.

The chemistry between them could be explained away easily enough. Lust was just a chemical reaction that could strike anyone, anytime, and for no reason more compelling than biological imperative. It was all about perpetuation of the species, nothing more.

Piper merely wished that meaningless chemistry wasn't so good at masquerading as emotional intimacy. When lust pretended to be love, it led to so much humiliation. A girl could get hurt out there when she desired someone.

Not Piper, though—not anymore. She'd been naïve to think that Kyle had taught her a thing or two about protecting her heart, but it was silly to blame herself. The Kyles of the world were nothing compared to Red. She'd know better, now. Piper would not be so blind ever again.

If and when the time came for her to venture out into the dating world once more, Piper would make sure she was shrouded in every piece of emotional armor there was, and she would be far, far smarter about staying in her own weight class. No more heavyweights for her, no way—the next man who got a chance to fight for her heart was going to have about as much piss and vinegar in him as a piece of Christmas fudge.

PIPER'S PARENTS CAME for another visit that weekend, bearing two house plants, a new toy for Sonny, and a stack of flat, square packages wrapped in brown paper.

Her mother was nearly vibrating with excitement when she handed them over.

"What are these?" Piper asked, surprised by how heavy they were. She laid them on the kitchen table and began to unwrap one.

"I dried and pressed cuttings from Grandma and Grandpa's yard," her mom said proudly. "Dad made the frames himself, from that old oak tree they trimmed in the side yard last year."

Piper placed them side by side, impressed with the beauty of the set—but even more with her mother's uncharacteristically fitting thoughtfulness.

"There's one more," her dad said. "Open it."

It was her grandfather's own painting of the house he'd built, amateurish and unskilled, the bright, primary colors giving it a folk-art look.

"Guys, you love this painting! I can't take this!"

"We've downsized," her mom claimed. "Besides, no one loved that old place more than you. We thought you should have it."

Piper blinked back a sudden wash of tears. "Thanks. I really appreciate all this."

Her dad jammed his hands in his pockets and rocked on his heels. "Who knows, kid. You're going to turn this setback around soon. Maybe you'll be able to get the house back someday."

"Maybe." But did Piper really want it back? Now that she'd given it up and grieved it, could she really return there?

The truth was, little by little, she was beginning to look forward. As much as she'd adored her grandparents' home, not having the burden of it hanging over her all the time felt…liberating. Piper could go anywhere she wanted now. Do anything. If not for Fredo, she might even allow herself to be happy.

Wondering if the poor cat was suffering somewhere made her tear up again. Sonny was so mopey without his buddy. Piper missed him, too. But *only* him.

Her dad broke into her gloomy thoughts. "You'll know what to do, Piper Mae."

She wrenched herself out of her funk.

"Hey, guys? I've been wondering." Piper ran a finger along the frame of the painting and turned to them. "Why'd you name me that, anyway? It's completely different from anyone else in the family."

"What do you mean? I thought it sounded pretty," her mother said.

"I sound like a hillbilly!"

"No, you don't." Piper's dad frowned. "It's a good, strong name. Pipers were the ones who led their clans into battle. And Mae—that's like that lady astronaut. Jameson, wasn't it?"

"It's Jemison, dad. Mae Jemison."

He brushed off the minor difference. "Regardless. With a name like yours, you could be fearless. Accomplish anything. And you have, kid. You really have."

"But…that's not true."

"Yes, it is. Your whole life, you've marched right at every new thing we threw at you, and you never once flinched. You've been a trooper from day one, Piper. Your brother wouldn't have had it half so easy without you."

"Dad!" Piper cried, unsettled and confused by his unexpected flash of support, "What are you talking about? Mom, what is he saying?"

Her father didn't wait for his wife to weigh in. He said, "I'll tell you something else, too. You never tried to cram yourself into anyone else's mold, even when it would've been easier for you. You didn't do it for me when I tried to get you to pick a different career than the one you wanted. And you didn't do it for that little pansy you were going to marry, either. What was his name?"

"*Kyle?*"

"Yeah, him. I'll tell you what—someone needs to kick that kid's ass."

"Dad, he must be a forty-year-old man by now."

"Does he know that?"

Piper's mother intervened at last. "Well, she's not going to tell him, hon. Piper's not talking to Kyle anymore. Remember? She has a new boyfriend now."

"And thank the Lord for that. You didn't contort yourself for him, did you?"

Piper sat down heavily, the fight seeping out of her like it had never been there. "I did. I molded myself right into his life."

Her mom met her husband's eyes over Piper's head. "I'm not sure I'd say that, Piper. Maybe you were just trying to love a difficult man the best way you knew how."

"Yeah, well, sometimes love isn't enough," she grumbled sourly.

Her father held her mom's gaze but told Piper, "You're wrong. Love is always enough. Love is…everything."

Piper looked between them, scowling. "What has gotten into you two today? Why are you suddenly being so philosophical?"

Her dad shifted his heavy stare to her. "We don't like to see you this way, kid."

"I'm fine."

"You aren't." He hesitated, then pulled out the chair next to her and sat down. "I talked to Perry, you know. After we saw all that nonsense on TV."

"So much for attorney-client privilege," Piper groused.

"He didn't divulge any details," he assured her. "But I asked him about that character you were involved with. Just to see what he thought."

Piper shot up so fast, her chair cracked into the wall behind her. "Oh, great," she said. "Listen—I can't hear this right now. There's absolutely nothing you can say that I haven't already told myself, okay?"

Her mother steadied her with a hand on her arm. "Hear him out, Piper."

"Why? So, he can point out how stupid I was to fall for a man like that?"

"Kid, you are many things, but stupid ain't one of 'em," her father fired back. "Hell, look at what you've done with your life so far. If you could make a whole career out of writing those silly books of yours, you've got a lot more on the ball than most folks."

"Gee thanks, Dad."

"Look…I don't know the man, but it's obvious that you care about him. So, after Perry and I talked, I checked the guy out. I have to say—I really think he cares about you, too. A man in his position just doesn't do the things you blamed him for."

"And how would you know?"

Her mother hissed, "Watch it, Piper Mae."

Her dad patted the table. "All I'm saying is, if what you had with him was the real deal, you owe it to the guy to give him the benefit of the doubt. You owe it to yourself."

"It wasn't," Piper said. "The real deal."

"Did you ever hear him out?"

"I didn't need to."

"In that, Piper Mae, we disagree. You'll never get over this if you don't."

Thirty-Five

R ED WASN'T USUALLY in the habit of thanking his lucky stars for a shitty night's sleep, not unless it involved a roll in the hay with Piper Mae Fulham, that was.

However, this morning he was grateful for the grinding weariness in his bones and his bloodshot eyes—they meant that he'd done everything in his power to prepare. When the questions came flying at him during the PKM board's emergency conference call, he'd be ready for them.

"MacLellan, I'm sure you understand that this train wreck over at Trident has the potential to severely impact PKM's main lines of business. It's one of the reasons I advised so strongly against this acquisition last year."

Red wasn't surprised by the comment or the speaker. The same man had 'advised strongly' against Red taking the helm at PKM, too. *Screw him.*

"I'm aware, yes," Red said. His throat felt like sandpaper. He motioned for Wayne to grab him some more coffee—though, at this point, it would probably only make him feel worse.

The disembodied voice coming from the console in the center of the conference room table wondered, "Well, what are you going to do about it?"

Another said, "Especially considering that most of what we discussed two weeks ago has now fallen apart."

Red stared down at the bullet points on the paper in front of him, representing so much work by so many loyal people. Employees, sure—but also friends. He owed them, big time.

He placed his finger on the first point and dove in. "Let's start with Rachel Wilbon," he began. "The papers were correct in identifying her as the source of the leak. She confirmed that much to the D.A. However, my legal team uncovered a strict nondisclosure agreement buried in her contract that expressly forbade her from speaking to the media about any of Trident's internal workings. We've been able to release her cleanly, without any threat of further legal repercussions."

"Well, that was lucky," someone said.

A reply came swiftly, "Was it? What about her Goldstein?"

"Who cares?" the first person retorted. "Rachel is a hack."

"Red," his father's dearest friend interjected, "Why did Wilbon even have a nondisclosure?"

Red grinned. Old Claude had just played his role in this play perfectly, much as he used to do for Red's dad.

"We think it was for two reasons. First, we learned that Rachel was in a romantic relationship with Jim Denton, who—you may remember—wrote for Trident under the pen name Phil Miller. He's also John and Lisa's only son. Rachel probably knew a lot of things they wished she didn't."

"I don't even want to know how you found that out," one woman muttered.

"Completely by accident," Red assured her. "Nevertheless, we also discovered that the rumors of Rachel's plagiarism were already percolating when she was up for the Goldstein. They undoubtedly wanted to keep *that* quiet. It seems the Dentons paid off the committee to make sure she won. Probably with the first of the stolen royalties."

That juicy tidbit came courtesy of Red's assistant, who sat, beaming, across from him. Once the Trident investors had begun jumping ship like a horde of diseased rats, poor Anika had been too swamped to pitch in.

Right on cue, a chorus of groans came over the intercom in front of him—and Red felt his first glimmer of hope. He glanced at Wayne, Anika, and Rob, arrayed across the conference table from him and ready for anything.

This could work. This was going to work.

"If that had gotten out, the Dentons would never have recovered," Claude pointed out.

Exactly. And the love of Red's life might've moved on to some other publisher, where Red might never have met her. It was hard to fathom.

"So why did Rachel let the cat out of the bag?"

Red explained, "I believe she was trying to save her job, plain and simple. Her contract stipulated that she was to provide Trident with a new manuscript within two years of *Moon*'s release, and she was already far past that deadline. PKM was pressuring her. She apparently thought that discrediting Trident might buy her more time to produce her next book."

"Or find someone to steal it from," Anika muttered sourly.

Red shook his head and dropped his finger to the next bullet point. "If there's nothing else, let's proceed to the next item—the Millhouse & Rock deal. Or rather, the dissolution of it."

"Can't say I'm surprised," one board member sighed. "It always seemed too good to be true."

Red rolled his eyes at Anika, who shot the intercom a manicured middle finger. He smiled and said, "M&R was never going to be the perfect fit for Trident, but they were high profile. At the time, that was going to work to our advantage. Now, however, I believe Trident will benefit from a different kind of arrangement."

The one Piper wanted. The smart one—the deal Red ought to have gone for from the beginning. He'd gotten lucky on this, Red knew. He'd only managed it because Anika had a friend, who had another friend—and that marvelous soul had set up a round of drinks in SoHo last night with two women he wished he'd met sooner.

Leigh Evans and Kiki Eastman, former book bloggers and founders of their own romance-only micro-chain of bookstores. They'd quickly moved from disbelief to deal-making, a quality that Red was completely in favor of. Talk about under the wire, though.

"What kind of arrangement are we talking?" someone asked cautiously.

God, they were playing into Red's hands perfectly. Anika looked as smug as could be.

"We've drafted an agreement with Eva East Books, giving Trident's romance titles priority placement in their stores and on their website. We'll do signings and readings and there's room to add in some merch, too. It's a boon for us, and for them."

The room was silent for a long, long moment. Finally, a man asked, "How in the hell did you swing that?"

Anika polished her perfect nails on her blazer and grinned broadly.

"I ran into Leigh and Kiki the other day," Red said casually. "We got to talking and discovered that our interests align." Well, he had got to begging and the ladies had got to laughing, but that hardly seemed relevant at this point.

Someone on the call snorted. Maybe two or three someones.

Red powered on. "Regardless, with your agreement, we can have this draft signed and back in the hands of their legal team later this morning. Wayne should've faxed you copies to review."

There was a rustle of static as the board members shuffled through their packets for the meeting, followed by a flurry of commentary and questions as they debated the particulars.

At last, Anika leaned forward and nodded at Red. "Move to pass the Eva East agreement. All in favor say *aye*."

"Aye."

"Aye."

A pause, and then a few more assents. Red waited for Anika to confirm the tally. She positively preened when she announced,

"Motion to pass the Eva East agreement approved. Red, what's the next item?"

Red fist-bumped his favorite lawyer in the world. "Now then," he said. "As most of you know, we've already turned over everything we had regarding the Dentons and their mismanagement of royalties to the district attorney's office."

"What's the status of that?"

"As I understand it, it's going to drag on a while. In the meantime, we have a key author to compensate and a business to stabilize."

"And here we go," a woman drawled.

That's right, Red thought. *Here we go.*

IN THE END, the board wasn't too broken up about shedding nearly every imprint at Trident except romance, the true money-maker. The harder sell had been trying to convince them to postpone one of their pet projects at PKM until the case against the Dentons was resolved.

All his directors, it seemed, loved the flashy new tech PKM was testing—but they'd have to wait another fiscal year before they got to see a real demo. They'd live.

Their muttering about it was rapidly eclipsed, anyway, once Red recused himself from the final vote on the grounds that he was in a personal relationship with a particular Trident author. He had to endure some pointed questions about his timing and intentions before they finally let him up off the mat and got down to business.

Still, Red had done it. He and his finest employees had managed to pass all the resolutions they should've put together from the outset—and they'd done it on no sleep and a whole lot of flying without a net. He wished he could feel proud, but the truth was he shouldn't have fucked it up to begin with.

When Rob finally sat forward to stab the button that disconnected the call, the team's relief was palpable. Red flipped over his agenda, scrawled a few words across the back, and held it up for Wayne, Anika, and Rob to see.

"*Raises for all my friends*," Rob read aloud.

"Huzzah!" Wayne crowed.

"About damn time," Anika smiled.

Rob looked too tired to join in the celebration, but he did manage a half-hearted salute. Red could relate.

"All right, you guys. The rest of this crap can wait for a while. Go home and get some rest. I'll see you on Monday, and then we can hammer out the details. Okay?"

"Don't have to ask me twice," Rob murmured.

As they filed out, Wayne hung back a step to squint at Red. "Need anything else?"

A miracle. Red needed a bloody miracle now, but he suspected he'd already used up his allotment—for this life, and the next. He wracked his brain, trying to determine if there was anything else he could do.

"No man, I'm good," he said.

HIS CELL BEGAN buzzing in his pocket just as Red headed down the hall to his office. He glanced at the screen and prepared to decline the call, but instead his eyebrows jacked up in surprise. *Tate.* What timing.

"Hey man."

"Avon calling," his friend sang.

"Sorry, dude. Bought at the office," Red fired back.

There was a chuckle, a muttered curse, and another sound that Red really hoped wasn't gunfire.

"You okay?" he wondered.

"Yeah, I'm tight. Listen, Luc told me what your week's been like. What the fuck, Red."

"You have no idea. I literally hung up with the board five minutes ago."

"Those fuckers," Tate growled. "What a bunch of crybabies."

"Even so. I had to do my song and dance, and I did. There's no going around them."

"I've told you a hundred times, brother. Never go around when you can plow straight through."

"I know, T. I plowed. Believe me, I plowed."

"Everything go okay?"

"Yeah. Seemed to," Red said.

"A'ight," Tate replied, all business. "Now. Luc and I want to know what you're gonna do about your lady."

Red groaned. "I mean—do you two fuckers just sit around gossiping about my pathetic ass all day? I would've thought you both had better things to worry about." Like hospital crises. And bullets, for Christ's sake.

"Quit your bitching. I don't have a ton of time, here."

"And I do?" Red balked.

"I know it sucks, but you have to go get her, buddy."

"Easy for you to say. Piper's not taking my damn calls, and unlike you, I don't have an automatic weapon at my disposal to make her."

"When did you become such a pussy?" his friend demanded. "This isn't a phone call kind of mission. Get on your fancy little plane, march up to your woman, and fight to get her back. What the hell's wrong with you?"

Red sat and absorbed that for a minute, then wondered, "How is it that you always end up playing Bad Cop?"

"Because Luc can't pull the shit off with his accent. Don't act dense. You know he's too sexy for Bad Cop."

Red had a feeling Piper would have plenty to say about bad cops being sexy. She might even like to roleplay the hell out of the idea, as long as she got to be the arresting officer. But not now. Now, Red needed to focus.

He said to Tate, "Okay, then tell me when you became such a staunch advocate of love and romance."

"The second it became important to you, motherfucker."

Red blew out a long breath. Even from the Middle East, his old roommate could be a pain in his ass.

"Tate, it's been a long day. I can't do this with you right now." The line crackled, and Red tried not to read too much into all the noise coming from Tate's end.

"Me either, as it happens. Good Cop should be calling you later, when his shift's over. Just…git er done, okay? I'll check in soon."

Red told him, "Be safe, brother."

"Safety's overrated," Tate said, then hung up.

Red sat behind his desk and considered his options. He'd been intending to go home and sleep for about fourteen hours straight, but…somewhere due south of him was the woman he loved. She was, currently, exceedingly unhappy with him.

Not rest for the wicked, it seemed—sleep would have to wait. Red had a heart to mend first and pulling that out of his hat was going to be his most challenging deal yet.

Piper was worth it, though. She was so, so worth it.

Thirty-Six

PERRY ASKED HER, "Did you get it?" It was hard to miss the excitement in his voice. He might be a kindly old man, but he did love winning.

However, Piper was a touch contrary these days. "Get what?"

"The wire transfer," he said, exasperated. "It should have gone through this morning."

She sighed, "I'll check."

Piper called up the banking app on her phone, and there it was. Her account balance had ballooned, as if by some kind of unsavory magic. And, okay—that was definitely a lot of zeroes. Too late to save her family's house, though. Too late to save her heart, either.

"Yup, all there," she told her attorney. "Thanks, Perry."

"It's what I'm here for."

There was a weighty pause, and Piper didn't need to guess what was coming next.

"Piper, you should talk to him. MacLellan."

As if there was anyone else they'd be discussing? "I have no intention of doing that," she said.

"I'm aware, but…"

She busied herself paying off a couple of bills and transferring some of her new funds into savings while her lawyer dithered.

Finally, Perry settled on, "I met with him, you know. When he came up with that *Eva East* rider for your contract."

"Did you?" she inquired dully.

"I did. And I talked to him for quite a while. Red and his legal team shared some very interesting information with me about their internal investigation. They were able to build quite a case against the Dentons and Ms. Wilbon."

"How nice for them."

"That was partly why I advocated for settling with PKM, instead of going to court."

They had been over this already. Piper saw no need to rehash it now. The man she'd fallen in love with had deliberately kept important details about her career from her, while simultaneously launching a full-frontal attack on her heart. He'd wanted her trust, but he didn't want to earn it fair and square. They were done, and that was that.

As far as Piper was concerned, Red MacLellan could take his team and his court case, and choke on them. The overgrown oaf.

"Piper, he's an honest man. He may have held off informing you of the situation for far too long, but that whole time he was trying to come up with a fix for it. I do not believe it was Red's intention to defraud you."

"Oh, terrific," she growled. "First my dad, and now you. He charmed the pants off you, didn't he?"

"He—"

"Well, that's just great. So glad you let him pull one over on you, too. I have to be honest, Perry. I thought you were a better judge of character than that." As soon as the words left her mouth, Piper wished she could retract them. She'd gone too far. That kind of pettiness wasn't like her, and Perry didn't deserve it.

Her attorney sighed. "I realize you are upset, but I'm going to pretend that you didn't just insult my intelligence or my legal acumen, Ms. Fulham."

"I'm sorry. But he *lied* to me, Perry."

"He withheld pertinent information until such time as he could present you with a solution."

"Why does everyone keep saying that?"

"Who's everyone? Just so I'm clear."

Piper sat in silence, feeling every inch the petulant child.

"Okay, hear me out. I'm not a fool. I understand that all of this is colored by the fact that the two of you have a personal relationship at stake."

"*Had*, Perry. Past tense."

"If you say so. But I know you'll feel a heck of a lot better about the new contract—and your new projects—if you can clear the air between the two of you. Bite the bullet and listen to what MacLellan has to say."

"And if I say no?"

"As your legal representation, I cannot compel you to do this. But as your friend…well, I hope I've banked enough goodwill with you over the years that you'll admit I have only your best interests at heart."

"Perry, come on. You're really going to play that card?"

"I've been on this earth a long time, young lady. You bet I am."

"*God.* You and Dad are two peas in a pod, aren't you?"

"Did you know that MacLellan disclosed your relationship to his board when they voted on the new deal?"

"He…what? He did?"

"Sure did. And then recused himself from the vote, saying he'd done all he could for the company, but that the decision was in their hands."

"I…wow. Okay," she stammered. A man did not disclose a personal relationship to his company's board of directors unless he considered it to be relevant and ongoing. Did he? Did Red really think it wasn't over between them?

"Were you also aware," Perry continued, "that he reorganized Trident and put off some big PKM projects in order to get you reimbursed as soon as possible? So you wouldn't have to wait for the court case to wrap up, or try to get the money out of the Dentons yourself?"

Piper bit her lip. "No. I was not aware of that."

"I didn't think so. Except…now you are. And you are going to have to decide what to do with that information, Cupcake."

AFTER THEY HUNG up, Piper tried to forget their conversation. She hit the internet and bought herself three impractical, badass pairs of shoes and sprung for the overnight shipping. She scoured her guest bathroom, then vacuumed all the snack crumbs from her laptop keyboard. She thought about investing. She thought about Eric Whittier and his sister.

None of it was enough to get her mind off Perry's words, though. Thanks to him and her dad, Piper wasn't going to be able to avoid the subject of Red any longer. So, for the first time since that horrible morning, she let herself relive what had actually happened.

When she'd first seen that news report on TV, Piper had immediately assumed that big, bad PKM had been looting little Trident's coffers. She couldn't conceive of John and Lisa Denton—or, for that matter, their son Jim or his fuck buddy Rachel—being outright thieves.

They'd smiled at her over coffee too many times. They'd asked Piper about her cats. Hell, a few times, they'd even emailed her funny cat memes. What kind of people did those things when they were stealing from you?

But Piper had jumped to an incorrect conclusion about PKM, and about Trident. In her defense, everything had happened so fast. She'd felt stunned, and when that wore off, fiercely betrayed. It was no wonder she'd kicked Red to the curb so abruptly.

As the full story unfolded, however, the true nature of the crimes committed against her had been revealed. Piper had to accept that she'd been wrong about PKM, and wrong about Trident. Loathe as she was to admit it, though, she had never reevaluated whether she'd given Red a fair shake.

In retrospect, she had to wonder if perhaps she'd been a tad hasty. Piper had not actually asked Red *why* he hadn't told her about the stolen royalties. She hadn't asked him a damn thing. She'd simply tossed the baby out with the bathwater, dried her hands, and went on her merry way.

Since then, she hadn't let herself read a single text or email from Red. She hadn't listened to any of the voicemails he'd left, either, just in case his sexy voice lessened her resolve. Where Red was concerned, Piper knew she was weak—and if she had any chance at all of resisting his pull, she had to go cold turkey.

Had that been fair, though? Red had asked her once if she was punishing him for Kyle's transgressions, and at the time she'd been dead certain she wasn't. Now things didn't feel quite so cut-and-dried. Red, after all, had always been straightforward about his feelings and clear about his intentions.

Abruptly, Piper saw that there were gray areas littered all over this debacle. Rocks and hard places. Impossible choices. She saw them, but she hadn't made any allowances for them. If she'd truly cared about Red as she'd claimed, she might have at least let him have his say.

Piper sat down heavily on the loveseat and sighed. Sonny rolled onto his back, so she stroked the soft black fur of his belly and considered the situation. Several weeks had passed since she'd started avoiding Red and he wasn't a patient man. It seemed entirely possible that he'd already given up and moved on to someone else. It was even likely, wasn't it?

Except deep in her heart, Piper knew it wasn't. Red would never have said the things he had if he hadn't meant them. He wasn't the type. Piper suspected he'd shown her a side of himself that not many people got to see. And if he liked her enough to do that, Red wouldn't give up on her easily.

He'd fight for her. Just like she should have fought for him—for them. Instead, Piper had thrown in the towel before she'd even broken a sweat. Guilt and shame washed over her.

Her attorney—her *friend,* as Perry had so helpfully pointed out—was an excellent judge of character. He was not the kind of person to be swayed by a movie-star face, or an excess of charm, or even a smarmy sales pitch. Perry assessed the facts, consulted his gut, and made his decisions.

Piper had never known him to be wrong, in all their long association. If Perry Shanahan had made up his mind to trust Red MacLellan, then he had a damn good reason to do so. Piper might be a dolt on her own sometimes, but she wasn't so rash as to ignore his counsel.

The thing was, Piper's hunches about people were almost always reliable, too. She could usually tell when people were shady, when they were lying, and when they were only out for themselves.

If she was brutally honest with herself, she *had* known all those things about Kyle—she just hadn't wanted them to be true. And maybe she'd even had some doubts about the folks at Trident— otherwise, why bring Perry in so soon after they'd signed her?

Which suggested Piper could read people just as well as Perry. So, if Red had sailed right past every one of her defenses and hadn't set off a single alarm on his way into her heart, then…*uh- oh*.

All this time, Piper had assumed he'd managed it because she was defective somehow. Broken in the parts that counted. But maybe she wasn't. Perhaps her Bad Guy radar was still somewhat operational. And if that was the case, Red hadn't set it off because Red wasn't actually a bad person. He was only a guy trying to do his best with a really shitty roll of the dice.

Piper slumped back into the cushions. Did she really believe that, or was she just looking for excuses to see him again? Was she trying to justify true assholery simply because she loved being kissed like she was the epicenter of someone's world?

She knew, with sickening clarity, that wasn't the case. Which implied…*crud*—it meant that if Red tried to contact her again, Piper probably needed to face the bossy bastard and let him say what he wanted to say. The only question was whether she could handle what came next.

Thirty-Seven

AT LONG LAST, Red found the information he needed buried on his own fucking desk. After getting the stiff-arm from Piper for too many weeks to count, encountering brick wall after brick wall trying to reach her, it figured that the solution would appear right under his nose.

He was sitting there flipping dejectedly through files, not really reading anything because what was the point? No one was around anyway, so it wasn't like he had an audience to pretend for.

But suddenly, deep within one Trident file, Red noticed a very large number—a number that could only be one thing. Piper's wire transfer. He yanked the page closer, staring down at it, and there in the bottom corner, was a notation.

Red followed the trail deeper into the packet and found a copy of the wire transfer that had settled PKM's case with Piper, and ensured she'd never have reason to speak to him again. And there it was, in innocuous black-and-white type: Piper's new contact information.

Red wanted to howl in triumph. Instead, he picked up the phone.

"Wayne," he barked, when his assistant answered, "I need the next flight out of New York."

"That's interesting. How exactly do you expect me to perform such a feat?"

"The way you usually do, I imagine. Call the hangar. Or an airline."

Wayne paused, and Red could hear his small desk clock ticking. "You are obviously not aware that the entire region has been grounded because of this storm," he said finally.

"Storm," Red reiterated, feeling like he was missing something.

"You remember the ice storm we're in the middle of? The reason you sent everyone home three hours ago?"

He did. Sort of. Had he been sitting here aimlessly fucking around for that long now?

"Which begs the question—what the heck are *you* still doing there?"

Red shook his head. "A train, then," he managed. "It'll take longer, but..."

"Red."

Red flinched. His intrepid assistant never called him by his first name unless shit had gotten real.

"There are no planes, trains, or buses. Where do you need to go so badly?"

"Maryland," Red told him glumly.

Wayne groaned. "Do you even know where you're going this time?"

"Yes." At least, he hoped he did. It was entirely possible Piper had used someone else's address to receive the wire and this was a dead end.

There was silence over the line, stretching long enough that Red began to wonder if Wayne had hung up on him. But, finally, the other man relented.

"Do me a favor, okay? Go outside and try to find a cab or something to bring you home. I'll see what I can do and call you in a little while."

ULTIMATELY, IT TOOK a couple of hours and a lot of angst for Wayne to find him a ten-year-old SUV for sale in the Village. It was a little dented around the edges, but the snow tires were new, the engine was sound, and it had excellent four-wheel drive—unlike Red's stupidly pretentious little sportscar or the Lincoln that Felix ferried him around in.

Red packed a bag and collared a second tenacious cabbie to take him over there, wired the seller his money while standing next to him on the sidewalk, and was on the road before nightfall. The streets of Manhattan were in abysmal shape, but luckily most of the residents had hunkered down for the night and he didn't have to jockey much for position.

Once on the highway, the going was slightly better, but still tortuously slow. Red and a handful of semis progressed at a crawl from the outskirts of the city all the way to the Jersey line. Halfway through Pennsylvania, the weather eased somewhat, but Red was exhausted—and was forced to stop in a hotel for the rest of the night.

In the morning, the last leg of his trek went well, but what should have taken him around four hours ended up taking more than ten. Red checked into another hotel, this one close to the address he was hunting, and made an effort to clean himself up. At least when he rang Piper's bell, he'd have had a shower and a shave, plus a boatload of coffee.

Now that he was so close to his destination, though, Red couldn't quite make himself go to her. He might say all the right things and still be turned away. He was probably lucky that Piper hadn't already taken out a restraining order on him since it was so patently clear she wanted nothing to do with him. But Red couldn't give up until he told her he loved her, face to face.

He could not allow even a single shred of arrogance to surface when he did that. Piper would have every right to murder him on the spot if that happened. So, before Red went to Piper's new place, he did the one thing that was guaranteed to make him feel like the lowest worm on the planet—he drove past her old house.

He parallel-parked across the street to check things out. Sitting there in his manly new ride, he didn't feel like much of a man. The guy he'd sent to make all Piper's home dreams come true had somehow managed to finagle her family seat right out from under her. And by the looks of things, he was already hard at work fixing the place up.

So much for Red taking worries off her plate. Instead, his good intentions had resulted in the worst possible outcome for Piper. He shut off the truck and got out, then leaned against the cold metal to take a few bracing gulps of air.

Because of him, Piper had lost her favorite thing on earth. Red was absolutely crazy to think this trip was anything other than a fool's errand.

Across the street, under a rhododendron in the front yard, a dark blob shifted and mewled. Red leaned forward and squinted, trying to make out what it was. A raccoon, perhaps, or a…cat? He stepped across the street and peered under the bush, hoping no neighbors were watching him.

The blob moved again, resolving clearly into the shape of a cat. A small, gray animal who looked an awful lot like…

"Fredo?"

Piper's pet darted across the grass and wound around Red's ankles, purring and shaking. Now he could see that it was definitely her cat, thinner and much worse for wear, with leaves and brambles stuck to his fur.

"Fredo! Oh my God, Fredo, I thought it was you," Red said, scooping him up. Then he laughed, remembering all of Piper's mafia jokes. "I *knew* it was you. You little stinker—what happened? Piper must be so worried about you."

Holding the cat securely in his arms, Red took one more look around, then crossed quickly to his truck. He settled Fredo on the seat beside him and took stock. Piper's beloved pet looked like he'd been living rough for quite a while. Red couldn't bring him to her looking like this.

So he pulled up the mapping app on his phone, got his bearings, and set off determined to get this part right, at least. When Fredo saw his mom and brother again, he was going to have a full stomach, a fresh bath, and a clean bill of health.

IT WAS EARLY afternoon by the time Red got the cat fed and watered and in to see a nearby vet. Red drove to Piper's new pad with his nerves jangling. He left Fredo in his cardboard carrier in the truck, then stood on her mat dumbly, staring at her door for the longest time before he could make himself hit the bell.

This was his last hurrah. Piper might turn him away. If she did, Red had to be able to turn around and leave, and never bother Piper again. Even if that went against every instinct he had. Even if it crushed him.

But the door finally swung open, and Piper stood inside looking as forlorn as Red had ever seen her. He wanted to fold her in his arms and make it all better, but he'd lost that right. He could only speak and hope it was enough.

Piper didn't seem the least bit surprised to see him, and she didn't move. Maybe Red was just that predictable, or maybe Wayne had warned her he was coming. Either way, it was now up to Red to get her to listen.

Despite his shower and his mission of mercy earlier, he must not have looked much better than her—because instead of slamming the door in his face, Piper simply sighed heavily.

"God, Red. You look awful."

"I'd like to claim it's because I've missed you so much, but I'm pretty sure those wounds are strictly internal." And, *crap*—he'd been determined not to come here hoping for sympathy.

"Save it," she muttered, but her irritation was tepid, at best.

Red scrubbed a hand over his face and tried to remember some of the things he'd been so desperate to tell her all this time. Nothing helpful came immediately to mind.

"What's wrong?"

"It's been a harrowing twenty-four hours," he admitted.

"Yeah, how are you even here right now? I thought all the airports up north were closed."

"They are. I drove."

"*What?*"

"As I said, harrowing."

"Jesus. You could have gotten yourself killed."

Red shrugged. Like that even mattered.

Piper studied him while he stood on her doorstep. He tried to ignore the sight of all the other doors and windows fronting that open-air hallway, tried not to think about the eyes and ears behind them, watching and listening to his abject humiliation. He deserved their judgment, after all. Every bit of it.

"Do I even want to know which one of my now-former friends gave up my address?" she asked bitterly.

"Don't worry," he told her. "No one ratted you out. I found it by accident, buried in the footnotes of some paperwork that crossed my desk yesterday."

"Damn it. The wire transfer," Piper grumbled.

"It's almost like you wanted me to find you, sweetheart." Red couldn't resist the jab, if only to wrench some sign of actual emotion out of her. He could work with a lot of things—anger, betrayal, and sadness among them—but if Piper had simply stopped caring altogether, he was dead in the water right now.

Piper scowled ferociously. Red was so fucking happy to just be looking at her, he didn't even have the heart to push his luck.

"Look, I know I didn't call ahead. If this isn't a good time, I can…" What? Take a nap on her doormat? Cry all the way home, like a wee little piggie? Hand over her cat and hie back to Manhattan?

Piper stared at him, waiting.

"This is where I'm staying," Red said. He handed her a brochure that he'd grabbed on the way out of the hotel lobby. "Maybe I can stop by some other time."

And maybe Piper would up and move again before he could.

She sighed once more. "Have you eaten?"

"I…" Red vaguely recalled some beef jerky at a rest stop somewhere, and maybe…a granola bar? Hard to say.

"No," he decided.

"All right. Come in," she relented, stepping back. "You big dolt. I'm sure I've got something."

"Hang on," Red told her. "I've got someone in the truck you're going to want to see first."

AFTER PIPER AND Fredo's emotional reunion, she parked Red in a chair in her tiny kitchen and went looking for food that was obviously not there. She managed to extract a yogurt drink that was past its expiration date from her fridge, and exactly one heel of 21-grain bread from her counter.

In the pantry, Piper tried to nudge a large jar of peanut butter behind a bag of flour where, presumably, Red wouldn't see it— but she wasn't terribly smooth about it.

The whole thing was so depressing, Red thought he could actually break down and cry in front of her. If he were a different sort of man, that was. Right now, though, his increasing worry that Piper wasn't eating properly was enough to take the immediate edge off his own misery.

"Don't worry. I can grab something later," he told her. "For now, I'm more worried about telling you a few things that I hope you'll want to hear."

Piper slumped into the chair across from him, looking wary. "I hate to break it to you, but I doubt I want to hear anything you have to say." Her words lacked bite, however.

"You did convey that rather nicely by avoiding me all this time," Red pointed out.

"And yet," she retorted, "Here you are."

"I don't give up easily."

"You don't say."

Red sighed. What was he doing here? Piper owed him nothing. He ought to leave her alone, and he might've—*if* she'd looked healthy and sane and glad to be rid of him. But something about her appearance and demeanor was registering in his brain as an uncanny echo of his own wretchedness.

Piper was as wrecked as he was. And a person didn't go through that unless their entire heart and soul was on the line. Red had a sudden, delirious flare of hope. If she'd loved him once, she might still. He just had to prove he was worthy.

"Piper, I'd like the chance to explain. If you hear it all and still want to toss me out on my ass, I'll understand. I'll walk right out that door and that will be that. I'll hate it, because I love you and I want to spend the rest of my life with you, but I'll do it."

She winced, then glared off into the corner like capitulating offended every cell in her body.

"Damn it, Red. I don't know why you're doing this," she finally growled. "Eat your damn bread. Then I'll listen."

He poked at the sad, seedy brown rectangle in the middle of his plate before breaking off a corner and shoving it in his mouth. Fredo was purring outrageously loudly from Piper's lap.

"I didn't find out the Dentons were stealing your royalties until after we started dating," Red began. "In retrospect, I realize that I should have told you right then. It killed me not to."

Piper arched one delicate brow, stroked her cat, and looked dubious.

Red swallowed another bite of bread and powered on, "I…had to be careful not to jeopardize our investigation, but also, you were so worried about all your house stuff. I thought if I could fix everything at Trident first, then tell you what happened, it would be one less thing for you to have to deal with."

She stared at him. "I have to say, I would never have pegged you for a Mary Poppins."

"I'm…sorry?"

"Helping the medicine go down with some sugar?"

Oh. Right. "Everything was going so well with us," Red said weakly. "I was terrified that if you found out before I could make it better, you'd blame me. I didn't want to let it affect us, but then Rachel leaked it too soon."

"Yeah, and why did she do that again?"

"Because I kept rebuffing her advances and was about to can her. She thought if she discredited me and PKM, maybe she could keep her contract a while longer."

Piper muttered, "That woman is not terribly bright, is she?"

"I had to shift some projects around to free up the money, but the PKM board did the right thing and agreed to Trident's reorganization, and to the Eva East deal." Red blew out a long breath. "I should've listened about Millhouse. You were right about them."

A delicate rose flush crept into Piper's cheeks, and she looked away quickly, her eyes shining. She had given him her heart, even though he was a head case. He would probably love her until he was cold in the ground, and then some.

"I'm really sorry, Piper. I tried to do things for you when I should've worked *with* you instead. I won't make that mistake again."

Piper lifted her chin and met his eye. Her voice was excruciatingly careful when she said, "What do you want, Red? Why are you here?"

"All I want is you," he said plainly, "and I came to get you back, my little dove. I don't know if you'll forgive me, or even if you still want me. But if there's a chance, if there's anything I can do, please tell me. Let me try."

BY THE RIPE old age of thirty-six, Red had already become a jaded bastard. Yet somehow, it had only taken one bookish female with a very dirty imagination to bring him to his knees. He'd have to remind himself not to take life for granted in the future. It had a tricky sense of humor.

At least he'd finally run Piper to ground, he thought, studying her. She'd tearfully accepted his apology, and finally allowed him to kiss her until neither of them could see straight. Then, she'd dragged him to her living room so she could curl up next to him on her small loveseat.

Red doubted she was pleased about the state he'd found her in. Piper had plainly not been expecting anyone, but he was half wondering when she'd last left the house. Now that he could think past his hammering pulse again, he realized that Piper wasn't wearing one of her usual, devilishly-enticing outfits. Instead, she had on a gray and black striped t-shirt with a hole near the hem; a baggy pair of fleece pajama bottoms in black, pink, and white stripes; and a thick pair of socks, *also* striped.

He'd laugh if he weren't so goddamn relieved that she'd actually relented. "Nice threads," Red commented, squeezing her shoulder.

Piper sagged against him, pulling her feet up so she could snuggle closer. She peered down at herself and muttered morosely, "Three stripes, you're out."

It took him a minute longer than it should've to get it. Red blamed Piper's proximity and the bewitching scent of her hair. Once it dawned on him what she'd said, though, he had to chuckle.

"Oh, God, woman. I've missed you. And your clever mouth."

Piper grinned up at him, and there they were—those insanely cute dimples he'd been dying to see. Red didn't deserve her, but he had to try. The alternative was simply too bleak to contemplate.

Thirty-Eight

PIPER'S RELIEF AT being reunited with Red was pervasive. Once she'd decided to forgive him, nearly every part of her life looked rosier. Her apartment was cuter, her cats were a dynamic duo again, and she had some new ideas for how to fix her ailing manuscript.

All that from twenty-four hours in his company. Old Piper might've balked at the kind of sway that gave Red, but she was done with that kind of thinking. The past was the past. Piper had learned her lessons from it the best way she knew how, but now it was time to leave it be.

Besides, Red was really turning over a new leaf, too. Piper suspected it wasn't nearly as easy for him as he liked to pretend, but the way he'd been communicating and considering her opinions on all kinds of things was hard to ignore.

She figured he really ought to be rewarded for making such strides. And when Piper thought about what she could do to show her appreciation, there was only one big thing that came immediately to mind.

She didn't want any unpleasant surprises this time around, however. If her idea was going to go off without any hitches, she needed a foolproof plan. A *Piper*-proof plan.

So, plan she did, in the way she knew best. She drafted the outline and wrote the story, then spent the afternoon fine-tuning it until it was perfect. Piper committed every last detail to memory, to be sure she wouldn't leave anything out.

When the time came to spring it on Red that night, she told him, "I want to try bondage again," in as clear and strong a voice as she could muster.

Red didn't look too shocked, but he also didn't move a muscle. "Now? Are you sure?" Even frozen, his whole being had gone on alert with her words.

She nodded. Piper was *so* sure.

"But what if you…" He stopped short before he finished whatever he'd been about to say.

"Have a meltdown?" she asked. "I thought of that. Maybe instead of doing it the same way as before, we could try something a little different."

"Whatever you want." Red's eyes moved restlessly over her face. His hands smoothed down his legs. "Piper…are you *really* sure about this?"

"Yes. In fact, I already got some things we'll need."

That knocked him back a step. Piper suppressed the victorious laugh that wanted to bubble out of her and took him by the hand. And to think, she hadn't even known her town *had* stores like the one she'd found earlier.

"Everything's upstairs. Follow me," she said.

Red was silent as he prowled behind her to her bedroom. Piper's heart pounded erratically inside her chest as she handed him the zippered satin pouch the store had given her. She watched Red's face as he examined the contents, looking for some sign that she'd done the right thing.

He made a low, growly sound and looked up at her. She had him. She knew she did.

Red pulled the long silk scarf free and tossed the pouch on her bed, then stood running the length of soft material through his fingers as he contemplated her. Piper didn't even wait for him to ask—she just started stripping. Red's eyes lit with fire.

"I thought—" She cleared her throat, trying to dislodge the tightness that had crept up with a sudden flash of nerves. "I thought you could bind my hands this time but leave my legs free."

His voice dropped low. "Okay. How do you want me to do it?"

She'd considered that. Piper turned around, presenting her wrists to him. "Behind my back, please."

Red stepped close and wrapped the scarf firmly around her, tying it quickly. She could hear him breathing deeply, could feel his exhales ruffling the hair on top of her head. She wouldn't back out now. He needed to know that she trusted him—and he'd given her the exact way to prove it to him, months ago.

"What else?" he murmured, his voice husky in her ear.

"Promise you won't leave," she said. "If you want to cover my eyes, keep a hand on me so I know you're still with me."

"Easy." Red reached again for the satin pouch and held it behind her back, rummaging through it. "Anything else?"

"Could you keep talking to me? I think it helps."

"Absolutely."

And he did. Red kept up a dirty running commentary on all of Piper's best attributes, murmuring in vivid detail about how she made him feel and what he wanted to do with her. His words were even better than the ones she'd written for him in her little story.

Pressing up behind her, Red cupped her breasts, kneading them gently and toying with her nipples. Piper dropped her head back against his chest and gave in to the sensation. Bolts of lightning streaked through her veins, leaving her hot and yearning.

She flexed her fingers, testing the restraint around her wrists. Caught between their bodies, Piper's hands encountered more than the air she'd expected. She could feel the fly of Red's jeans— and so much more. She gasped, startled.

He chuckled darkly—the hound—and stepped neatly back out of her reach.

"How are you feeling?" he rumbled once more.

"Excellent," she fired back. "How about you?"

Red laughed again, then trailed a scrap of black satin up her thigh. Good—he'd found the blindfold.

"May I cover your eyes now, little dove?" Piper's nickname on his lips sounded utterly filthy, and a deep thrill shuddered through her.

What did it matter if she could see? She had her eyes squeezed shut anyway. Piper nodded quickly, holding still so he could tie the blindfold and rearrange her hair. His hands slid down over her hips, warm and safe.

"I'm going to step back, beautiful girl. Just two steps, and then I'll be with you again. Is that all right?"

She hesitated, but Red was doing everything she'd asked. "Yes," she agreed.

"I'm right over here," he assured her. Piper stood quietly, listening to some indistinct rustling next to the bed. There'd been one more thing in that bag she'd given him. Maybe he—

Abruptly, Red was touching her again, fastening what felt like a whisper-light chain around her waist. Piper shifted as it tickled her and discovered that another short chain hung from the first. This was not the toy she'd given him. This was something entirely different. Where had he gotten it?

Red's hand stroked down her belly, then grasped the weighty metal device grazing the very top of her sex. He twisted it in his fingers, and the pendant began vibrating. Its maddening hum spread quickly through the cradle of her hips.

Red growled low in her ear, "You didn't think I'd let you have all the fun, did you?"

The chain around Piper's waist was torturous. It wasn't heavy enough to provide any real friction, but it was inescapably *there*— caressing her hips with every move she made and every brush of his fingers. The sinful pendant added a whole other layer of anticipation, not quite low enough to hit where it could really do her any good, but making its presence known, nonetheless.

Piper should've anticipated that she'd never be able to tame Red all the way. Standing there letting him kiss her neck and shoulder, feeling his hands smooth over her burning skin, she knew she'd never want to.

Red MacLellan was the romance hero she'd always hoped to write, but never dreamed was real. To think that he not only existed, but was hers, was almost too much to believe.

"You're a goddess," he told her.

Piper managed only an incoherent whimper. She couldn't, for the life of her, remember any of the witty, sexy banter that she'd scripted for herself, not now that he'd managed to turn her scene inside-out on her.

Red slid his hand across her stomach and down, pressing the humming metal against her pubic bone as he cupped her. His long fingers stroked and rubbed, his other hand molded to her breast, and his teeth nipped her ear.

Piper's knees buckled under the onslaught. Red wrapped an arm around her waist to hold her upright, and at last she could reach what she wanted and get her revenge. She wriggled her hands into position and then she had him.

He groaned at the feel of her hands stroking his cock through the thick denim of his jeans. Red didn't pull away this time, though. Instead, he ground his hips forward into her grip, aiding Piper's cause while he continued to work his fingers and the pendant over her.

"Fuck. I love you so damn much," he ground out.

Piper was so, so close. Hovering right at the precipice.

"Red, please. I don't want to finish this way," she gasped. "I want to feel you inside me."

In an instant, he'd whirled her around. Piper felt him fumbling with his pants and putting on a condom, and then, just as suddenly, he reached behind her and freed her hands. Red sat on the edge of the bed, lifted Piper bodily onto his lap, and sank into her with one deep, heart-stopping thrust.

She wrapped her arms around his neck and dove for his lips. He was ready for her, sucking Piper's tongue deep into his mouth while he drove into her. Hot, hard and in control—that was Red. *Her* Red. The insidious pendant hummed against her skin each time they pressed together.

Maybe they were still working through the long stretch of deprivation, because he sent Piper hurtling over the edge in only moments. Her body gripped Red's while the shockwaves quaked through her, and then her big, strong man was ruined, too. He stopped thrusting, gripped her hips tightly against him and roared out his release.

They remained like that, panting and damp with sweat, for several quiet minutes. Red slipped off Piper's mask with shaking fingers and cupped her face. His eyes brimmed with emotion.

"Hi," he whispered.

Piper bit her lip, abruptly shy. "Hi."

"You sure know how to spoil a guy."

"I love you," she told him.

His eyes dropped down, and he searched for the clasp of the chain around her waist. "And I love you. I am curious, though."

Piper could've predicted that. In Red's orderly world, all things had defined causes and effects. This would be no different.

"What brought this on?" he wondered. "Not that I'm complaining one bit, but it was unexpected, to say the least." Once he found the clasp and released it, Red pulled the chain free, turned off the device, and tossed it aside.

Piper tracked its location, not wanting it to get lost in the sheets. She had no idea where he'd procured it, but they were definitely going to be using that baby again.

"I know. I wanted to thank you for not giving up on us, and it seemed like an obvious choice. Plus, I feel like I kind of owed you one. Or even two," she said.

Red closed his eyes. "How can you say that? After everything that's happened?"

"I just…feel guilty that I didn't hear you out sooner. I should've trusted you. I'm sorry."

"No, don't say that." His eyes popped open and searched hers. "After what happened to you before, it was totally understandable."

"But I still could've made a better effort to find out the whole story," Piper said wearily.

Red disengaged carefully from her, then laid back and rolled them to the side. "It's done, little dove. Let's not give it more traction than it deserves. We just have to agree to do better in the future."

She sighed. "You're right."

He stroked a hand down her arm thoughtfully. "Listen, there are some things I wanted to run by you. Since your advice about *Eva East* was so good, I thought maybe I'd better check with you before I screwed anything else up." Red's mouth pulled the side in a sardonic little smirk.

Piper laughed.

"No, really," he said.

Her eyebrows went up, gauging his seriousness. "Okay. What's up?"

"Now that Trident is stabilizing, we've been making some new hires," Red explained. "We snagged this terrific woman named Daisy to replace one of Rachel's old cronies in the design department. And we've gotten new editors and formatters, but…"

"What?" she prodded.

"I had another idea." Red looked uncharacteristically sheepish.

"Well, spill it!"

He took a deep breath. "I was looking at some market research a couple of weeks ago, and the numbers surrounding the mystery genre are really interesting. I thought we'd keep Trident romance-only, but what if we added a small mystery imprint, just to test the waters?"

Piper kissed him. "Not a bad idea." Another kiss. "Mystery readers are nearly as voracious as romance readers."

Red's lips followed hers when she pulled away. He murmured against her mouth, "So I'm not crazy? It doesn't sound bad?"

"No, not at all. It sounds very savvy." She kissed him again, but he resisted her efforts to take it deeper.

"Mmmm. Now we just need to track down some authors. Don't suppose you know any of those?" he wondered, idly tracing her ribcage with his fingers.

Piper sat up and pointed at him. "As a matter of fact, I do. Lyla Lawson. She was already with Trident, too—I run into her at conferences all the time. Her books are *insane*. You can't put them down. And I bet if you could get her back on board, she'd know other writers you could check out."

"Excellent." Red grabbed Piper and pulled her back down against his chest. "Tomorrow, maybe you could give her a call and feel her out. I'll tell Rob and his team to reach out, too. And later, we can think up a name for the new imprint. Something cool and mysterious." He traced up the underside of her chin with his tongue.

"Why not now?" Piper giggled.

Red gripped her rear end in his large, hot hands and squeezed. "Now, we have stuff to do."

Thirty-Nine

GUILT WAS A powerful thing. Red was pretty happy he didn't often have to feel it, because the way it gnawed at you really fucked with your ability to be happy.

When he couldn't take the heat anymore, he finally said, "Piper, honey, maybe I can talk to Eric Whittier for you. If we can find another house for his sister before she moves into your old place, I bet he'd consider selling it back to you."

Piper had diluted the majority of Red's anger at the contractor once she'd explained that Eric's offer had arisen out of kindness, rather than a desire to take advantage. Still, it bugged Red that the way things had shaken out was not what he'd intended when he'd hired the man.

Piper shook her head, though. "There's no need," she said. "I already talked to him. I don't want the house back."

That was a surprise, but not necessarily an unwelcome one. "But why?" Red asked. "It was so special to you."

"Now that I've had time to think about it, I've realized that most of the trauma I felt was because we'd broken up and because Fredo got lost. Not because I gave up my home." It was definitely lowering to be put on such an even par with a skinny little cat, but Red let it pass.

"We were *not* broken up," he insisted, vehement now. "It was a brief hiccup. That's all."

"A hiccup."

"Barely a blip."

"I…see," Piper muttered, eyeing him like he'd lost some IQ points. "Anyway. It occurred to me that even if my grandparents loved their house, it was mainly because of who was in it. They never would've wanted me to feel tied down or burdened by the place. Especially if there was somewhere else I'd rather be."

That sounded promising. Red barely dared to hope, "*Is* there somewhere else you'd rather be?"

"You might say that," Piper smiled. "I've recently become rather enamored of city life."

Red snorted. "Sell me another one, little dove."

"Okay fine. On occasion, I enjoy certain parts of the Northeast."

He debated whether it was the right time to spring what he'd done on her but figured it didn't get much better than this. "That's very interesting," he drawled. "As it happens, I may have something to show you in a certain part of the Northeast very soon."

"When will you know for sure?"

Now or never. "Fly up to see me next week," Red replied. "I'll know by then." What he wasn't sure about was how Piper would take it.

RED ARRANGED FOR him and Piper to fly out to Shelter Island by seaplane before she even got a chance to set foot in his loft. The real estate agent had couriered over keys and a remote control for the gate the day before. Like clockwork, they soon found themselves walking across the driveway pavers of the pretty shingled cottage, with its incomparable view of the harbor.

The breeze blowing in off the water was brisk, making Piper's cheeks rosy as she looked around. In summer, they'd be sheltered in a green, grassy enclave. The garden off the kitchen would deliver up its herbs and vegetables and flowers, and there was a little red barn that Eric Whittier had already agreed to turn into an office for Piper.

"What is this?" she asked, a hesitant smile flirting at the edges of her lips.

Red took her hand. "Let's go inside." She followed him up the steps to the front door with a frown.

"You have keys," she pointed out.

"I do."

Inside the foyer, she gasped, completely unable to mask her admiration. Red could hardly blame her—he'd fallen for it in two seconds flat, too.

Then she wheeled on him. "Wait. *Why* do you have keys?"

Here goes nothing. "Well, after we visited my parents' house, I started thinking that it would be nice to have our own place. I had a real estate agent look around, and a couple of weeks ago, he showed me this."

Piper blinked rapidly, her clever brain sifting through the many tempting tidbits he'd just laid out. Her mouth simply said, "And?"

"And I bought it." Her eyes turned into saucers and her mouth dropped open. Red's chest expanded with excitement.

"You bought it. Just like that."

"I wanted to show it to you first," he explained, "but then this bidding war happened…"

Piper muttered, "Oh, Jesus."

Red tossed up his hands. "I'm kind of competitive."

"You don't say," she said drily. "I hadn't noticed."

"Anyway, I won. So…" Piper grabbed for the carved bench he'd found for the front hall and sank onto it. "Welcome home," Red told her.

"Red, you—" she looked around with disbelief. "—you bought us a *house*?"

"What can I say? I seem to have a flair for over-the-top romantic gestures."

Piper just snorted at that.

"Don't get me wrong," he laughed, "I'm as surprised as anyone." When she didn't get up and immediately start investigating, Red began to get worried. "Piper? Do you like it? I'm sorry I didn't ask you, but there was no time. I had to jump on it. And it just seemed so much like you that I…"

She jumped up and threw her arms around him, stretching up onto her toes to smash her mouth clumsily against his. Red wrapped his hand around the back of her head and guided her into place, so he could kiss her more easily.

"I love it," she managed to say between long swipes of his tongue. "I already love it so much."

"I love you," he said. And then, "Even if you weren't here, you were the deciding factor, you know. We noticed that the owner had a ton of romance books in the library, so my agent—accidentally on purpose—let slip that you were the other buyer. It worked. And the seller left a ton of them for you. Come see."

In the little library, Piper went straight to the window seat set into a deep alcove and stared out at the steel-gray water. "Oh my God. This place is like something out of a movie."

On a shelf, Red found the package he'd sent to the agent. He brought it to the small table in the center of the room with a pointed *thunk*.

"What's that?" Piper asked, spinning around and studying the wide, flat box cagily.

Red smiled. So suspicious. "Open it and see."

Her elegant fingers released the ribbon and carefully dismantled the wrapping, then extracted the album within. Red suppressed a chuckle at the cover—Daisy, the new hire in Trident's design department, had really outdone herself.

Piper scowled down at it, taking a long moment to realize that it was, in fact, her and Red's faces photoshopped onto the enlarged, old-school romance novel cover. From *The Perils of a Pirate's Woman*, Red believed. Out of print now, but a huge seller back in its day—likely due to the entangled, overwrought specimens of passion on its cover.

He'd have to see if he could find a vintage copy somewhere. Shouldn't be difficult, given how many printings it'd gone through. This version was rarer. One printing. One copy.

He'd renamed this edition *Falling for You*. Well, actually Wayne had come up with that one after Red's early efforts had fallen totally flat. As Piper examined it, her face settled into its customary expression of delighted curiosity.

Red congratulated himself. This was absolutely the way to do what he'd been aching to do for a while now. If only the printing hadn't taken so long.

Piper cracked the cover and turned to the first page. At the top was a large, posed publicity shot, taken for the press releases when she'd signed her new contract with PKM. At the bottom, was the beginning of their story.

"*Once upon a time*," she read aloud, "*A lonely but dashing pirate met a glorious sorceress.*"

Piper looked up at him with laughing eyes, so Red gave her a jaunty salute. "Ahoy," he said.

She paged through the next couple of pages. More photos, more sentences about the way her staggering beauty made otherwise-strong men weep. One or two asides detailing Red's undeniable virility and roguish good looks.

Piper paused for a long moment on a photo she'd never seen, another Wayne contribution. They'd been in Red's office, their heads bent over a galley on his desk—the first one from her new series, the first that PKM would launch into the world.

Red thought it was perhaps her best novel yet, and that was a high bar to clear. His assistant had snapped the photo to prove a point to him, to underline how obvious it was to everyone else that Red was head over heels for the woman beside him. Good thing he'd told them already. There was no hiding it now.

"*The pirate needed the woman to work a very specific spell,*" Piper read. "*One that would ensure untold treasures filled his coffers for years to come.*"

Another page. Another picture, this one from Red's own phone. *"The sorceress, being far cleverer than he, decided to work a different spell—one to heal the pirate's wretched heart."*

In the photo, Piper was in front of her laptop but gazing out the window of her living room, deep in thought as she worked on some story or another. Here in this room, she was staring up at Red, somber now, with suspiciously watery eyes.

"Keep reading," Red urged. "You'll never guess what happens."

Piper huffed out a laugh. "Plot twist?" she asked.

"Yes. And it's even more fiendish than one of yours."

On the last page, there was a picture of him down on one knee, holding a ring up to her. In it, Piper was smiling down at Red, hand over her heart—another wonder from Trident's new, expert designer. Wayne had gleefully shot the photo of Red, making him pose over and over until it was declared perfect. Daisy had then grafted it onto a picture they'd unearthed of Piper at a conference earlier in the year, being charmed by a fan's cute little dog. Now there was no dog—only Red, heart on display.

She gasped and looked up at the place he'd been standing only a moment before, then rapidly reoriented herself to Red's current position, on his knee, ring in hand.

"You accepted a ring from me once before," he said. "Can I convince you to do it again?"

"Holy cats," she sputtered.

"I don't just want a part of you anymore. I don't want only some of your days. I want all your days—I want to start every day with you and end each one with you, too." Red explained. He lifted his grandmother's beautiful art deco diamond toward Piper as an offering.

"Oh, Red." She dropped to her knees in front of him and grabbed his arms. Under his sweater, the bulky bandage on his bicep crinkled, and Piper's eyebrows pulled together. "What's that?" She poked at it, tilting her head in confusion.

She hadn't agreed to be his wife yet. Hell, Red hadn't even gotten a chance to *ask* her to be his wife yet. That was Piper for you.

He sat back on his heels and pulled his sweater and t-shirt over his head. The big square of gauze was taped to the inside of his arm, and he'd be glad to be rid of it soon. It itched like crazy.

"Oh my God! What did you do to yourself?" she cried.

"Don't worry, little dove. It's not bad."

"It sure looks bad."

Red grinned, "Why don't you take it off and see?"

He'd spent hours adding to his tattoo that week. Now, his curling treasure map had a second section, making it look like an antique book. The new page wrapped around the inside of his bicep.

The red dotted line led to a beautiful woman seated at a table with a quill in her hand, books stacked beside her and in piles on the floor. Crouching beside her was a red-haired man with an open treasure chest, two artful, scrolling P's decorating the side of it.

He was offering her a gold necklace with a heart dangling from it. They stared at each other in affection. On the ground beneath them, lay a carpet decorated with a large red X.

"Red!" Piper gasped, "What did you—good Lord. You added the books, didn't you? And then some."

"I did. Plus, the 'personal thing' you mentioned. At least, the only personal thing that matters."

"Treasure?" she teased.

Red rolled his eyes. He *still* had an undelivered ring in his hand. "You, Piper."

"That's me? You made me so pretty. Thanks."

"X marks the spot," he said.

"It sure does."

"So, what do you say, Piper Mae?" He winced a little at his unintentional rhyme but powered on. "Will you marry me?" Funny, Red sounded so calm. His heart was pounding, though.

Piper launched herself at him unexpectedly, nearly toppling him backward and knocking the black velvet box containing her ring a couple of feet away on the rug. "Yes," she sobbed. "Oh, yes."

Red held onto her with one arm and managed to get hold of the box once more. He fumbled the ring out of its nest and slipped it onto her trembling finger.

"That's some plot twist." Her voice was impressed but muffled, since her face was pressed into his chest. His skin felt suspiciously damp, and he suspected Piper was trying to hide that she was crying.

Which only made *his* eyes a bit watery.

"They lived happily ever after," he murmured into her hair. "In case it wasn't obvious."

"It's how all the best books end," she told him.

He knew that now. Red didn't intend to ever forget it.

Epilogue

A COUPLE OF weeks later, they found themselves at Anika's wedding reception in town, huddled in a corner with some of the PKM and Trident employees. They were all too stuffed full of Persian delicacies to even consider dancing yet.

Red kept a possessive hand on Piper's back as they made small talk with Rob, Wayne, and some others. The bride and groom were out on the floor, grinning from ear to ear and engaged in some complicated routine with the bridesmaids that involved a long knife, cash, and a significant amount of raucous cheering from the respective families.

Red's cell buzzed insistently in his pocket, but most of the important people in his life were standing right next to him, and he doubted any critical work was being done at either company tonight—everyone was here celebrating.

In the off chance it was Tate or Luca, he pulled it out to check the screen, and lo and behold—Good Cop was calling.

He leaned down to murmur into Piper's ear. "It's Luca," he explained. "Do you mind if I take it?"

"Of course not! Tell him I said hi."

Red ducked into the hotel hallway and accepted the call. Switching erratically back and forth between Italian and English, Luca launched into a convoluted tale about a woman he'd dated a year earlier. There was something about students and professors that Red couldn't quite follow, but he understood the insults his buddy leveled against himself well enough.

Secchione—smart, but dense. A few more declarations of Luca's stupidity, involving both testicles and fava beans. And then a whole lot of exclamations of frustration, invoking a *porca*—a pig—over and over. Red knew them all because over the years, Luca had *used* them all on both of his old roommates.

Now it seemed the tables had turned. Luca was in the romantic hot seat, and Red got to be the one who gloated and dispensed dodgy advice. He'd have to negotiate with Tate, though, about who got to be Bad Cop.

Red's ears perked up when Luca grew more lucid and held to English for several sentences straight. Whoever the dubiously-lucky lady was, his friend had mostly tracked the missing woman down—and he claimed that she was somewhere right here in Manhattan.

"What did you say her name was?" Red interjected sharply.

He ducked his head back into the reception and his eyes tracked instantly to his newest Trident designer. He'd just introduced her to Piper. He suspected Piper was busily thanking the woman for helping to create the special book that had led to her and Red's engagement. It was obvious the two women were hitting it off like gangbusters.

"Daisy." Luca uttered the name reverently, like a blessing or a prayer. "Daisy Montgomery."

Red listened to Luca's answer, then gazed at Daisy again, stunned. She was holding Piper's hand and admiring her engagement ring with a sad, wistful look on her face.

He'd promised his wife-to-be that he would be less controlling—that he wouldn't try to manage things from on high, like some pig-headed puppeteer. Her words, not his. Even so, Red probably shouldn't march right up to Daisy and fix this right the fuck now. Especially since he wasn't crystal clear on all the particulars.

Maybe there was a very good reason for her to lie to his friend. Maybe she'd ghosted him because she'd had to. Still, this was Luca he was talking to. Red had to do *something*.

So, he smiled and said, "You know how I keep saying it's been too long since you visited?"

"*Si*, I know. I've been busy with—"

"Well, you've run out of excuses. Piper and I are having an engagement party in a few months and I need you to be at it. Tate probably can't get leave. It's up to you."

"I don't know if I can. My research…" Luca muttered distractedly.

"I'll sweeten the deal, then, since the bonds of our friendship clearly don't matter enough to you. I'm serving on the board of a hospital here in town, and there's a surgeon you should meet. Have you heard of Harlan Green? His research is similar to yours."

Luca was silent so long that Red wondered if the call had been dropped. But then his friend said, "Harlan Green. Of course, I know of him. He's there? Near you?"

"He is. I've talked to him. I can introduce you. *At my engagement party.*"

"Okay, okay." Luca's thick accent was waning as he stuck to English longer. "I'll come. I'll meet your Piper, I'll meet your Doctor Green, and perhaps…"

"Perhaps you'll find Daisy, too." Red smiled. *Yeah, that ought to do it.*

Review

Did you enjoy **The Titan Was Tall**? If so, please consider leaving a review at the retailer where you purchased this title.

Book reviews can be as simple or as detailed as you wish, but all of them help authors sell more books, and assist other readers in finding the stories they want to read.

Almost any book can be reviewed by simply logging into the website where you purchased the title, then scrolling to the bottom of the title's product page to find an area called "Leave a Review."

Up Next

The Doctor Was Dark

Triple Threat, Book Two

Take this oath and...

Shove it. As far as Luca was concerned, his promise to first do no harm could take a flying leap off a tall building. A doctor of his caliber should've known better than to make assumptions, though—and the biggest one he'd made was thinking he could ever live without Daisy. Now that he's finally tracked her down, he's prepared to move heaven and earth—and maybe even harm a person or two—in order to win back the one who got away. If only it were that simple.

It turns out the woman he fell for a year ago was not at all what she seemed. Back in America, his supposedly sweet, uncomplicated graduate student is actually a ferociously-talented professional, and twice as seductive as she was before. Daisy is also his old friend's newest hire—and she's not exactly thrilled to see Luca show up unexpectedly at her boss's engagement party.

When she discovers that Luca wasn't exactly forthcoming about his professional pedigree either, it becomes clear that Daisy's made some hasty assumptions of her own. Luca will have to wield every instrument at his disposal to heal her hurts. Forget his best bedside manner— winning Daisy a second time is going to require all of Luca's heart, too.

Can he convince Daisy that love is still the best medicine, even on a new continent and in their real-life roles? Or will Luca find himself heading back to Italy empty-handed and sick at heart?

There's only one way to find out.

The doctor will see you now.

The Doctor Was Dark

One

IT COULDN'T BE him. There was no way, not on God's green earth, that Daisy's erstwhile fling—her freak in the sheets, her flame who shall not be named—was here and standing a scant seven yards away from her at this engagement party.

Luca, after all, was only a humble family doctor who practiced medicine in a sleepy part of Florence, Italy. He was the kind of guy who doted on his grandmother in his spare time—when he wasn't setting hapless expats on fire from the inside out, that was.

Luca barely had to lift a finger to do it, either. He was that good.

But Daisy had left that man behind a year ago, and at the time, she'd thought it was the only thing she could do. She and Luca had only worked as a couple during their brief time together because he hadn't known her from a hole in the wall.

He didn't know her people, such as they were. Okay, make that *person*—the plural was totally unnecessary. Daisy had exactly one person that she could sort-of call family, and occasionally she didn't even have that much.

The point was, Luca hadn't known anyone at all who knew Daisy, and that was what had made him so perfect for her. Well, besides his shiny black hair. And his full, seductive mouth. And his long, strong…everything.

Because he didn't know anything about her, Daisy had been able to be herself with him. *Only* herself. She'd been lighter and freer than at any other time in her life. She'd been *fun*, for fuck's sake, without the albatross of her stupid past dragging her down.

She'd planned to carry the golden memory of her affair with the gorgeous Italian throughout the rest of her life. It was going to be a vivid window into what might have been, if she'd only been dealt a better hand. A kinder one.

Instead, he appeared to be here, in Daisy's hometown, in the flesh. Where he should not be.

There was no conceivable reason why Luca, *her* Luca, should be standing in the middle of her boss's engagement party, looking as urbane and polished as a GQ fashion spread. Maybe she was hallucinating.

Daisy scowled down at her drink, a bright-red Shirley Temple with a healthy shot of bourbon in it. The bartender had called it a *Dirty Shirley*, but now she wondered whether he'd added something a little more illicit to it than liquor.

Did she feel like she'd been drugged? Daisy rapidly assessed her motor function and the clarity of her vision. Both seemed fine. She shook her hair out, but the room stayed steady. None of her extremities were remotely numb.

Well, with the possible exception of her toes. But she was almost positive that was because she rarely wore heels and it was about nine degrees outside. The swanky apartment she was in was obviously heated, but it was still old, and a chilly draft was lingering near the floor despite the many people standing around chatting.

And her heels, while hot as sin, were brutal to stand in for long periods of time. Both perfectly reasonable explanations for foot malfunctions.

However, if it turned out that her eyesight hadn't taken a sudden, ill-timed plunge into near-blindness—if that *was*, in fact, Dr. Luca in the flesh over there—then Daisy was happy to be wearing these shoes.

She was happy for her fire-engine red flamenco dress, and thrilled that she'd taken the time to wash her hair yesterday. She'd even worn some shiny, sticky lip gloss in a nod to her surroundings.

Okay, fine—she hadn't started out wearing it. She'd only dug it out from the bottom of her bag and slathered it on five minutes after arrival, once she'd gotten a look at the other high-dollar attendees.

Still, it suddenly felt fortuitous that Daisy was so bad at cleaning out old purses, and terrible at throwing shit away, in general. Especially since she didn't even think that lip gloss belonged to her. The brand sounded more like something you'd scrape off the bottom of your shoe than something you'd want near your piehole.

She'd probably been holding it for Poppy sometime when they'd gone out on the town. Daisy couldn't remember actually doing that, but given her friend's affection for cosmetics, it certainly seemed possible. And, since she'd only moved back to New York from Boston a couple of months ago, that meant the lip gloss couldn't be very old.

Poppy wasn't the type to keep a lip gloss around for years. Daisy, sadly, was. But that was irrelevant.

Watching Maybe-Luca mingle with the other guests like he belonged here, Daisy pressed her coated lips together, and hoped like hell that the glop she'd used on herself looked normal.

She was afraid the odds of getting out of here unseen by her one-time flame were slim to none. Daisy knew she was…noticeable. For one thing, she was taller than a lot of the women there, and hardly blending into the woodwork with her bright red dress.

For another, her distinctive coloring had always garnered her second and third looks from people. It wasn't that there were no other people of color at this WASPy party—it was just that Daisy was hard to categorize.

Was she white? No. Black? Also, no. She was…well, she didn't know exactly what she was, but she had her theories.

Other people didn't seem happy not knowing what box to put her in, however. So, their eyes lingered on Daisy's face, and the gears turned behind their eyes as they tried to figure out where she fit in.

She wished one of them would clue her in, if they figured it out. As it was, the extra attention had always made her uncomfortable. Still, Daisy was no shrinking violet, and she wasn't going to cower in a corner just because some idiots didn't know what to make of her.

She had bigger fish to fry at the moment, anyway.

Daisy edged closer to the man she'd spotted—the man who might be Dr. Luca—as her boss ushered a little couple into his orbit. The pair was short and squat compared to Red's daunting 6'6 build, but the future groom was definitely not in intimidation mode tonight. Instead, he looked positively thrilled to be celebrating his engagement.

Daisy turned her attention to the new arrivals, hoping for some clue that would confirm her suspicions. The small man had full, brushed-back silver hair and chunky black glasses, and the woman on his arm was all smiles, her wrists covered in a startling number of jingling gold bracelets.

"Luca," Red boomed, establishing somewhat that Daisy wasn't seeing things, "May I introduce Dr. Harlan Green, and his wife, Dr. Shari Green?"

Luca, also a tall man at 6'2, leaned down slightly to shake each of their hands in turn, but it came off as a formal, sophisticated bow.

"I'm honored," he said, and Daisy's chest constricted when she picked up a trace of his accent. How could this be happening?

Harlan Green was nearly bouncing in his dress shoes, he was so excited. "Trust me, the honor is all mine. When MacLellan told me Gianluca Delledonna was his college roommate, I just assumed he was…"

Red turned and raised an amused brow at the diminutive man.

"Full of it," Shari Green supplied merrily.

"He often is," Luca chuckled back, sharing a mischievous grin with Daisy's boss that made it obvious the two men were more than passing acquaintances. *Oh, God*—what were the freaking odds? She was so screwed.

"However, I never expected…" Harlan Green tried again.

Red just shook his head, cutting him off. "I promised, didn't I?"

Luca looked like he was at a loss for words, blinking rapidly as he underwent the other doctor's scrutiny. Finally, he turned instead to Harlan's wife, inquiring smoothly, "I'm certain I heard a 'Dr.' attached to your name as well. What kind of medicine do you practice?"

Shari toasted him with her champagne flute. "Psychiatry," she declared with a flourish. "I doubt you want to talk shop with me right now, though. This guy's the one with the goods." She bumped her husband's shoulder fondly with hers.

"Why don't we leave these two to make friends?" Red asked her. "Have you seen that dessert table yet? I can't stop eating the cream puffs. I'm due for another drive-by, for sure."

With that, there was a flurry of handshakes and back-slapping, and then Daisy's boss was steering his charge resolutely away, bound for the far corner of the party.

Daisy felt like the worst sort of lurker as she watched Harlan Green move in. He was clearly determined not to waste his opportunity. She risked shifting another few steps closer, keeping herself out of Luca's peripheral vision as best as she could.

"Dr. Delledonna, I've been following your research, and the chance to meet you in person was too tempting to resist. I hope you'll forgive me for ambushing you here."

Luca made a sound that would translate as "Nonsense!" in any language.

"And I must admit—I had another goal tonight, if MacLellan did end up producing you."

Luca cocked his head, drawing Daisy's attention to the tendons in his tanned neck. The same tendons she'd once licked up and down. "And what was that?" he said.

Green backtracked slightly. "I don't know if you've heard of the research I've done on cancer cells and the body's immune response?"

"Of course. The paper your team published last summer was fascinating. We discussed how it might apply to our theories for weeks."

"That's just it," Green exclaimed, delighted and clapping his hands. "What if we were able to work *together?*"

"I…" Luca's face was alive and focused, homing in on the other man with alert interest now. "That would be…"

Dr. Green interrupted him. "I'll be blunt. I've got an opening at Weill Cornell and I want you. You wouldn't have to pick up more than a class or two for the first couple of years, until your work is really up and running. I can promise you state-of-the-art lab facilities in the same wing as mine, plus a highly-skilled pool of students and residents to assist you."

"That's…"

"Dr. Delledonna, if you know about anything I've done in the last ten years, then you know this is a match made in heaven. Together, you and I could potentially find a cure for gastric cancer."

Daisy held her breath, waiting to see what Luca would say. What Green was offering would require Luca to move to New York, wouldn't it? She felt like the floor had dropped out of the room, only to be replaced with a spinning carnival ride.

At last, Luca's broad chest expanded with a deep breath. "If we're going to do that, you should call me Luca," he rumbled in his smooth baritone.

Immediately, the men launched into making arrangements, pulling out phones and scheduling meetings, and Daisy knew in her bones that Luca intended to take the job.

Red's fiancée Piper popped up at her elbow, nearly making her jump out of her skin. "See something you like?" the woman grinned.

"Cripes, Piper! You scared me!"

"Sorry. But the question still stands."

Daisy sighed. "I…think I might know the guy with the dark hair," she admitted reluctantly.

"Luca?" Piper smiled. "Red suspected you might. They're such good friends, but I just got to meet him for the first time yesterday." And then the bride elbowed her with a conspiratorial wink. "He's something, am I right?"

No way was Daisy going to get into *that* discussion. But as long as Piper was here and feeling chatty, she supposed she could do some digging. "Who's the other guy?"

"Oh, that's Dr. Green. He has it bad for Luca. I'm a little surprised he's keeping his composure and not falling on his knees begging, though."

"Why?"

"We met him for dinner a few weeks ago. When it came up in conversation that Red was friendly with the famous Gianluca Delledonna, Green nearly drooled in his moo goo gai pan."

Daisy felt a little light-headed. Her voice sounded weak when she asked, "Famous?"

"Oh, sure. He's, like, an international badass in cancer research. And so charming, too. If I wasn't getting hitched to my own tall drink of water, I'd totally want to steal him from you."

Daisy didn't even know where to begin with that bit of insanity. "He's not mine. You can't steal something that doesn't even belong to me."

"Save it, sister. I'm not blind. Luca may as well have a big neon sign around his neck, blinking *Taken As All Get Out.*"

"Piper!"

The party's honoree just snorted, supremely unapologetic. "Anyway, I'd better go cut that damn cake. My future mother-in-law is beckoning, and I've already avoided her for as long as I can." With a friendly half-hug, Piper began moving through the crowd, but she called over her shoulder, "Hey, text me next week! The four of us can go out together sometime!"

Daisy stood there, blinking stupidly after her and wondering how her evening had veered so far into absurdity.

DAISY COULDN'T FOOL herself that she'd remain incognito at this party for long, or that she and Luca would never run into each other around town. New York might be a big place with about a bazillion people crammed into it, but the shared association to Red and Piper was too much of a coincidence.

The fix was definitely in, but Daisy was confounded by how her boss—or Luca, for that matter—had managed to figure out the connection.

True, Luca had known she was affiliated with the NYU study abroad program in Florence last year, and she must have mentioned at some point during the semester that she lived in Manhattan.

However, in the intervening twelve months, Daisy's life had undergone a massive upheaval. When she'd come back from Italy, she'd opened her own solo graphic design shop, then had to shutter it months later when the building she leased space in kicked all its tenants out to revamp into luxury lofts.

From there, she'd ended up in Boston, helping her college friend Poppy at a contemporary art museum she worked for.

Daisy had only come back to New York recently, when she'd landed the gig at Trident Publishing. Red's company, PKM Conglomerates, had bought the small, struggling press and managed to turn it around—barely—and in the process he had met and fallen for Piper, a successful romance author there.

Daisy had helped him propose to Piper by putting together a picture book he'd conceived about their relationship. Now, strangely, the couple seemed to have decided she was a friend of theirs.

That wasn't a bad thing, necessarily. They were good people, decent and non-irritating. She just had to wonder why they'd spend a single minute bothering with her.

Regardless, for Luca to have tracked Daisy to her current job after all the recent changes in her life was too far-fetched for words.

It had to have come from MacLellan. Maybe he'd seen the Florence job on her resumé when she was hired at Trident. Maybe he'd overheard something when H.R. called her references. In any case, for Red to have connected the dots all the way, Luca *had* to have talked to him about Daisy.

A panicked sound escaped her throat. Daisy needed to get out of here, quickly, but it felt like her feet were glued to the floor. She was utterly paralyzed from her face to her toes, watching the suave man across the room. The man it had killed her to leave behind. The man who still haunted her dreams.

God, he looked good.

As if Luca could feel her eyes on him, he suddenly raised his chin and looked over Dr. Green's head, searching the room with a small perplexed divot between his dark brows.

He turned slightly to the side, taking in the sight of Red and Piper cutting their cake and joking with their guests.

And then Luca pivoted in Daisy's direction. She shrank back, trying to commune with the potted plant behind her, but it was too late.

He'd seen her. Their gazes clashed, her breath locked up in her throat, and her heart flapped around like a wild, panicked bird in her chest. His lips were moving, but she couldn't process whatever he was trying to say.

Luca's face was pale with shock. His hand shot out, reaching unsteadily toward her. "Daisy?" he croaked.

She swallowed and spun, dodging the banana palm and banging her shoulder into a corner as she fled toward the front door.

Behind her, Luca cried out, *"Daisy, no!"*

To read more, please purchase The Doctor Was Dark from your favorite bookseller!

FREE BOOK

Get a glimpse of Morgan, Meg, Molly and Mina—*before* their happily ever afters take place!

Sign up for the author's Reader's List and get a free copy of the Lost & Found prequel novella "Girls Night Out."

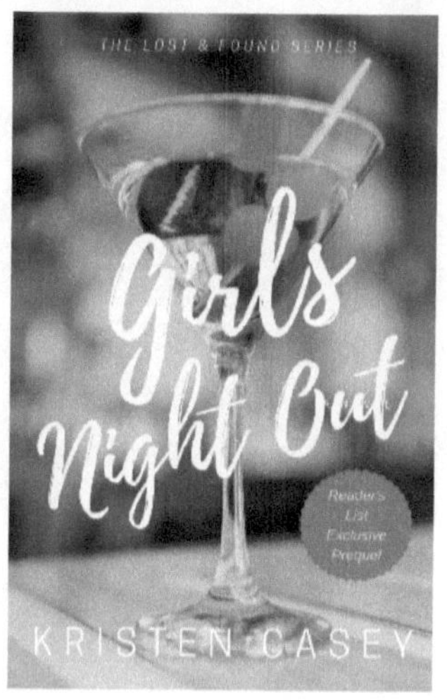

Visit Here to Get Started:

http://eepurl.com/ctGk1j

Also by Kristen Casey

The Lost & Found Series

Girls Night Out
Finding Home
Finding Love
Lost in Love
Lucky in Love
Christmas in Cambridge
The Flynn Sisters Box Set
Finding a Husband
Heroes & Husbands
Finding Forever
Forever and a Day
Forever Starts Now
The O'Connell Sisters Box Set

The Black Watch Security Series

False Flag
Heat Seeking Missile
Brothers in Arms
Fight or Flight
Search and Destroy
Squared Away

Acknowledgments

You might have noticed that Titan is nearly twice as long as some of my other books. It came as a bit of a surprise! It meant that I worked long and hard to bring you Red and Piper's love story, and so did my wonderful team.

Thanks go to Deborah at Tugboat Design, whose gorgeous cover totally captures the feel of this book. She is always a joy to work with, and she makes it all look easy.

The story would be in a lot worse shape if not for the meticulous beta reading provided by Helen Snay. As always, her insight and careful eye are so valuable to me, but not nearly as valuable as her friendship and sense of humor.

As well, I owe my family a huge debt of gratitude for their bottomless patience and unflagging support this time around. Sometimes I was too distracted by imaginary people to listen to tales of your days, and sometimes dinner was an hour-late pizza, but you never complained, and I thank you.

Last but definitely not least, my readers: Your joy and enthusiasm for each new book are what make this the most rewarding career I could ever dream of. Thank you, from the bottom of my cat-loving heart.

About the Author

Kristen Casey writes the kind of heartfelt, steamy books she loves to read—full of relatable characters and snarky dialogue. She lives in Maryland with her husband, two kids, and assorted cats, and in her free time enjoys all things crafty—especially projects she finds on Pinterest.

Sign up for her newsletter to receive exclusive content, sales, and new releases emailed right to your inbox.

Follow her on social media, for even more fun stuff!

Goodreads: Kristen_Casey
Facebook: AuthorKCasey
Twitter: @AuthorKCasey
Pinterest: KristenCase0461
Instagram: Kristen.Casey.Books
BookBub: Kristen Casey
TikTok: KristenWritesRomance

Reading Order of Kristen's Books

The Lost & Found Series

Girls Night Out (Prequel exclusive to subscribers)

Finding Home (Book 1)

Finding Love (Book 2)

Lost in Love (Book 2.5 – Includes short story *Lucky in Love*)

The Flynn Sisters Box Set (Includes *Christmas in Cambridge*)

Finding a Husband (Book 3)

Finding Forever (Book 4)

Forever and a Day (Book 4.5 – Includes *Forever Starts Now*)

The O'Connell Sisters Box Set (Includes *Heroes & Husbands*)

The Triple Threat Series

The Titan was Tall (Book 1)

The Doctor was Dark (Book 2)

The Hero was Handsome (Book 3)

The Triple Threat Box Set (Includes *The Masquerade was Magic* and *The Hero's Brother*)

The Black Watch Security Series

False Flag (Book 1)

Heat Seeking Missile (Book 2)

Brothers in Arms (Book 3)

Fight or Flight (Book 4)

Search and Destroy (Book 5)

Squared Away (Book 6)